To M[...]

My Glasgow Pal

With Love - Best Wishes

from

[signature]

X

26/9/08

WHAT'S FOR YE, WON'T GO BY YE

Avril Dalziel Saunders

The Derwent Press
Derbyshire, England

www.derwentpress.com

WHAT'S FOR YE, WON'T GO BY YE
By
Avril Dalziel Saunders

ISBN: 1-84667-013-6

Cover art and book design by:
Pam Marin-Kingsley
www.far-angel.com

Published in 2006 by
The Derwent Press
Derbyshire, England

www.derwentpress.com

I dedicate this book to my dear family.

*My parents who gave me a secure and loving
upbringing in spite of the trials and tribulations
suffered by ordinary folk and the effects that it had
on them due to The Second World War.*

*My husband and soul mate, who inspired and
encouraged me to write this book*

*My wonderful son, lovely daughter-in-law,
two beautiful daughters and fine son-in-laws,
they are all very caring, a great joy to me and
make me very proud.*

*My gorgeous grand daughter who has
made my life complete*

*My brother, who is a great optimist and
always looks forward, never back.*

I love all of these people with all my heart.

CHAPTER ONE

The year is 1950. The place is a council house in a tenement in the Possilpark area of Glasgow. Like so many families during and after the War, they are all living in cramped conditions. Due to the men all being away from home fighting in World War II, the wives have been left to bring up the 'we'ans' and fend for themselves. Some young married women carried on living in either single-ends (one room in a tenement), one room and kitchen, or, if they were really lucky, two rooms and a kitchen. Most had an outside toilet on the staircase that had to be shared with at least three other families. Other young married women opted to move back with their mothers, meaning that, when the men finally came home, you could find two or three daughters, plus husbands and kids, all squashed into a three bedroom council flat. At least they had the luxury of a large bathroom with a big cast iron bath and hot and cold running water. The men had been away in far away places such as Egypt, Germany, France, Palestine, Iraq and Japan, fighting for world peace for at least six years. Therefore, these young married couples never had the chance to start building their nests together. This was the case for the parents of two-year-old Linda MacGregor.

Douglas and Margie met in 1939 when she was 18 and he was 19. Unbeknownst to her, he had spotted her with her friends many times over a few months, but she didn't seem to notice him. When he was on late shift, he would deliberately walk the long way round to his home in Ruchill from his job in the flourmill, in the hope of seeing her again. He felt his heart fluttering every time he caught sight of this young, beautiful Judy Garland look-a-like.

Three months previously, he had had a nasty accident at the mill where he worked, his hand being drawn into the cutting machine. The noise of the machinery drowned out his screams for help. Just in time, one of his colleagues came to the rescue and quickly switched the machine off, though it was too late to save Douglas' right index finger. Douglas looked upon that as a lucky escape. Had it not been for the quick thinking of his workmate, his whole arm could have been torn off or, worse still, he could have been killed.

He was 5ft 8ins tall, dark and very handsome. Margie was blonde, fair skinned, very pretty, bubbly and petite, insisting that she was 5ft and a half inches tall, but others would have argued that she was more like 4ft 11ins. One evening, they practically bumped into each other. She was blethering away and giggling with three other girlfriends as they excitedly exchanged stories about the latest heartthrob in the cinema.

'S-S-S-Sorry', she mumbled bashfully, as she noticed this good-looking young man for the first time. She felt her heart thumping as he smiled at her. She carried on walking but, as she glanced back, he was still standing there, smiling shyly at her. She didn't know why or where she got the courage from, but she turned and went back, asking him why his hand was bandaged.

'Oh! It's only a wee cut', said Douglas, scared that the thought of his wounds might put her off him. He was delighted, he finally got to talk to this girl that he had been admiring from afar for at least three months. This was the start of a wonderful, happy romance.

During the next few months, Douglas MacGregor and Margie Nixon got to know each other better. They went for long walks, all the way from Possilpark, through Ruchill Park to Jaconelli's Café in Maryhill Road. They sat at the back in a wooden booth and tucked into Jaconelli's famous Glasgow delicacy of ice cream and raspberry sauce, commonly known in those parts as a 'MacCallum'. They talked and dreamt about their future together. They were very worried about the impending war and how it might affect them. They were only too aware that Douglas could be called up to serve in the British Forces.

Then the 'black outs' came. All the lights had to be turned off at nighttime, making it difficult for the German planes to find and bomb the shipyards, ammunition-making factories and populated areas. The warden did his rounds, making sure that windows were covered with black-out material. Even the slightest gap would make the windows visible to the skies above, endangering the lives of many. In the dark winter months, Douglas and Margie ventured out to meet each other, in spite of not being able to see their noses in front of them. Douglas lived in the middle part of Bilsland Drive. It started at Maryhill and ended in Possilpark at the crossroads of Balmore Road, opposite the Mecca Picture House. Margie walked down Balmore Road.

Douglas always stood on the corner of Bilsland Drive and Balmore Road, waiting for Margie in the pitch black, whistling 'Stardust'. She listened for this and found her way to him. Needless to say, 'Stardust' became their song. They went to the Mecca Picture House to see the latest films and newsreels. Often, on the way back, the sirens went off, warning that German planes were approaching on a bombing raid. They then had to run to find the nearest underground shelter. It all became a way of life for them and everyone else in Britain at this time.

Her mother had arranged for her first job of sewing shrouds when she was 14, but she hadn't liked the place. Her boss was a dour, bad tempered man who made her work long hours, demanding his pound of flesh. There were no unions in those days, and she worked in a back room in an old, creepy warehouse block. She was an intelligent girl who dreamt of staying on at school and becoming a teacher or a secretary, but her mother needed her to work to help support the family of six brothers and sisters. Margie left this job after a year and trained as a seamstress making kilts. She enjoyed this job. She was very talented and could make anything just by looking at a magazine picture. She never needed patterns. This came in handy during the War years, when everything was rationed and you couldn't buy clothes for love nor money. She would make beautiful evening dresses for herself and her sisters from the blackout material used to cover the windows. In 1940, Margie helped the War effort by changing her job to work as a machinist, sewing uniforms for the Forces.

Her father had an executive manager's job with a big engineering firm in Renfrewshire. Margie remembered the depression in the 1930s when their doorbell rang constantly, with people on their doorstep pleading with Mr. Nixon to give them jobs to feed their families. Mr. and Mrs. Nixon could easily have had a better life and a privately owned house, but he was an alcoholic who disciplined his wife and children with a rod of iron. Mrs. Nixon opted for a three bedroom council tenement flat because her husband didn't give her enough money to pay the bills. She struggled to manage the finances and feed the family while he went out every night with his boozing buddies, buying the rounds and drinking all his wages away.

Mrs. Nixon, (Peggy), had come from a well-to-do family from Bishopbriggs. They lived in a big red stone-built house with a sweeping drive. Her family owned a large clothing store in the Cowcaddens area of Glasgow. She was a quiet, well brought up girl who led a sheltered life. She met John Nixon in 1912, when she was 27 and he was 29. They courted for almost three years. Early in 1915, Peggy found herself pregnant. To be unmarried and 'with child' was a terrible, unforgivable sin in those days. This was a pure embarrassment to her family and they disowned her, regarding her as a black sheep. At the age of 30, she and John married. She gave birth to John junior ten weeks later. She affectionately referred to him as her love child.

They set up home in a room and kitchen in Possilpark. This consisted of one bedroom and another room for their living area. There, she cooked over an open range fire and washed by means of an old stone sink with one cold tap. If she wanted hot water, she had to boil it in a large kettle over the open fire. Bath time was once a week. She brought the big tin bath into the kitchen and placed it in front of the fire, boiling pots and kettles of water to fill it. A kettle was kept on the boil to top up the bath water.

In the corner of the kitchen was the 'hole in the wa' bed'. This was a recess where a double bed fitted snuggly, with a curtain in front for privacy. In families, the children usually slept here, often four to a bed, two at the top and two at the bottom. Peggy and John shared a toilet outside on the stair with three other families. This was all a far cry from the privileged upbringing that Peggy had been used to, but she never complained and got on with her life.

When John junior was 15 months old, she gave birth to a daughter, Betty, followed 16 months later by another son, Donald. Then, one year later, a third son James. In 1921, Margery (Margie) was born. Three years and ten months later, Mary was born. This family of eight lived in these cramped conditions until 1929, when they were re-housed in a brand new council flat with three bedrooms, a living room, a kitchenette and a big bathroom. This was sheer luxury for them. Peggy was a very good mother. Her house was spotless and her children immaculate. No one would have guessed the struggle she had to make ends meet because of John's selfishness. If he had been a responsible husband and father, he could easily have afforded to buy a nice house for them. In spite of his executive position and top wage, sometimes he came home on payday with no money, having drunk the lot treating his boozy pals.

It was a happy household, mostly due to the fact that Mr. Nixon was very seldom there. He left very early in the morning and wouldn't get back until past 10pm, after the pubs had closed. That's when the atmosphere changed. Everyone knew to stay out of his way. Peggy would have his dinner ready and agree with him in all his points of view. She was a peace-loving woman and knew better. The family loved their mum, they would do anything for her, and came to despise their dad for the way he treated her.

The girls remained terrified of him and never answered him back, whereas the boys, although frightened of his aggression, would give as good as they got. As John junior matured into a teen-ager, he would disagree with his dad and get into terrible rows with him. Donald and James were fun-loving and angered their father by taking things flippantly.

One freezing cold Friday night near Christmas in 1937, it had gone past mid-night and John senior still hadn't come home. Peggy assumed that he had gone back to one of his pal's houses to carry on boozing and celebrating the festive season. At 2am there was a knock on the door. Peggy could see the outline of a figure through the top glass on the door. She knew it couldn't be John, as he only stood 5ft 4ins. She woke up John junior and they very cautiously opened the door to find a tall policeman standing there. John senior had been found lying in the snow, dead. He had chronic bronchitis. The drinking and the freezing cold had taken their toll and ended his life at the age of 54.

After Mr. Nixon's death, the household atmosphere was more relaxed. Inwardly, Peggy felt quite guilty about feeling contented. She wasn't aware that Mr. Nixon had taken out a large insurance policy years before, or that he also had a savings fund through his company. His will stated that the children were to receive £100 each and Peggy £400. This was a vast sum of money in 1937.

Their wealth was short lived, though. At the ripe old age of 22, John junior was now the head of the house and he suggested that all the kids sign their share of the money over to their mother. They all respected John junior's new position and did as they were told. Although he was nothing like his father in that he was more caring and only drank in moderation on special occasions, John junior liked the good life. He persuaded his mother to buy a motorcar, convincing her that it was to help make life easier for her and the family. Of course, it was for no such thing. John junior was a ladies' man, and a motorcar was an attraction that very few young men had in 1937. He therefore had his pick of all the young ladies. His younger brothers, Donald and James, were pranksters. Unbeknownst to John junior, they often took the motorcar out when he was working evening shift.

Margie liked a bit of fun too. One cold evening, she was standing at the tram stop in Cowcaddens, waiting for a tram to take her home after another long day at work. Suddenly, she heard this 'toot, toot, tooting' coming towards her and doubled up laughing on seeing Donald behind the wheel of the motorcar, with James sitting beside him. They shouted to her to jump in and go for a hurl. She looked at the other folk waiting at the tram stop, gave a cheeky grin, and climbed into the back seat. She had never been given the opportunity to sit in the motorcar before, as John junior always kept it to himself. She felt like a million dollars sitting in the back. They giggled and laughed, deliberately driving down streets where they knew their friends would be, tooting all the way. Of course, John junior never knew anything about this. Their mother had an idea what was going on, but she was very discreet and never asked any questions.

To further justify the family's need for a car, John junior took his mum for a drive one day. They set out about 10am on a beautiful spring Saturday morning and drove over all the bumpy roads into the country. They got as far as Carbeth when disaster struck and the car broke down. They had to wait for four hours for the country bus to take them back to town. Then they got on a tramcar, finally getting back home at 9.30pm that night. Peggy was absolutely exhausted. That was the end of the motorcar. John junior sold it for a mere pittance, as it would have cost too much to repair.

Betty was learning John junior's tricks by this time. She worked as an assistant to an old photographer friend in his small business located in a room above a local tailor. She convinced her mum that she needed the best jewellery and clothing to make an impression on the clients. She also talked her mum into helping build up the business by loaning them money to buy expensive photographic equipment. She promised faithfully to repay her mum every penny back as soon as she got on her feet. Of course, this never happened. Between them, John junior and Betty soon dwindled away their mum's nest egg.

By 1939, all the family members were working. Margie cared so much for her mother that she gave her all her wages every week and got pocket money back in return. She helped the family out a great deal by making all their clothes. In the evenings, they would all sit around the big roaring fire telling ghost stories. Margie was gifted in that she could play the piano by ear. Some evenings her sisters would ask her if she knew the latest song. Margie would pluck at the piano to get the gist of it. Then, in no time, everyone was round her and singing.

One summer evening in 1939 Margie told her mum, 'I've met this very handsome boy, he looks like Tyrone Power and his name is Douglas MacGregor He comes from Ruchill.'

Peggy, being young at heart, said, 'Invite him round for dinner!'

This would not have been allowed if Mr. Nixon were still alive, as the girls were not allowed to talk to boys, never mind having a boyfriend.

The next Friday evening, Douglas arrived at their tenement on the top floor. He had a great pride in his appearance and was immaculate in his navy double-breasted suit and gleaming black shoes. He wanted to make a good impression on Margie's mother. He nervously handed her a bunch of carnations and thanked her for inviting him. Peggy made him feel very welcome and gradually he began to relax. Betty, Mary, John junior, Donald and James all made it a point of being there to give Margie's new beau the once over. Peggy was a good cook. She had made Scotch broth, followed by the Scottish delicacy of steak pie, champed tatties and steepy peas. Margie made her favourite dessert, apple pie and custard. She took great pride in her custard, it always turned out perfectly, with no lumps. They rounded their delicious meal off with Margie's home-made rock cakes and tea.

At the table, John junior asked Douglas what he did for a living. Then Donald asked what football team he supported (in Glasgow this was a sure, but polite, way of finding out what religion one was). James asked him if he knew of any jobs going at the mill, while Betty and Mary, completely blown away by Douglas' good looks, piped up with 'Have you any brothers?'

Douglas lived in Ruchill, He was born in 1920, in a room and kitchen in Agnes Street in Maryhill, the sixth of ten children. The same as Margie's family, they had been allocated a brand new council flat in Ruchill in 1929. Ironically, it was the exact same type of flat, top floor, right hand side. Just like Margie's tenement, they had the factor living below them. This was the rent officer for the area. He had a wee window from his back room on to the stair landing. People would queue up the staircase to pay their rent. This made life more difficult for people who lived close to the factors, as the stairs were always busy and had to be perpetually swept and cleaned.

Life had been hard for Douglas. His father, Angus MacGregor, was a cobbler. He had a wooden leg that he had made himself. He never talked about it, but his children believed that he had been run over by a tramcar when he was a boy.

Angus came from a privileged family, but he never reaped any benefits from it. Around 1870, his paternal grandfather and uncles inherited from their father a large departmental store in Buchanan Street in Glasgow.

Angus' father, James, was disowned from the family when he married Isabel in 1888. She was a parlour maid for a rich family who owned a big mansion with vast grounds in Great Western Road, Glasgow. She lived in the tiny attic room of her employer's house, which she shared with the kitchen maid. The MacGregors regarded James as having married beneath himself. He loved Isabel, and nothing was going to stop him from spending the rest of his life with her. Not letting anything beat him, James worked hard and started up his own coach-painting business in Bishopbriggs. He worked long, hard hours to support his wife and family. His labours paid off, as the business became very successful. They lived very comfortably in a stone-built cottage on the road out to Kirkintilloch. Isabel loved her husband and children, and their home was full of happiness.

Then tragedy struck in 1898 when Angus was only nine and his sisters seven and five years of age. Their father James took very ill and died quickly from lead poisoning, contracted from the paint used to paint the coaches. He was only 34 years of age. Isabel tried to cope, but in those days, there was no help. She pled with the wealthy MacGregor family, but her pleas were ignored. She had no option but to put her three beloved children into a home. It broke her heart. She visited them as often as she could afford the fare to the children's home in the country.

Angus and his sisters were very unhappy there. They mourned for their dad and missed their mum. The stern matron at the home bullied and beat them regularly. She forced them to scrub floors, clean toilets, chop up wood, light the fires, and made them go without food for days. One evening, Angus rounded up his two young sisters and they ran away, over the fields heading for Glasgow.

He didn't know where their mother lived anymore. They wandered through the back streets of the town, scavenging for food. It was thought that during this time he was run over and lost his leg. They then were split up to lead truly miserable existences, living unhappy childhoods in different homes.

Angus left his home when he was 14 and went to work as a message boy for a small bakery. There were two other lads working there, and they all shared a room above the premises. They all worked different shifts, each taking their turn to sleep in the only bed in the room. Angus tried in vain to find his mother, but he never did find out whether she was dead or alive.

When Angus was 16, he was lucky enough to get a job as an apprentice joiner. Jimmy, an old labourer who worked for the firm, took pity on him. He and his wife were never fortunate enough to have children of their own, so they took Angus under their wing. When they heard the story of Angus' two sisters, they went to the authorities and pleaded with them for help in tracing the girls. Angus and his two sisters hadn't seen each other for seven years.

When the two girls were eventually found, they were both thin and bedraggled. They both had had miserable childhoods in separate children's homes. The oldest girl was pushed out of the home and into the street when she reached the age of 14. She was found begging for food and crawling with lice. She slept rough in side alleys. The younger sister was 12. She was found, very unhappy, in a children's home 20 miles from Glasgow. Angus felt responsible for his sisters and felt that he had failed them. Jimmy and his wife took them all under their wing. They didn't have much, but they showered them with love and affection. At last, after all those years, the young MacGregor children felt the comfort and love of a normal family home life.

When Angus was 19, he met Kathleen. She was 16 and a dark-haired beauty. She had beautiful Mediterranean olive skin and big flashing brown eyes. She was a quiet, well-mannered girl. They were soon head over heels in love. They didn't have much money, as he was an apprentice joiner and didn't earn much. They saw each other as much as they could and spent their time together strolling hand in hand, talking. Angus was anxious to settle down and make a home life with beautiful Kathleen. He plucked up all his courage and proposed early one evening as they sat on the swings at the local park. Kathleen was overjoyed. She knew that Angus was the man of her dreams, so caring and loving. He treated her so well and he was also very sensible for his young years. They kissed passionately and then went home to **her** parent's house, where Angus very nervously asked Kathleen's dad for her **hand** in marriage. He had no hesitation in giving them his blessing. Her **parents** were delighted. They liked Angus, and were impressed with his **manners and** how well he treated their daughter.

What's For Ye, Won't Go By Ye

Angus and Kathleen started to make plans for the future. They couldn't afford anything grand, so in 1909, when he was 20 and Kathleen was 17, they got married in her church, with only Angus' two sisters, old Jimmy and his wife, Kathleen's parents, and her sister present. Shortly after that, Angus saw his two sisters emigrate to a new life in New Zealand.

Angus and Kathleen lived in the back room of her parents' house in the Gallowgate area of Glasgow. Within months, Kathleen was pregnant. They were all overjoyed. His apprenticeship had just finished and Angus was at last earning a decent wage. He planned to get a nice house for his wife and unborn child. Less than a month later, when he went to collect his wages on Friday night, he was told to collect his cards, as there just wasn't enough work to go round. He was the youngest and last to finish his apprenticeship, so he would have to be the first to go. His heart sank, what was he going to tell Kathleen?

Kathleen's dad was a shoemaker. The old man who had trained him as a boy was due to retire. Kathleen's dad made enquiries and soon Angus was training to be a shoemaker alongside his father-in-law. He really enjoyed this new trade and, just after the birth of their first son, Angus junior, they moved into a room and kitchen, one floor up in Agnes Street in the Maryhill area of Glasgow. It wasn't much. They had a big open-range fire in which she did all the cooking. Their means of light was a gas mantle above the fireplace. At night, they carried candles on saucers to go into their other room or when they went out on the landing to the toilet which they shared with three other families. The washhouse was a little brick building in the backcourt with an old stone sink. She went down there once a week on her allocated day with her washboard, big bar of soap and the week's washing. In spite of everything, she was blissfully happy.

Kathleen shopped around for second hand furniture. She bought a smoker's chair for Angus, which had wooden sides and shelves to keep his pipe, tobacco and newspapers, a small brown leather easy chair for herself, a small table with folding flaps for them to eat their meals from, and two dining chairs. The recess in the kitchen already had a bed in it, so they used that for the time being. They had plans for saving hard for a big double bed for the bedroom for themselves, as they knew eventually the 'hole in the wa' bed would be for their offspring. Kathleen was extremely fertile and gave birth to another son ten months later. She went on to have six more children in these cramped conditions in Agnes Street.

In 1929 when she was37 and pregnant with their ninth child, they moved to their brand new council flat in Bilsland Drive. Kathleen was in bliss to have her very own kitchenette where she could cook and do the family washing. There was a big bathroom with hot and cold running water. No more would they run out into the staircase to use a shared toilet. In the new flat, Angus and

Kathleen had one bedroom, the three girls shared a double bed in the second bedroom, and the five boys had the big bedroom with two double beds. They felt like millionaires. Kathleen gave birth to their ninth child, Alex, shortly after the move. In 1935, at the age of 43, she gave birth to her tenth and last child, Andrew. She was aware that something wasn't quite right, and, by the time Andrew was six months old, he was diagnosed as a Mongol, now more commonly known as Down's Syndrome. Kathleen and all the family loved and encouraged baby Andrew. They couldn't understand why people seemed embarrassed and avoided talking to them when they took him out.

Angus was very firm with the family. He disciplined them and they all had a chore to do. They referred to him affectionately as 'Pop'. With such a big family, everyone had to muck in. Kathleen was very organized and had a daily menu. The family only had to think of the day of the week and they knew what their meal would be for that evening. On Saturdays, it was mince and tatties. They had a very large oak dining table that Kathleen had bought second-hand when they moved to Bilsland Drive. It had thick, round, carved legs on casters, one on each leg and one in the middle. It also had many flaps to pull out, but no one ever saw it at its full potential, as the room wasn't big enough. This big square table could sit twelve people around it, no bother. On Saturdays, all the children would line up behind their Pop and they would sing as they marched round the table, 'Glory be to Saturday, the day we get the mince, the mince, the mince, the mince, the mince!' Kathleen also bought, second-hand, a beautiful ebony sideboard with twisted, carved legs, and a Victorian display cabinet that was a tall, square glass box on long, thin legs. She loved her new house and was so proud of her bargain buys.

She worked hard, up at 5am to get the fire going and to make breakfast for all the family. No sooner had she got the family out to work and school, she then had to start on the washing. Out would come the mangle. It would take about three hours to wash and wring all the bedding and clothes. She would then go down three flights of stairs to hang it all out in the back green. After that, she would start on the cleaning. Then, it would be time to go to the shops to buy the evening meal and come home again to prepare it. Before she knew it, everyone was home and hungry. The boys would lay the table and the girls would do the clearing up after. Saturday afternoon was Kathleen's day to catch up on her sleep. Angus and the older boys would go to see their local football team, 'Patrick Thistle', play. The girls would look after the younger children and Kathleen would have a three-hour nap in peace before getting up to start making the mince and tatties.

What's For Ye, Won't Go By Ye

Douglas was a bright boy. He was top in his class, won lots of books, and every prize giving. He had thoughts of going to a university, but he knew his family could never afford it. All his older siblings had left school at the age of 14 to work and help the family. He was very disheartened when, at the age of 14, his mum found him a job as a message boy in Cochrane's Grocery Store in Maryhill Road. She needed the extra money to help pay the bills and buy clothes and food for the younger members of the family. Although it wasn't the job he had dreamt about, he put everything he had into it and carried out all his duties efficiently. He soon became the darling of all the housewives. He would pack all the groceries into his homemade wooden barrow and run like the clappers, delivering the messages to all the different houses. He was always polite and would carry the entire heavy shopping right into the kitchen. The old dears would insist that he stop for a cup of tea. They then would press a farthing or, if he was lucky, a ha'penny into his hand. He could almost double his wages some weeks in tips alone. When he reached 16, he was promoted to work behind the counter. He enjoyed cutting ham in the big machine and digging into the big mound of butter with the wooden butter patter, then battering it into individual pats.

When Douglas was 17, his friend Archie, who worked at the local flourmill, told him about a job that was going there. It was shift work. Douglas knew the pay would be a lot better than what he was earning at Cochrane's. He went down there, but was dismayed to find a long queue of at least 40 men all waiting to be interviewed for this one job. He took his place in the queue, and then six more men turned up to join the queue behind him. Six hours later, he was ecstatic to be told that the job was his. They told him that they were impressed because he had turned up for the interview looking so smart and that he seemed an intelligent, polite lad and was the right age for them to train. He ran home, his heart pounding with excitement, he couldn't wait to tell his mother the good news He burst in the door jumping up and down with joy and broke the good new to her. She laughed and hugged him and told him how proud she was of him. He started work in the flourmill the following Monday.

With the older children out working, the family could now afford a holiday. The following summer, in 1938, the entire family packed their hampers and rented a flat with two rooms and a kitchen in an old tenement in Arbroath, on the east coast of Scotland, for two weeks. This was a special treat, to live by the seaside. They tasted for the first time the local traditional delicacy of Arbroath smokies, or herring, hung out and smoked. It wasn't much of a holiday for Kathleen though. With such a big family, it was just a change of sink! Every morning Kathleen made the breakfast for them all. After they had all eaten, it was the girls' job to clear up and wash the dishes. Kathleen then nipped down to the shops to buy something for dinner. After their work was done, the girls took the younger boys down to the seaside, while the older boys and Angus went out to place a 'holiday' bet with the bookie on the corner before going to the pub for a pint at opening time. When Kathleen returned, she peeled potatoes and vegetables, made a big pot of homemade soup, and prepared the meal. Usually she managed to get down to the seafront around about 4 o'clock. She spent an hour breathing in the sea air before heading back to finish the dinner preparations. The Arbroath holiday became an annual event.

In 1939, Douglas told his mum that he would like to introduce her to a lovely young lady he had met, called Margie. Kathleen was very apprehensive, as he was only 19, and she was slightly possessive with her sons. Margie was a bag of nerves when Douglas took her up to his house. There were so many MacGregors and so many names to remember. Kathleen questioned her about her family, her job, and life in general. Margie felt a bit uncomfortable with Kathleen, but Angus soon put her at ease and made her laugh, telling her stories about Douglas when he was younger. Douglas' brothers all liked Margie and she got on very well with them. His younger sister, Dot, appeared to be jealous of Margie, as Douglas had always spoiled her, and now she was feeling a bit left out. Margie soon brought her round and they became good pals. Andrew was four by now and a very loving child. He was full of impish pranks. For devilment, he called Margie, 'Maggie'. She pretended to be angry with him and he went into fits of giggles and laughter.

Margie went to the MacGregor household every Sunday evening. The whole family sat round the big table for the weekly game of cards. Pop sat with his back to the fireplace. Kathleen sat the corner, still wearing her apron. In the pocket, she had a wee bag of sweeties. She discreetly ate one after the other. It was as if she was telling the family that she had given to them the best part of her life and the sweeties were hers, and not to be shared. Pop always made up card game rules to suit himself. He changed them every week and was a bad loser. It always ended with him accusing his sons of cheating.

Margie and the girls sat and giggled, threw their eyes in the air and exclaimed, 'MEN!'

The second youngest son, Alex, was ten years of age now. It was his job to lay the table for supper after the card game. Being so young, he got away with a lot, as, after raising all these children over the years, Angus had mellowed. Alex picked up the cards and, with a cheeky grin and giggle, flicked them over his dad's nose. No one else would have dared to do that, but Alex had a way with him. He was a very loving boy and it was difficult to tell him off. He put out on the table milk, sugar and butter in the Sunday best cut glass dishes, two plates of sliced cheddar cheese, two plates of sliced meat, salt, pepper, sauces, pickles, plain Scottish bread, home made black buns or dumplings, cups, saucers and cutlery for everyone.

After they all had tucked in and had had enough to eat, Margie and Douglas' sisters cleared everything away and did the washing up. Then, about 10.30pm, Douglas walked Margie home. They strolled arm in arm all the way down Bilsland Drive, past the Mecca Picture House and up Balmore Road. The walk took them about 25 minutes. When Margie was safely indoors, Douglas about turned and ran all the way back home in about ten minutes. He was now on permanent early shift at the flour mill and had to be up for work at five the next morning. He usually got in to find Kathleen making a mound of 'pieces'. This was the next day's sandwich lunches for all the workers in the family.

Douglas loved is mum and would do anything for her. He appreciated how hard she worked. Often, in the middle of the week when money was scarce, he would be thinking where he was going to get the money to take Margie to the pictures. He would ask his mum for a loan until payday on Friday. She was an excellent manager and always had a few bob tucked away. She would go into her apron pocket, take out her brown leather purse and slip him half a crown (12 and a half pence), saying 'Don't let Pop know!' Douglas would then get down on one knee and serenade her with, 'For cherish her with care and smooth her silver hair, for when she's gone you'll never find another. And wherever she may be, God send her back to me, for a boy's best friend is his mother' She loved his charm and with a wee tear in her eye, she would laugh and say, 'Get oot o ma sight noo!' He would then tear down the road to meet Margie on the corner by the Mecca Picture House.

In 1940, Douglas became concerned when his eldest brother, Angus junior, was drafted into the Royal Air Force. Shortly afterwards, Jack (who was only eleven months older than Douglas), signed up for the Royal Marines. Douglas' other brother, George, worked for Rolls Royce. His skills were needed in the war effort, so he escaped being called up to fight in the Forces for Britain.

Douglas felt sick at the thought of being separated from Margie and his family by war. He knew it was only a matter of time until he was called up. One Sunday evening, as they strolled home in July of 1941, Douglas took Margie in his arms and asked her to marry him. Margie was ecstatic and yelled, 'Yes, of course I will, you know I will!'

The next day was Glasgow Fair Monday and so the shops were closed. They got a bus into Paisley and looked round the jewellers' shops there. Margie eventually chose a beautiful 'three in a twist' diamond engagement ring. 'She'll keep it on', Douglas told the jeweller. Margie beamed with happiness and couldn't wait to get home to show the family.

They set the wedding date for February of 1942. Margie made herself a lovely white forties style wedding dress from material that she bought with coupons she had asked around for and begged for. Betty was her bridesmaid, and she managed to borrow a dress from one of her clients whose wedding photos she had taken three years previously. Douglas' brother was on leave from the Marines and he was best man. They married in the vestry of the parish church in Possilpark. All the immediate family attended the service, followed by a meal at the Ca'dora restaurant in Glasgow.

They rented a furnished room and kitchen in Amisfield Street in Maryhill. They were so happy to be together, they put the worrying thought of Douglas going to war to the back of their minds. Only three months later, the letter they were dreading arrived. Douglas was ordered to report for a medical exam the following week. He went through a thorough examination, then, just as they were about to pronounce him fit, he was asked what happened to his finger? He told the army doctor about his accident at the flour mill two years previously. Well dammit man! exclaimed the doctor, you're no damn good to the army without a trigger finger! They signed his papers as unfit to serve in the Forces due to his missing right index finger. When he told Margie, she breathed a sigh of relief. Her eldest brother, John junior, had not been called up, as he was an engineer in the shipyards. Donald and James were already serving abroad in the forces.

Douglas received another letter six weeks later, ordering him to report for a second medical He thought there must be some mistake as they already turned him down! When he got there, he was told that a panel had checked all the papers of the men who failed their medicals and it was decided they should be seen again. This time, he was passed as fit and was signed up for the Royal Artillery.

Margie couldn't believe it. She cried her eyes out and wished that Hitler had never been born. Douglas was to report for training in four weeks' time. He decided that she should move back in with her mother, as he feared for her living alone with all the bombing raids that the Germans were carrying out over Glasgow in their attempt to bomb the nearby Maryhill Army Barracks and the shipyards on the Clyde.

So, only seven months after they married, a tearful Margie, overcome with grief, said good-bye to her beloved Douglas at the Central Railway Station.in Glasgow. He was off to train in an army camp in Bedfont, Middlesex. Like all the other young women there to see their men off, she clung onto him as he leaned out of the carriage window. She screamed 'no!', as the train gently started up, with steam belching from its funnel. She ran along to the end of the platform, sobbing uncontrollably, as she watched the train disappear into the distance. She couldn't understand why they had to send him so far away, when there was an army barracks only two streets away from their little nest in Amisfield Street. It didn't seem right to her that the barracks here in Maryhill were full of English soldiers, and that the Scottish soldiers were all sent to England. This, of course, was the army's method of getting the full attention of the soldiers, making it very difficult for them to sneak back home.

Margie settled back at her mother's flat with John junior, and her sisters, Betty and Mary. She carried on working and helping her mum, just like she'd never been away. She and Douglas wrote to each other every day and slept with each other's photos under their pillows. Two months later, Douglas was allowed home on a two week's leave. Her stomach churned with excitement as she waited for his train to arrive at the station. It came chugging in forty minutes late. She stood there anxiously watching all the soldiers arriving home on leave and kissing and cuddling their sweethearts. Then she spotted Douglas. They ran towards each other and he swept her up into his arms, giving her a long, passionate kiss. They were so happy to be together again. Although she hated the idea of him being a soldier, she thought he looked handsome in his uniform with his kit bag, stamped Private D. MacGregor, over his shoulder.

He told her all about his training, and how difficult he was finding it. He was at the rear on the big guns, shooting down aircraft. Because of his missing index finger, the gun shuddered every time, but his sergeant wasn't interested in the mere problem of a missing trigger finger! He also told of the devastation and carnage in Bedfont when a German bomber tried to bomb the army barracks and missed, flattened a whole street of houses instead. Douglas' eyes filled up as he told how they had to dig out the bodies of people that they knew: the little old couple in the corner shop (who always kept black market cigarettes under the counter for the servicemen), women, children and babies. Douglas told her how brave the local Feltham Fire Brigade was. They coped with this sort of thing night after night. It was a horrifying sight, and left its mark on Douglas' brain. Douglas stayed with Margie in the small room in her mother's flat. Margie managed to get some time off, and they spent the two weeks relishing and appreciating every minute of being together. Douglas knew that when he went back, it would be the start of the serious business of war. He was to be posted to the White Cliffs of Dover to operate the anti-aircraft guns on top of the cliffs.

All too soon they were back at the Central Railway Station with a heavy feeling in their stomachs. At the back of both their minds was the unthinkable thought that they might never see each other again. They clung to each other, Margie was again sobbing uncontrollably. Douglas was scared, he hated the thought of leaving his wife, family and his homeland. He put a brave face on for Margie, though inside he felt sick. The scene upon the platform was of mothers and young women hanging onto their soldier sons, husbands, boyfriends and brothers, as if trying to pull them back and defy Hitler's war.

Margie sunk herself into her work and waited eagerly every day for the postman. Douglas was on active duty and now letters were few and far between. Christmas and the New Year came and went. Late one Monday night towards the end of February 1943, there was a knock at the door. Families all hated hearing their doors go at odd hours when they weren't expecting anyone. They all looked at each other with worried and frightened expressions, hoping against hope that it wasn't a telegram with bad news about Douglas or Margie's two brothers. Gingerly, they all approached the door and John junior slowly opened it. Standing there beaming was Douglas! He had been allowed two weeks' leave before his new posting. Everyone screamed in delight. He held Margie in his arms like he was crushing her and gave her a long, lingering kiss. The rest of the family cuddled around them in a tight family hug.

Douglas was glad to be back and enjoyed the home comforts while he could. He told Margie and her family how he had to sleep rough under canvas beside his big anti-aircraft gun on top of the White Cliffs of Dover in the freezing cold. A siren went off to alert the soldiers when the German planes were approaching across the English Channel for another bombing raid. They would all leap into action, watching for the dark shadows of the planes across the night skies and attempt to shoot them down. Douglas hated himself for doing this, but he was all too aware that if they didn't, then innocent British people would have their homes bombed to the ground, be seriously injured or, worse still, die. One night he had a narrow escape when a German bomb hit the cliff face. Luckily, no one was seriously injured. At the back of his mind was always the thought that he was responsible for killing someone's son, brother, dad or husband, maybe someone that, like him, was forced and had no option but to go to war for his country.

During his leave, Douglas was very spoiled and well looked after by Margie and Peggy. He and Margie walked round to his parents' house to surprise them. Kathleen grabbed Douglas and sobbed her heart out. She would do anything to have all her boys back home. Food was scarce due to the rationing, but Kathleen sat Margie and Douglas down at the big table with the rest of the family. Kathleen then prepared a feast out of nothing.

Douglas knew that within the next six months there would be a definite chance that he would be posted abroad, but the soldiers were never told until a week or two before. The whole family was upset when he had to return to the South of England. Again, there were the usual sorrowful scenes at the station, with everyone saying good-bye to their menfolk. During this time, Margie was feeling unwell. She put it down to the strain of coping with the worry of her young husband and fearing for his life. Peggy wondered if Margie wasn't expecting a baby? Within a couple of weeks, Peggy's comment proved true, Margie was pregnant with her first child. She wrote immediately to tell Douglas. He was overjoyed but, at the same time, worried that he wouldn't be there to take care of her. He knew any day that he could be sent abroad. He yearned to see Margie.

On his days off, Douglas used to help a local older gentleman named Mr.Mason. Douglas told him about Margie. The old man insisted that Douglas bring her down to stay with him and Mrs. Mason, as they had four bedrooms all to themselves. Douglas wrote to Margie with the good news. She packed her bag and set off for Central Station to catch the train to London. Peggy was very worried about her going there, as they knew how badly London was being bombed. She also worried about the condition she was in. The train was packed, there were no seats, and Margie sat on her suitcase for the whole nine-hour journey. Had she said that she was pregnant, someone would have given up his or her seat for her. Being as she was a small and slim girl, nothing was showing. She didn't want to make a fuss, although she felt ill for the best part of the journey.

When she arrived in London, Mr. Mason was waiting for her, recognizing her immediately from the photograph he had in hand that Douglas had given him. After another hour and a half's journey, Margie arrived at the Mason's house in Bedfont. She was overwhelmed. They lived in a big semi-detached four bedroom house with a big back yard and front garden. They were very kind to Margie and looked after her like she was the daughter they never had. Out in the garden Mrs. Mason kept rabbits. There were hutches upon hutches of them. Margie thought how beautiful they were and took one out to pet it. Noticing that one hutch was empty, she asked Mrs. Mason why there was no rabbit in that one. 'That's because you've just had it for dinner', she exclaimed. Margie was shocked. She had never eaten rabbit before. She had eaten her dinner and not asked questions, not wanting to appear rude by asking what her meal was. She soon learned that the rabbits were not pets, but a means of survival.

Margie enjoyed staying there, as it meant that she saw a lot more of Douglas on his daily and weekend leaves. After four weeks, Margie was preparing to go home. She realised that Douglas' new posting abroad was imminent and she missed her mother very much. Mr. and Mrs. Mason tried to talk her into staying, telling her that they would look after her, and there would always be a place for the baby too. They were upset when Margie left. They told her to keep in touch and let them know all about the baby when it was born.

Five days after she got back home, Margie got a letter from Douglas saying that he was boarding a ship that day. He wasn't allowed to tell her anything more. She felt her heart miss a beat. This meant that, at this moment in time, he was somewhere out at sea. Four months passed. Soon it was Christmas and she heard nothing. She waited every morning for the postman. On the Morning of 30th December 1943, she finally got her long awaited letter from Douglas. He was in Egypt. He sent her a photo of himself in khaki shirt and shorts, standing by the pyramids. That night, she kissed his photo and held it close to her heart before putting it under her pillow. As she did so, she felt a twinge. She called to her mother, who confirmed that she was going into labour.

Peggy called in the midwife, who decided that Margie should give birth in the nearby Oakbank Hospital. Twenty-six hours later, and just before midnight on 31st December 1943, Douglas junior was born. He screamed his head off and weighed in at a healthy 6 pounds, 8 ounces. Margie was delighted. She couldn't wait to write and tell Douglas that he had a handsome son. Betty arranged for lots of photos to be taken at her studio. Margie sent them all off to Douglas. He was ecstatic when he saw the photos of his son. He just wished that the war would come to an end. He wanted to get back to his wife and son in their own house and be a proper family.

One evening in their flat in Possilpark, the sirens went off. Margie wrapped baby Douglas in a big blanket and went with John junior and her sisters to the air raid shelter. Peggy refused to come down, saying she was fed up with running up and down the stairs at the beckon call of the Germans. Margie worried for her mum as she heard a doodlebug above. These were flying machines with no pilots. When their engine cut out, you knew it was over an area that was about to be bombed. She listened as the engine cut out directly above them. When the clearance siren stopped, they all scrambled anxiously out of the shelter to out to see what devastation there was. They were amazed to see everything was untouched. A few hours later, they were told a doodlebug had landed in the school opposite. Fortunately, it hadn't gone off. The bomb disposal squad gingerly defused it and made the area safe. That same night, Peggy's sister-in-law and three children were killed when a doodlebug bombed their home in Clydebank. After that, as soon as the sirens sounded, Peggy made for the shelter with everyone else.

Baby Douglas was the apple of everyone's eye. Peggy was a proud grandmother for the first time. Betty and Mary raced home from work every night and took turns to cuddle and spoil him. John junior would walk up and down the floor with him, soothing him to sleep during the teething months. Douglas junior was surrounded by love. There was a big fuss when he cut his first tooth. His first word, da-da, brought tears of happiness to Margie. She wrote and told

Douglas of their son's progress, how he was crawling at seven months and then toddling at eleven months. She hoped that her letters were getting to him. Douglas junior was also the first-born grandchild in the MacGregor family. Angus and Kathleen were so proud that they had a grandson to carry on the MacGregor name. As he grew into a toddler, he became close to his Granny Peggy. She was like a second mammy to him, probably because she was always there. If he fell over and hurt his knee, she would kiss it better for him. She would save up her coupons to buy him sweeties.

In the spring of 1944, when she was 19, Mary joined the Wrens. Peggy was at her wits' end, especially as Mary had volunteered. She was sent to Portsmouth for training. Fortunately, she was never sent to trouble spots. She enjoyed being in the Service and looked upon it as a great adventure. She spent most of her time socialising in the southeast of England, going dancing and showing off her jitterbugging skills.

That summer, Margie and baby Douglas joined the MacGregors on their annual trip to Arbroath. The girls loved having a baby to fuss over and took it in turns to hold him and push his pram. Alex was 14 by this time and asked Margie if he could take the baby for a walk. Margie agreed, and told him that he could take the baby out while she helped his mother in the house. This was at 10 o'clock in the morning. By noon, there was no sign of him. By 3 o'clock, Margie was frantic, thinking that something had happened to them. Baby Douglas had been due a feed at 2 o'clock. She knew he would be hungry and needing a nappy change. Everyone split up and went to look for Alex. By this time, it was quarter to four. Margie was looking along the seafront road when, in the distance, she recognised baby Douglas' pram, being pushed by Alex. He was speeding towards her. The baby was crying and hungry. Margie breathed a huge sigh of relief and angrily asked Alex where he had been all this time. She told him how worried they had all been, adding that she had only meant for him to take the baby round the block for fifteen minutes or so, not for almost five hours! Alex couldn't see what all the fuss was about. Margie nearly passed out when he said that he had gone to Carnoustie, an all round distance of twelve miles. When the baby had started to get restless and cry in the last half hour, he decided to run and get him home as soon as possible. Alex seemed to think he had done well, and didn't understand why people were not congratulating him for his efforts!

The same year, Douglas was posted to other places in the Far East. He and the other young soldiers saw terrible scenes that no one should ever have to witness. They saw destruction, the death of innocent people, and their own best friends being killed. They buried their pals' bodies in unmarked graves. They knew that it was only by sheer fortune that they were still alive. They didn't hold out much hope of ever seeing their loved ones again. They cursed Hitler for his dictatorship and sheer greed.

While in Iraq, Douglas got very ill with malaria. He laid sweating and hallucinating in a hospital tent for days and wasn't expected to live. He amazed the doctors as his temperature gradually came down and he made a full recovery. In 1945, he had a close shave with death in Palestine after boarding a troop train. As it was about to pull out of the station, the frantic command came for everyone to jump off at the double. Four carriages full of soldiers obeyed the command. Two minutes later, as the train chugged out of the platform with the driver and crew still aboard, it blew into smithereens. It had been booby-trapped and the word had got to the officer in command just in time.

Two months after that, Douglas got the wonderful news that they all had been waiting for: World War II was over! Hitler had been defeated and they would be going home. Back in Britain everyone was so relieved, there were street parties that went on for days. There was a great feeling of peace and neighbourliness. Maybe now they could get on with a normal life.

CHAPTER TWO

Margie's two brothers were discharged from the Army and came home within six weeks of each other in the spring of 1946. Donald had had a hard time in France, as did Douglas' brother, Jack. They were both lucky enough to have survived D-Day. 6th June 1944, when the German Army swept through Northern France, taking prisoners and shamelessly killing thousands. They were rescued in an armada of small sailing ships and fishing vessels. These were captained and crewed by ordinary people, who took their own lives in their hands to sail across the English Channel to and from France to save marooned servicemen on the French beaches.

Margie and Douglas' brothers didn't realise that they had both been in the same predicament until they finally got back home again and exchanged stories. James had a terrible experience in Italy. He had hidden from the enemy by lying under water in the banks of a river, breathing through a reed. He had lain there for hours. This had left him with a weakness and wheeze in his chest after that.

John junior took his brothers out to celebrate their homecoming. They met up in the pub with all their pals and exchanged stories of their experiences. The majority of these young men were not even twenty-five. They had experienced scenes that were to stay with them and haunt them for the rest of their lives. They put on very brave faces, but, in reality, most of them were affected. They looked at life with different perspectives.

Later that evening, John junior, Donald and James crawled up the stairs to their mother's flat, intoxicated and laughing. They could be forgiven for getting drunk, they hadn't been together in over four years. They found the door key after searching through each other's pockets and managed to negotiate the lock and open it. Everything was quiet. The family members were all fast asleep in their beds. John junior was hungry and went to see what he could find in the kitchen. He saw a big pot sitting by the side of the cooker and said to his brothers, 'Our luck's in, mother's made a pot of soup'. He warmed it up on the stove and carefully ladled the soup into three bowls. The young men tucked in before climbing into their beds to sleep off their drunken stupors. The next morning told it's tale in their aching heads, but they agreed that it was all worth it, as it was great to be back together again as a family.

John junior said to Peggy, 'That was a rerr pot of soup you made mother, we fairly appreciated it when we got home last night!'

Peggy looked puzzled and said, 'What soup?' Then the penny dropped. She said, 'You daft galoots, that was the mince pot that I left steeping after last night's tea!'

Donald and James had both missed their sweethearts so much while they were away fighting for their country, they decided to make up for all the lost time and set a date to marry their girls in a double ceremony in the local parish church. Mary was discharged from the Wrens and got home just in time for the wedding. Material was scarce. Nevertheless, the two brides looked beautiful in their stunning white, lacey Forties style dresses that Margie had redesigned from old wedding dresses donated by friends. Donald's bride-to-be had a calf-length dress with a 'V' neck, three-quarter sleeves and big, padded shoulders. She set it off with a dainty little white hat with feathers, tipped to the front of her head. James' bride chose a full-length dress with a stand-up open neck collar and buttons down the front. She had long sleeves that went into points on her hands. Her neat little veil was held in place by two beautiful, big white roses. Both girls' bouquets were made up of white roses, gip and long, hanging green fern.

Douglas junior was two and a half by now. Margie made him a little MacGregor tartan kilt along with a white shirt and matching tartan bow tie. Kathleen gave him a wee leather sporran that had been handed down through all her boys. He loved his new outfit and Margie was so proud of him.

After the church service, there was a big party at the Nixon's house for the family and all the guests. Food was still on ration, but Peggy had managed to persuade family and friends to part with some of their coupons. She had two plates piled high, one with ham sandwiches and the other with cheese sandwiches. She also made three round fruit cakes, graduating in size. She placed them one on top of another, with the smallest on the top, and then iced them together. On the smallest cake, she arranged some iced rose petals. The brides and grooms were delighted with their surprise wedding cake.

After all the toasts and speeches were completed and they had all had their fill of food, Margie's sisters coaxed her to play the piano. They sang all the wartime favourites, *Pack up your troubles in your old kit bag*, *It's a long way to Tipperary*, *We'll Meet Again*, and *There'll be Blue Birds Over the White Cliffs of Dover*. When Margie was playing these songs, she could not help but think of Douglas. She missed him so much and felt sad that he wasn't with them to join in the family celebrations.

Douglas arrived back in England not long after. He had been made up to corporal and was proud of his stripe. He enjoyed singing and had a lovely tenor voice. He learnt a lot of songs whilst in the army and used to entertain his fellow troops with his renditions and yodeling. The word soon got round about the 'singing and yodeling corporal'. He was invited to sing on a live radio show in England for the Forces, but sadly, he missed his moment of fame. He had damaged his right knee in Palestine and it had gradually worsened It was now so bad that he couldn't take any weight on it and needed to be operated on. He was admitted to the army hospital in Chertsey, Surrey and stayed for two weeks. He was then sent back to the barracks at Bedfont on crutches. He knew that he would be discharged from the Army within the next 18 months and couldn't wait to get back home and start a proper married life with Margie and his son. He went round to visit Mr. and Mrs. Mason, who were both delighted to see him again. They offered two rooms in their house for himself, Margie and their young son to live in. There was lots of work becoming available in the southeast of England, and he would have no problem getting a good job when he left the Army. Mr. and Mrs. Mason felt that the young couple deserved a chance in life, and they wanted to help them get a good start to their long awaited married life together.

Excitedly, Douglas wrote to Margie to tell her of Mr. and Mrs. Mason's generous offer. Margie thought about it long and hard but, in the end, she told Douglas that she couldn't move away from her mother. It would have broken Peggy's heart and upset both her and Douglas junior if they were parted, as the grandmother and grandson both adored each other.

At last Douglas got the news he was waiting for. Just before Christmas in 1946, he was discharged from the Army. Margie was ecstatic. She couldn't wait for her man to come home. She dreamed that they would all soon be all together as a family, in their own wee house. That Christmas was the happiest one in years. They hung up paper chains, put up a small Christmas tree and hung bobbles on the branches that they made out of paper. There was happiness, contentment and a feeling of peace all around. Douglas was getting to know his son. With great joy and delight, he helped him hang up his stocking and leave out a biscuit and a glass of milk for Santa Claus. On Christmas morning, Douglas, Margie, Peggy, Betty, Mary and John junior watched and laughed as 'wee Douglas' peered into his stocking. There was a toy gun, an orange, an apple and a two shilling piece. He then looked over to the corner and he spotted a big box. He ran over to it. In spite of still being sleepy, his eyes were wide with excitement and amazement. When he tore it open, he found a wee red and blue trike. He climbed on to it and in no time he was peddling up and down the lobby, wearing his dad's helmet on his head and a beam on his face. Douglas and Margie had treated their son to the trike out of the money Douglas received on his discharge. They all sat round the table for Christmas dinner, which consisted of homemade broth, brisket beef, potatoes and steepy peas. This was followed by a homemade fruit dumpling and custard. In the evening, Margie played the piano as they all sat around her and sang. The family was complete again at last. They had all waited so long for this day and they were relishing every minute of it.

The following week, being New Year, the families all got together at the MacGregors' on Hogmanay to celebrate the men's homecoming and the start of a new and peaceful year. It was wee Douglas' birthday, and everyone brought him presents and wished him a happy third birthday. Douglas bought him toy soldiers. Margie made him a smart pair of tartan trews and a shirt. Peggy knitted him a Fair Isle jumper and Kathleen knitted him a balaclava, socks and mittens onto which she sewed a long tape that went through his coat sleeves to ensure that he wouldn't lose them.

Angus was very proud of his Scottish roots and New Year's was always a big event in the MacGregor household. Angus and Kathleen were very superstitious, and their superstitions had to be obeyed and carried out. The house had to be spotlessly clean and all rubbish thrown out before the bells chimed midnight. This stood for getting rid of the past and looking forward to the future. The kettle had to be on the boil as the bells were chiming midnight, this was to welcome new visitors into the family. The first person to visit after the bells had rung was known as the 'first foot'. They had to be dark and carry a lump of coal, some whisky, and some shortbread. This superstition meant the dark person was a miner giving you coal to burn in your fire to keep warm and have hot water. The whisky and shortbread were food and drink. With coal, food and drink, you were very wealthy! They all gathered around the radio to hear Big Ben chime in 1947. This was a special year, all the men and women were home from the War, and families all around Britain were reunited with their loved ones. As the first chime sounded out, they all raised their glasses, with whisky for the men, sherry for the women and blackcurrant cordial for wee Douglas and Andrew, who was now 11. They spared a thought for the poor families who had lost loved ones because of this cruel war and were not so fortunate as to be all together again like them. Then, they wished each other a happy, healthy and prosperous year ahead.

The next day Pop, Douglas and all his brothers all went to the 'Old Firm Game'. This was the traditional Rangers vs. Celtic match, played on New Year's Day. Throughout the match, Alex was complaining of a headache. Pop and Kathleen had been worried about him. He was working at the shipyards as an apprentice welder and, six weeks earlier, had a bad fall into the hold of a ship.

As they left the game, Alex hurried on ahead. They had trouble keeping up with him. He ran up the stairs to the house and rapped on the door impatiently.

When Kathleen answered it, he swept past her, saying that he needed to lie down. Kathleen made Pop and the boys some tea and sandwiches. After about half and hour she asked Douglas to go in and see if Alex wanted something to eat before she cleared the lot away.

Douglas opened the door of the big room. Alex was lying on top of the bed and Douglas knew immediately that something was wrong. Getting closer, he saw blood stains on the bedclothes and screamed an agonizing, 'NO!'

At that, everyone came rushing through to the big room. Poor Alex! He had suffered a fatal brain hemorrhage. It would have been his 18th birthday the following month. The whole family was in deep shock. He was such a lovable, mischievous, likable lad, and they just couldn't picture life going on without him. Margie was devastated. She felt she had lost her best pal. Alex had kept Margie company while Douglas was away, and wee Douglas loved him.

There was an air of immense sadness about the MacGregor household that New Year. As a mark of respect, all the neighbours kept their blinds down for the first week of the year until after Alex's funeral

Douglas and Margie settled into the wee back room in her mother's house with their son. Peggy liked Douglas a lot and really appreciated how helpful and obliging he was. He was always there to do all the odd jobs about the house and took care of the old grandmother clock that had belonged to Margie's dad. It had been left to rot after he died. His Pop also had a beautiful ebony grandmother clock with an eagle on top, Douglas loved clocks, but he was never allowed near Pop's clock. He had always hoped that one day he would own one as grand. He took Margie's dad's clock out of the cupboard and mended all the parts with care until it was working perfectly. He lovingly cleaned and polished the wooden case, the face, and pendulum until they shone. He hung it on the wall in the corner of the living room and every quarter of an hour, when the chime rang out, he glowed with pride.

Margie's best school chum, Daisy, and her husband, told Douglas that there was a job going at his local engineering firm. He said that if Douglas were interested, he would put in a good word for him. Douglas jumped at the chance and, less than a week later, the job was his. The pay wasn't good, but Douglas was aware that the training he was getting was invaluable and hopefully would enable him to get a better job with another company at a later date.

Betty got married and she and her husband moved in with his family in their council house in Scotstoun in the west of Glasgow. Peggy shared the other small room with her 21 year-old daughter Mary, while John junior (oblivious to the cramped conditions of the rest of the family), continued to selfishly claim 'the big room' all to himself. Two double beds could have fitted easily in this big room.

It was an extremely cold winter that year. Margie bought her sister Mary's heavy Wren's overcoat from her and she was delighted with it. Mary was never in. She loved going out and enjoying herself. She was very pretty and had no shortage of boyfriends. Margie was aware that Mary didn't pull her weight and could easily do more to help her mother. She would never offer to wash a dish. Peggy and Margie did all the cooking, shopping, washing and cleaning.

John junior announced that he was going to marry, and that his new bride would be moving into 'the big room' with him. Peggy was delighted that he was settling down at last. He liked to flirt and had plenty of girlfriends. He was almost 32, and she had worried that he would never meet the right girl. At the same time, she was feeling very apprehensive about them moving in with her. She felt that the house was getting too overcrowded and could lead to problems. Regardless of her feelings, Peggy was very soft hearted and never said anything to John junior.

Margie and Douglas were delighted to discover that she was expecting another baby, due in the spring of 1948. Douglas was elated, as this time he would be there for Margie. He only ever saw photos of his firstborn and never had the privilege of holding his son in his arms until wee Douglas was three years old.

Margie worried that it would be difficult for Douglas and their son to bond and, at times, she sensed that her husband was showing signs of feeling left out. She said to Peggy, 'You know mother, I'm concerned that the War has changed him. He's not the same man. Sometimes, when I hug and kiss wee Douglas or buy him something new, Douglas appears to be jealous. I get the feeling he's thinking that while he was away fighting a war, his baby son has taken his place, although that's not so. Maybe things would have been different if he'd never had to go, and had always been there for his son!'

Douglas had come through a very difficult time. Margie understood this and did her best to welcome him home and help him adjust back into family life. It wasn't easy for them, living under the same roof as the rest of the family. Their bedroom was cramped with a double bed, cot, small wardrobe and a dressing table. There just wasn't room to move.

Poor Peggy never argued or got involved in any of the family disagreements between her daughters and new daughter-in-law about the hot water or whose turn it was to use the kitchen for laundry or cooking.

On more than one occasion, when Margie went to the coat stand in the hallway, she discovered that the big Wren's overcoat was not there. She became extremely annoyed when told that Mary had gone out earlier wearing it! She thought that Mary was selfish, as she had paid her for it, and it was an ideal coat to cover her pregnancy and keep her warm in the winter.

John junior's new bride missed her own mother terribly and was finding it difficult settling into the Nixon house. Luckily, within three months of them getting married, her mother managed to find them a room and kitchen to rent in the close next to hers in Auchentoshan Terrace in Springburn.

Margie thought that life would be a bit easier for everyone then, as her mother could at last have her bedroom to herself. Mary could move into Douglas and Margie's room and hopefully, at last, as John junior wouldn't be there to call the tune any more, she, Douglas and their son could move into John's 'big room' in preparation for the forthcoming birth. There was plenty of room for their double bed, wee Douglas' single bed, a cot, a dressing table, a large wardrobe, pram and even a settee and two chairs. She was so excited to think that at last, they would all have some living space.

Immediately after John junior and his wife moved out, Mary sneakily moved her belongings into 'the big room', announcing that she was getting married, and her new husband was moving in. Margie was upset and furious that she had been kept in the dark and had not been consulted. She disappeared into her wee room and cried for hours, surely anyone could see that her and Douglas' needs were greater! No one even knew Mary's husband-to-be!. John junior had brought him up to the house a couple of times with him. Unbeknownst to anyone, Mary had gone out on a couple of dates with him. No one could understand why she was marrying someone she hardly knew and hadn't courted properly. Margie was the one who helped mother with all the household chores. Douglas was paying the rent, meaning that Peggy had her widow's pension all to herself. Margie felt the others never pulled their weight and they tended to take advantage of their mother. Margie recalled that when she moved back with her mother in 1942, she asked her if it was OK. The rest of the family moved themselves and their spouses in and out of Peggy's house as they pleased, and never respected their mother by asking her permission. Margie was annoyed at her brothers and sisters for taking their mother's good heartedness for granted. As usual, Peggy kept out of it and let them get on with it. She was becoming more involved with her spiritualist church and spent most of her time there. It was an ideal get-away from all of them.

Mary and her new husband were married in a quick civil ceremony and soon settled into 'the big room'. Very soon, it became apparent why Mary had decided to steal back her big Wren's overcoat from Margie. She couldn't conceal her bump any longer. She never discussed with her mother or Margie the fact that she was six months pregnant when she got married. They had their suspicions about it, but it was never brought up and they never dared to ask. Mary carried on as normally as possible. She gave birth to a son in January. Ten weeks later, in early April, Margie gave birth to her daughter, Linda. Douglas and Margie were overjoyed. They now had their perfect family of a son and a daughter. Wee Douglas was four by now and too big for the cot. He slept in Peggy's room at night to make way for the new baby.

Douglas and Margie were window-shopping in town one Saturday afternoon when Margie spotted a beautiful, coach-built bouncy pram. She had never seen anything like it. During the war years, everyone had to rely on second hand prams.

Douglas said to her, 'would you like that pram for Linda?'

Margie said, 'Oh yes, but it's six guineas, that's an awful lot of money!'

Douglas replied, 'We'll use my discharge money in the bank. We can manage on my wages now. I can earn £5 per week with overtime!'

They came out of the department store half an hour later, the proud owners of the big blue and white pram. She was the envy of all the young mothers for miles.

The atmosphere was getting very heated in the household. All the young parents and their offspring made the house very crowded. Margie went into the kitchen one morning to boil up the baby's nappies. She turned on the tap and was mystified to find there was no water. As usual, Peggy was at the spiritualist church. Margie knocked on Mary's bedroom door to tell her that there was something wrong with the water. Mary's husband was a bit of a 'know-it-all'. He answered the door and aggressively informed Margie that he had turned the water off, because he had bought the coal that heated the water and he wasn't having her using their hot water! Margie was dreadfully upset. She was a kind person, just like her mother, and would never have hurt anyone. She had done so much for her mother and the family over the years and couldn't understand why anyone could be so cruel as to deny her hot water for her young family.

When Douglas came home from work and heard what had happened, he was furious. He turned the water back on and went straight to Mary and her husband's bedroom door, banging it loudly. He informed Mary's obnoxious husband that he and Margie were paying the rent of the house. He also pointed out that Margie also attended to the general housework and cleaning of the home, with no help from Mary. If they wanted to have a say in any household matter, then they would both have to start paying their way and pulling their weight. Mary and her husband were very sheepish after that. They didn't realise the expense and upkeep of running a home. In their naivety, they thought that buying the coal and paying for their own shopping was all that was involved.

What's For Ye, Won't Go By Ye

It was 1950. Mary had given birth to another son in October 1949, but Margie and Douglas had kept out of the way of her and her husband since the 'coal and hot water' argument of two years previously. Instead of sitting by the warm cosy fire in the living room in the evening, they stayed in their wee cramped room. They had heard that the Glasgow Corporation was building housing schemes to help all the young families who never got a decent start to their married lives because of the War. The first houses were expected to be ready by 1952-53. Margie went down to the council offices and put their names down, hoping against hope that one day she and Douglas would get one.

Peggy had a soft spot for Margie and Douglas. She often said to them, 'What's for ye, won't go by ye!' and brought them wee treats to their room, maybe a bag of buns or a cake. She didn't like the friction and bad feeling, but she understood their predicament. She wasn't too keen on Mary's husband herself. She was aware that he was argumentative and that he was causing disruption in the family. Margie and Mary only spoke to each other when it was necessary. The children had the freedom of the house though, and wee Douglas, Linda and their cousins used to go into the living room and sit by the big fire where Peggy read to them and told stories.

Wee Douglas loved his wee sister and looked after her. He pushed her up and down the lobby on the trike. One time, he took her down to the backcourt to play with the other kids in the neighbourhood, promising faithfully to Margie that he would look after her. Linda loved this and stared in wonderment as the children set up a pretend shop using pebbles for money. Wee Douglas pressed a pebble into her hand and said, 'go and buy some sweeties'. The big girl took the pebble and gave her something wrapped in old bread paper. Linda opened it and started to eat it. She screwed her eyes up and pulled a face, thinking to herself that it didn't taste too nice. At that moment, Margie appeared in the backcourt to hang out her washing. She was wearing a cross-over paisley patterned apron and a green turban on her head. She ran over to Linda and scooped her finger into her mouth, pulling out the earth that Linda thought were sweeties.

'I thought that you were looking after your wee sister, Douglas!' she said sternly.

'Sorry mammy', he said, 'I forgot to tell her it wisnae real sweeties'.

They played hide and seek after that.

Then, one wee lad said, 'Let's shout up tae oor mammy's windae fur a jeely piece!'

This was a jam sandwich. When the children got hungry, instead of climbing all the stairs up to their homes, they shouted up to their mothers from the backcourt, 'Mammy, throw us o'er a jeely piece'. The busy mothers made them one big plain bread jam sandwich and wrapped it in waxed bread paper. They threw it from the kitchen window for their kids to catch. The youngsters all sat down and tucked in. This would keep the hunger pangs at bay until their dads came home from work and they had their evening meal. Linda loved to play with the big children. She was the youngest and they all wanted to be her 'mammy' when they played at 'wee hooses'.

Linda enjoyed going to the co-op with her mammy. The inquisitive wee girl always made a beeline over to the big bunker and watched in wonderment as the assistants shoveled out the potatoes. One day she felt very daring and decided that she would nip outside while her mammy's back was turned. She wandered around looking in shop windows and then thought that she would be very grown up. She crossed the busy road to look in the toy shop window. Very sensibly, she went to the zebra crossing and stood there waiting for the trams and motorcars to stop. Just as she was about to put a foot out, a big hand came down on her shoulder.

'And where do you think you're going to young lady?' said a man's voice.

Linda looked up to see the biggest policeman ever, his head seemed to be way up in the sky. He took her by the hand and asked her what her name was.

Linda told him, then she said, 'my mammy's in the shop'.

She took him to the co-op but there was no sign of Margie, who, by this time, had discovered Linda missing and was frantically searching for her. The policeman asked Linda if she knew where she lived. Linda nodded.

'Can you take me there?' the policeman asked.

Linda nodded again. She took him up the hill past the library. Halfway up the road, Rita, the next-door neighbour, came running down the hill. She shouted out, 'Oh Linda! thank goodness you're safe! Your poor mammy has been looking everywhere for you for the past hour, she's so worried'.

The three of them hurried home to find everyone out in the street. They cheered when they saw Linda. Margie was just coming round corner at the bottom of the street after another fruitless search. She heard the commotion and caught site of Linda with the policeman. She ran towards her wee girl then grabbed and held her so tight, sobbing her heart out.

'Oh, I thought I had lost you, my wee pet', she said through tears. She thanked everyone, including the policeman and Rita, for their help before going upstairs for a very welcome, nerve calming cup of tea.

Every Saturday at teatime Margie, and Douglas got the kids dressed in their best outfits and set off on the walk to visit Granny and Grandpa MacGregor. Douglas' brothers and sisters, and their spouses, gathered round the big table to play cards and dominoes. It was the same routine as it had always been, with Pop making up his own rules and accusing everyone of cheating, then nipping down for a pint with his sons while the lassies laid the big table for supper. After they'd all eaten and Linda was tired, Margie put her coat on her. Then, just as they were about to leave, it started as usual. Pop and his sons got into a heavy debate. It went from football to religion to politics. This went on for an hour or so. By this time, Linda had fallen asleep. Douglas, Margie and wee Douglas walked home by the light of the moon, Linda fast asleep in her daddy's arms. They eventually got back to their cramped room, and wee Douglas crept quietly into his Granny's bedroom.

By 1953, everything was getting too much for Douglas and Margie. Their children were growing and they badly needed to get a place of their own. Their marriage was feeling the strain of it all. Douglas was irritable and Margie felt that he blamed her for not taking up the opportunity that Mr. and Mrs. Mason had given them. They would have had so much more space, a garden for the children, and Douglas would have had a better paid job. Margie's concern for her mother had stood in the way of their future. Now, she felt that they had no option but to find another place to live, as the pressure of living under the same roof with Mary and her disagreeable husband was telling on their relationship.

After yet another argument with Mary over her husband and his selfishness, Margie set out to look for a place to rent. She tramped around the streets all day with Linda while wee Douglas was at school. It was a fruitless search, there was nowhere to rent anywhere, and you had to be 'in-the-know' to have any chance at all of getting a roof over your head. Margie felt angry that the War had caused so much disruption in their lives. They could have saved and bought their own place by now with the wages Douglas earned in the flour mill, had he not been called up to fight. Like so many other families, they were promised so much when the War was over. Sadly, these promises never materialised but then, they were the lucky ones, they were still alive! Just as with World War I, thousands of families lost loved ones during World War II. Their lives were wrecked, and they got no help or sympathy from anyone. Soldiers' hospitals and homes, such as Erskine Hospital in Renfrewshire and the Star and Garter Home in Richmond, Surrey, took in the unfortunate ones who were seriously injured and had no chance of living a normal life ever again. The hospitals relied on charity to keep them. It seemed that the country and the government took all that they could from their loyal people. but didn't give back in return.

Margie and Douglas were at the end of their tethers. Douglas said that he couldn't stand living there any longer and, after having angry words with Margie, he left for work, slamming the door in temper. Fifteen minutes later, the postman came. Margie looked at the postmark, it read 'Corporation of Glasgow'. Her heart started to thump as she cautiously opened the envelope. It requested her to come along that day to the corporation offices in Possilpark. She took wee Douglas to school and practically ran to the offices with Linda. Trying to curtail her excitement, she presented her letter to the woman at the front desk, who told her that Mr. Grant would be with her shortly. After about ten minutes, a short and stocky pleasant man with a big grey moustache and thick grey hair appeared. He had a big smile on his face. Margie felt that something good was about to happen at last! He informed her that they had reviewed thousands of applicants and although it was hoped they would all be re-housed eventually over the next five years, the Corporation had to prioritise who were the most needy. She felt her heart sink, convinced that he was going to tell her to wait another five years.

Then he said, 'As you and your husband have a young son and daughter and are living in cramped conditions, we have decided that you are a needy cause. This will benefit you and allow your sister and her family to spread out and have more space in your mother's house'.

He presented her with a slip of paper and asked her if she could meet the housing officer that afternoon at 2pm in Glengarry Street in the new housing scheme of Milton.

Margie practically kissed him. She danced out of the offices on cloud seven. Linda didn't quite understand, but she laughed and skipped down the road with her mammy. Margie quickly arranged for her mother to pick up wee Douglas from school. She didn't tell her mother anything, as she wanted to tell her husband first, before anyone. She walked all the way up Balmore Road towards Lambhill with Linda. She knew this road very well, as she had walked it many a time with Douglas when they were courting. It was her favourite walk with the children when they were in the pram. Just before Lambhill, she turned right towards the new housing scheme. She was in awe. There were streets of brand new tenement flats. She nipped herself to make sure that she wasn't dreaming. Margie walked all the way along the new main road. Two streets down she found Glengarry Street. There were rows of cottage style terraced houses with back and front doors and back and front gardens. She didn't know if their new house was definitely to be in Glengarry Street, but she hoped and prayed that this would be where it was.

A crowd of people was gathering. The housing officer appeared and took them all into the kitchen of one of the houses. He pulled the folding kitchen table up from the wall, then he took all the papers from the anxious people. He marked their presence off in his big black book. He then invited them, one by one, to pick a piece of paper out of a box. The piece of paper had a number on it. Margie could feel her heart beating as she waited to find out what this all meant. He carefully laid out keys on the table. When everyone had a piece of paper in their hand, he checked the number on each person's piece of paper, wrote it in his book against their name, and gave them the house keys with the matching plot number on them. He congratulated them all, one by one. Margie couldn't believe that she was holding the keys of her brand new house. She picked Linda up, squeezed her close, and started to cry with happiness and sheer relief. She and Douglas would at last have a normal married life! She looked around and it was a similar story with all the others. Everyone was exhilarated as they excitedly asked each other which plot they had got.

The housing officer told them that they were free at this point to swap houses with each other, and two people did just that. Linda knew something good was happening, but she wasn't quite sure what! Margie had a grin from ear to ear.

She said to Linda, 'Come on, let's go and find our new house!'

They approached the end of their terrace house. There was a 20-foot front garden with concrete steps up the middle. They climbed up the steps. Margie put the key in the lock and turned the key to open the door. To the right was a big living room with a tiled fireplace and windows to the front and back. Straight ahead was the kitchen with a cooker, a pantry, a press, a coal bunker, a boiler for boiling washing and a folding table. The back door was at the side and opened out to a side garden. At the back there was a 100-foot garden. Upstairs, there were two good-sized bedrooms, a big bathroom with a massive galvanised bath, sink and toilet bowl. Margie and Linda held hands.

Linda said, 'Is this our house, Mammy?'

Margie nodded with glee and then the two of them jumped up and down, holding hands, laughing and squealing with excitement. Margie felt like they had won the pools!

They got back home just five minutes before Douglas returned from work. Margie swore Linda to secrecy. He came into the room with a depressed look on his face, remembering the mood of things when he left that morning.

Margie said, 'Are you talking to me now?'

Douglas mumbled, 'Yes'.

She then said, 'Oh that's good! It would be awful lonely in that big house without you'.

He looked at her with a questioning frown. She then presented him with the keys.

'What's this?' Douglas said.

'It's the key's to our new home!' she replied.

'What do you mean' he said, with an even more puzzled look on his face, wondering what she had been up to.

Margie explained everything to him and wee Douglas. Douglas couldn't believe it at first. Then, he grabbed Margie in his arms and held her so tight she gasped for breath. It was like a dream, at last they were going to have a home of their own. Wee Douglas and Linda stood there looking on. Douglas scooped them both up, one in each of his arms, they all laughed and cried tears of happiness. They went and told Peggy, who was extremely delighted for them, and she felt that they more than deserved this happiness. Inside she felt sad. Margie was a very good daughter and she was sorely going to miss them all.

The following Saturday, Peggy took Douglas and Margie down to a furniture and household goods warehouse in The Gallowgate. She had held an H.P. account there for years and she went guarantor for Douglas and Margie to open an account. It was the only way that they would be able to furnish their new house. They picked out twin single beds and new bedding for the children, a sideboard, dining table and four chairs and a green leather settee. The manager very kindly agreed that a van would pick up their new possessions from the warehouse on the day that they were due to move in, and he also arranged that it would stop off at Peggy's house and pick up the rest of their belongings en route.

Moving in day arrived and the big brown furniture lorry pulled up at the close in front of Peggy's flat. There wasn't much, only the double bed, utility dressing table, two basket chairs, a big brown bakelite radio, wooden mantle clock, boxes of clothes, books and a few toys. Peggy gave Margie some of her pots, crockery and cutlery to help give her a start. Margie and Linda climbed into the cabin of the lorry with the driver, while Douglas and his son got in the back beside the furniture and the driver's two mates for the 15 minute journey out to towards the countryside and their new abode.

Margie felt her heart burst with joy and pride as the lorry pulled up at their new end of terrace house. Wee Douglas and Linda ran up and down the indoor stairs, then round and round in the front door and out of the back. They ran into the garden, which was overgrown with weeds and grass. They got the fright of their young lives when they saw a brownish tail sticking out the top of the long grass and creeping slowly towards them. Then they heard 'Toby! Dinner'. At that, the tail turned into a big tabby cat who jumped, turned, and raced to their new next door neighbours' house for his dinner. Toby was to become their friend and the lion in their imaginary jungle of long grass.

Margie soon had the house looking like a wee palace. She made curtains for all the windows, and flowery cushions and chair backs to match for the settee and chairs. Times were hard, as money had to be put aside every week to pay for the H.P. on the furniture. With the help of Margie's brother Donald, Douglas transformed the rear of the large back garden into a potato patch. Further down, they planted peas, tomatoes and rhubarb. This was all a great help in feeding their family. The children loved to pull a stick of rhubarb out from the garden and eat it raw, dipping it into a 'poke' of sugar. By Wednesdays, the cupboard was almost bare in waiting for payday on Fridays. There were no luxuries, spam mashed potatoes and peas were common on a Thursday evening for dinner. When the cornflakes ran out, wee Douglas and Linda had to have saps for breakfast. These were slices of bread cut up into small one inch squares with a tablespoonful of sugar and hot milk poured over them. A piece, or sandwich, of butter and sugar was a rare treat when there was no jam in the house.

They had to be very careful, though, as sugar, sweets and dairy products were all still on ration. Margie made stewed rhubarb, sometimes with custard, and, if she had the ingredients, she baked a rhubarb pie. Even if Margie was lucky enough to have the odd three or four pence to spare, it didn't matter, as it was no good without a coupon. Douglas changed his job to work for an engineering firm in the Trongate area of Glasgow. Towards the end of the week, he sometimes had to walk the 12 miles to work and the same back home again, because he didn't have the tu'pence for the tramcar fare.

Linda was five and due to start going to school, in the mornings only, at Easter. She was so excited and couldn't wait to be grown up like her big brother. Margie thought that with the two children off to school, it would be the perfect opportunity for her to get a part-time job to help with the family finances. She went down to the Candleriggs area of Glasgow with Linda in tow. There were many factories there and she tramped around them all, repeating the same story that she was looking for morning work as a seamstress. Her luck seemed to be out, as there were more people than there was work for. Finally, just as she was about to give up, she decided to try a company who made children's clothes in a big, old-fashioned building off of George Square. She spoke to a stout Jewish man. He had a tape measure round his neck and smoked a big cigar. To her delight, he asked her when she could start. As Monday was Linda's first day at school, Margie agreed to begin on Tuesday. Douglas' sister Dot had to go to the school everyday at noon to pick up her own daughter Anne, who was eight months older than Linda. Dot said that she would be more than happy to pick Linda up from school at the same time and look after her until Margie returned from work at 2pm. Dot and her husband Tom had been allocated a brand new flat in a tenement block two streets away. He had a secure, well-paid job with the Electricity Board

The big day arrived and Margie dressed Linda up in her little navy blue gymslip with the school badge sewn on the front, white blouse, school tie, shiny black strappy shoes, white ankle socks, navy brimmed hat with school badge sewn on and elastic under her chin to hold the hat firmly in place. Off they went, Linda skipping excitedly all the way. They got to Miltonbank School, built from prefabricated corrugated tin. They reported to the big classroom at the end. It was actually two classrooms, with the dividing wall opened up. They stood there with almost ninety other children and their mothers, anxiously waiting for Mrs. MacDonald, the head teacher, to appear. At last, she came through the door. She apologised for the delay, then went on to explain that this was a boom year for five year olds. Schools up and down the country were witnessing problems finding places for them all. On average, there used to be only 35 children to a class. The births had been so high in 1947-1948 due to the men returning from war, that there was now an average of 80 to 90 children. There just wasn't the space or teaching staff to cope. So, because of this, they were only taking in half of the children at Easter. The rest had to come back in August.

Everyone waited with baited breath to find out who the lucky ones were to be. They started calling out children's names. Margie knew that Linda would be very disappointed if she didn't get in this time, as she was so looking forward to it, trying on her school uniform in anticipation. The suspense was unbearable. Mrs. MacDonald had called out 34 names, and Linda's wasn't one of them.

As she got to the 35th, she said, 'I'm afraid that's it for this term, the rest of you will have to come back in August when we hope to have more resources and teaching staff'.

Linda didn't quite understand what was happening, and asked Margie why they were leaving and why she wasn't staying at school. Margie gently explained to her that she would have to come back again in four months. Margie was relieved that Linda was such a happy, easygoing child.

She said to her mother, 'But I WILL be going to school, won't I? I just have to wait a little longer!'

Margie looked down and her heart went out to her, standing there immaculate in her school uniform. 'That's right, my wee hen', she said, 'That's right!'

Meanwhile, Margie had the problem of the job she was due to be starting the next day. Dot came to the rescue. She told Margie to go to work as planned and she would look after Linda every morning for her.

The next morning, Margie was up at 5am. She went outside to the back of the house to get coal to light the fire so that there would be hot water for everyone when they got up. She made Douglas an egg sandwich and a cup of tea for breakfast, packed his lunchtime pieces into a red box tin, and saw him off to work at 6am. She had to leave the house by 6.40am at the latest, as she had to drop Linda off at Dot's before catching the 7am bus into Glasgow city centre to start work at 7.30am. She dashed upstairs and got herself ready first, letting the children sleep for as long as possible. She then woke wee Douglas up at 6.15am and, while he was washing and dressing himself, she pleated Linda's long dark shiny hair and then washed and dressed her. By 6.30am, they were sitting in the kitchen having breakfast. Wee Douglas was ten years old now. Margie was thankful that he was an extremely smart and sensible ten year old. He still attended his old school near his granny's house, and travelled four miles there and back on the bus everyday by himself. The night before, his dad had given him his very own door key on a long string to hang round his neck. He felt very grown up! Margie checked that all the windows were closed and everything was secure. Then she told wee Douglas not to touch anything and to leave the house by 8.20am, making sure that the front door was firmly closed behind him. He had over an hour to spare, so he settled down to read his schoolbooks and swot up for his spelling test that day. Wee Douglas was a very inquisitive, studious boy and enjoyed learning.

Margie hugged and kissed him, told him to be careful, and then set off apprehensively with Linda for Dot's house. She hurried up the road with mixed feeling and emotions, hating herself for leaving her children to go to work but, at the same time knowing that if she didn't help with the weekly income, there was no other way that they were going to make ends meet financially. Fortunately the bus stop was across the road from Dot's house, so she was able to give Linda a big hug and kiss and explain that she had to go to work to get 'more pennies'. Linda sat at her Aunt Dot's window and watched her mammy get on the big double-decker green and yellow corporation bus. She waved as it pulled away. Margie saw her wee daughter waving and felt her eyes fill up. She felt like stopping the bus and running back, but she knew that wasn't an option and she had to go to work.

Linda liked her Auntie Dot a lot. Uncle Tom had a good income and they were a bit better off. Her cousin Anne was a spoilt child. Linda was amazed at how rude she was to her mammy and sometimes felt like giving her Auntie Dot a hug to make up for Anne's bad manners. Anne had a bedroom full of brand new, expensive toys and games, bought for her by her Granny and Grandpa MacGregor and Dot's unmarried brothers and sisters. They tended to over-favour Anne.

Wee Douglas and Linda didn't have much, but what they did have, they appreciated. Linda loved her hand-me-down, home made wooden doll's pram and her baby 'Roddy' doll that she had been given for her first Christmas. Wee Douglas had a 'gird' that his Aunt Betty's husband made for him in the shipyard where he worked. This was a metal hoop with a metal looped handle. The object was to get it spinning and see how far you could run with it. Wee Douglas used to get all the way to the shops three streets away without it stopping. When his daddy timed him and told him how fast he was, he felt like a champion!

Auntie Dot got Anne ready for school and the three of them set off down the road. Linda really wished that she could be a big girl like Anne and go to school too. They took Anne into the playground and waited until the bell rang. The children all lined up and marched into their classrooms. Then, Linda and Auntie Dot headed back home again. Auntie Dot told Linda that she could play with Anne's toys while she caught up with some housework. Linda went to Anne's bedroom and she was in heaven, especially as Anne wasn't there to boss her around and tell her not to touch anything. She got out Anne's big new bouncy doll's pram and life size baby doll. She loved it. Then she had a shot at her rocking horse. She rocked to and fro, thinking to herself how lucky she was to have all these toys to herself. She was beginning to like the idea of having all this fun every morning while Anne was at school.

Mid morning, Auntie Dot called Linda 'ben the hoose' (through to the living room) for eleven's. On the round marble table, Auntie Dot had put a cup of tea for herself, a glass of milk for Linda, and a plate with four Abernethy biscuits on it. After they had eaten, Linda went and put everything back as she had found it in Anne's room. Then they set off back to the school to pick Anne up at 12 noon.

Anne came through the gates and said to Linda threateningly, 'I hope you huvnae been touchin' ma toys!'

Auntie Dot told her that she had to learn to share. When they got back home again, Auntie Dot prepared them sausages and chips for lunch and Anne went straight to her room to check everything. Linda said nothing as, even at five years old, she thought, 'what she doesn't know won't hurt her'. Anne was a spiteful child. She nipped and kicked Linda and pulled her hair when Auntie Dot wasn't looking. When Auntie Dot came into the room, they were locked together fighting on the settee and she had to pull them apart. Anne put on a pet lip and whimpered to her mammy that Linda started it. Linda was scared of Anne so didn't say anything and Auntie Dot believed Anne. As Auntie Dot left the room, Anne smirked sneeringly at Linda behind her mammy's back. Linda was a caring, loving girl and was never rude like Anne, but she didn't like being bullied by Anne. Whenever Anne picked on her, she plucked up all her courage and tried to give as good as she got. Unfortunately, she was always the one that was caught and got blamed of hitting 'sleekit' Anne.

Margie got home from work at 2pm and Linda was so happy to see her mammy. She had hated the two hours with the spoilt brat Anne. She skipped down the road home, hanging onto Margie's hand. She told Margie all about how she enjoyed playing with Anne's toys all to herself, her mid morning milk and biscuits, then sausages and chips for lunch, but that she didn't like it when Anne came home because Anne was mean to her. Margie worried about this. She didn't like the idea of Anne physically hurting Linda. She considered having words with Dot, but she knew that this would only lead to bad feeling and she didn't want to fall out with Dot. Peggy visited that evening and when she heard of Margie's predicament, she immediately offered to come over in the mornings to look after Linda to allow Margie to get to work. Of course, this was a much better arrangement, as Peggy was sure that she would enjoy the change of spending the mornings at Margie's with her granddaughter.

The next morning, Peggy arrived in time to see her daughter off. Margie breathed a sigh of relief and went to work more relaxed, safe in the knowledge that the children were with their granny. Now wee Douglas didn't have to see himself off to school and Linda did not have to get up at an unearthly hour. Peggy prepared wee Douglas' breakfast for him before sending him to school. Linda got up just after he had left. Margie much preferred her mother to look after the children, but hadn't liked to ask her because she felt her mother deserved a life of her own. Peggy, however, was only too happy to help. Linda loved her Granny Nixon, she made her feel like a special girl.

The extra money that Margie was earning came in handy. It wasn't much, but it helped keep the wolf from the door. She worked very hard in the factory, sewing children's tartan trousers and kilts. She was on piecework, which meant that her earnings were according to the amount of garments she completed. On Fridays, wee Douglas and Linda used to get excited, they knew it was payday for their mammy and they always got a treat. When Margie got home from work she emptied out the messages (shopping) from her bag and the children waited patiently for the white paper poke (bag) to appear. In it was a selection of 1d and 2d sweeties, usually two MB bars (a fondant bar covered in milk chocolate), lollies and toffees. In a good week, Margie treated them to a Napoleon hat each from the baker in Dundas Street. This was a pastry cake in the shape of Napoleon's hat, with fruit inside. At 5pm on Fridays, wee Douglas got ready and went off to the Life Boys in Possilpark. He looked forward to the day when he was 12 and could transfer to the Boys Brigade. He got back home about 7.30pm. At 8pm, Capaldi and Victor Cornachio's ice cream van came down the street, tooting their horn.

Wee Douglas was sent out to get two three-penny wafers and two tu'penny pokey hats (cones), one Mars bar and one bottle of ginger. Ginger was the standard name for pop. Usually he chose American Cream Soda (which had a lovely vanilla smell and flavour) or Irn Bru, which was a popular Scottish soft drink, reputed to make you strong and guaranteed to be the best cure for a hangover on a Sunday morning. With the 3d back on the previous week's bottle, this all came to 1/9d, and what a treat it was! They all huddled around the roasting coal fire while Margie cut the Mars bar into four equal pieces and poured out four glasses of ginger. The children took a teaspoonful of ice cream from the top of their pokey hat and stirred it into their glass of ginger to make an ice cream drink. They giggled and bet each other whose was going to fizz up the most, only to panic as it threatened to come over the top of the glass.

Linda made friends with two sisters across the road, Lorna and Anita. They came over to play most days, or Linda went to their place. They clip-clopped around in their mammy's high heel shoes, playing with their dolls. The old wooden doll's pram, along with the toy tea sets, were all brought out as they played at 'wee hooses'. Another favourite game was when they got one of their mammy's old silk stockings and put a rubber ball right down into the toe. Then they stood with their backs against the wall singing, 'Ah've a loddy in America, Ah've another in Dundee-ie-ie, Ah've another in Australia and he's comin' hame tae merry me-ie-ie', while they banged it up and down against the wall. When they tired of that, out came the old Kiwi or Cherry Blossom polish tin, full of pebbles. They marked out an area of boxes with chalk, numbered them and played peever (hopscotch). Linda loved her skipping ropes and occasionally Margie would join in with the girls and teach them some of the old rhymes that she remembered from when she was a young girl.

Lorna was six months older than Linda and Anita was six months younger. Lorna was at school in the morning. Linda listened intently while Lorna told her all about her mornings at school. Linda couldn't understand why she wasn't able to attend the same school as Lorna. She was only five years old and thought it very mean and unfair that grown ups insisted Catholics and Protestants attend different schools. She couldn't see the logic in it. Surely it would make more sense to go to the same school as your friends, that way you can all be together. It was bad enough that every one went to different churches on Sundays, why did they have to go to different schools too?

One afternoon when Margie got home from work, she persuaded Peggy to stay on later to have tea with them.

About 4pm, Mrs. Cuthbertson from next-door came round and blurted out in excitement, 'Have you heard? They've struck coal at the bottom of the street where they're building the new school!'

Apparently the developers had found an old coal mine. Coal was the main source of energy. Everyone had coal fires and this was their only means of hot water and heating. The word soon got round and everyone was down there, men, women and children, with buckets, basins, bags and spades. They were there well into the evening, digging for all they were worth and filling every vessel they could find with coal. The photographer from the 'Daily Record' turned up and took pictures of all the blackened, smiling faces. There was a wonderful, happy atmosphere as everyone celebrated their little bit of prosperity and the extra money that they would have in their pockets for the next week or two because they wouldn't need to buy any coal.

Margie got talking to another young mother who lived at the top of the street. Her youngest son was ages with Linda. Linda watched as he played up and down the street on his big, dark red three wheeler bike, wishing that she could have a shot, but too shy to ask. The young mother whispered to Margie that she had bought her son a brand new bike for his birthday next week, and asked if Margie was interested in buying the old one for Linda. Margie knew how Linda and wee Douglas had longed for a bike and had no hesitation in saying yes. The next week, they were the proud owners of the big three wheeled bike. Wee Douglas peddled round and round the block and raced to the shops for his mammy while his daddy timed him.

Wee Douglas was pally with the twin boys a couple of doors down, they were about eighteen months older than him. An older girl in the street told them that one of the farmers was clearing out his potato field and had said to spread the word that anyone was welcome to help themselves. They, and a few other lads in the street, cycled round to the field. The news spread like wildfire and you couldn't see the field for people filling their bags. The next thing they heard were the bells ringing as two police cars raced across the field. It was all a rumour! The farmer had said no such thing and the police were coming for them. They all jumped on to their bikes and peddled 'L for leather!' Everyone else had two-wheeler bikes and managed to make a quick escape, but wee Douglas was on his tricycle, panicking and peddling for all he was worth with two bags of potatoes for his mammy hanging from each side of his handlebars. He ran into the house, shoved the potatoes into a cupboard, and breathed a sigh of relief that he hadn't been caught.

Another time, when they were out playing football on some spare ground, they heard the sound of the police car bells ringing. A megaphone was instructing everyone to get indoors immediately. As the bells grew nearer, everyone was peering out of their windows, wondering what on earth was going on. The next thing they saw was a big, black bull galloping down the street, with the police car in hot pursuit. The bull had escaped from a nearby field and was running wildly round the streets. It was finally captured after four hours when it ran out of steam and was successfully lassoed. Fortunately, no one was injured. It could have been serious, but everyone was laughing hysterically at the antics of the police chasing the bull round and round, up and down the streets with their bells ringing.

In June 1953, it was the coronation of Queen Elizabeth. The school children were all presented with a round green tin with toffees inside and a picture of the Queen on top. Linda never got one, because her date for starting school had been delayed until August. Wee Douglas generously shared his with her. On the actual day, some roads had street parties. Douglas, Margie, Dot and Tom decided to take the children for a picnic to celebrate. They cut through the fields where the cows and sheep were grazing and walked along the canal bank towards Bishopbriggs. Boats were sailing by with their Union Jacks proudly flying, and there was a sense of peace and happiness in the air. They got to the canal lock at Mavis Valley. The lock-keeper had a quaint whitewashed cottage. He and his wife had turned their front room into a shop that sold groceries, hardware and confectionery to the passing boats and villagers. The families walked on for another ten minutes to the Bluebell Woods. Margie pulled up a tiny shoot from a Rowan Tree and wrapped it in her hankie, planning to plant it in the back garden when she got home.

The men found a clearing with a big, flat tree stump and decided this was the perfect place for a picnic. Dot and Margie started to unpack the picnic boxes. Out came a nice red and white gingham tablecloth, which Dot placed over the tree stump. Then came the plates, cutlery, bread, butter, gammon, tomatoes, cheese, fruit, cooked sausages, cake, biscuits, milk, sugar, soft drinks and two flasks of tea.

Dot said to Margie, 'Could you pass me the cups, please?'

Margie said, 'You've got them!'

'No, I thought you were bringing them!' exclaimed Dot.

They looked at each other in disbelief, realising that they had all this lovely food and drink, but nothing to drink from.

Douglas said, 'I'll go back to the lock-keeper's shop and see if they sell paper cups'.

Tom and wee Douglas went along too, leaving the women to carry on getting everything ready. Linda and Anne found a big log and a plank of wood and made a seesaw. They were singing, 'see saw, Margery daw', when suddenly they heard a loud THUMP! THUMP! THUMP! coming towards them. They looked at each other in terror, not knowing what it was. Margie and Dot ran over to the girls. They were all frozen on the spot with fear. Suddenly, out of the woods bounced a massive hare which carried on bouncing straight past their makeshift picnic table. The women and girls were so relieved that it had not stopped. Fortunately, none of the food was damaged.

The men came back five minutes later saying, 'They didn't sell paper cups, but guess what? The lock-keeper's wife has loaned us her best china tea set!'

They all had a good laugh about the hare and the idea of having a picnic in the middle of the woods with a posh china tea set.

Wee Douglas and Linda enjoyed the summer with their Granny Nixon there every morning. One beautiful sunny morning, she took them for a walk up to Springburn Park. They skipped on ahead and raced each other, playing tag. As they neared the boat pond, they ran to get a place in the queue for the paddleboats. Linda sat at the front of the boat while wee Douglas turned the paddle handles. They raced their friends round the pool and shouted in excitement until the man shouted, 'Come in No.6, your time's up!' That was the cue for them to paddle over to the side and give their boat up for the next person in the queue.

Next they climbed the slopes up to the swing park and stood at the side of the swings waiting for one to be free. After ten minutes, they usually managed to get a swing each. Wee Douglas sat on the swing next to Linda and showed her how to get the swing going by herself.

She tried hard, but she was only five, so inevitably the cry would come, 'Granny can you give me a push please?'

Granny Nixon was always so obliging and pushed Linda for 15 minutes.

Then she said, 'Come on you two, it's picnic time. You'll have to get off the swings and give someone else a shot!'

Granny took a tartan rug from her message bag, She spread it out and they all sat on it. Then she placed a flask of tea, a bottle of milk, cheese sandwiches and Abernethy biscuits in the middle. They all tucked in, the children had milk and Granny had tea. It was 1pm and getting hotter. They sat and relaxed in the shade.

Then Granny said, 'Who would like an ice cream pokey hat?'

'MMMEEEE!' both of the children echoed together.

They enjoyed their ice creams with raspberry sauce, but had to eat it quickly as it was melting fast in the heat. At 2.30pm they started the long, three-mile walk home. They were all tired out and collapsed onto chairs, exhausted, when they got in. Margie was delighted to see them and they told her all about their exciting day.

She said to her mother 'Well, they'll certainly sleep tonight!'

Peggy replied jokingly, 'Never mind them, I'm ready for my bed now!"

Margie realised that her poor mother still had to get a bus home after her tiring day. She said, 'Why don't you stay and have a rest?'

Peggy replied, 'No, if I fall asleep, I won't have the energy to get up and go home, so it's best that I get on my way now'.

Before she left, she shouted to the kids, 'Maybe we'll go for a nice walk out to Lambhill tomorrow'.

To this, the children replied, 'YEESSS!'

Margie left the children resting while she walked her mum to the bus stop. She gave her mother a big hug and told her how much she loved her and appreciated what she was doing to help her.

Peggy just laughed and shrugged saying, 'Oh, I enjoy my mornings with the kids. It's given me a new lease of life!'

Margie counted her blessing that she had such a lovely and understanding mother, she was a godsend to her!

Before they knew it, it was nearing the end of August and the big day finally arrived for Linda's first day at school! Margie arranged to take the day off work to make sure that she definitely got admitted this time. Linda skipped along, asking her mammy if she was just going to look again or would she be allowed to stay this time? To Margie's relief, Linda was accepted. She gave her a big hug and kiss, and walked away with a lump in her throat. Linda was too busy to notice her mammy going. She was looking round the class at individual blackboard slates and all the coloured chalks and crayons.

She made friends with another little girl called Fiona. They were first in the queue at lunchtime for their very first school dinner. They stood excitedly chatting and skipping up and down, off and on the steps into the dining hall, as they waited for a teacher to open the door and let them in. Mrs. MacKinnon appeared. She was very pretty, with long, dark, wavy hair and a full pink, flowery frock with a broad, white belt and white, wedged high-heeled sandals. She ordered Linda and Fiona to come with her. They followed her along the long winding corridor, holding hands and bursting with excitement, wondering what surprise Mrs. MacKinnon had for them. She took the two five-year-olds into the staff room and brought out a thick, black leather belt with three fingers on it and then she told them to hold out their hands. The wee lassies were trembling with fear as the big heavy belt came thudding down on their hands, leaving big, red, swollen marks up their wrists. They were too shocked and frightened to cry, they still didn't know why they had been punished.

Then Mrs. MacKinnon said, 'You know you do not stand on the steps going into the dining hall, you queue below the steps!'

Perhaps Mrs. MacKinnon wasn't aware that it was their first day at school and that no one had told them that they weren't allowed to stand on the steps, but they weren't going to question the teacher! That day, Linda realised that school wasn't all fun and play. She was a girl with sensitive feelings, but she was also hardy and would not give in that easy!

Her teacher was Miss Pollard, she was young and blonde and always wore a blue flowery smock overall. She very seldom smiled and the children felt intimidated by her. One day, another teacher came into the room and whispered something to Miss Pollard, which brought a big happy smile to her face. Linda thought her teacher looked so different and pretty when she smiled. If only she would do it more often! Linda enjoyed learning and always tried very hard. She never wanted to experience that 'big black leather monster' again. She worked hard at her arithmetic and writing exercises. She carefully practiced her letters between the two dark blue lines, taking the letters 'b' and 'h' very carefully up to the light blue line above, and the 'p' and 'q' to the light blue line below, up light and down heavy, she was proud of her efforts. After one writing exercise, she queued up at Miss Pollard's desk, quite confidently expecting a star for her good work. Instead, the teacher picked the unsuspecting Linda up and, in front of the whole class, she put her over her knee, lifted up her gymslip and whacked her twice on the bottom, simply because she had not joined an 'o' up properly. Linda felt humiliated and wanted to run out of the class, but she knew that this would probably mean another whack. Linda had really looked forward to starting school, but she hadn't bargained for some of the teacher's brutality. She couldn't understand why they didn't just explain things properly rather than belt the kids. She was beginning to think that school wasn't such a good idea after all! It didn't put her off, as she was keen to learn.

At the end of that year, she was surprised to be told that she was to attend prize-giving. She wondered why she was the only one in her class to be asked. At five and a half, she was too young to sit exams and the children didn't get to go to prize-giving until they were seven and attended school full-time. Margie took her to the local church on the afternoon of prize-giving, still unaware what was going on. They were sitting at the front. The headmistress called out 'Linda MacGregor'. Margie was very proud and egged Linda on to go up and get her prize. The headmistress presented Linda with a book called, 'Victoria and the Golden Bird', and explained that this was a special 'Progress Prize', as Linda had worked so hard in her first year at school.

None of her classmates were there, but a big cheer went up from wee Douglas' friends at the back, and he could be heard saying, 'That's my wee sister!' Linda was confused and couldn't understand why she got a prize, as she was always convinced that Miss Pollard didn't like her. She came to the conclusion that Miss Pollard had a guilty conscience, and this prize was all about that horrible, humiliating day when she put Linda over her knee. Presenting Linda with this prize was Miss Pollard's way of making herself feel better about her sins. Margie and Linda sat on and proudly watched and cheered as wee Douglas was presented with three books for coming in first in exams.

Linda became ill with tonsillitis. It came and went for the best part of a year and was pulling her down. Eventually, the doctor suggested that as her tonsils were so swollen, she should have them removed. Margie had to paint Linda's tonsils every day with a black liquorice substance to keep them from becoming inflamed. Linda was admitted to Stobhill Hospital. She was only six and she was put in a big, twenty-bed ward full of women. Margie felt upset leaving her wee girl there all alone. There was a teenage girl in the next bed. She talked to Linda and put her at ease. Linda felt nervous at first, as she didn't know anyone, and there was only half an hour visiting in the afternoon and the same again in the evening. That night, Margie, Douglas and wee Douglas all went up to visit her. She had settled in by now and had found a play room with lots of toys. She was beginning to enjoy it, at least it was better than school! Everyone told her that after she had her tonsils out, she would get lots of ice cream to eat. This was something she looked forward to.

The day of the operation came and a nurse approached Linda's bed, put a white hospital gown on her, and gave her a pre-med jag in her arm. She felt quite drowsy after that and vaguely remembered being wheeled on a trolley through the corridors and into a lift. She was brought to a room where other children were all sitting cross-legged in a circle on the floor. They called out the names and, one by one, the children got up and walked towards the big, brown double doors, where a man in a green outfit and mask could be seen.

'Linda MacGregor', called the nurse.

Linda attempted to get up, but her legs buckled beneath her. Every time she tried to get up to walk, she fell back down again. She was having trouble focus ing and could hear the other children laughing loudly as if they were in the distance. The next thing, she was scooped up into the arms of a nurse and placed on a long table. That was all she remembered until she woke up in bed, feeling awful, vomiting up black stuff while the teenage girl in the next bed was telling her what a brave girl she was, and could now look forward to lots of ice-cream!

After a couple of days, she was beginning to feel much better. Granny Nixon visited her every afternoon while Margie was at work. She brought her a miniature pink and blue plastic doll's pram about three inches long, with a doll inside it. Linda loved it and played with it all during visiting time while granny talked to her and kept her company. The bell went to tell everyone that visiting time was over.

Linda said to her granny, 'You'd better go now!'

Peggy laughed, saying, 'Oh, you want rid of me!'

The real reason was, that as soon as the visitors went, Linda was allowed up out of bed and could go into the playroom. After ten days, Linda was home again, healthy and fit. On doctor's orders, she was kept off school for another two weeks in case of infection. After that, she went back at school, much better for having her tonsils removed.

It was Saturday afternoon. Douglas met up with his brothers and Pop, as he did every week, to go and see their football team, Partick Thistle, play. Sometimes they had to travel to away games, but today, it was a home game at Firhill Park. Margie, meanwhile, caught up on the week's housework and washing. She put on the boiler to boil the bedclothes and white cotton, then lifted the Acme wringer and fixed it into place between the deep and shallow sinks in the kitchen. Wringing the clothes by hand was back-breaking, and it took the best part of the day to complete the week's washing. She tried hard, working against the clock to get it done in time to hang out in the afternoon, as it was frowned upon to hang clothes out on a Sunday. In between doing the washing, the grocery bus came into the street, so she stopped everything to go out and queue up to get her weekly 'messages'. By four o'clock, she was feeling exhausted, but it was time to start the Saturday night dinner and boil the beef to prepare the soup stock for Sunday's dinner.

The children were setting the table at half past five when Douglas came home, slightly slurring and tipsy. He had a few drinks with the boys after the match and was in a good mood because his team had won. Margie served up corned beef, cabbage and mashed potatoes, followed by her delicious homemade apple pie and custard. After dinner, Margie cleared the table while the children started the washing up. Margie sat down, shattered after her hard day's work and thought to herself, *If I didn't have to go to work during the week to make ends meet, I would have more time to spend with the children at weekends.* She knew they needed the extra money, so she had no option. Meanwhile, Douglas put his feet up on the mantelpiece and dozed off into a boozy sleep after his hard day of watching football and drinking in the pub. This was the 1950s, and, in spite of the hard work and labour women had put in during World War II, it was still a man's world!

CHAPTER THREE

It was just after 7am on a cold Saturday morning in January 1955. There was a loud rat-a-tat-tat on the front door. Douglas jumped out of bed, pulled on his trousers, and ran downstairs to find his older brother, Angus junior, standing there unshaven and looking very anxious and distressed.

'It's mother', he said. 'She has taken very bad and is in Ruchill Hospital'.

Angus junior had run the five-miles to their house. Douglas pulled the rest of his clothes on in three minutes flat. The two men managed to get a No 47 bus down to the corner of Bilsland Drive and ran all the way to the hospital.

Kathleen was in a bad way. She was unconscious, and the doctor told them it didn't look good. All the family took it in turns to sit by her bedside and talk to her, hoping that she might rally round, but, at 3.30am on Sunday morning, she passed away. She was only 63 and had died from complications of the womb. It became apparent that she had ignored warning signs over the previous six months. She had borne all these children in her short life and had loved and cared for them all, but neglected her own health. If she had sought medical advice earlier, it might have saved her.

Without Kathleen and her organising skills, the family was in turmoil. No one could pluck up the courage to tell Andrew, who was now 19. Kathleen had had great patience with her Downs Syndrome son. She taught him to help her in the kitchen preparing food, peeling potatoes and vegetables, and laying the table. He could lay the table for the exact amount of people simply by saying their names on his fingers. Pop took Andrew aside and explained gently to him that his mother wouldn't be coming back to the house. He told him that she was now with the angels, looking down on them. Andrew looked sad and puzzled, but seemed satisfied.

He then said, 'Well, when I peel the potatoes, who's going to cook them now?'

Pop was relieved that Andrew understood in his own way, but he had a heavy heart and was deeply distressed that he had lost the love of his life at such an early age. Kathleen was much missed. She was a wonderful woman and her absence from the house was prominent. Within a few months Pop, Andrew, Angus junior, George, Harry and Ina, who all still lived at home, had got themselves into a new routine. It would never be the same. No one in the family could match Kathleen, but they realised that they had to move on and do their utmost best for Pop's sake.

Kathleen often used to say to Pop that her biggest worry was if something happened to her, what would become of Andrew. She couldn't bear the thought of no one being there to care for him. Pop always reassured her that there would never be a problem, as the family would look after him. Andrew loved to play board games. Kathleen used to play Ludo, Snakes and Ladders, and Draughts with him. Pop realised that this was good for Andrew, it helped him to concentrate and learn numbers. He carried on his wife's good work and taught his Downs Syndrome son to play cards and dominoes.

Another thing Kathleen had taught Andrew was how to make pom-poms. She used to cut out lots of cardboard circles with holes in them. Then she got all oddments of wool from friends and family. He loved to wind the odd bits of different coloured wool around the two pieces of cardboard. When it got too thick and the wool wouldn't go through the middle, he would come to Kathleen and she cut the edges for him while he tied the wool tightly around the middle and fluffed the wool into a big colourful ball.

All the babies in the neighbourhood had a pom-pom hanging from the bood of their prams that Andrew had made for them. This was another job that Pop carried on with. He saved all the cardboard from food packets and made a stock of different sized circles with holes in the middle. Ina took over in the kitchen with Andrew as her helper. The brothers always made sure that Andrew was well dressed. Dot and her older married sister, Emily, knitted for him. He loved his Fair Isle jumpers and different coloured waistcoats. Margie and Douglas took him for days out with wee Douglas and Linda. In fact, everyone rallied round to make sure that they kept their promise to Kathleen, and Andrew was well cared for.

It was March, 1955, and still cold. The children loved it on chilly nights. Margie had the fire glowing red hot. Douglas piled on the coal and they pulled the big green settee and their chairs in closer. They looked into the fire and saw tunnels and faces in the red hot coals. Douglas made them all giggle when he told them stories of when he was a boy and the pranks that he and his brother Jack got up to. They were very close in age. Jack was only 11 months older than Douglas. Douglas recalled how Jack was a toe-rag at school and always getting into playground scraps, whereas their eldest sister, Emily, was very quiet and stu dious. Jack didn't need persuading to be the centre of attraction in the after school scraps. No one in their right senses would want to be on anyone else's side other than his. If anyone dared to pick on Douglas, then they had Jack to answer to.

At least twice a week, the headmaster would send for Emily to tell her that Jack was in disgrace yet again, and give her a letter to take to their father. Emily was an emotional girl and just burst into tears. On the way home, Jack convinced Emily that he had turned over a new leaf and pleaded with her to tear up the letter and throw it away. He knew what he would get from his father for misbehaving at school. Emily was an honest, church-going girl and believed him every time, so to save her brother from a beating, Pop never got the letters and, of course, Jack's behaviour never changed.

Even Jack's experiences in Dunkirk never altered him. He was a lovable rogue. He had the rugged good looks of Humphrey Bogart. He had black, combed back and Brylcreemed hair, tanned Latin type skin, penetrating blue eyes, with a permanent cigarette in his hand and a stub behind his ear. Douglas told the kids about the time he took Jack to meet Margie's family for the first time. Margie and Douglas had just got engaged and he warned Jack to be on his best behaviour and not to embarrass him in Peggy's house. Halfway through the evening, Jack went to the toilet and discovered the toilet seat was loose.

He came back into the living room wearing the toilet seat around his neck and asking, 'Do you like my new collar?'

It broke the ice and everyone howled with laughter. He always dressed smart in a double-breasted suit with large lapels and wore a soft hat. He could easily have passed for a Hollywood gangster from the movies.

Jack married a widow with three children. They went on to have two more girls. In 1954, they moved to a three bedroom maisonette in Auchinairn, which was about a 35 minute walk from Douglas and Margie's house. He was a wonderful father to all five children. He liked his tipple of whisky and was a regular in the local tavern, but he worked hard driving tankers and was an excellent husband and provider. He had a devilish sense of humour and at parties, he always took control and had everyone doubled up with laughter. Linda loved her Uncle Jack. He was such a happy man. He made her giggle and was full of fun and love. He used to call Linda his wee dark eyed beauty, and questioned why none of his kids had dark eyes.

The children's other favourite story was one Douglas had made up. He told them when he was a message boy at Cochrane's, he used to run with his barrow full of messages (shopping) to each delivery, and one woman gave him a big 'jeely piece' (jam sandwich). He said he bit into it so hard that his finger disappeared. At that, he wiggled his half finger that he had lost in the flour mill when he was 18, and the children all laughed uncontrollably. Wee Douglas, Linda and all the nieces and nephews believed this to be true until they were old enough to know better.

These nights were cheery, and often they sat on the floor in front of the fire, playing Ludo or Snakes and Ladders. The children loved this, especially when Douglas pretended to be upset because he was losing and mockingly accused them of cheating. It never occurred to them that they won the game just before 8.30pm and their bedtime. They went to bed laughing, happy and contented. They had a happy family life, finances were tight but the love was warm.

Douglas tried to hide his feelings, but he took the death of his mother very badly. He had moments of depression and got upset thinking about her and his young brother, Alex, who he missed so much. He felt that he had missed out on precious years with them that had been stolen from him while he was fighting for his country in World War II. Margie was always there for Douglas. She was very understanding and helped him the best she could. She listened to him while he talked about his boyhood days, Alex, and his mother, and how no one appreciated how hard she worked until it was too late. The one thing he never mentioned were the horrors that he had seen during his many years in the Army. How he had witnessed friends and fellow soldiers cruelly killed before his eyes. How he had to pull dead bodies out of bomb sites, some unrecognizable with their limbs blown off. Those times he left Margie standing in tears at the Central Station as he went back to camp, the nagging worry that he was being posted to the war-torn Far East and might never return or see her, wee Douglas, or any of his beloved family again. He buried these depressing memories deep in his troubled mind.

Margie noticed that Douglas was tending to have an extra beer or two. She was used to him going to the pub with Pop and his brothers after the match on a Saturday, but his drinking was becoming more regular. He was paid on Fridays when his shift finished at 4.30pm, but he never got home until after 8pm. She could smell the beer on him as he entered the house and he was slurring slightly. He never, ever told Margie how much he was earning, so she had no way of checking what he was spending. She was becoming increasingly worried about his behaviour and his drinking. He had always been a peaceful, loving and caring man. She felt that his experiences in the War and the death of his brother Alex had a serious effect on him and changed his moods. Now, with the death of his mother as well, it seemed to be more than he could cope with.

Margie was a quiet woman, who preferred to go along with things rather can cause a scene, so she never challenged Douglas or the fact that he was spending money they couldn't afford on alcohol.

In the late spring of 1955, Douglas decided on a change of career. He had a friend who was a postman, and he told Douglas about all the perks and overtime, and how he could be earning so much more. Douglas applied and soon he was standing proud in his uniform. At 5am, he reported for work at the George Square sorting office from Monday to Saturday. The postmen stood in line to attention, and were inspected by the PHG. Their shirts had to be spotless and ironed, ties straight, trousers pressed with seams, shoes polished and peaked caps gleaming. When the PHG was satisfied that they were a credit to the G.P.O., they would carry on with sorting the letters and preparing their rounds. They could usually finish by 12noon and there was always the chance of overtime for sorting duties.

Now that Douglas was home in the afternoon for the children coming in from school, Margie was able to extend her hours at work until 5pm. Friday was payday and what a difference! With his overtime, Douglas was able to give Margie an extra £1/10/- (£1.50p) per week and, with her earnings now at £2/10/- (£2.50p) per week, she could do so much more. Over the next few months, they were able to buy extra furnishings on hire purchase, including a red standard lamp and matching table lamp, two big and colourful square rugs for the living room, and nice new bedding for the children, fluffy pink sheets for Linda and blue ones for wee Douglas. They could now afford little luxuries like tomato sauce, butter instead of margarine, and biscuits.

Douglas also had more money in his pocket. It didn't occur to him that if he gave all the money to Margie and then got pocket money back, that their problems could all be solved. She wouldn't have to go out to work, nor would she be so exhausted. She would also have some time to enjoy her home and family. Instead, it became a regular occurrence on Friday and Saturday afternoons for him to go to the pub with his boozy post office pals. Margie never dared to ask him how much money he had. He made it clear to her that this was none of her business. Judging by his inebriated state most weekends, it was quite apparent that he wasn't short of a bob or two.

Linda and Douglas got to the stage where they dreaded coming home from school on Fridays. They couldn't understand the change in their father. He turned from a very loving, caring individual into a fearful monster. Linda finished school at three o'clock and he would start on her the minute she got home, lecturing her with the stench of booze and the thick smoke of Capstan full strength cigarettes in her face. The frightened child edged into the corner as her drunken father came closer and closer, telling her how bad she was. She hadn't done anything wrong, but she dare not speak up or disagree, as that would break his temper and lead to a beating. She knew, in any case, his big strong hand was going to come towards her sooner or later as it always did, leaving his fingerprints across seven-year-old Linda's swollen, tearful face.

Wee Douglas didn't finish school until half past three. In a way, it was a relief when he came home half an hour later, as Douglas left Linda alone and started on her brother. Linda couldn't comprehend the change in her father's nature. He had always been a loving and protective daddy. She couldn't bear to see her brother being beaten up on a regular basis every Friday by their dad. Wee Douglas was such a good and caring brother. He didn't deserve this treatment. She hid in the recess under the stairs crying as her dad bullied her brother by pressing his face close to his, staring into his eyes like a madman and shouting orders at him as if he was a sergeant major. Her dad made wee Douglas march and stand to attention, telling him how useless he was and that he'd never be a man or make anything of himself like his dad, who had been 'dux' of his secondary school. She screamed and tried to stop him from battering her brother's head back and forth off on the back door, for which she received a severe slap around the head.

This went on until Margie's footsteps were heard coming up the side path towards the back door.

Then Douglas would say to the kids, 'Get upstairs quick! Wash your faces and not a word about this to your mother!'

He made it sound like he was doing them a favour by not telling their mother. They knew that it would be more than their lives were worth to say anything to her, as they would only get hell for it the next time. They just wanted to get their old dad back. They still loved him, but they didn't like what he was becoming.

Margie could never have perceived that this was going on. She had noticed that wee Douglas was becoming increasingly nervous and was burying himself in his school studies, but she put that down to the fact that he had his qualifying exams coming up and wanted to make sure he passed to get to the high school. Linda started wetting the bed. Margie couldn't understand this at all and thought it was just a phase that she would eventually grow out of.

On Saturdays, it would be Margie's turn. Douglas came in, staggering and slurring, and started in on the poor woman. She had been working all day, trying to catch up on the week's housework and shopping. Margie tried to ignore him, but this only made him more aggressive. Finally, all hell broke loose and Margie was in tears as he ranted and raved on at her. She was not a strong-minded person and took the abuse. Her way round it was to get out of the house and go for a walk until he had collapsed into a drunken slumber. She then slipped back home and carried on with her housework. She just wished the Saturday away until Sunday morning came, when he was sober again. On Sundays, he would carry on as if nothing had happened, coming into the kitchen and pulling Margie towards him in a loving embrace, giving her a long, lingering kiss. She smiled with relief that he was back to a loving husband and father again.

Every Sunday, Margie took comfort that he was 'normal' and put the Saturday showdown out of her mind. She was too frightened to tell Douglas all the nasty things he did and said, in case it started him off again. She was a peace-loving woman and very much in love with him. She never stood up to him and never told anyone what she was going through. This only made the situation worse. She thought that by not confronting him about his drunken rages, that she and the children would have a quiet life. She didn't seem to grasp that by doing nothing about it, she was actually enabling him to become worse and worse. She was embarrassed that the neighbours might have heard his drunken shouts, and swore the children to secrecy, telling them not to mention their dad's tempers to anyone. Of course, she was totally oblivious to what was going on every Friday and what her children had to put up with. This carried on weekly. Douglas was indeed a changed man. It was as if he was trying to vent on his wife and children for the hell he suffered in his Army days and for the death of his mother and brother.

It was July 1955 and Margie's factory had an outing on the 'Showboat'. This was a paddle steamer with lots of entertainment. It left from Broomielaw in Glasgow, sailing 'Doon the Watter' past Erskine, Greenock, Gourock, Helensburgh, Largs, Innellan, Kirn, Dunoon, Rothesay and up the Kyles of Bute, before finally returning to Broomielaw about 10.30pm. Some of Margie's workmates took their spouses and children, but a lot of the girls she worked with were young and went on their own. Margie took along Douglas and their children. There was a live band on board, and all the food and drinks were paid for by her work. Margie was very worried that Douglas would give her a 'showing up' when he started drinking. Douglas loved to be the centre of attraction. As he got more and more drunk, he got chatting to all the young girls from Margie's factory. He disappeared for over an hour while Margie stayed with her children.

The next thing Margie heard were the tones of his lovely tenor voice. The band backed him as he crooned, 'If I ever needed love'. Granted, he had a wonderful voice and sang it better than Eddie Fisher, but Margie was getting really embarrassed by his pushy, uncharacteristic behaviour. Thoughts were going through her head of how she was going to face her work mates on Monday.

At last, the paddle steamer tied up back at Broomielaw. The children were very tired, but Douglas was in no fit state to help. He staggered back and forth, Margie on one side of him and his 11 year old son on the other, both trying to hold him up. They managed to get a No. 45 tramcar up to Colston and walked through the dark Colston Road and over the little railway bridge, taking a shortcut through the fields to home. By this time, Douglas was really menacing and gearing up for an argument. Margie was trying to get him to go to bed, telling him that it was after midnight and the children were very tired. At that, he suddenly took his heavy Crombie coat off and swung it at Linda. It was so heavy it knocked her off her feet. The big buttons caught her round the face, just missing her eyes, leaving big swollen marks on her cheeks. Wee Douglas shouted at him and grabbed the coat from his grasp. He found the strength to argue back with his father when his mother was there, but deep down he knew that he would suffer for it at a later date. Margie was utterly shocked. She had never seen him being violent towards the children. She didn't know that this was a common occurrence on Fridays after school when she wasn't around. Her adrenalin flowed and she stood up to him, telling him how evil he was to harm his poor defenceless seven-year-old daughter. He suddenly went quiet, as if he was in shock at what he had done. Then he turned round on his heels and went up the stairs to bed. Margie bathed the tearful Linda's face and gave her lots of big hugs and kisses, and told her that daddy wasn't himself.

The next morning Douglas was very sheepish. He tried to behave like nothing had happened and, if it had, he pretended that he didn't remember anything. He got up and made a full Scottish fry up breakfast for everyone consisting of square-sliced sausage, black pudding, fried dumplings, ham, eggs and tattie scones with fried bread. He insisted on Margie having a day off and a nice rest while he boiled the stock and started peeling all the vegetables to make a big pot of Scotch broth. He followed this with steak pie, peas and potatoes. His mother had taught him a lot and he was a good cook. He pulled Margie into his arms and gave her a lingering kiss, telling her how wonderful she was and how much he loved her. He hugged and kissed Linda, saying to her 'How's ma wee chookie?' He laughed and joked with wee Douglas and created a happy atmosphere in the house. They all felt the tenseness melt away and Margie fell for it. She was so much in love with Douglas. She imagined that at last, he had shocked himself, seen sense, and was going to get back to his old self again. She forgave him, although Douglas never at any time brought the subject up or uttered the word, sorry.

Margie came home from work one evening just before Christmas, 1955. She was proud and beaming as she told Douglas that she had been made up to supervisor and, with her promotion, came a raise of £2 per week, with immediate effect. The following week, when Douglas gave Margie her housekeeping money, it was £2 short. He just shrugged it off by saying it was a short week. In actual fact, because she had a raise of £2, he had cut her housekeeping by the same amount, giving him more money for the booze. Margie carried on in her usual mild manner and not complaining. It never struck her as unfair that all her money was going into keeping the house and paying the bills and less and less of Douglas' money was contributing to anything other than the pub.

The children had their chores to do. During the week after school, at least two afternoons per week, their father was usually leaving for an extra overtime shift as they got home. Wee Douglas peeled the potatoes and vegetables for dinner. Then he went round the back of the house to get some coal in and lit the fire for his mum's coming home so that there would be some hot water. Linda went to the shops for any groceries that her dad told her to get and laid the table for dinner. After dinner, they cleared the table and washed and dried the dishes. On Saturdays, wee Douglas swept the floors and polished the furniture. Linda cleaned and scrubbed the bathroom, polished the linoleum in the two bedrooms and the surrounds in the living room, then went to the shops with her mum to help with the weekly messages (shopping). Wee Douglas also started taking an interest in the garden, more so because he was embarrassed about the state it was in. It was so big. His dad never did anything to it because, when he wasn't working, he was in the pub. Margie didn't have a spare minute, so who else was going to do it?

One Wednesday when the children came home, Douglas said to his son, 'I have to get back to work for overtime and I haven't got my bus fare because I'm skint, go and ask your Auntie Dot to lend me £1, but don't tell your mum!'

Wee Douglas dutifully did as he was told. This became a regular habit and it embarrassed wee Douglas to have to ask Auntie Dot every Wednesday for a £1. Every Friday, he was sent back to return it to her. Dot always looked bewildered when she handed over the £1. She shook her head and gave wee Douglas a look as if she was telling him that she couldn't understand how his parents had run out of money when the both of them were out working, yet she had only one wage coming in and she managed OK. Of course, she hadn't a clue about her brother's drinking binges and that poor Margie was working her fingers to the bone and practically financing the upkeep and expense of running the home and feeding her family by herself. Meanwhile, Margie was kept totally in the dark about Douglas borrowing money from his sister every week.

New neighbours moved in next door. Tess Harrison was a tall, stout and kindly Highland lady with rosy cheeks and thinning black hair, pinned back with Kirby grips. Her husband, Alan Harrison, was a few inches shorter than his wife. He had dark, wavy hair and a round, smiling, happy face with the most amazingly piercing green eyes. He was the local bookie who stood on the corner taking bets. They had five children, three girls and two boys. All were very well dressed in the best of fashion, and ranged in age from six months to nine years. They were never short of a bob or two. They were the only family in the street with a car, a black Morris Oxford. Alan Harrison liked his beer, and soon, Douglas had a new drinking pal. It wasn't long before Douglas was borrowing money from Alan to finance his alcoholic cravings. He was giving Margie less and less housekeeping money, lying through his teeth with excuses like, the tax man had been under taxing him so he has to pay a lot more tax to catch up on his arrears. Margie innocently and blindly believed him and accepted that he had less income. She struggled on, working all the hours that God sent, to make ends meet and pay off the hire purchase that they had taken on when they thought that life was going to be rosier with more wages coming in.

Douglas could only afford to go to the pub on Fridays and Saturdays. This seemed to affect his moods. Some days he would be back to his caring, mild-mannered self, making everyone giggle and laugh with his funny little rhymes and jokes. The children next door loved him and were always pleading through infectious laughter, 'Mr. MacGregor, tell us about your finger again or say that wee rhyme for us'. His good moods were few and far between. During the better spells, life was so much more pleasant, but they were short-lived. The least little thing would set Douglas off. One Saturday, Margie bought wee Douglas some new socks and underwear. Her husband went into a rage like a madman, eyes staring and face almost purple, demanding to know why she hadn't bought him socks and underwear, too. He was like a Jekyll and Hyde. It wasn't as if he needed any items of clothing. Considering the conditions and how tight money was, Douglas had a wonderful wardrobe consisting of three, three-piece suits, one each of black, navy and brown, a tweed sports jacket, a blazer, umpteen pairs of flannels and shirts, a Crombie coat, and three pairs of shoes. He didn't need extra clothes for work, because he was provided with a uniform.

Meanwhile, Margie had only one grey skirt, one white and one blue blouse for work, which she protected by wearing a navy-blue over-all, and one grey heavy coat. She had two flowery frocks and a pale green suit for her Sunday best. The green suit had a straight skirt and a three-quarter length, swagger-back, swing-style jacket, one pair of black high heeled shoes for work and one pair of brown suede high heeled shoes for best. The children had their school uniforms, with trench coats, a couple of changes for after school, one pair each of sensible shoes, sandshoes and black Wellington boots. Wee Douglas' Sunday best outfit consisted of a brown small check suit with short trousers. Linda looked forward to Sundays, she got dressed up for Sunday School in her best turquoise coat with square sailor's collar and tassels, MacGregor tartan kilt that Margie had made for her, white blouse and straw hat with brim and imitation flowers. She tied the blue ribbon tiers in a big bow under her chin.

Margie's and the children's lives revolved around Douglas' changing temperaments. He was becoming very greedy. If there was anything going, he had to have it. He never noticed that the rest of the family was going without, while he seemed to have the best of everything. If he thought someone got something and he didn't have it, then he would start again, causing unhappiness and unrest in the home like a spoilt brat.

Deep down, Douglas was a caring person with a good heart. His past experiences of his hard life had badly affected him. His way of dealing with this was to drink himself into oblivion and put it out of his brain. This turned him into a monster. The children were too young to understand what their dad had become, and that he needed help. All they knew was that they were very scared of him when he had been drinking. They began to hate him when he was in this state.

On the other hand, when they got up on Christmas Eve morning and saw all the Christmas decorations that their dad had put up for them, they were squealing with delight and excitement. Douglas was very artistic and loved any excuse to decorate the place. In his sobriety he loved to spring surprises and make his family happy. He never saw the delight on wee Douglas' and Linda's faces, because he had already left for work at 4.15am. He came home that Christmas Eve at 4pm, drunk as a skunk. He had plenty of money in his pocket, as his delivery round was mostly businesses, and the tips were very good at this time of the year. Needless to say, it was all thrown over the counter of a bar, and Margie never saw any of his seasonal windfalls. He staggered back and forth and tried to balance himself as he went into his postman's sack. He took out a beautiful, big basket arrangement of fruit that the fruit shop on his rounds had given him for Christmas, and presented it to Margie. The kids laid the table and the family all sat down to dinner of corned beef, cabbage and mashed potatoes at 5pm.

Linda had a bronchial cough. Douglas got angry with her coughing at the table and told her to stop it, telling her that she was putting it on. Poor Linda tried to hold the cough in until she couldn't breath. She felt herself going dizzy and had to let go a loud bark. Douglas got very angry. Margie made excuses for Linda and tried to calm him down but, by this time, he was into one of his evil, drunken moods and criticised the poor hard-workingwoman. He knew she wouldn't argue back and continued to bully her.

The next thing she knew, the basket of fruit was coming towards her at great speed. It just missed her nose as it crashed into the wall. He shouted that she didn't deserve anything and cast up how good he was to her, that he furnished the house, kept her and the kids, and that they would have nothing, if it wasn't for him. The children hid behind their chairs in fear as he ranted and raved. Finally, he went upstairs and collapsed onto the bed in his usual drunken state. Margie and the kids picked up the fruit and placed it back in the basket. They were relieved that he was now asleep and they would have peace of mind for the rest of Christmas Eve.

What's For Ye, Won't Go By Ye

The kids went to bed early, at 8.30pm. Wee Douglas wanted a chemistry set for Christmas. Linda got a doll for her past two Christmases, and she hoped that, this time, she would get the dolly's go-chair that she had been longing for, to put them in. Douglas got up at 10pm, gave Margie a big hug and kiss, and carried on like nothing had happened, as usual. Margie never mentioned a word about his earlier, disgraceful behaviour. They got the children's presents ready. A chemistry set for wee Douglas and a big walkie-talkie doll for Linda. Margie had bought a doll's go-chair for Linda the week before, but Douglas told her to take it back and exchange it for a big doll, because they couldn't afford a doll, too. He said that it wouldn't be right to give her an empty go-chair. Margie put an apple and an orange into each of the children's stockings, along with a shiny half-crown apiece. There was also a chocolate selection box for both of them. There was a geometry set in a tin box for Douglas and some toiletry bottles for Linda that Margie had got as presents from a girl at work. Margie never got to keep any of the presents given to her for Christmas. She didn't have the money to buy any presents back for anyone, so the presents that had given to her, she gave back out to others. She had to be very careful that she didn't give the same present back to the person who gave it to her in the first place. None of her pals or Douglas' brothers and sisters was aware of her plight and shortage of money. They all assumed that, with both of them working, Douglas and Margie were quite comfortably off

On Christmas morning of 1955, wee Douglas and Linda got up at 6am. Their dad had already left for work at 5am, as Christmas Day was not a holiday, and the post had to be delivered. Linda threw the living room door open and hoped against hope that there would be a dolly's go-chair in there. She looked at the big box and tore open the lid to find, another doll! She never showed her disappointment and sat the doll upright in the box, along with her two other dolls, putting the lid in the end as if it was a handle and played with her make-believe go-chair. Margie's heart sank. She realised that a go-chair to put her two dollies in that she already had was more important to Linda than a new doll. She knew that she had done the wrong thing. She wished she had kept the go-chair and never listened to Douglas. Wee Douglas was delighted with his chemistry set and spent the morning experimenting with the litmus paper.

The following week was the big one that the MacGregor's looked forward to, when all the family gathered up at Pop's to bring in New Year 1956. This was the night that all children in the family loved, they were allowed to stay up until the wee sma' hours to welcome in the New Year. Wee Douglas loved the fact that he could stay up all night on his birthday. Margie made him new warm navy short trousers and knitted him a jumper for his twelfth birthday. Betty knitted him a navy blue balaclava. He couldn't wait to put on his new clothes for the

New Year's party at his grandpa's. Margie made sure that they had a sleep from about 5pm until 9pm. Then they got up and dressed in their best clothes.

Wee Douglas was in his new jumper and trousers, and Linda in the lovely pink taffeta party dress that Margie had made her two weeks before, for the Sunday School Christmas Party. Margie fastened up the buttons at the back of Linda's dress then took her down to see her dad.

Douglas said, 'My, yer a wee toff!'

Margie told her, 'Ye'll be the belle o' the ball tonight!'

Linda felt like a million dollars in her posh party frock. At 10pm, they wrapped up with their warm coats, woolly hats, gloves and Wellie boots, Douglas picked up his new portable record player in its posh brown leather case. It weighed a ton! They opened their front door to be met by 12 inches of snow and started to plow their way through it.

'Dad, are we getting a bus to Grandpa's?' wee Douglas enquired.

'No, the buses have stopped for the night' came the short, swift reply.

'Well, how are we getting there?' Douglas asked again.

'By shanks' pony', came the firm answer from his dad.

The walk normally took 45minutes. The children ran through the snow, scooping up handfuls and making snowballs to throw at each other. The cold, icy snow was so deep it was going down the top of Linda's boots, soaking her socks and making her feet tingly and numb. Fortunately, Margie had thought ahead and put big warm wooly socks on the children and carried their nice dressy socks in her bag for them to change into when they got to Pop's. They all plodded on through the snow, Douglas struggling over to the one side with the weight of his portable record player.

After about 20 minutes, they were all getting colder. Linda couldn't feel her nose, it had gone numb, along with her feet. They walked backwards so that the cold icy wind wouldn't nip their faces. Suddenly, Linda spotted the orange hire light of a black taxi in the distance.

Linda shouted, 'Here's a taxi coming daddy', hoping that he would stop it.

He waited until it was almost alongside them, then, as if he had just suddenly made up his mind, he stuck his hand out and gave a loud piercing whistle. To their delight, the taxi ground to a halt. They all climbed into the warm cab while Douglas put the record player in the luggage compartment beside the driver. Wee Douglas and Linda sat in the pull-down seats opposite their mum and dad. In no time they were at their grandpa's house.

Dot and Tom were already there with Anne. So was Emily and her husband Bert and their five-year-old daughter, Maureen. Dot and Emily had got there in the afternoon to help their spinster sister Ina, with the New Year's meal. There was great excitement when everyone saw the portable record player. Douglas had his Al Jolson and Eddie Fisher 78 records inside the box. Wee Douglas reminded him to put in his favourite 78 record of Davy Crocket. Angus junior dug out his Jimmy Shand and Winifred Atwell 78 records. They all took off their wet boots and socks, dried their feet, hung their wet socks by the side of the fire to dry, and put on their posh socks and shoes.

Dot, Emily and Ina came through from the kitchen with a homemade sponge with icing and twelve candles on it, singing Happy Birthday to wee Douglas, and everyone joined in. Then they brought some presents out from behind their backs. His grandpa gave him a fountain pen and a bottle of ink for school. His uncles had clubbed together and bought him a Brownie camera. Auntie Dot gave him a new snakeskin belt for his trousers. Auntie Emily gave him gloves, and Auntie Ina gave him socks. Wee Douglas was delighted with all his gifts. He asked his grandpa for some paper and sat beside him at the big table, practicing writing with his new pen.

Andrew laid the big square table for 16 people. He put out all the fancy pickles, beetroot, pickled onions, and chutney. At ten minutes to midnight, George ran down to the midden with the bin to get rid of last year's rubbish. Angus junior got all the glasses ready for the New Year's toast, whisky for the men, sherry for the women and blackcurrant cordial for the children. Linda loved this. She called it her New Year's drink because it was only at this time of year that they got this luxury. Ina got the kettle ready so that it would be boiling for midnight. As the chimes of Big Ben struck twelve on the radio, they all raised their glasses and wished each other a happy, healthy and prosperous New Year. This was the first year without their mother. There was a moment of emotion and tears as Pop gave an extra toast to the memory of his dear wife Kathleen, and son, Alex.

The sisters brought through the steaming hot plates of homemade Scotch broth, followed by the traditional steak pie, home made steepy peas and mashed potatoes. After that, there was trifle. Everyone tucked into their midnight feast and were soon bursting at the seams. Andrew cleared the table and put out16 cups, saucers and spoons, along with the big brown teapot that held 12 cups at a time. Then he brought through cherry cake, sultana cake, Madeira cake, black bun, and shortbread, and laid them on the table for the duration of the evening. They all blethered for a good half hour after the meal, remembering the happy times and the sad times of the previous year.

Then Dot said, 'C'mon, lets get the music on and have a dance!' Douglas set up the record player as she shouted, 'We want the Gay Gordons!'

The women and children all lined up in the big hall while the men stayed sitting at the table with their beer and drams. The children giggled and screamed loudly in excitement as their mothers and aunties twirled them round and danced up and down the lobby as the sound of Jimmy Shand and his band blasted out. Then it was straight into the Bluebell Polka. Dot sang at the top of her voice, 'Somebody stole my Gal', as Winifred Atwell battered it out on her piano. After half an hour of this, when it was going on for 2.30am, the doorbell rang.

'Oh, I wonder who'll be our first foot this year?' questioned Angus junior.

He opened the door, and Mr.and Mrs. Bruce from next door were standing there with a lump of coal, bottle of whisky and a piece of black bun. 'We've come to join the party!' they exclaimed.

The MacGregors were delighted as Mr. Bruce crossed the threshold. He was tall, with dark wavy hair, and that made him the perfect first foot.

'Let's hope you bring us luck and we'll have a better year than the last one', said Pop.

George suggested they all go into the big room where there were easy chairs plus a nice big comfortable brown leather three-piece suite and they could all relax and have a wee singsong. Uncle Tom got his accordion out of the box. He didn't sing himself, but he accompanied everyone else. He was self taught and never struggled to pick up a new tune. Douglas led the singing with his rendition of, 'Old Scotch Mother Mine' with a tear glinting in his eye. Everyone listened intently, deep in thought of days gone by. Dot had a wonderful operatic voice. Douglas had helped to coach her and showed her how breathe. She sang 'Bonny Scotland' and reached the highest notes with total ease. The family went ecstatic and gave her an encouraging round of applause. It is traditional at Scottish parties for everyone to sing a song, and the MacGregors just loved to air their vocal chords. They were a musically talented bunch!

Pop was sitting in the brown leather easy chair in the corner. He quietly started singing 'I'll take you home again Kathleen'. Everyone listened intently and could feel the sorrow in his heart. It was time to liven the party up. Dot and Douglas got the MacGregor choir going with 'Nelly Dean'. Their voices blended into a beautiful melody, as if they were professionally trained singers, the ladies with their soprano voices and the men with their deep baritones. Douglas harmonised in his lovely tenor voice. Then he took them straight into, 'Who killed Cock Robin?' They sang their hearts out and hung on to the last line, When they heard of the death of poooooooooor, Cooooock Robin!' They looked at each other in sheer disbelief and glee at how good they sounded.

They all fell about laughing as Dot said, 'Hear, we should make a record!'

The children sang their street songs while the adults listened and encouraged them. Then Angus junior sang his comical song, 'Here comes the factor, the factor, the factor. Here comes the factor, the factor fur his rent. Catch him by the tail o' his coat, tell him he's a nanny goat, and throw him doon the ster' The children all fell about laughing and asked Uncle Angus to sing some more funny songs.

What's For Ye, Won't Go By Ye

Soon it was 4.30am and everyone was getting very tired. They all got on their heavy socks, Wellie boots, coats, hats and gloves, and got ready for the long walk home. Linda and Anne walked in front holding hands, followed by Dot and Margie, while wee Douglas walked with Tom and his dad. He was 12 now and felt like a grown up. The girls were tired and begged their daddies to carry them, but both dads were the worse for drink after celebrating the New Year. The men were struggling and staggering, taking it in turns to carry Douglas' heavy record player. They told the girls that they were too big to be carried. The families cut through the lane at the railway bridge at the bottom of Bilsland Drive. Just as they were coming out the other end at Balmore Road, two taxis were travelling down towards them. Douglas and Tom stuck their hands out and whistled for them to stop. With a sigh of relief, the weary partygoers opened the taxi doors and collapsed into the seats. They were home in ten minutes and the children were tucked up in their warm cosy beds. Margie dreaded coming home after Douglas had been drinking, because this was usually the time when his temper broke and the insults would start. She busied herself about, putting away the children's wet clothes and boots, and hoped that he would fall asleep. She breathed a huge sigh of relief when she heard his snores coming from their bedroom. She crept up the stairs and got undressed in the bathroom so as not to disturb him. Then, gently, in the darkness, she climbed into the bed beside him. She was terrified he would wake up, but being up all night drinking, he was very tired and, thankfully, dead to the world.

The following Saturday, Dot and Tom took their turns at being hosts for a New Year's Party in their house. All the family met there, along with Dot and Tom's friends and neighbours. Douglas, Margie and the kids didn't have far to go this time, only two streets away. Auntie Dot sat everyone down to a three-course meal. The party was the same rig a-ma roll as New Year's at Pop's. Douglas took charge of the singing, everyone thought he was a great guy. The life and soul, they would say as they told Margie what a handsome, talented man her husband was.

Big Aggie, who lived in the flat below Dot and Tom said, in her deep gruff masculine tones, 'It's a shame, with a voice like that and the looks to go with it. He should be famous!'

Margie was very proud of her husband's talent and good looks. She loved him so much and somehow, in her mind, this seemed to outweigh the drinking and verbal abuse no one knew about.

Everyone had their own songs to sing. Big Aggie sang 'Moonlight Bay' in the sweetest voice. They were all amazed and couldn't believe that this was the same woman. Ina gave her best rendition of 'It Had To Be You'. Tom's friend, Dan, sang, 'When I Grow Too Old To Dream', and his wife, Doreen, sang 'If I Had My Life To Live Over'. Woe betide anyone that sang some else's song, they were told in no uncertain terms, 'That's so and so's song your singing', and they would be stopped in their tracks! Douglas' favourite was 'The Northern Lights Of Old Aberdeen'. He saved that for the finale. He knew that everyone would request it and pressure him into singing it, how he loved the attention! The evening seemed to go so quickly and at midnight, the guests started saying their farewells. Douglas and Margie were the last to go. Douglas was slurring and hugging his sister Dot, telling her she was the best wee sister. Everyone was laughing at Douglas's capers. Dot told him he was a daft midden. How could anyone believe the monster that this Mr. Nice Guy turned into behind closed doors?

They started off down the road. Douglas couldn't walk, he was all over the pavement. Margie got on one side of him, wee Douglas on the other, and Linda had both her arms propped up at the back of him, pushing him along. The walk home took a lot longer than normal and was especially worrying as they had to go down a steep, hilly street that was slippery with ice. It was difficult enough to steady themselves, never mind carry a very drunk man too. As they rounded the corner into their road, Margie was very worried that the neighbours would see. It was almost 2am and Douglas was starting to get loud and insulting. They got indoors and Margie kept telling him to keep quiet, as other people in the street were sleeping.

He retaliated by questioning her in a drunken slur, 'Why should I be quiet in my own house?'

Then he started shouting, telling her what a terrible woman she was and that she wouldn't have got anywhere and was nothing without him. It wasn't long before all hell let loose. Douglas again started a drunken rage, throwing things around, telling everyone how wonderful he was, how he kept them and provided for them and that they should all be very grateful to him. The children loved their dad, but they didn't like him. In fact, they began to hate him, especially for the way he treated their mother when alcohol took over his body. Linda and wee Douglas hid under their covers listening to the shouting and abuse that their mother was taking from their dad.

Wee Douglas whispered, 'I wish he was dead'.

Linda found herself agreeing and said, 'Why does he have to be so horrible? I hate him and wish he was dead too!'

The constant effects of being bullied and beaten by his drunken father at the weekends, and being told he would never make anything of himself or be as good as his father, made wee Douglas very determined. He was a quiet, studious boy and never stood up to his dad physically. Academically, he made his mind up that he would prove his dad wrong. He worked very hard at his schoolwork. He had transferred to the local primary two years previously when they had built a new extension to the annex for the growing number of children. Wee

What's For Ye, Won't Go By Ye

Douglas and Linda didn't have the privilege of going to school together. Linda went to the annex that was two streets to the south of their house. The new extension where wee Douglas went was four streets to the north of their house. He had lots of school pals and they called him 'The Professor', because he was always top of the class and loved explaining scientific things to them. Wee Douglas was proud of his nickname.

One day, he got his friends together and said he was going to make a rocket that went into space. His pals were fascinated and didn't doubt him for a minute. Wee Douglas was aware that it would probably raise suspicions if they went to one chemist for everything, so he gave his pals notes of the different ingredients needed and they all split up and went to different chemists. They agreed to meet in the field at the back of the tenements by the doctor's surgery at 7pm on a cold February night. Wee Douglas prepared the rocket in a tin stuffed with gunpowder. He told his pals to stand back as he lit the string. BANG! A huge explosion ripped through the air with a tremendous thump. House lights went on everywhere as everyone rushed to their back windows to see what was happening. People soon flooded into the street. Wee Douglas and his pals scampered, then casually mixed with the crowds inquisitively. The police were called in and the local paper was there. Wee Douglas got home and his mum and dad were discussing it with Tess and Alan Harrison from next door.

'What on earth could it have been?' said Margie.

'It couldn't have been electric, as all our electricity would have gone out', said Alan.

'Did you hear that big bang Douglas?' inquired Tess to the boy.

'Aye', said the lad, 'Whit wis it?'

'That's what we'd like to know', said his dad, 'and anyway, go and wash yourself, your face is black. Where've you been?'

'Oh, Jist oot playin!' said wee Douglas, grateful that he and his pals had lived to tell the tale.

The next day, the headlines in 'The Daily Record' said 'Mystery explosion rocks Milton'. It then went on to give different expert opinions on what it could have been and what caused it. Wee Douglas decided to put that bad experience out of his mind and pretend that it never happened.

June 1956 and the day of the qualifying exam results came. Wee Douglas was delighted to be told that he had come top yet again and would be going to the high school. He couldn't wait to get home and tell everyone. Margie was delighted and very proud. His dad congratulated him but, for some reason, he couldn't help but show a sliver of envy. He was happy for his son but, at the same time, it was as if he resented him getting the education and chance in life that he hadn't.

The qualifying dance loomed and wee Douglas' class was taken down to the gym at every opportunity to learn the Canadian Barn Dance, the Military Two Step, the Pride of Earn, and the Dashing White Sergeant. Their teacher, Mr. Kennedy, brought in his portable record player and played his own 78 records. He told the boys that they had to choose girls from their class and ask them to be their partners for the night of the dance. If they agreed, then they were to collect the girls from their houses and escort them to the dance. Wee Douglas plucked up all his courage and asked Caroline Reid. She was a beautiful, well-mannered girl with long, shiny black hair, immaculately dressed in her school uniform. To his delight, she shyly accepted. Margie bought Douglas a new charcoal coloured suit for the dance as a present for doing so well in his exams. He was delighted. It was his very first 'grown up' suit, complete with long trousers.

On the night of the dance, he put on his suit, crisp white shirt, bow tie, complete with a carnation in his lapel buttonhole, and Brylcreemed hair. His dad missed this, as he was out working overtime. Margie swelled with pride and felt her eyes fill up as she looked at her wee boy.

She said to him, 'You're growing up son. Soon you'll be a man!'

She told him to remember his manners when he took Caroline to the dance, to let her go first, open doors for her and tell her how pretty she looked.

She then gave him a quarter pound box of Cadbury's Milk Tray and said, 'Give them to Caroline when you arrive at her house'.

Linda and her mum stood by the window and watched proudly as he left the house to pick up his date for the evening. He got to Caroline's door and nervously rang the doorbell. Her mum answered the door and invited him in. Caroline stood there looking absolutely radiant in a pale blue lacy dress. It stuck out with dozens of pale blue and white petticoats that bounced as she walked. It had little cap sleeves and she had pale blue nylon short gloves. She wore a white orchid on her shoulder and her hair was pulled back into a lovely ponytail with a big blue bow. Wee Douglas thought she looked stunning.

He said, 'You look lovely Caroline', and thrust the chocolates into her hand. He felt that he was the luckiest boy in the class.

'You see and look after my girl, Douglas MacGregor!', said Mrs. Reid ,as she opened the front door for them to leave.

'Oh! Don't you worry Mrs. Reid, I will', wee Douglas replied.

They arrived at the school gym hall. The teachers had decorated it up with big coloured crepe paper bows and a big sign at the top of the hall wishing everyone good luck. They all had the time of their lives. Wee Douglas wasn't used to this type of socialising. He spent his time between studying, the Boys Brigade and occasionally meeting up with his pals. Halfway through the evening, they were all given a plate with four small sandwiches, two cheese and two ham, an iced fairy cake, a chocolate biscuit and a small bottle of pop. The girls had dance cards and wee Douglas made sure that his name was marked down on Caroline's card for the last dance.

Near the end of the evening, a lady's choice was announced. The boys were lined up on one side of the school gym and the girls on the other side. As he sat there, Douglas was aware of Big Eileen thumping across the floor towards him. He shut his eyes and thought, *Oh please God, no!*

At that moment, he heard a familiar voice say, 'Can I have this dance please?'

It was Caroline! 'Big Eileen' was standing to Caroline's right, asking the boy next to him to dance. Wee Douglas was relieved and got up on the floor with Caroline. All too soon the evening was over. They walked shyly down the road together and talked about how they would miss their friends and their old school. When they got to Caroline's front door, wee Douglas remembered his manners and shook her hand, thanking her for a lovely evening. He knew he wouldn't see much of her anymore, as after the summer holidays, they were off to different secondary schools.

Linda had a totally different attitude from her brother, who buried himself into schoolwork and tried to prove himself to his dad academically. The beatings from her father made Linda stronger in character. She thought to herself, *One day I will stand up to him and put a stop to this, for my mum and brother's sake.* She was young, but she hoped that one day her mother would find the strength and face up to him or, better still, that her mum would tell someone and get help. Margie felt ashamed and embarrassed and warned the kids not to tell anyone their business. Linda hated life when her dad was drunk. Life was hell for them all. She vowed to herself that she would never put up with a man like that and would always defend herself against any bully.

The summer holidays were upon them. Granny Nixon couldn't come to visit so often, as Mary had just got herself a part time job three mornings a week and Granny was looking after Mary's four children. Granny Nixon called in on Tuesday and Friday mornings, which were Mary's day's off. Wee Douglas was always up first up in the mornings. He washed and dressed and while he prepared the breakfast of cereal and toast, Linda got up and ready. After breakfast, they had their household chores to do. The sooner they got them done, the sooner they got out to see their pals. One morning, wee Douglas was in their mum and dad's bedroom vacuuming. Linda came in to polish the linoleum surrounds. She then climbed up on to her parent's bed and started jumping.

'WHEEEHH', she said to her brother, 'this is great fun!'

Douglas got up on to the bed and the both of them were bouncing up and down, screeching in delight to see who could touch the ceiling first with one hand. Suddenly, there was a huge crash and the bed slid down to an angle. The terrified kids climbed off to investigate. The feet on the baseboard of the bed had collapsed and broken off under the strain, causing the bed to slope down six inches at the bottom. Sheer panic set in. How were they going to explain this to their parents? Wee Douglas thought he had the answer. He got all his strength together and lifted up the double bed, instructing Linda to slip the feet into place. When they were satisfied that it looked ok, they left the room and got their chores finished in record time. They wanted to be out of the house when their dad got home. He might have been going on a back shift and would want to go to bed to catch up on some sleep.

That night, as Linda and her brother were tucked up in their beds, they lay awake waiting and petrified in case their dad suspected that they had broken the bed. They heard their dad get into bed and listened, but nothing happened. They breathed a sigh of relief. About fifteen minutes later their mum came upstairs. They waited anxiously, hoping that the feet of the bed would stay in place. They lay there holding their breath in pure dread. They could hear their mum talking to their dad as she climbed into bed.

The children groaned, 'Oh no!' as they heard the crash of the bed collapsing.

Their mother shouted, 'What's happened?'

They heard the commotion in their parent's bedroom. Wee Douglas was in a terrible state, worried that his parents might suspect that he had something to do with it, while Linda burst into a fit of uncontrollable laughter. Douglas got up and threw the covers over her head to stifle the noise. He got angry with her and told her to shut-up, otherwise they would be in serious trouble. Linda calmed down, but every time she thought about her mother jumping into bed and it giving way, she started again. Her laugh was so infectious that soon her brother was joining in. They put their heads under the bedcovers and giggled themselves to sleep. The next morning, before their mother went to work, she told them about what happened the night before, telling them what a fright she got and that their dad would have to mend the bed, as they couldn't afford a new one. The children felt very guilty but said nothing, they were just happy that their parents didn't suspected anything and that their secret was safe.

There were quite a few children in the street and they all gathered to play together. They went round to the field by the doctor's surgery. Builders had left behind planks of wood, bricks, plasterboard, and logs from chopped down trees. They made see-saws out of the logs and planks of wood and built 'a wee hoose' out of the bricks, putting a sheet of plasterboard on for the roof. About ten of them climbed inside and sat there proud of their achievement. They also got ropes and threw them over the branch of the biggest tree to make a rope swing. At other times they played street games like kick–the-can, What's the time Mr. Wolf, rounders, and skipping ropes.

While all the other kids were enjoying themselves, Kevin, a wee five year old, stood in his Rangers football stripes with his ball under his arm, watching. He then turned away to practice his goal kicks and keepie-uppies. Kevin's dad, Mr. Donaldson, encouraged him no end and proudly told friends and neighbours, with great confidence, 'One day my Kevin will play for the Glasgow Rangers!' Mr. Donaldson worked for an engineering firm and drove the company van. On Saturday afternoons he took his son Kevin and ten year old daughter Rena, along with all the kids in the street, to the Vogue Cinema in Possil to watch the children's matinee at 1pm. He piled them all into the back of his van and dropped them off. He then returned at 3.30pm to pick them all up again and take them home. If Linda and wee Douglas got their chores done on time and Margie didn't need them for the afternoon, then they were allowed to go.

All too soon it was the end of August. Linda was due to start her new year at school and wee Douglas at his new secondary school.

Linda's dad said to her, 'You're eight now, and you've managed without your Granny Nixon for most of the holidays, so there's no need for her to come all the way here every morning. You can see yourself out to school'. He put a key on a string for her to wear round her neck and said, 'This is in case I am at work doing overtime when you come home from school. Your brother doesn't get out of school until four o'clock now and he has a half hour's bus journey home'.

Linda felt very grown up having her own front door key. She was excited because it meant that, if her dad wasn't home, she could come in the front door after school. This was something that Douglas absolutely forbade. He instilled into the family that the front door was for guests only and they had to use the back door. Margie took wee Douglas and Linda into town to get their uniforms. Margie had a tear in her eye as he came out of the changing room in his new high school uniform. It consisted of long grey flannels, a blazer, school tie, and scarf. Her boy was growing up! Next, she took them to the shoe shop. Wee Douglas chose a pair of black slip-ons with thick, sturdy soles. Linda got round her mum and talked her into a fancy pair of black patent leather, strappy shoes for school. These were much to her dad's disapproval.

'We'll see how long they last!' he commented.

They went to bed early the night before school started up again. Margie laid their uniforms out. Douglas got up for work in the early hours at his usual time. Margie always got up with him to make him breakfast and then went back to bed for another hour. At 6am she got up, washed and dressed herself and prepared breakfast for the children. Then she went upstairs and pleated Linda's hair into two thick pleats tied at the bottom with red tartan ribbons. She told the children to be careful, to make sure everything was off and to lock the door properly. She then kissed them goodbye before running up the road to catch the 7am bus into town. Wee Douglas got up and washed and dressed himself, and then gave Linda a shout. He checked that she had her blouse buttoned up the right way. He tied her tie for her.

Then, as if he was her guardian, he said, 'You'll do. You look nice and smart!'

He left for his first day at high school at 8.15am. Linda didn't have to leave until 8.45am. She felt strange leaving by the front door. She stood on the step and put her hand behind to pull the door shut. Then, sheer panic set in. She couldn't move. She had shut her skirt in the door and it was so tight, she couldn't turn round to get her key in the lock! She began to get upset. What was she to do? She didn't want to be late on her first day. Her new teacher was the deputy head Mrs. Mackay, and she was very strict. Linda mustered up all her strength and managed to pull her skirt out far enough to allow her to turn and put the key in the lock and free herself, but not before she had ripped a hole in her new skirt the size of a two shilling piece. Luckily, it was hidden in the pleats. She ran all the way to school and got in the gates just as the bell was ringing. Linda settled in easily in her new class. Mrs. Mackay was strict, but Linda didn't have a problem with that. It felt good to be one of the oldest children in the annex. You got all the important jobs to do, like cloakroom duties, school dinner and milk monitor.

When Linda got home, she tried the back door and it was locked. This meant that her dad had gone to work. She went round to the front door, took her key out and opened the door. She was happy about having the house to herself. She went upstairs to change out of her uniform and then came down to the kitchen. She poured herself a glass of milk and reached up to the shelf for the biscuit barrel. It was very light, for inside there were only three pieces of broken Abernethy's and crumbs. She helped herself to one piece of broken biscuit. She noticed a note on the table from her dad with half a crown beside it. She was to go up to the shops and get a quarter stone of potatoes, half a pound of spam and a tin of peas for that night's tea. When her dad was home on weekdays he usually prepared something more substantial like soup, mince, stew or chops with cabbage, cauliflower or fresh peas. When he was working, they had to make do, as Margie didn't get in until after 6pm.

Wee Douglas came home excited and enthusiastic after his first day.

'How was high school?' Linda asked.

He ran upstairs to change out of his uniform and shouted, 'I'll tell you in a minute'.

He came down to the kitchen and poured himself a glass of milk. He took out the colander and, as he peeled the potatoes for tea, told Linda all about his first day.

What's For Ye, Won't Go By Ye

Linda listened intently as he said to her, 'You don't just get one teacher at high school. You can get up to eight different ones in a day, and you have to change classes after every lesson'.

'How do you know which class to go to next?' she inquired.

'Oh, it's dead easy!' said her brother, 'Our form teacher, that's the teacher that we report to every morning, draws out a timetable of all our classes on the blackboard and we copy it on to a sheet of paper'.

'What if you get lost, it's a big schoo', said Linda.

'You soon find your way round, no bother', said wee Douglas. 'The prefects took us on a tour of all the different floors and blocks'.

It was mid October. After only seven weeks, Linda's strappy black patent leather shoes had a hole in the sole of each shoe. She didn't know how to tell her mum, because she knew that she couldn't afford to buy her another pair so soon. She was sitting on the floor in front of the fire in the living room with her legs crossed when her dad suddenly noticed the big holes in the soles of her shoes.

Douglas said, 'Look at the state of your shoes'. He then turned his attention to Margie and said sternly, 'I told you that they would never last her!' Then he instructed, 'Take her out and buy her boy's shoes. She won't wear them out so soon!'

Linda was shocked at the thought of wearing boy's shoes. She knew that she would never be able to live it down at school and would get teased unmercifully. Margie did what she was told and took her out that Saturday afternoon to the big warehouse where she held an account. She asked the young assistant to bring her sturdy, lace-up boy's shoes, explaining that Linda went through shoes so fast that her dad had insisted on this. The assistant climbed up the big ladder and brought down a box from the top shelf. She opened the box. She walked back towards them and looked apologetically at Linda, as though she sympathised with her. She brought out a pair of brown, thick, round toed, heavy shoes.

Linda was horrified and said to her mum, 'You're wasting your money, because I won't wear them!'

When they got home, Linda put the box of boy's shoes in at the bottom of her wardrobe and there they stayed. She continued to wear her strappy shoes with the holes. She saved any cardboard that she could get her hands on from empty cereal and detergent boxes. Every few days she cut out a cardboard insole to put inside her worn shoes. On rainy days, she wore her Wellie boots. There was no way that those embarrassing boy's shoes were coming out of the box!

All the kids were discussing what to wear for Hallowe'en. They loved this time of the year. They dressed up in fancy dress and went round the neighbour's doors, asking, 'Anything for my Hallowe'en?' They were invited in to do their party piece, usually a song, a poem, a dance or a magic trick. They were then rewarded with a piece of fruit, some nuts or sweets. If you were very lucky, you could even get a thru'penny bit.

Douglas said, 'Here son, you can wear my postman's uniform'.

They all had a good laugh, as the big jacket and trousers drowned him and the skipped hat came over his eyes to rest on his nose. He put the postman's sack across him. It would come in handy for all his goodies. Linda's dad took the soot from the chimney and blackened up her face. She put on an old flat cap and jacket belonging to him. With a brush over her shoulder, she looked very comical as a chimney sweep.

All the children were in the street for Hallowe'en. Linda giggled as she spotted Raymond, a boy from her class, with a turban, cross-over apron, his mum's high heels and red lipstick on, carrying a white handbag. Douglas told his children to be home again by 8.30pm. They came in happy and weary and sat to show their parents all their gifts. Between them, they had ten apples, six oranges, enough mixed nuts to fill a big fruit bowl, some loose hard-boiled sweets and 1/9d. It had been a very successful night. The best laugh for Linda was next day at school, when she saw Raymond. His lips were still red. Although he had scrubbed and scrubbed, he had found it impossible to completely remove the red lipstick stain on his lips.

Margie's brother Donald and his wife, Janet, moved into a house above the shops two streets away. They had three children; two boys and a girl. Donald had a lovely, caring nature. He always had a smile and a nice word for everyone and loved a good joke. Janet was a difficult woman. Most people said it was only because of Donald's good nature that they were still together, as no other man would have put up with her. She liked her luxuries and Donald worked hard to give them to her. She didn't have any time for her children. Donald came home after a hard day driving buses and cooked the family dinner, as she never made any effort. She liked her whisky, and it wasn't uncommon for her to be sitting in her living room in the afternoon in her dressing gown with a bottle of Whyte and MacKay at her side. Often, Linda would call in for her cousin, who was only seven, only to find her struggling in the kitchen on her own with the family wash. They were one of the few lucky families to have a washing machine. Margie still had to wash everything by hand while Linda used to 'caw the handle' on the wringer for her mother. Every Saturday, Linda fed through the sheets, towels, shirts and other clothing. Linda used to feel sorry for her wee cousin. The electric wringer looked so dangerous and she worried that she would hurt herself, as she had no supervision.

Linda's selfish aunt shouted through to her wee daughter, 'Are you getting that work done, or are you standing there blethering?'

Her oldest cousin got away with blue murder, as he was the apple of his mother's eye. Aunt Janet treated her second son very badly. She used to belt him and lock him up in his bedroom all day with no food. When Donald came home after work, he let the tearful lad out of his bedroom.

Janet would then say, 'That boy needs to be taught a lesson, he's got no manners!'

Donald and Janet were one of the first to get a television. Everyone was fascinated. How wonderful it was to watch live pictures on a screen in your front room. Donald invited wee Douglas and Linda, along with all the neighbours' kids, to watch Children's Hour at 5pm on BBC, the only channel available. Douglas drew the curtains and turned off the lights, just like they did at the pictures. There was a blue glow in the room from the screen. Fourteen kids sat cross-legged on the floor in front of the television in anticipation and watched, mesmerized, as a roundabout appeared on the screen announcing Children's Hour. Aunt Janet, drunk, snoozed on a chair by the fireside while Donald made dinner. The programme finished at 6pm.

As the kids left, they shouted, one by one, 'Thanks Mr. Nixon'.

Then they ran off to tell their parents all about their experience of watching television forthe first time.

Saturdays were busy days. Margie and the children were up and dressed by 9am. Linda helped her mum on Saturday by now doing the shopping on her own. She wrote a shopping list out as her mum called out what was needed. While her mum caught up with the week's wash, Linda went to the shops. She struggled back with two message bags and four carrier bags, stopping every so often for a rest and a change of hands. The string from the handles was digging into her hands, making a red dent across her palms. She got to the back door and put the bags down just as Margie opened it.

'Oh my wee hen', Margie exclaimed. 'How did you manage all that? You're such a good wee lassie!'

Linda put all the shopping away and then it was time to help her mum put all the washing through the wringer. Wee Douglas usually spent his time digging and planting in the back garden on Saturdays. He put the washing line up for his mother and tied the rope tightly, stretched in a triangle between three poles. By the time Margie hung out the clothes, it was mid-day and time to go into town to pay the HP bills and shop for anything else they needed. Sometimes Linda went with her mother if she needed her help. Margie always went into the butcher's in town to get the meat for Sunday lunch. One particular Saturday she decided to buy tripe for Saturday night's tea. Linda wasn't a fussy eater, but she didn't like the look of this white stuff at all. They got to the bus stop in town just after 6pm when the shops were shutting. They were home for quarter to seven, about twenty minutes before Douglas staggered in from his day with Pop and his brothers at the football match.

'What's for tea?' he demanded, oblivious to the fact that Margie looked deadbeat.

'Tripe and onions', she said.

He nodded in approval. Linda laid the table, feeling very apprehensive about this 'tripe'. Margie passed the plates, floating in milk with tripe and onions, through the hatch to the living room table. Linda felt her stomach churn. She attempted to eat a bit but couldn't swallow it. Douglas got annoyed and lectured her about all the starving kids in the world and how lucky she was to have food.

He demanded that she try it. 'How can you say you don't like it if you haven't even tasted it', he shouted.

He instructed Margie to spoon it into her mouth. At that moment, Linda lost control. She couldn't help it. Her whole stomach turned inside out and whoosh, she threw up all over herself and Margie. Her dad seemed to calm down at this point and stared in disbelief at what had just happened.

Margie said, quite firmly, 'There's no use in forcing her Douglas. She obviously can't eat it!'

After that, there was never any arguments about tripe. When the rest of the family had it, Linda got something different.

Christmas 1956 was approaching and Asian flu was raging through schools and workplaces. Margie noticed the buses to and from work were half empty. A lot of people were absent from her factory and Douglas had to do more shifts to cover the postal duties of those who were sick, all due to Asian flu. It was serious. Some people were very ill and even dying from it. Linda's class at school normally had forty-three pupils. During this epidemic, there was only an average of twenty five children present at any time. The MacGregors thought they were lucky, as they seemed to be escaping the demon virus.

Then, just one week before Christmas, as the schools broke up for the holidays, Linda began to feel unwell. She had no energy, felt very weak, and the smell of food making her vomit. She couldn't eat. Margie called in Doctor MacDonald, who confirmed that she had the dreaded Asian flu. She lay in bed very sick. She dozed in and out of sleep, feeling woozy, like everything was a dream and she wasn't really present. At one point, she was hallucinating and felt herself drift out of her body. She was confused as she looked down from the ceiling and saw herself lying in bed. She was so ill she just wanted to die to get away from the suffering.

What's For Ye, Won't Go By Ye

Christmas Eve came and Linda was too sick to care. Margie and Douglas were very worried about her. They tried to cheer her up by hanging her Christmas stocking up on the end of her bed, instead of on the living room mantelpiece. On Christmas morning, wee Douglas thought he would surprise her by carrying their joint Christmas present up the stairs to their bedroom. It was a black, second hand, two-wheeler 18-inch Hercules bike. Linda didn't bat an eyelid. She could have cared less. She was more concerned about the smell of the Christmas dinner cooking downstairs. It was making her feel awful. She asked her brother to shut the bedroom door to try to keep the cooking smells out. Wee Douglas sat by his sister and put a cold wet face cloth on her forehead to cool her down. He tried emptying her Christmas stocking and showing her the contents, but she showed no interest whatsoever. She dozed back off to sleep. Douglas crept out of the room and went out to play and show off their new bike. After Christmas dinner, Margie tried to get Linda interested by showing her the big chocolate medallion in her Christmas stocking, telling her she would enjoy it when she was better. The thought of the chocolate made Linda feel worse and she told her mum to take it away and let her sleep. She was so weak, she was only sipping fluids and couldn't even sit up. Margie and Douglas became increasingly worried about their daughter, so they called Doctor MacDonald back in.

He said quite confidently, 'It's only been just over a week. Give her another four or five days!'

On the morning of 30th December, Linda woke up.

Weakly she said to her brother, 'Ask mammy if I can have a piece of toast, please?'

Wee Douglas ran down the stairs, jumping the last four and shouting loudly to this mother, 'Linda wants some toast!'

Margie came tearing up stairs, relieved that her girl was requesting some solid food. She gave her a big hug before nipping back down to the kitchen to make toast and a cup of hot, sugary tea. She brought it upstairs to the bedroom, propped Linda up and wee Douglas and Margie sat on the side of Linda's bed, grinning with happiness as she slowly ate every bit of toast and drank the tea.

Wee Douglas said, 'I'm really glad that you're better for my birthday tomorrow Linda'.

Douglas and Margie brought their daughter down to the settee in the living room to celebrate both her brother's birthday and New Year's Eve. She was still weak and lay there with a cover over her, dozing off now and again. They wouldn't be visiting Pop's house this New Year, but the main thing was that Linda was getting better. As Big Ben chimed midnight, Douglas raised his glass to Margie and wished for a healthy and happy 1957. Linda had given them both a real fright and now they could put that all behind him. Margie wondered if the scare of Linda's illness would bring her husband to his senses and make him realise that family life is more important than booze. Only time would tell if this would have any permanent impact on him.

CHAPTER FOUR

It was Easter Monday 1957. The sun was high in the blue sky. Linda still had not mastered the art of cycling her two-wheeled bike. Wee Douglas persevered with her, he helped her climb up onto the saddle, then told her to look straight ahead and start peddling. She gripped the handlebars tightly and, with a determined look on her face, she did as she was told. Her brother had his hands on the handlebars and the saddle to steady her. He let go of the handlebars but assured her that everything was OK, as he was holding the saddle. She cycled up the street for about twenty yards.

Suddenly she heard laughter and shouts of 'Well done Linda, you did it!'

She glanced round to realise that her brother wasn't right behind her but, further down the road. She panicked, wobbled and stopped the bike, feeling quite scared.

Then, a big satisfied grin came across her face. 'I've done it!' she shouted to wee Douglas, 'I can go a bike'.

After that, there was no stopping her. Every spare minute she had, she was out on her black Hercules bicycle.

Mrs. Harrison shouted over the fence to Margie, 'I'm going into Maryhill to buy the kids some new clothes for the first Sunday in May, does Linda want to come along for the ride?'

Linda excitedly nodded her head, she enjoyed going out with the Harrisons, and she especially loved to mother their babies. She always wished that her mum would have another baby so that she wouldn't be the youngest. She longed for a wee brother. Linda went outside to wait for them all, assuming that Mr. Harrison was at work with his car and they would be walking to the bus stop. The next thing she knew, a black taxi pulled up. Mrs. Harrison didn't like to complicate her life by attempting to struggle on and off buses with her brood, so she had rang for a taxi. Not only were they the only family in the street with a car and a television, they were also the only ones with a phone. They all piled in the cab. Mrs. Harrison and her eldest child Marilyn sat with their backs to the driver on the pull-down seats. Linda sat on the long back seat with the three other children and baby Patrick on her lap. They giggled and chatted loudly on the way.

When they got to the children's wear shop. Mrs. Harrison bought almost everything in sight. The assistant just had to show her something and she said, 'I'll have it'. After about two hours of them all trying on different outfits, she finally decided she had everything she needed. The assistant wrapped up all the purchases. There were twelve big bags. *How on earth are we all going to fit into a taxi with all these bags?* Linda thought. Mrs. Harrison asked the assistant to ring for a cab for her and, within five minutes, it was standing outside waiting. As they all piled in, the driver tied six of the bags into his luggage compartment. The rest went into the cab with them, squashed up against their legs.

'I'm hungry mammy', said five-year-old Michael. 'Can we have fish and chips?'

'Oh yes, please mammy!' echoed the other children

Mrs. Harrison asked the driver if he minded stopping at the fish and chip shop in Maryhill Road.

He said, 'Nae problem, Missus'. As he stopped outside the shop, he said, 'Here, Missus, you've got too many bags 'n' we'ans. Whit dae ye want? Gie's yer money 'n' ah'll get it fur ye'.

Tess Harrison pushed a five-pound note into his hand and said, 'Six fish suppers and whatever you want for yourself'.

He brought the steaming hot bags out and handed them to Mrs. Harrison with her change. When they got home, Linda helped the younger children out of the taxi. She then assisted Mrs. Harrison to carry the bags up the stairs to the house. Linda politely thanked her for taking her along.

Just as she was about to leave, Mrs. Harrison called her back and said, 'Here's your fish supper Linda, and a present for the first Sunday in May. Thanks for being such a good help to me today'.

Linda thanked her and ran home quickly. She threw the back door open, plonked the fish supper on the kitchen table, and babbled out in breathless excitement that Mrs. Harrison had given her a present.

'Open it then', said Margie.

Inside were the loveliest expensive red nylon knickers with white lace frills. Linda couldn't believe it. She loved girlie things and, up until now, she only had plain cotton underwear. That was all her mother could afford to buy her. She never dreamed that she could own such pretty frilly knickers.

It was the Glasgow Fair Fortnight in July 1957. Margie's factory closed down, as did most businesses in the city, for the annual two week holiday. Douglas was lucky enough to swap his holiday with another postman so that he could be off at the same time. Granny Nixon had a friend who owned a two bed roomed flat in Kinghorn in Fife. She was going away for a week and said that they could have her flat for a holiday. There was great excitement as they packed their swimming costumes, bucket and spades. Granny Nixon came to stay the night before. On the Saturday morning, they rose nice and early at 6am. They had to get washed, ready, eat breakfast and catch a bus into Buchanan Street Station to be in time for the 8.45am train to Kinghorn. Douglas and his son walked down the platform with the cases. They searched for an empty carriage. Most of the carriages had one or two people in them. They wanted one to themselves so that they could relax for the entirety of the journey with no disturbance from others. There was no corridor on the train so, once you had chosen your seats, you couldn't move.

They were getting near the front of the train when Douglas shouted 'This one will do'.

They all climbed in, helping Granny Nixon up the big step. Douglas told Granny and Margie to sit on the seats by the window at either side of the door with wee Douglas and Linda beside them. He then pulled the leather strap, let the window down and stood at the door looking out as if he was waiting for someone.

He winked at the children and said, 'This'll make the carriage look busy, no-one else will come in and we'll have a wee party all to ourselves on the way to the seaside'.

They could hear the steam engine starting up, then there was a loud hoot, a belch of steam, and the train chugged out of the platform. The children dashed from side to side, looking at all the places they were passing.

Douglas said, 'Listen to what the train's saying'. They listened intently, then their dad started saying to the beat of the wheels on the tracks, 'Tuppence a mile, tuppence a mile…'.

They all joined in as the train whizzed past fields with cows and sheep grazing. Soon they were approaching the Forth Railway Bridge across the River Forth. Douglas dug deep in his pocket for some big bronze pennies. He gave everyone one each. Then, as the train approached the bridge, he let the window down and told them that they were to throw the pennies as hard as they could over the bridge and into the water and make a wish. One by one, the pennies went flying out of all the train carriages, thrown by travellers who kept up this long-going superstition. Just before the train pulled into Kirkcaldy, which is famous for manufacturing linoleum, Douglas dropped the train carriage window down and convinced them all that they would be able to smell the linoleum. Linda sniffed but couldn't really smell anything different, but, not wanting to admit it, she agreed with her daddy.

They got to their destination. It was hot and the sun was shining brilliantly. They walked up the cobbled streets to their little flat on the first floor of an old house. It was spotlessly clean. There was a big range fire to cook on, a big double bed in each of the two rooms and a 'hole in the wa' double bed in the kitchen. This was a great novelty for wee Douglas and Linda. They had never seen a bed in a recess before. There was a lovely big garden at the back with a vegetable plot. While Margie unpacked, Douglas went to the pub and the children went out to the shops with their Granny Nixon to get some groceries. Wee Douglas and Linda carried the shopping bags back to the house for their granny. Margie had finished unpacking and their daddy was back from the pub, having only had a couple of pints. He was on his best behaviour in front of his mother-in-law.

That afternoon, they all went down to the beach. The children had their red metal buckets and spades with them and couldn't wait to start making sandcastles. Once there, they hunted for a space on the crowded beach. They found a spot just big enough for the five of them and then Linda changed into her blue stretchy elastic bathing costume, while her brother donned his navy blue swimming trunks. Douglas rolled up his trouser legs and shirtsleeves. Margie and Granny Nixon took off their nylons and shoes and, holding their summer dresses up above their knees, they went into the North Sea for a paddle with the children. The adults came back and left Linda and wee Douglas playing in the water.

After ten minutes, wee Douglas came back and started making a sandcastle for Linda. His dad helped him pat the sand pies into place. They dug out a moat and wee Douglas ran down to the sea with his bucket to fill it. Margie shouted to him to bring Linda back, as they were about to open their picnic. Margie had made sandwiches with the gammon and salad that Granny Nixon had bought, with a special treat of assorted tea breads for after. Wee Douglas looked for Linda but couldn't find her. He ran back to his parents and told them he couldn't see her. Douglas ran down to the water's edge, but she was nowhere to be seen. He started shouting her name out.

A man came up to him and told him there was a child way out in the water. Douglas' heart almost stopped as he saw a child resembling Linda wading out further and further, he knew she couldn't swim. He shouted out to her as he made his way towards her. Linda couldn't hear him at first and carried on going. As he got further out, she eventually turned round. She saw all the people waving and shouting but she was unperturbed, not realising that they were trying to attract her attention. She was not understanding what all the commotion was about. By this time, she had already made her own mind up that she had gone out far enough and turned to walk back through the water.

She panicked as she discovered that it wasn't easy getting back, as the water was very heavy and pushing against her. She saw her dad coming towards her and, to her great relief, he scooped her up and got her back to the beach safely. Linda was embarrassed at the attention she had drawn to herself, as people came up and asked if she was OK. She couldn't see what the big deal was when her mum and granny hugged her tightly and asked her what she was thinking about, doing something so silly. To her mind, she had only gone in for a paddle. Unbeknownst to her, the seabed suddenly dipped and the water was very deep. When she was told she could have drowned, she felt a bit foolish and froze at the thought of her naivety. She learned a very important lesson on the first day of her holiday and promised never to leave the water's edge again.

Every morning, the crowds gathered round as the Salvation Army band played on the beach.. Linda loved singing and joined in the songs, 'My Cup's Full And Running Over', 'I Will Make You Fishers Of Men' and 'Away Far Beyond Jordan', were three of her favourites. In the afternoons there was a Punch and Judy show on the beach. The children all sat cross-legged in front of the tall blue and white-stripped tent. Linda got there early to make sure that she got a good view. The man came round and gathered the pennies from them before it started. The beach was alive with the laughter of happy children as they watched the antics of Mr. and Mrs. Punch and the crocodile.

All too soon, the week was over and it was time to return to Glasgow. The last bit of excitement of the holiday was the return trip over the Forth Railway Bridge and throwing the pennies over again. The steam train pulled into Buchanan Street Railway Station. They climbed down out of the carriage, tired but happy with the memories of their first family holiday.

Margie and Douglas still had another week's holiday from work and promised the children that if the weather were nice, they would spend a day out at Rothesay on the Isle of Bute to visit their grandpa. Pop always rented a house for the month of July on the island for himself, Dot, Tom, Anne, Ina and Andrew, and had invited them over too. They had agreed that if the weather was nice, they would come for a visit on Friday.

During the week, they took the children on tram and bus trips all over Glasgow and its surrounding areas. They went to Rouken Glen Park, they had a sailing trip across the River Clyde on the Renfrew Ferry and, another day, they visited Milngavie to see the water works. On Friday morning, Douglas got up at his usual unearthly hour. This was a habit he found hard to break. He opened the back door and stood out in the garden.

He then came in and said to Margie, 'It looks like it is going to be nice today. Let's get the kid' up and we'll go to Rothesay for the day'.

Wee Douglas and Linda quickly got ready, munched through their corn-flakes (or toasties as Margie always called them), and were ready to leave the house by 7.30am. They got the bus down to Glasgow Central Railway Station to catch the boat-train to Gourock. This then linked up with a boat to take them for the half hour sail to Rothesay. The queues at the station for the trains were unbelievable. They wound round for what seemed like almost half a mile through the station and down through the tunnel underneath into Hope Street. They didn't get on the first one, but managed to get on the 9.15am train. It was approximately a forty-minute journey to Gourock. The train pulled into the pier. Everyone alighted and joined the long queue for a boat. It was a hot sticky day. The water was calm and still, the sky was blue, and boats were sailing in and out of the harbour continuously. This was their busiest time of the year, during the Glasgow Fair Fortnight Holiday. The family boarded 'The Jeannie Deans' paddle steamer at 11am for the crossing. They sailed out of Gourock Pier to two loud hoots from the steamer's chimney.

Douglas took the children down to the engine room and they watched in amazement as the giant polished cogs turned and made the ship move. The children then split up and explored the ship on their own. To them, it was so big. There were at least four different seating areas, two decks, a bar and a restaurant. Their parents had told them to return before the boat docked at Dunoon. The boat sailed in the harbour. Wee Douglas and Linda watched fascinated as a man on the boat threw the rope to another man on the pier. The man on the pier then pulled on the rope as if he were pulling the whole boat with all the hundreds of passengers on board all by himself. He then tied it up to a big iron mushroom-shaped thing They watched from the deck as the boat half emptied, then, just as many people boarded again for the trip to Rothesay. Half an hour later, they sailed into Rothesay. They spotted Pop and the family standing on the pier. Pop had a good idea that they would come and visit, as the weather was so good. He and the others had sat by the pier watching the different ships coming in.

When Auntie Dot saw them up on the deck waiting to disembark, she started calling out their names and waving enthusiastically as if she hadn't seen them for years. Linda got off the boat and ran over to her Auntie Dot.

Anne said to her, 'There are shows on the front'.

'Oh, can we go mammy, PLLLEEEASE?' pleaded Linda.

They all went for a stroll along the prom. Linda and Anne got excited as they were getting nearer the shows. The 'Chair-O-Planes' were swinging out right over the water.

'Oh that looks scary', said Linda.

The adults took a seat in 'The Frying Pan'. This was an area of seating in a circle with an entrance/exit at either side. Pop had nicknamed it this because it resembled the shape of an old frying pan. Pop gave wee Douglas, Linda and Anne a silver sixpence each. They went for a ride on the 'Dodgems', wee Douglas in one and the girls together in another. They chased and bumped each other to the sound of Bill Haley belting out 'Rock around the Clock'. The girls then had a go at hooking the ducks. Linda won a plaster-of-Paris rabbit ornament. Wee Douglas won a trick camera that squirted water, for knocking a coconut off the stand. They all had a penny each left, so they went to the roll-a-penny stall. One by one they put their pennies onto the big wooden block and then let it go, hoping that it would land in a winning square. Linda went first and squealed with glee as her penny wobbled and then fell backwards onto the 'Win Tuppence Box'. Anne went next, but her penny rolled right off of the edge. Douglas managed to win a penny, so they had their three pennies back again. Linda gave Anne a penny and they tried again but this time they all lost! When all their money was spent, they made their way back to the bench where the adults were sitting.

Auntie Dot had gone on up to the house to prepare lunch for everyone. She told them all to come home in hour. The men decided to go for a pint before lunch while Margie and Ina took Andrew, wee Douglas and the girls for a walk through 'Skipper Woods'. The children ran through the trees chasing each other, and everyone played hide and seek before making their way to the house for lunch. Auntie Dot had prepared a lovely cold meat salad and potatoes in their jackets, followed by Neapolitan ice cream and tinned fruit. By the time they finished it was 3.30pm.

They decided to make the best of the day and wander up to the meadows where there was a swing park, sports pitches and lots of space to run around. Anne brought a football with her. Grandpa watched as the adults and children got onto the football pitch and split themselves into two teams to play football. Linda kept jumping up and grabbing the ball.

Uncle Tom bellowed at her, 'Right, that's it. You cin be a goalie, yer no supposed tae pit yer hons oan the ba'.

Auntie Dot laughed and shouted to him, 'Don't take it so seriously Tom, it's only a game!'

After twenty minutes, the adults were tired out, so they called a halt to the game and went for a walk through the country paths to Loch Fad. It was so beautiful and peaceful and there were a few people fishing.

Douglas looked at his watch and said, "We better start making tracks it's just after half past six. By the time we get back down to the pier it'll be about half past seven and the last boat's at quarter past eight'.

They started walking back to the pier and then Dot said, 'The day has gone so quick, there's so much more for you to see. You haven't even seen Ettrick Bay, Kilchattan Bay or Port Bannatyne. You have just got to see the view over the Cumbraes from the golf course at the top of Canada Hill to believe it. You'll have to come for longer, maybe a whole weekend next year'.

Everyone was weary as 'The Talisman' paddle steamer pulled away from the pier. They stood on the deck waving to all the family back on the pier.

'I really enjoyed today', said Margie to her husband. 'I would love to come here for a holiday sometime'.

'I did too', said Douglas. 'Let save up and come here for our fortnight's holiday next year'.

Linda overheard them and her face beamed with delight as she told her brother.

It was 9am Sunday morning and the children were getting washed and dressed for the day. They could hear voices downstairs.

'That sound's like Uncle Donald', said wee Douglas.

Linda listened intently at the top of the stairs as she heard him say, 'I've got Kevin and May in the car. Get the kids ready and I'll take all of you for a run'.

She ran back into the bedroom to tell her brother, 'Quick get ready, Uncle Donald's taking us out in his car!'

They were downstairs in record time and had some shredded wheat before getting into Uncle Donald's little black box car with their mum and dad. Douglas sat in the front with Donald. Margie got in the back with the girls while Kevin and wee Douglas sat on the floor at her feet. They headed out through Bishopbriggs and Kirkintilloch for the Campsie Hills.

'This is a lovely way to round off our holiday', said Margie.

'Aye, it's back tae auld claes 'n purridge tomorrow', Douglas replied.

The little car approached the road at the bottom of the Campsie Hills and then started to climb. It chugged and chugged but eventually, when they were just over half way up, it would go no further.

Uncle Donald said, 'It's nae good, she's no' goin' to make it. There's too much weight in the car. We're going to have to turn back'.

He proceeded to do a three-point turn, backing onto the edge of the narrow road. Margie looked down. There was a drop of at least 200 feet and she was terrified.

Her voice quivered as she said, 'Oh, we're too near the edge. I'm feart Donald. Let us all out'.

Donald just laughed as Margie clung to the kids. He was an expert driver, having driven all sorts of transport during the War for the Army. Soon they were tearing back down the hills again. Margie was glad when they reached the bottom and confessed to her brother that when he turned the car on the narrow road, that was the most frightening moment of her life.

'Whit war ye scared aboot? said Donald. 'Dae ye no' trust me?'

Margie didn't answer him. He stopped the car outside a tearoom in Lennoxtown and Margie was more than ready for a welcoming cup of hot, calming tea.

Margie and Douglas returned to work the following day. There were three weeks left of the school holidays, and wee Douglas and Linda were left back in charge of the housework.

What's For Ye, Won't Go By Ye

Wee Douglas said, 'Let's hurry up and get all our chores done, then we'll go up to the Catholic school for our free milk'.

Most of the children in the housing scheme went up to the big Catholic school every morning during the holidays. They were entitled to claim their daily allowance of the third of a pint of milk that they normally got every day during school term. It was something to do and you got to meet up with your friends of both religions.

The children had really enjoyed their holidays with Granny Nixon in Kinghorn and the days here and there, finally finishing up with a Saturday trip to Rothesay to visit their dad's side of the family and a run in Uncle Donald's car on the Sunday. Their dad hadn't had time to have a 'skinful'. He would never have misbehaved in front of his mother-in-law in Kinghorn or in front of his father, brothers or sisters in Rothesay. After they paid for the holiday and all the different trips, there wasn't much money left to squander on booze. He only managed the odd pint here and there, and what a difference it made! He was the kind, loving father that they all knew and loved. Wee Douglas and Linda hoped that he would now realize that he didn't need to drink until he was 'steamin'.

That Saturday, Mary, her husband David, and their three sons and daughter came to visit. They had good news. They had just been allocated a lovely three bed roomed corporation house with back and front door and big back garden, in the west side of Glasgow. It was a lovely area. Margie was delighted for them, but she was going to miss her mother. She realised that she wouldn't see her so often. They had qualified for the house on Peggy's long tenancy with the corporation. The new house was in Peggy's name, as they didn't have enough points on their own to be awarded a house in such an elite area.

All the troubles of the past years were now water under the bridge. The men went out to a tavern in Bishopbriggs for a pint while the children played and the women blethered. Mary was having a moan about the price of all the school uniforms for the three boys. She wouldn't be able to salvage any of their previous uniforms to pass down, as they were all starting a new school. She didn't know how on earth she was going to afford to buy them all shoes.

'I have a pair of shoes that you can have' Linda piped in.

Margie looked at her and said to Mary, 'Well, you might as well have them. They've been lying upstairs for a almost a year now. Linda refused to wear them and they're far too small for her now!'

Mary was delighted. Cousin Neil was very small built and, although older than Linda, they fitted him a treat. He was as pleased as punch with his new shoes.

'Are ye sure, Margie?' said Mary.

Margie nodded her head and smiled.

Mary said, 'I'm awful glad I brought the subject up. Thank you very much Margie AND, thank you very much, Linda. I know I shouldn't say this, but I'm delighted that you didn't wear these shoes. You've taken a load off of my mind and solved a big problem for me!'

Linda was MORE than delighted to see the back of those horrible boy's shoes.

All too soon it was the beginning of the school term again and a really exciting one for Linda. She had left the annex for five to nine year-olds and was moved up to the main school at the other end of the housing scheme. She had heard that the teachers were a lot stricter, and Mr. Hutchinson, the headmaster, was the scariest man on earth. Wee Douglas and she got up early, along with their mother, for the first day of school. They had their breakfast of cereal and Linda made toast, putting it in greased bread wrappers for them to take to school for a play-piece.

After Douglas left, Linda sat in her dad's armchair (which was strictly forbidden) and sorted out her pencils into her new wooden pencil case. She put them into her new briefcase and then put her toast into the little buckled pocket in the front. She took the two shilling piece her mammy had given her for her dinner money and, just as she was about to put it into the zipped pouch on her brief case, it slipped and went down the side of the chair.

'Oh No', Linda screamed.

She put her hand down the side, but couldn't feel anything. Then she put her arm down, up to the elbow.

'Phew' she sighed, as she felt a coin.

She pulled her arm free and was delighted to find that she had plucked out a half-a-crown. She was sixpence better off now! She felt really smart in her pleated navy skirt, white blouse and school tie. She put on her navy trench coat with its check lined hood. Lastly, before she went out, she arranged her navy school beret with the badge on the front over her long pigtails. She set off nervously up the hill. As she got to the end of her road, she met the twins and three other girls in her class. They were all chatting and comparing stories that their older brothers and sisters had told them about the big school.

'I've heard that Mr. Hutchinson has a really thick leather belt with four fingers, but he only straps the boys', said Irene Green.

Linda was thinking how grateful she was that she was born a girl, when Elizabeth Sweeney piped up, 'And Miss Ryder is a bit of a nutcase. If she's in a bad mood, she takes the whole class out and straps them all really hard'.

'My brother told me that we are allowed out at lunchtime. He also said that when we come out of dinner school, everyone goes across the field to the ice cream van. There's also a black van that sells home made candy, cakes, and toffee apples outside the Catholic school', said Lorna Burns optimistically.

Linda was glad to hear that there seemed to be some good things to look forward to and that it wasn't all doom and gloom.

As Linda and her friends wandered in through the gates, she felt very small again, as compared to her last class in the annex where she was one of the oldest children. They were told that they were to go to the far away playground on the right side of the school. The school was split into two halves, with four classes in each half and the canteen/gym in the middle. Each side had its own playground. She knew that she was to be in Class II, as they had been told before they left the annex what their new class number was. She had butterflies, but took a deep breath and tried to look confident. At five minutes to nine, a whistle blew. An elderly woman teacher appeared, looking out over them from the top of the concrete stairs. She shouted sternly for everyone to stand still and not to move.

Then she bawled out, 'Class III'. At that, about a quarter of the children in the playground formed a single line and marched up the stairs.

The same thing happened when she shouted, 'Class IV'. Only the new pupils from Classes I and II remained standing in the playground, staring at the woman teacher and wondering what was going to happen next.

She shouted, 'My name is Miss Ryder! Well! You've all seen the routine. When I blow the whistle, everyone stops where they are, and no one moves. Then, whatever class number I shout, form a single file and march up the stairs. Do you all understand?'

No one answered, they just nodded nervously.

'I SAID, DO YOU ALL UNDERSTAND?' she bellowed.

'Yes', the children shouted back..

'YES WHAT?', Miss Ryder demanded.

'YES MISS', they all yelled back as loudly as they could.

'CLASS II', she bawled out.

This was Linda's class! She quickly joined her classmates in a single file and marched up the stairs to a smaller playground. There she saw Classes III and IV standing to attention in straight lines, in order of boy/girl. Another teacher, this time a younger, more pleasant looking woman, was standing over them. She instructed Linda's class to form a line of boys and a line of girls. Class I soon followed them. When there were eight lines of pupils, Miss Ryder instructed Class IV to go to the cloakroom and then into their class. They were to be followed by Class III.

Then she said, 'Miss Honeywell and I will be your teachers'.

Linda clenched her fists and prayed with all her might that Miss Honeywell would be her teacher.

Miss Ryder continued, 'Class I, make your way to the cloakroom and Miss Honeywell will show you to your new classroom, the rest of you wait with me'.

Linda's heart sank. She thought to herself, *will I really have to put up with this awful woman until next summer?*

The desks in Miss Ryder's classroom were separated and in single file. She sorted the children out into boy/girl order. She told them that this way she expected them all to work and learn. She wouldn't tolerate any carrying-on or nonsense. She added that if she thought anyone was getting too friendly with their neighbour, then she would move them.

Linda had been placed in the middle, second row from the front. Miss Ryder dumped a load of text books on Linda's desk and told her to hand them out to the rest of the class. One of the boys was ordered to hand out three exercise jotters each to everyone. The stern teacher told them that they had to be covered by the next day, or else they would be facing the belt! They spent that morning hearing about all the work that they would be expected to learn that year. At last, it was lunchtime and Linda was never so pleased to hear the bell. Everyone stood up and made their way to the classroom door.

'SIT DOWN!' bellowed Miss Ryder. 'WHO SAID THAT YOU COULD GO?'

Everyone ran back to their seats immediately and sat down.

'Now', she continued, 'you go when I say you can. UNDERSTAND?'

'Yes' replied the terrified kids.

'YES WHAT!' she demanded.

'YES MISS!' they obeyed, at the top of their voices.

'Sit smartly' Miss Ryder said, 'don't slouch. No one's going anywhere until you are all sitting up with your arms folded'.

She stood quietly in front of the class, checking them all with pursed lips and her eyes searching round the room. Eventually she said, 'OK, class dismissed!'

The children made their way to the hall for school dinners. There was a lovely aroma as they approached. Classes I through IV stopped for lunch half an hour before classes V through VIII, as the hall wasn't big enough to take them all at once. They stood outside in line and then the dreaded Miss Ryder appeared again.

'Right! We need four monitors to assist the dinner ladies', Miss Ryder said.

All the children eagerly raised their hands and shouted, 'Me Miss, Me Miss!'

She seemed to ignore them and picked out children from the back.

Then she looked right at Linda and said, 'You. You'll do'.

Linda couldn't believe it, her first day and she was a dinner monitor, she went inside. There were square tables that seated four, placed in four long rows. Each monitor got a row each and they had to serve the two-course meal and clear away the dirty dishes and cutlery. Monitor duty lasted for the week. Every Monday, four new people were chosen. It took half an hour to serve everyone and clear everything away. Then the monitors got their meals. The bonus was that they got extra helpings. Linda was starving by this time and welcomed the extra mince and tatties, followed by a double portion of caramel cake and custard.

That afternoon, Miss Ryder sent Linda on some chores to other classes and told her what a good, smart girl she was. She made Linda class monitor and told the rest of the class that she expected them all to listen and learn as quickly as Linda did. Linda felt really proud of herself and was beginning to think that Miss Ryder wasn't all that bad and, as long as you did what you were told, you wouldn't get on her bad side. She went home that day full of excitement, telling wee Douglas, her mammy and daddy how she was school dinner monitor, that Miss Ryder gave her special jobs to do in class and had made her the class monitor. Margie was delighted that Linda had settled in but wasn't surprised as she remembered how well she took to school in the first place.

Before Linda knew it, it was Friday lunchtime and the end of the week. She tucked into her school dinner after serving her row of tables and clearing away the table. She was really quite sorry that this was the last day of her lunchtime monitoring duties. She had really enjoyed the job and got on so well with the dinner ladies, especially Mrs. Mac, a stout kindly lady with a round happy face. She went out to the playground after lunch to meet up with her pals.

Irene Green said to her, 'You're a teacher's pet'.

'What do you mean? Linda asked.

'Well, Miss Ryder gives you all the good jobs, like handing out books, class monitor and dinner monitor. She's really nice to you and horrible to everyone else!' Irene spat.

Linda did wonder why she got these jobs, but she didn't do anything special to get Miss Ryder to like her. Next thing, Irene Green grabbed Linda's beret and threw it to another girl, and soon all the children in the playground, including the boys, were throwing her hat around. She desperately tried to jump up and down between them to catch it. Linda got quite upset, but refused to let anyone see her cry. She went back into the class after lunch and Irene Green still had her beret. She kept looking over at Linda and with an evil smile, showing her the beret in her hands under the desk.

Linda wasn't frightened of her, but she didn't like the fact that the rest of the class seemed to be siding with Irene and laughing at her. None of her friends had ever been mean to her before and she didn't know how to handle it. After school, she ran after Irene and asked her for her beret back. Irene told her she would never see it again and started throwing it about to everyone. Linda decided that she wasn't going to make a fool of herself again by trying to catch it, so she walked away. Irene shouted names at her as she walked away and some of the other children joined in. Linda ran home in tears.

She went in the back door of her house. Her daddy was in the kitchen, drunk. He was making stew and dough balls, but he could hardly stand up. Linda's heart sank. She thought her dad had given up drinking, but it looked like back to normal Fridays again.

She tried to sneak past him, but he shouted, 'Where do you think you're going?'

'Upstairs, to change out of my uniform' Linda said. She was petrified he was going to beat her.

'Don't bother. Go to the newsagents now and get me ten Capstan cigarettes' her father said.

Linda took the half a crown from him and did as she was told. She ran up through the lane, still upset about the other children bullying her. The last thing she needed was to come home and find her daddy the worse for alcohol. She knew she had to be very careful of his tempers and rages when he was in that state. As she hurried to the shops, the half a crown accidentally slipped from her hand and rolled back down the lane. She frantically chased it and thought her world had come to an end when it went straight into a stank and plopped into the water below. What was she going to tell her daddy! This would definitely mean a hiding for her. She walked around trying to kill time and wondering how to tell him, when she saw her brother going into the house.

She plucked up the courage and walked in the back door. He had already started on wee Douglas, lecturing him and telling him how useless he was.

Douglas went to slap his son around the head when Linda blurted out, 'Daddy, I'm sorry. I couldn't get your cigarettes, I lost your money'.

He turned round on his heels, 'What do you mean, you lost my money. How could you lose it?'

'It slipped from my hand and rolled down a stank' she cried.

'You shouldn't have been so b****y careless, what am I going to do now!' he snapped at her.

She stood shaking with her head bowed, 'I don't know daddy'. She daren't tell him that she knew that there were two shillings down the side of his armchair, because she would have got a smack for sitting on it in the first place. And another one for losing it. Plus, he would have wanted to know how she paid for her school dinners and she would have had to confess to finding a half a crown in his chair!.

He slapped her hard across her face, took another half a crown from his pocket and said to wee Douglas, 'Right, you go and get me my fags. I don't trust her. God help you if you don't come back with them!'

He slapped Linda again and told her to get upstairs and change. Linda thought the only good thing that came out of it was that she saved her brother from his usual Friday beating.

What's For Ye, Won't Go By Ye

After five minutes, her daddy shouted, 'What are you doing up there? Get down here now and set the table for tea'.

She went downstairs and her daddy said, 'I'm going up for a kip. Wake me up in an hour, before your mother gets home'.

Linda was so pleased that he had decided to go to bed. That meant that her brother would not be getting the brunt of her father's Friday drunken rage this week.

Linda was worried all weekend about her beret. She thought about telling her parents she had lost it, but knew that would mean a telling off and probably a belting from her daddy for being so careless. In the end, she kept it all in to herself and said nothing. Last. week she was nervously excited about starting at the big school, now, after only one week, her stomach was churning and she was dreading going to school to face the bullies on Monday morning

Linda woke to the noise of the wind and rain battering on her bedroom window. She hoped that it would be the middle of the night and she could roll over and go back to sleep. The next thing, her bedroom door opened and her mother was standing at the end of her bed with a comb and elastic bands in her hands, ready to pleat Linda's hair. It was 6.30am. Linda sat up, half asleep, and was swaying back and forth as Margie tugged at her hair.

Margie said to Linda, 'I'm sorry, my wee hen, for disturbing you so early, but I have to get to work'.

Margie finished pleating her daughter's hair and slid in a blue clasp at each side of her head.

Then she said, 'Right, I must away. You can have a wee rest now, but see and be up by half past seven so that you leave yourself time to get dressed and have breakfast. You don't want to be late for school!'

Linda groaned quietly to herself. The thought of school made her feel quite ill. She would do anything to get out of going, but she knew she had to face it sooner or later.

She got her coat on and automatically reached up to the peg for her beret. It started to prey on her mind again. She pulled her hood up and went out into the drecht weather.

As she walked up the hill, Irene Green and her friends got behind her and starting taunting, 'Where's yer beret, Linda?'

Inside, Linda felt scared and her tummy was tumbling over, but she wasn't going to give in and let them see that they were frightening her. She ignored them and hurried on up the road. Inside the gates, the word got round the school and matters escalated. Linda went through the morning pretending that they weren't bothering her, but deep down controlling herself from bursting into tears. She had got used to putting a brave front on. She was petrified of her daddy when he had been drinking and would beat her and her brother, but she never gave in or let him see that it bothered her.

Thank goodness for her two trusty pals! One of them wee Sadie, who was a cheery soul who came from a very poor family. The first time Linda went round to Sadie's house, she was horrified. Linda's family wasn't by any means well off, they just managed to make ends meet some weeks, thanks to the secret £1 borrowed every Wednesday from Auntie Dot. Sadie, however, lived in squalor. She had nine brothers and sisters. She was only nine years old and had two brothers and three sisters younger than her. Their house was very basic. They had bare floorboards. Sadie's bedroom had two old wooden double beds where her and her five sisters slept. There was nothing else in the room. Their hand-me down clothes were all piled in a cupboard in the room. That's the reason why Sadie usually came to school in ill-fitting clothes, she just grabbed what she could from out of the cupboard. Her two brothers' bedroom was similar and had one big old-fashioned double bed. The walls of the rooms were badly soiled and scribbled on. The living room had bare floor boards and a threadbare red patterned rug in front of the fire, two torn and well-used armchairs and an old fashioned brown settee that you sunk into because the springs had all gone. There was a gate leg table in the corner. By the fireplace was a cot where Sadie's four-month old baby sister slept during the day. At night, Sadie's parents took the baby into bed with them.

In spite of her poverty, Sadie was a good friend. Linda was very caring and felt very sorry for her. She always shared her play piece with her everyday at playtime, as Sadie never had one. Sadie only got the free school dinners. On Mondays, Linda usually had sixpence given to her by her Grandpa after her visit with him on Sundays. Linda always split it so that she and Sadie had thru'pence each. They trotted up to the ice cream van or the candy man after lunch and treated themselves. Linda always stood by Sadie when the others were being mean and mocked her for being poor. Linda's other friend, Myra, was a chubby jolly girl. She was the youngest of a family of boys, well spoiled, but not nasty with it. The three girls all got on very well together and never got involved with troublemakers.

After lunch, Linda was playing skipping ropes with Myra and Sadie. She told her friends to wait a minute until she ran to the toilet. She turned to dry her hands and a tall lassie in the year above stood in front of her and blocked her way.

She sneered at Linda and said, 'You're a wee coward. Ye were too feart tae ask fur yer beret back'.

'No, I wasn't. I'm going to get it back later', Linda replied as her heart pumped with terror.

'Well, ye'll no want it back noo, it's been trampled in dog's dung!' she said callously.

Linda felt mixed emotions of anger and fear. She loved her mum and knew how hard she worked to buy her the uniform for school and she remembered her sitting sewing the badge on the beret and being so proud when Linda donned it for the first time. The older lassie made a grab for Linda's pigtails and threatened to put Linda's head down the toilet and soak her pigtails in pee. At that, something snapped inside Linda. She was enraged. All the anger that had been building up for what she was suffering at home from her drunken daddy's beatings and the bullying from other children seemed to come to a head. She had had enough! She wasn't big enough to stand up to her daddy yet, but she was determined that this girl wasn't going to get the better of her.

Linda's temper broke and she grabbed the older girl. She put her arm across her throat, holding her against the wall.

She screamed at her, 'Well, go on then, do what you said you were going to do!'

The older lassie breathed in sharply, eyes staring at Linda as if pleading for mercy. She was scared out of her wits. Linda suddenly calmed down and let her go, but not before warning her not to ever think about threatening anyone again. The big lassie ran out of the toilet. Linda stood for a minute shaking at the thought of what had just happened.

She pulled herself together and went out to the playground. The big lassie was standing with a crowd. They were listening intently to her and glancing every now and again over to Linda. One of them started walking towards Linda. Suddenly, the bell went and Linda breathed a sigh of relief. She was never so happy to hear that wonderful sound. She didn't want any trouble and couldn't believe how all this had got out of hand just because horrible Irene Green had stolen her beret.

Linda sat in class. Miss Ryder told the children to take out their exercise books for dictation. The boy behind Linda tapped her sharply on the back with his ruler. Linda turned round and he slipped her a note. She placed it inside her jotter and opened it. It read, 'So you think you're big for kneeing Annette Cruikshank in the toilets? Well I'll be waiting for you in the field in Elder Street after school. You can show me how brave you are'. It was signed 'Norah'. Linda couldn't believe this, it was all escalating. She never kneed Annette Cruikshank. She only held her against the wall and warned her off. If she hadn't defended herself, Annette would have had Linda's head down the toilet. Annette wasn't harmed in any way. The only thing that was hurt was her pride. Linda felt sick inside. She didn't need or want any of this, she wasn't interested in fighting any-one. She wasn't that type of person. She was a good, caring person who would help anybody. She just wanted to enjoy life. She looked across at Norah, who stared back at her menacingly. Norah was one of the popular, outspoken girls in the class and she would have no problem getting everyone on her side against Linda. She obviously believed Annette Cruikshank's cock and bull story.

Wee Sadie and Myra stood by Linda.

Myra said, 'What are ye going tae dae?'

Linda thought for a moment and then said, 'Well, I'll just have to go through with it and stand up to her'.

Soon the whispers were all round the class that there was going to be a big fight in the field after school between Linda and Norah. The bell rang for the afternoon playtime. Linda didn't really want to go out because she knew by this time the whole school would be taunting her. They would never go against bossy Norah. Strangely enough, Norah left her alone in the playground, apparently she told her pals that Linda wasn't worth worrying ruining their break for.

The word had traveled, however, and boys and girls were approaching Linda and saying, 'Is it true that you're fighting Norah Banks after school?'

Linda swallowed her pride and said quietly, 'Aye'. Then she came out with a more confident, 'Aye! She's no' gonnie tae get away wi' sending me threatenin' letters!'

Linda was shocked at her own confidence and didn't know why she had said that. As four o'clock approached, she began to feel sick inside and wished she had never got into this mess. The bell rang. Linda, wee Sadie and Myra got their things together. They headed out to the playground. Linda was ready to face the music.

She said to her pals, 'I don't stand a chance, the whole school will be on Norah's side'.

Just then, Simon Ronaldson shouted over, 'Hi Linda, I thought you were gonna fight Norah?'

Linda said, 'Aye, I am. I'm going to the field now'.

He replied, 'Well you'd better hurry up and catch up with her. She made a run for home as soon as the bell went!'

Linda couldn't believe it. She started running down the road with wee Sadie and Myra, pretending that she was running after Norah. The word got round that Norah had fled and soon Linda had about fifty or so pupils running with her, chanting for Norah's blood. Linda got to the field to find practically the whole school gathered there, waiting for the big fight.

Linda shouted with make-believe confidence, 'Well, I'm here, where is she?'

Secretly, she was relieved when she was told by the angry mob that Norah had run off. She was hoping against hope that Norah wasn't going to come back. Gradually the crowd dispersed, labeling Norah a yellow coward.

What's For Ye, Won't Go By Ye

The next day at school, Linda was the hero. Irene Green gave her back her beret. (It hadn't been trampled in dog dung). Everyone wanted to be her friend.

Elizabeth Sweeney said, 'No one will ever attempt to mess with you again Linda, if they value their life!'

It turned out that Norah assumed that Linda would back down and run after reading the note, making Norah look good. Instead, Linda faced up to her so Norah took fright and ran. Norah had now lost all her pals, credibility and respect. She was now a lonely figure in the playground. At the afternoon break, Linda felt sorry for Norah, as the other kids were being horrible to her and calling her a coward. The tables were well and truly turned.

Linda didn't like this, so she went over to Norah and said, 'You'll know not to send notes like that again'.

Norah nodded nervously.

Linda said to her, 'Well, I'll forget it, will you?' Norah looked relieved.

Linda then said, 'You're welcome to come over and join in our game of rounders'.

Soon they were all yelling, laughing and screaming as Linda and Norah both ran rings round the other team, beating them hands down. Norah was grateful to Linda for being so forgiving. Everyone else in the class respected Linda's decision. Linda had control and no one dared to attempt to intimidate or bully anyone again. Linda, wee Sadie, Myra and Norah all became firm friends.

When Margie came home from work that evening she asked Linda, 'How was school, anything exciting happen?'

'No, just the usual', replied Linda, followed by, 'What are we having for tea tonight?'

Christmas was approaching and most of the children were talking about buying their teachers a little gift. Linda knew that it would be a waste of time to ask her parents for money to buy Miss Ryder a Christmas present, as there wasn't enough money in the kitty to go round at the best of times. The Sunday before the school broke up for the festive holidays, Linda visited her grandpa. He gave her and her brother half a crown each for Christmas. Their three uncles, who still lived at grandpa's house, gave them half a crown each. They had ten shillings each and they felt very rich. Linda knew exactly what she was going to do.

On Monday morning, she said to her little pal Sadie, 'After lunch let's go to the shops. I want to buy Miss Ryder a present'.

They gulped their dinner down and, at half past twelve, they ran down the road to catch the shops before they closed for lunch at one o'clock. Linda bought a beautiful big box of milk chocolates tied with a blue ribbon and a big blue bow for 4/6d. They started walking back to school. She was happy and excited about giving the chocolates to Miss Ryder. When she looked at wee Sadie's face, she could see that poor Sadie was feeling a bit upset because she couldn't afford to buy the teacher a present. Linda related to this well, as without her grandpa's and uncle's Christmas money, she wouldn't have been able to buy anything, either. On the spur of the moment, she grabbed Sadie's hand, turned round and hurried back to the shops. She took Sadie into the chemist and she asked the lady assistant what toiletry sets she could get for around 4 or 5/-. The lady brought out five sets and Linda told Sadie to choose one. She picked a gardenia scented one with talcum and soap for 4/11d. Linda had 7d left over from her 10/-, so they went back into the newsagents and she bought 7d worth of sweets for them both before they hurried back to school. They presented Miss Ryder with their Christmas presents. She was delighted but looked at them in suspicious amazement, as though her mind was working overtime thinking where on earth the girls got the money from to buy the gifts.

The school broke up on Wednesday and, on Thursday morning before Margie went to work, she asked Linda to go to the shops after she had finished her chores to get bread and potatoes.

'Just use the money your grandpa and uncles gave you'. Margie said. 'I get paid tomorrow, so we'll go out at the weekend and I'll put it towards buying you some new clothes'.

Linda held her head down and sheepishly told her mammy that she didn't have any money left.

'Why, where is it?' asked Margie.

'I've spent it on a present for my teacher'

'What, the whole 10/-?' inquired her mother, who was getting unusually annoyed.

'Well, wee Sadie didn't have any money, so I bought her a present to give to Miss Ryder', Linda said.

'YOU WHAT!' shouted Margie. 'We don't have money to give away. That would have been a really good help for us. Not only did you buy your teacher one present, but you buy another one for someone else to give her. Are you stupid? You've never ever bought me a present and I'm your mother. What has Miss Ryder done to deserve this honour?'

Linda felt awful. She only bought her teacher a present because she didn't want to be the odd one out of the girls in her class. She thought that she was being kind by buying another one for Sadie to give. She never thought about spending the money on her own mother. She felt really mean and guilty now and wished that she hadn't done it, but it was too late now. Linda was grateful that her mammy didn't tell her daddy because he would have belted her from here to Kingdom Come.

What's For Ye, Won't Go By Ye

It was the summer of 1958. Linda was really excited and counting down the weeks until her forthcoming holiday in Rothesay. He brother Douglas junior (as he was now known because he was fourteen and a half and growing up fast), was going on holiday to Whitley Bay with the Boys Brigade at the same time. Linda and her brother got their morning chores done as quickly as they could and, by eleven o'clock, she was out on her bike. She loved her bicycle even though it was only a second-hand one. Linda was popular because she was lucky enough to have a bike. None of her classmates had one. They used to come round to her street and Linda taught them how to ride it and let them have a shot.

Her friend Janette, who lived in the next street, had a posh pink bike with straight handlebars. They went to different schools, but they always met up in the holidays to go cycling. Their favourite route was through Bishopbriggs, Kirkintilloch, and all the way to the Campsie Hills. They came back via Mingavie and Lambhill. They would be away for almost seven hours, getting back about six pm, just in time for tea. Linda always made a point of doing this on Fridays. Douglas junior and she had learned that it was always better to have an excuse not to be around when their dad came home drunk on Fridays. Their dad was always furious that they weren't there, but, if they timed it right and got back at the same time as their mother, he wouldn't have a go at them because Margie never knew of the verbal abuse and beatings they were getting. The children made a point of dodging their father when he was drunk by not being alone in the same room as him. If their mother left the room, they followed her out. They knew that he would whisper drunken warnings to them, telling them that he was going to deal with them later for being so disobedient and not coming home earlier

Linda's cousin Anne knocked on the door one morning and asked if she could have a ride on Linda's bike. This was one thing that the spoiled Anne didn't have. She had everything else, but Auntie Dot refused to let her daughter have a bike. They lived on the main road where the buses went up and down, and she was worried Anne would have an accident. Linda was her usual generous self and allowed Anne to cycle her bike up and down the street and round the block until she finished her household chores. Anne never did any chores. She didn't even know how to wash a dish, never mind scrub a toilet. Linda went out to the street to look for Anne and tell her that she was finished. She could see her in the distance, cycling towards her.

Linda took her bike back and Anne said, 'Where are you going now?'

'I'm going for a long cycle out to the country', replied Linda.

'Can I come, give us a backie, go on', Anne pleaded.

Linda agreed, as usual, and took Anne for a cycle out to Milngavie. It was a stifling hot day and they stopped for a rest by a burn and paddled their feet.

After an hour, they cycled back home, Linda standing all the way and peddling like mad, while Anne sat comfortably on the saddle. They approached the big steep hill leading to Linda's house.

Linda said to Anne, 'Watch this. I can cycle down here with my eyes shut and guess where the turning is into my street. I've done it hundred's of times!'

Anne screamed as Linda missed the turning. They went over the handlebars of the bike and ended up stuck in a high hedge. Linda had a white frilly blouse on. She looked down and it was red with blood. Her left arm hurt too. She put her hands up to see where the blood was coming from and felt her chin was all raw. She was numb with shock but bravely got up and helped Anne, checking that she was OK, before pulling her bike out of the hedge. Anne only had a graze on her hand. Linda had cushioned her fall. The wheel of her bike was bent and the handlebars were wonky. They walked down towards Linda's house.

Linda said to Anne, 'My daddy will be back from work. Please don't tell him about me shutting me eyes. He'll be dead angry with me'.

Anne promised not to say. Linda got home, put her bike round the back of the house and went in to see her daddy

He looked at her in disbelief. 'What on earth has happened?' he demanded.

'I fell off my bike', Linda answered.

He wasn't very happy, as he was preparing to go back to bed for a couple of hours before going on overtime that evening. He marched Linda round to the doctor's surgery. It was closed but he rattled on the door.

The doctor came out and took a look and said, 'She's split her chin open and it needs stitching. My equipment is broken, so you will have to take her to Stobhill Hospital'.

There was no quick way of getting to the hospital. No buses went direct. The only one that went anywhere near took over an hour as it went into the town first before going to the hospital. Douglas walked with Linda through the fields for a short cut, complaining all the way about how he was losing overtime and asking how an earth she managed to fall off of her bike. He told her that he wouldn't be fixing her bike and she could forget about ever going out on it again.

Thirty-five minutes later, they arrived at the casualty department. Douglas went to the reception and told them what had happened. Then they sat in the waiting room for about an hour. A stout dark haired friendly nurse came to the door every now and then and called patients' names. Linda waited, hoping that it wouldn't be much longer. She was feeling uncomfortable and her arm was hurting, although her dad hadn't mentioned this when he checked her in.

Douglas said to her, 'I can forget about my overtime now'.

Linda felt badly for upsetting her daddy's day.

'Linda MacGregor', called the nurse.

What's For Ye, Won't Go By Ye

Linda got up and followed her through to a cold, white room which smelled strongly of disinfectant. The nurse helped her up onto the couch and told her that the doctor would be here soon. Ten minutes later a round, jolly bald man appeared. He looked at the notes and then at Linda.

He kindly asked, 'Now then Linda, what have you been up to?'

'I fell off my bike', she replied.

'Well that was a silly thing to do, wasn't it?' he smiled. 'Let's get this cleaned up for you. We'll put a butterfly stitch in your chin. It won't hurt and we'll just put strips of thin tape on it to hold it together. It would be too difficult to stitch it properly', he said to Douglas. 'They would only tear through the skin with jaw movement'.

Linda sat patiently while the nurse cleaned her up, then the doctor and nurse butterfly stitched her wound and put a thick plaster round her chin to restrict movement and help it to heal.

'Just sit still for a minute Linda, I will need to give you a wee jag. Look away, it won't hurt', said the nurse.

'Right, that's it! You're all patched up', said the doctor. 'Do you feel a bit better now?'

'Well not really', said Linda, 'my arms hurts'.

He looked at her arm, and touched it in several places, asking her where it hurt. He sent her for an x-ray. She had to go back in the waiting room and sit for another hour with her daddy. Finally they called her in and broke the news that she had cracked a bone in her wrist, so they would have to plaster that too, and put her arm in a sling. Linda walked out of the hospital four hours later looking like she'd been in the wars. When she turned into her street with her daddy, all the kids were running up and asking Linda what had happened. Mrs. Harrison next door looked at her with great sympathy and tried to make things better the only way she knew by giving Linda half-a-crown. Linda was delighted, for this was a lot of money!

Margie knew nothing, as no one had a telephone to tell her, but she wasn't allowed to have telephone calls on the company telephone anyway. Linda sat on the wall and waited for her mammy to come home. She saw her in the distance and ran towards her. She loved her mammy so much, she missed her when she was out at work and always felt so happy to see her.

Margie stopped in the street with shock when she saw Linda. 'What's happened?' she said in a panic.

Linda told her all about the accident and the hospital (but carefully missed out the bit about shutting her eyes).

Margie hugged and kissed her and said, 'Oh my wee pet, and I wasn't even here. That's it, you're not to go out on your bike again when I'm not around!'

Margie felt really guilty and blamed herself. She was a very maternal woman and hated leaving her children everyday to go to work. She felt that if she had been there to look after Linda, then this accident would never have happened. She was in a dilemma, for they needed the money and the bills had to be paid. Douglas sat quietly and never mentioned anything about making life easier by working more overtime and handing in more housekeeping so that Margie could cut down to part-time and be around for her children. There was no solution, so things carried on as normal with Margie working long hours to help pay the rent and bills. Douglas only gave her basic housekeeping, his overtime money disappearing over the bar in the pub.

Douglas junior was looking forward to attending Boys Brigade camp and excited about going to Whitley Bay in England. He was to be responsible for bugle wake-up calls in the mornings and was frantically practicing. Linda used to sing along with him 'Charlie, Charlie, get out of be-e-ed, Charlie, Charlie get out of bed. Get out of bed, get out of bed and fold your blankets, this is another day, to serve the Queen.' Between this and his bagpipe playing ,it was a very musical household. Of course, the noise had to stop when their daddy came home from work. He sent his son over the fields to the canal bank to practice, convincing him that the sound was much better in the open air, and had nothing to do with the fact that there is nothing worse than someone learning the bagpipes! It wasn't long until Douglas junior had mastered the pipes. Every Friday night on the bus home from Boys Brigade, he made quite a tidy sum from the drunken men. He got it off to a T.

He went upstairs on the bus and, sure as fate, some drunk would say, 'Is that the bagpipes ye've goat ther' son? Cin ye play thim, geeza wee tune?'

Douglas would stand up, tune up his chanter, then go up and down the passage giving the passengers a rendition of 'Scot's Wa Hae', 'Mairi's Wedding', 'Heilan' Laddy' etc. As he passed by them they slipped money into his pocket, sometimes getting the odd two bob bit or half a crown.

Two weeks later, Douglas junior set off to Boys Brigade camp and Linda went to Rothesay with her mammy and daddy for their annual holiday. They had a room and kitchen to rent for two weeks. Granny Nixon came along too. They sailed into the bay on board 'The Waverley' paddle steamer. They looked down at the quay and saw Auntie Dot with Uncle Tom and Anne. Linda and Anne were very alike and were often mistaken for twins. Margie had made them tartan trews and they had identical cardigans from a shop in Springburn that knitted everything to order on machines. Linda was wearing her tartan trews and new cardigan.

Margie looked down and said, 'Oh look, Anne's wearing her tartan trews and new cardigan too'. Then she said, 'What's that on her arm, is it a sling or is she pretending to have a sore arm because you both look so alike?'

They got off the boat to find out that Anne too had broken her arm. She had been playing on the passenger ramps on the pier and slipped and fell between two of them. Anne and Linda caused quite a commotion with both of them having 'stookies' and slings on their left arms. People took pictures of them and were asking how both twins happened to break their arms at the same time. The girls got fed up explaining that they weren't twins and ended up letting people believe what they wanted. They didn't complain when they were given free rides at the fairground because the men took pity on them, nor when the cafe owners gave them a free ice cream each. In fact, they were quite enjoying being the centre of attention!

Douglas junior brought his sister back a black shiny purse that clipped shut. He had put a shiny penny in it for luck. Linda loved it and put it by her school dinner money. Just before school started up again, she visited the hospital to have the plaster removed and her arm examined. It had healed well, so she was OK to go back to school without the sling. Although her arm still felt very weak, the doctor told her that everything was as good as new and she would soon get the strength back. It felt good to be able to get her arm out in the fresh air again and have a good scratch at it. She had a little scar on her chin but, unless she lifted her head right, back no one noticed it.

Linda wondered what her new teacher would be like, what new things she would learn, and what would happen this year at school. She was ready to face another term!

CHAPTER FIVE

It was the spring of 1959 and the class above Linda's was preparing for their qualifying dance. She could hear them all giggling and talking as they walked past her classroom en route for the gym to practice their dancing skills. Linda was envious because she loved to dance but, as it was year-about for a dance or an outing, she would be going on a day trip the following year Mr. Ross, the teacher from the qualifying class, came into their classroom one Friday afternoon and whispered something to their teacher, Miss MacCormack. The class carried on writing their exercise, peering up occasionally to see if they could catch a gist of their conversation. After a few minutes, Miss MacCormack told the class to put their fountain pens down.

She said, 'Mr. Ross is organising the qualifying dance for the year above. It turns out that they have too many boys and are five girls short. We need to pick five girls from this class to go to the older children's dance'.

The girls eyes lit up in delight. They all thrust their hands in the air, begging the teachers to pick them.

Miss MacCormack said, 'I think the fairest way is for you to put your names in a hat and we'll choose the first five out'.

She tore some sheets of paper into quarters and gave all the girls a piece, instructing them to write their name on it and then fold it into quarters. She went into the book cupboard, took out a box and placed all the names into it. Giving it a shake, she invited Mr. Ross to pick out the first name.

'Maureen Souter', he announced. Maureen Souter was a tall gangly girl and she clapped her hands in excitement.

Miss MacCormack picked the next name. 'Hazel Johnstone', she called out.

Mr. Ross then picked out Jean MacIntyre's name, followed by Joan MacDonald's, which was pulled out by Miss MacCormack. It was time for the very last name. The girls all sat there in anticipation. Just at that moment, in walked the headmaster, Mr. Hutcheson. Mr. Ross invited him to pick the all important last girl's name. Linda closed her eyes and prayed while the headmaster slowly took out the paper and unfolded it.

He seemed to be taking an eternity, everyone was in suspense, then he called out, 'Linda MacGregor'.

Linda opened her eyes in delighted amazement.

Myra and Sadie both said, 'Oh, you're dead lucky Linda. We wish we had been picked to go with you!'

'Now', said Mr. Ross, 'the five girls who have been chosen should report to the gym for dancing practice straight after the afternoon playtime'.

Linda was so excited she could hardly contain herself. She couldn't wait to tell her mammy.

She went to the gym with the others. The girls were all told to stand along one wall and the boys along the opposite wall.

Mr. Ross said to the boys, 'Now you will each be escorting one of these pretty young ladies to the dance. I want you all to go across and ask one now. If she says yes, then the both of you go over and sit on the bench together. If she says no, then you'll have to keep asking until you find a partner'.

Linda felt it a bit intimidating when all the boys came towards the girls. After all, they were all older than her and she didn't know any of them.

A shy lad with a mass of brown curly hair approached Linda and asked politely, 'Would you mind if I escorted you to the dance?' Linda felt pleased. She liked him and was relieved that none of the scruffy lads had asked her, she would have been too embarrassed to say no.

She shyly nodded her head and said yes. They went to the bench and sat down together. Linda recognised him from school, but didn't actually know him. He told her that his name was Tim Roberts and that he already knew who she was.

He had a twin sister called Tina, who came over and said to Linda, 'Oh, I'm so glad that you are going to the dance with Tim, he's liked you for ages'.

Tim blushed like beetroot and told his sister to be quiet. The rest of that afternoon, and the last hour of daily lessons every day for the two weeks leading up to the big night of the dance, were spent learning popular dances.

It was a lovely Friday evening in the middle of June. Tim was due at the door to collect Linda and take her to his qualifying dance. Margie had got away from work early especially to help Linda get ready. Douglas was on his best behaviour, no drinking that day, because he knew that his wife was coming home early and he didn't want her to find out the truth about his Friday afternoon binge drinking. Margie had made her daughter the most beautiful blue net party frock that sat in layers. The top had a beaded detail around the neck and shoulders. Linda wore a pretty multi-coloured layered paper nylon petticoat underneath that allowed the dress to float and move gracefully as she walked. She had silver dance shoes with white ankle socks and, the biggest treat of all, her very first bra. The bodice of the dress was very fine net over blue taffeta and when Linda tried it on for a fitting, Margie became aware that her girl was growing up and needed a little support. Margie did Linda's hair in curls with a big blue bow at the back. She stood back to admire her daughter and couldn't believe how beautiful she looked.

Douglas said, 'Aye hen, ye'll break a few hearts this night, yer almost as good-looking as yer faither!'

Just then the doorknocker went. Margie opened it and there stood Tim in his smart navy blue suit and bow tie.

'I brought this for Linda', he said shyly to Margie, showing her a lovely white orchid in a box.

Margie said, "Oh, that's really lovely Tim. Come in. Linda's ready, I'll just pin the orchid on to her frock".

Linda stood very quietly as her mammy pinned on the flower. Margie, Douglas and Linda's brother stood at the front door as Tim and her left for the dance. They watched them nervously walk up the road.

Margie said to Douglas, 'What a polite, well mannered lad'.

They got to the school hall, where the girls got together excitedly to compare their outfits. Mr. Ross had a portable record player in the corner and the music struck up.

'OK, take your partners everyone for The Gay Gordons', he called out.

The children dutifully danced all the steps that they had been taught and after an hour, they stopped for refreshments consisting of sandwiches, fairy cakes and bottles of pop with straws.

Margaret Brown boldly went up to Mr. Ross and said, 'Please sir, we've done all the dances you've taught us, now can we change the music to something a bit more modern?'

'Like what?' said Mr. Ross.

'Well, I've brought my Cliff Richard 45s that I got for my birthday with me', Margaret answered.

'Cliff who?' inquired Mr. Ross.

'He's the latest singer and he's fab', said the determined schoolgirl.

'Oh, go on then. It is a party after all', smiled Mr. Ross.

The girls all squealed with delight as the sounds of Cliff Richard echoed throughout the hall. The boys came over and danced with the girls. So much for all the dance rehearsals and Jimmy Shand music! The teachers seemed to enjoy it too and joined in with the children as Cliff Richard took over the party, belting out his big hits. Tim and Linda shared the last waltz at the end of the evening. Then he politely fetched her coat and held it for her before seeing her safely home again just after ten o'clock. Linda never saw Tim again except from a distance, because he went on to his new secondary school. His twin sister Tina told Linda that he really wanted to meet up with her again but didn't have the courage to come to her door and ask her.

What's For Ye, Won't Go By Ye

It was a summery Saturday morning in June. Betty, Duncan, Mary, David and their children were coming to visit in the evening. Linda went into town with her parents. They were buying food and drink for their visitors that evening. Douglas junior gave Linda 6/8d and asked her to buy him Cliff Richard's new record, 'Travelling Light', while she was in town. She went from shop to shop with her parents, waiting for her chance to get her brother his record. Linda didn't like to let her brother down, and reminded them that they had to find a record shop before going home, but her daddy told her that they had to get back home before their visitors arrived so Douglas junior would have to get it another time. They were taking a short cut through Woolworth's in Sauchiehall Street to the bus terminus when they could hear 'Travelling Light' being played. It was Woolworth's own version by a singer called Dick Jordan.

'Just get him that one', said Douglas, 'It's only 4/-, you'll save him 2/8d'.

Linda didn't think she was doing the right thing, but did what her daddy told her. They got home and she handed the record to her brother.

'This isn't Cliff Richard', said Douglas junior disappointedly.

'I know', replied Linda. 'Daddy says that you'd be better off with that one because it was cheaper!'

As the evening got underway and the men swallowed back the beer and the women sipped their sherry, the atmosphere became very merry. Linda was outside in the garden with her cousins. Douglas junior was sitting with the adults, sipping over his half pint of very weak shandy.

His dad told him, 'Now you're almost sixteen. It's time that you got a taste for the stuff!'

Little did his dad know that his son got the taste a long time ago during the family parties when he used to hide in the corner, finishing off the dregs in the beer bottles. He had also had his first puff of a cigarette when he was twelve. His grandpa had given him a big tent and Douglas set it up in the garden with the opening away from the house. He and his seven pals sat in there sharing a packet of five Woodbines between them. Linda, who was seven at the time, untied the flap and gasped as the she was met with a big cloud of smoke.

She said, 'I'm tellin' mammy you're smokin!"

Barry Wood called her back and said, 'Do you want to see a trick Linda?'

She said, 'OK then'.

Barry said, "When I inhale this cigarette, watch my ears. Then press my stomach and you'll see the smoke coming out of my ears'.

Linda did as she was told and as she watched his ears, he burnt her hand with his cigarette. She ran out of the tent crying as all the big boys laughed. Douglas junior was concerned and ran after her.

'Are you OK Linda?' he asked.

She sobbed as she showed him the burn on the back of her hand. Douglas got angry.

He ran back to the tent and said to Barry, 'That wis a damn stupid thing to do to my wee sister. You've really hurt her hand. I hope yer proud of yersef!' He ordered everyone out of the tent as he said, 'Right, Barry. You're no comin' in here again if yer gonna do daft things lik' that. Linda, show him yer hand'.

Barry sheepishly looked at the burn on her hand and apologized to Linda. The other lads felt awful because they had laughed and hadn't realised how painful it was. Linda never told her mum because she didn't want to get her brother into trouble. After that, whenever Douglas junior or his pals were in the tent for a puff, Linda never went near them.

The family party was going well and, after the usual family sing-song led by Douglas, he switched on the record player and played his Eddie Fisher records and other favourite songs of the 1940 and 50's. As usual, he was the life and soul of the party. He told everyone to stand up while he drunkenly pushed back the couch and chairs.

He got Margie up on the floor to dance and then pulled Mary, David, Betty and Duncan up, telling them, 'C'mon, it's a party. Let's see ye dancin!"

The men all had a good skin full. David always concealed it well and alcohol never seemed to change his moods or personality. Duncan was normally a very shy person, but when he drank alcohol, he used to get silly and annoying, wanting to give everyone bear hugs. All the children hated being near Duncan when he was drunk. He didn't mean any harm but, not having any children of his own, he didn't realise that they didn't liked being grabbed and held restricted. He scared his nieces and nephews and sometimes reduced them to tears, so they always went to play in another room and kept out of his way. Poor Duncan could never see where he was going wrong. He felt hurt when the children avoided him and embarrassed if they got upset when he crept up behind them to playfully grab them. He didn't realize his own strength and that he was actually hurting and frightening them. He used to do the same with the women. He always wanted to put his arms round them, not realizing that some women don't like to be pawed like this. Whenever they were in company and Duncan had a drink in him, the women used to cringe and say, 'Oh no, here comes pawey!' It was all very innocent. Duncan wasn't a good communicator, he found it difficult to hold a conversation, and it was just his way of being friendly.

Everyone had a great night. Just after midnight, Betty, Duncan, Mary and the children climbed into David's car. David might have downed a few beers, but he didn't appear any different from the beginning of the evening. He drove them all the ten miles home, dropping Betty and Duncan off at their house on the way. Luckily, no buses or trams ran after midnight and not many people had cars, so the roads were empty.

Margie started to clear away all the dirty plates and glasses, as she hated to get up in the morning to the mess left by a party from the night before.

Douglas swung the kitchen door open and, with an evil stare, he slurred, 'I saw you trying to get off with Duncan!'

She tried to ignore him, but he swung her round, knocking a glass out of her hand as he did so.

'Do you hear what I'm saying, you're a loose woman'.

Margie went to pick up the broken pieces of glass.

Douglas kicked the glass out of the way and demanded, 'Look at me when I'm talking to you!'

Margie shook with fear for she knew she couldn't reason with him in this state. All she wanted was for her husband to go to bed and sleep, and then wake up his caring self again in the morning.

Margie hated when her sister's husband Duncan came near her. She used to feel herself coming out in a cold sweat. She hoped that he wouldn't put his arms round her because she couldn't stand it, for she knew it would provoke her husband's jealousy. At the same time, she didn't want to be rude to him. She could not talk to her sister Betty about it, as she didn't want to offend her or fall out with her. Margie tried to explain to Douglas that she didn't encourage Duncan in any way and that she didn't like him touching her. Douglas carried on shouting and blaming her for egging Duncan on. Poor Margie was in tears. The happy evening had ended in the usual way, with Douglas drunk and shouting, accusing and arguing.

She plucked up her courage and nervously said to him, 'Douglas, why don't you go to your bed and have a good sleep, you'll understand better in the morning'.

At that, he went into a rage. He grabbed her arms and shouted, 'No one tells me what to do in my own house!'

Douglas junior and Linda got out of their beds and ran downstairs to the kitchen.

Linda screamed, 'Let my mammy go!' as she pulled at her dad's hands.

Douglas junior shouted at him, 'Leave her alone, you know what Uncle Duncan is like when he's drunk. He paws all the women and no-one likes him. If you want to sort it out, then speak to Uncle Duncan, not mum. He's the one causing the problem'.

'Mammy hasn't done anything wrong', sobbed a tearful Linda. 'She hates Uncle Duncan's cuddling her, we all do. He frightens and hurts us. You should tell him not to do it, Daddy!'

Realising he was outnumbered, Douglas looked at his family with a horrible scowl on his face. He dropped his grasp on Margie and stormed out of the kitchen, going upstairs to bed.

'Are you OK, mammy?' asked Linda.

'Aye pet, I'm fine. I don't know what gets into your daddy sometimes!' answered Margie, trying to put on a brave face for her children.

'I won't let him hurt you mum', said Douglas junior, hiding his own anguish at the secret beatings from his drunken father.

Spring 1960 and Mother's Day was approaching. Linda and her cousin Anne had been saving up their pocket money to buy their mums each a nice gift. They had 10/- and were really looking forward to it, because they were being allowed to get the bus into town on their own to look round the shops. They went to Woolworth's and Boots in New City Road. In Boots they spotted nice blue see-through plastic toilet bags with talcum, soap and hand cream, they were 7/-. In Woolworth's, Linda saw a little trophy cup with 'World's Best Mum' on it for 1/9d. They bought the toilet bag and the trophy cup for each of their mums and felt quite pleased with themselves.

'We've got 1/- each left', said Linda. 'We can get a 3d bag of chips with thru'pence for the bus fare home. That means we still have sixpence to spend'.

As they approached the fish and chip shop, Anne said, 'I don't have any money left, Linda'.

Linda said, 'How come? We both had 10/- and we both spent the same'.

'I don't know', said Anne.

'Oh, never mind', said Linda trustingly, 'I'll get your chips and pay your fare home'.

Anne allowed Linda to spend her last 1/-, leaving her with nothing. The bus approached Anne's house.

'I'll get off here', Anne said, as she quickly stood up and hopped off the bus.

Linda looked at the seat next to her, and there lay Anne's purse! Linda held it up and tried to shout after her, but the bus had left the stop and Anne was oblivious to Linda calling her name. As she held the purse she heard something move about in it. She opened it up and stared in disbelief at the shiny 1/- inside. She couldn't believe that Anne had lied, making Linda spend her last so that she could still have a shilling left. Linda was upset by Anne's deceit.

She went home and told Margie and said, 'I think I will keep the shilling! She can't say anything, because she told me she had no money left!'

'You'll do no such thing. Two wrongs don't make a right', said Margie. 'You take the purse and give it back to her now, with the shilling inside. She will know that you have found her out and it will be her that will feel embarrassed for being so mean to you'.

Linda did exactly what her mammy told her to do and, as she handed the purse over to Anne, Linda gave Anne a look that clearly told Anne that Linda knew she had tricked her. Anne looked uncomfortable at being found out but, in her usual sleekit way, said nothing.

What's For Ye, Won't Go By Ye

It was exam time at school. These were the big exams that decided what school you were to go to. If you passed, you went to Possil Senior Secondary (known locally as High Possil), where lessons were more academic. You had the option to leave and go to work at the age of fifteen, or stay on for a five year course to take 'O' levels and 'Highers'. If you failed, you went to Colston Junior Secondary. Lessons there were more basic, domestics for girls and trades for boys. You only stayed at Colston for three years, although any pupil there was given the opportunity at the age of fifteen to go to the Senior Secondary School to take their 'O' levels exam if they wished.

The day of the results came. The children all sat quietly with their hands clasped, as the headmaster, Mr. Hutchinson, came into the classroom. He spoke for a minute in whispers with Mr. Kinnear, and then he turned to the class.

'Right, children, Mr. Hutchinson said. I'm here to tell you what school you will be going to in August'.

Linda took a deep breath. She desperately wanted to be told that she had passed and would be going to Senior Secondary, the same as her brother. She knew it would make her mammy so proud. She couldn't bear the thought of telling her parents that she hadn't passed and would be going to Junior Secondary. Mr. Hutchinson read out the names of everyone going to High Possil. Linda waited and waited, then to her sheer relief and delight, he called her name. The only sad thing was that her two pals, wee Sadie and Myra, were going to Colston. They congratulated Linda.

As Mr. Hutchinson went to leave the room he said, 'Can Linda MacGregor and Norah Banks stand up, please'.

Linda got worried that he had made a mistake.

He then said, 'Give your parents these letters. I want them to come and see me'.

Linda wondered what was wrong. She dreaded giving the letter to her parents in case she was going to get a telling-off for something she hadn't realised that she had done. She decided she would play safe and leave the letter until her mother came home, because if her father wasn't happy with the contents and her mother wasn't there, then his temper could flare up.

When they sat down to tea that evening, her stomach was churning over.

She tried to look composed as she said, 'Oh! I forgot. I have a letter to give you from school'.

She handed it to her mammy, but her daddy took hold of it before her mammy could grasp it. Linda eyes watched and examined his expressions as he read the letter.

'The headmaster wants us to go and see him tomorrow about Linda going to Secondary School', he said to Margie. 'What's all this about Linda?' he said sternly.

'I don't know, daddy. He did tell me today that I was going to High Possil'.

'Then why does he want to see us?' insisted Douglas.

'I don't know, daddy', Linda repeated.

Linda tossed and turned that night, worried and upset about what the headmaster was going to say to her mammy and daddy. Margie arranged the afternoon off work and met Douglas after he finished his shift. They went up to see Mr. Hutchinson. Douglas became quite uptight about the appointment. He knew how scary Mr. Hutchinson was, because he had been his teacher when he was a boy.

Linda came out of the school at home time. Her parents were at the school gate talking to Norah Banks' mammy and daddy.

'Oh well, here goes', thought Linda to herself.

She held her head down and looked up with her eyes only at her daddy, waiting to hear the worst.

'Congratulations Linda', her parents said together.

Linda looked puzzled. 'For what?' she enquired.

'Mr. Hutchinson thinks that you have done really well, especially in the last two years. He said that you have the intelligence to go to The Academy, so he wanted our permission to upgrade you to there instead of High Possil'.

Linda could see that her parents were so proud and delighted. 'Is there anyone else going from my class?'

'Yes, Norah Banks', said Margie. 'You'll have a wee pal there'.

Linda was happy that she had pleased her parents, but she dreaded going to the posh school in another area away from all her school friends.

May 1960 and it was Linda's class school qualifying trip. Her parents, aunts and uncles had all given her money to enjoy the day. All together she had 11/6d in her purse. She felt very well off. Auntie Dot came to see her off and pressed another 1/- into her hand. The big blue and cream bus pulled up and took the two classes of twelve year olds to the Trossachs. The children sang and the teachers joined in. Eventually they got to Callandar, where everyone got off the bus at the park. One of the teachers, Miss Beattie, organised a game of rounders. Linda loved that game. She was excellent at fielding and catching the ball. She got big cheers from her team as she ran and caught the ball time after time, knocking out the other team's star players. Linda's team won the game easily.

It was 1.30pm and they were all hungry and thirsty. The teachers went into the boot of the bus and brought out big boxes. They handed everyone a brown paper bag with a corned beef sandwich, a fairy cake, a biscuit and an apple inside, plus a bottle of fizzy ginger. The children sat on the grass down by the river and munched away as they giggled and chatted excitedly. Linda was really enjoying her day out. Soon they had finished eating.

What's For Ye, Won't Go By Ye

Miss Beattie clapped her hands twice and announced, 'Children, you have half an hour to look round the shops. Make sure that you go to the toilet before you come back on the coach. Be back here at half past two sharp!'

Linda went to the little gift shop on the High Street. There, she bought her mum and her Granny Nixon a lovely lace handkerchief each, her dad a yellow tartan handkerchief, and her brother a pen. She was very pleased with her purchases. This was her very first day trip without her family and she couldn't wait to see their faces when they opened their presents. She climbed wearily back onto the bus and flopped down on her seat.

As the bus pulled out of the park, the children all started singing and Linda joined in at the top of her voice. She loved singing and dreamt of being a famous singer one day. She always sang the minute she opened her eyes in the morning. She knew all the modern songs as well as her mammy and daddy's favourites. Her rendering of Connie Francis wasn't always welcome at half past seven on a Sunday morning. Her dad was trying to sleep off his Saturday night hangover and he banged through the wall, telling her to keep the noise down. Margie just giggled at her daughter's efforts. Linda had a powerful voice for her age. She never got any encouragement, so she lacked the confidence to sing solo in company. She just sang along with the others.

As the bus trundled along through the country roads and past Loch Katrine, Mr Kinnear informed the children that this was where their drinking water came from.

'It's the best in the world', he told them.

'Talking about drinking water', said Mrs. Beattie, 'we have some ginger left. Who all wants some?'

The children all raised their hands anxiously, it had been a long hot day and they were all thirsty.

'Don't worry, there's enough to go round. Just take the flavour that you are given. If you don't like it,then see if you can swap with someone', she said.

One by one the teachers made sure all the children had a little glass bottle of ginger.

Suddenly, someone shouted, 'Look in that field, it's Highland cattle!'

Wee Sadie whisked round and, as she did so, her bottle clashed with Linda's mouth. The pain was excruciating. Linda couldn't bear to have her top front tooth touch her tongue or her bottom lip. The bottle had chipped the bottom corner off of the tooth. Linda was in agony for the rest of the journey home.

When Margie saw her tooth she was upset. 'Oh Linda, you have always had such beautiful straight white teeth. I hope the nerve doesn't die, because it will discolour your tooth'.

Linda wasn't worried about that, she just wanted the pain to go away, which it did do within a few days. Luckily, her tooth kept it's lovely gleamy whiteness, she just had a cheeky little bit missing from the outside corner.

Avril Dalziel Saunders

The school broke up at the end of June. Linda was heartbroken because she loved her primary school. She didn't want to leave all her friends and go to her new snobby secondary school. Her cousin Anne didn't pass for senior secondary the previous year,so she was already at Colston. Auntie Dot was a wee bit envious that Linda had done so much better than Anne,but she did congratulate her.

During the holidays, Linda met up with her Catholic friends. She only got to see them in the summer time because they went to different schools. A new boy came along whose name was Patrick O'Grady. He was a year older at thirteen and Linda really liked him. She felt herself attracted to him. He seemed to like her too. Linda blushed when the others in their little gang teased them about fancying each other. There were nine of them, four girls and five boys. They took bottles of water and went for long walks in the sunshine out to the country and up to Springburn Park.

Uncle Donald's wee daughter always tagged along. Somehow Linda felt responsible for her because her Aunt Janet was in another planet. They sat in the park laughing, chatting, and forgetting about time when Linda suddenly looked at her watch and realised that it was five past four. She had to be back for half past four on her dad's instructions. She jumped up, the others asked her what was the matter. When she told them, they all made a move and hurriedly walked home. They knew how strict Linda's dad was and didn't want to see her get into any trouble. One by one, the friends left the gang at different corners, until there was just Linda, her wee cousin and Patrick left. Linda was running out of time and decided to take a short cut through the fields.

As they passed the back of Patrick's house, he said, "Well, this is where I leave you'.

Linda shyly said, 'Bye, bye'.

He then said, 'Is that it then?'

Linda looked puzzlingly at him. He came towards her, put both arms around her then put his lips on hers. Linda went to pull away but he pulled her back and held her close, pressing his warm lips onto her tightly shut lips. Her wee cousin stood at the side with a big admiring smile on her face, her eyes quickly swishing from Patrick to Linda. She was wishing that she was older and Patrick would kiss her like that.

Linda slowly pulled away from Patrick and said, 'I have to go now'.

He said, 'See you tomorrow, same time, same place?'

Linda shouted back, 'Aye, see you then', as she glided away, floating on air, ecstatic with the experience of her first kiss.

'Whit wiz it like, Linda?' asked her wee cousin.

'Oh, I cannae explain, it wis like nothing I huv ever felt before,but it was really, really nice!'

She went indoors, where her dad was waiting and immediately she was back to reality when he asked her why she was eight minutes late.

'Oh, sorry daddy, my watch stopped', she said, lying through her teeth and thinking to herself, if only he knew.Of course, Linda would not have been allowed out at all if Douglas suspected her of kissing a boy, never mind a Catholic boy!

In July 1960, Linda went on holiday with Auntie Dot, Uncle Tom, Anne, Grandpa MacGregor, Andrew and Aunt Ina. As usual, they were in Rothesay for a month. Her mammy, daddy and Granny Nixon were coming down to their but 'n' ben at the Glasgow Fair Fortnight in the middle of July for two weeks. Linda stayed two weeks with her Auntie Dot and then two weeks with her mammy and daddy.

Anne and Linda were walking along the seafront one bright and sunny morning.

'Dae ye fancy we take a wee rowin' boat out?' said Anne.

Linda hesitated, she knew that their parents would never allow them to go out in a boat on the bay on their own. 'Oh, a don't know Anne, we'd get intae awful trouble if our mammys and daddys found out'.

'C'mon, they'll never find out', Anne said, persuading her.

Linda stopped and thought for a minute, then said, 'Oh all right then. Ah suppose it won't do any harm not tae tell them'.

They went up to the man at the jetty, paid him 3d each, and hopped into their rowing boat, sitting side by side and taking one oar each. The man gave them a push out into the bay and then they attempted to row on their own.

'Oh, you're no' daeing it right', said the bossy Anne. 'We're going roon' in circles. Let's count and dig into the water together'.

The two girls counted, one, two, one, two, and soon they were out into the bay.

'This is great fun', said Anne. 'Look. There's a big paddle steamer sitting at the pier, which one is it?'

'It's the 'Jeannie Deans'', said Linda.

'C'mon, we'll go over and get a better look', said Anne.

The two girls rowed over towards the pier, ignoring signs saying that rowing boats were not allowed beyond this point. They pulled up near to the big paddles and were fascinated by them. Suddenly, the ship gave a big 'HOOT! HOOT!' and the paddles started to move. They started to row their wee boat to get away, but found themselves being sucked back towards the paddles, which dwarfed their rowing boat. They frantically started screaming and rowing for their life, their adrenalin was flowing. By a strange miracle, they were able to break away and get clear seconds before the big ship pulled out. Their hearts were pounding as they rowed back towards the jetty and voluntarily returned their boat with ten minutes' hire left to go.

'Are ye sure ye want to come in lassies? Ye've still got time left', said the man in charge.

'Positive', they echoed together.

'We've had enough', said Anne.

'Aye, our arms are tired', said Linda.

They breathed a sigh of relief as they walked away.

'That was a lucky escape, never ask me to go out in a boat with you again', Linda told Anne.

Next thing, they saw their mammys walking towards them.

'Hello girls, what have you been up to? Are you enjoying yourselves', enquired Margie.

'Oh, nothing much', said Anne.

'We've just been taking a look at the big ships', Linda said, trying to convince herself that she wasn't telling any lies.

'How would you girls like to go to the 'Go As You Please' in the Winter Gardens? It starts in half and hour. We're meeting everyone else there', said Margie.

'Great', said the girls, 'That'll be good fun'.

Linda loved talent contests and although she was aching to get up there and sing her heart out, she could never pluck up the courage to get on the stage. The family never recognised that she had a talent, so they never gave her any encouragement. It was the usual thing, the dads and grandpas getting up to do their best rendition of Frank Sinatra or Dean Martin and embarrassing their kids. Or the mums and grannies getting up and performing there best opera or Doris Day piece. Then, a young girl with her best pink party frock on and long, mousy brown hair in ringlets, tied with a big matching bow on the top of her head, got up and started to sing Connie Francis' latest song, 'My Happiness'. Her parents had obviously prepared her for the big event and were egging her on and behind her every step of the way. The whole hall erupted, clapping, cheering and going mad with appreciation. Linda watched her mum and dad shouting their enthusiasm. The girl was the same age as Linda. She was good, but Linda knew she could have done the song better, stronger and with more feeling. Linda felt very envious and thought to herself, *If only my mum and dad could recognise that singing is what I really want to do, and encourage me like that girl's parents.* She knew that their confidence in her was all she needed, but Margie and Douglas never took their daughter's singing seriously.

What's For Ye, Won't Go By Ye

The big day came when Linda was to start The Academy. She donned the new uniform that her mammy had bought her. Maroon blazer, white blouse, school tie, grey skirt and new black leather slip on shoes. She felt really smart. It was also Douglas junior's first day at the Academy. He was transferred there to sit his Highers exam, as High Possil didn't have the facilities for the advanced exams. He was allowed to wear the same uniform of charcoal trousers, black blazer and white shirt. He just needed a new school tie. Norah and her older brother had arranged to call for them at eight o'clock. Linda was speechless when she answered the door to find Norah in a navy blue skirt and blazer.

'Why are you wearing these colours?' Norah asked Linda.

'My mammy said that was the school uniform. My big cousin wore these colours when she went to The Academy'.

'No, it changed a year ago. It's now a black or navy blue blazer and skirt', Norah told Linda.

Linda was concerned that she was wearing the wrong colours for her first day at her new school. She stuck out like a sore thumb in the playground, but fortunately, she wasn't the type that let it get to her.

They were introduced to their form teacher, Miss Millington, a neurotic French teacher in her late forties. She told them the rules of the school and drew out their timetables on the blackboard, explaining to them that they had to find their classes between each lesson as quickly and quietly as possible. They were only allowed to use the staircase by the girl's playground at the west end of the school. The boys had their own staircase by their playground at the east end of the school. They were forbidden to talk to the boys when passing them in the corridors. They were not to be late for school. Prefects were on all the gates and, if they arrived at the gates after nine, their names were taken and they were sent to Miss Blake. She was the gym mistress and ruled the girls with a rod of steel. She enjoyed every minute of bringing her heavy, four-fingered leather belt heavily down on the wee girls' hands and wrists, ignoring their pleas that their tram, car or bus was late.

Lunchtime came and they queued up at the opposite side from the boys outside what looked like an old Army hut, at the end of the school grounds. The smell of school dinners filled the air. When they were allowed in, they sat at long benches of eight, boys at one side of the hall and girls at the other. The four pupils at the end of each bench were ordered to collect two meals each, one for themselves and another for those left at the table. They were in and out of there within twenty-five minutes. The food was good and everyone seemed to enjoy it.

There was time to spare, so Linda and Norah, along with some new school friends, went outside for a walk to have a look at the area around their school. They found a wee shop that sold everything: crisps, gingerbread, Albert cake, sweets and soft drinks. One of the girls bought a slice of Albert cake for 2d,

116

which was sponge cake with white icing. She was so enthusiastic about how delicious it was, that Linda and Norah decided that tomorrow they would bring 2d each and try it for themselves.

Back in the playground, the bell went for the girls to line up for class. Out came Miss Blake, the gym mistress. She walked up and down the lines, inspecting the girls like a sergeant major, stopping every so often to straighten a tie, order someone to pull up their socks, get their shoes polished or tidy their hair. She was in her late fifties and very masculine in appearance. She wore a tweed jacket, calf length pleated skirt, lace-up brown shoes and a short grey haircut. She clasped her hands behind her back and took large strides.

She stopped right in front of Linda and bawled out, 'Why are you wearing these colours, girl?'

Linda stuttered to try to explain.

'Stop stammering girl'. 'These are not the school colours', Miss Blake bellowed.

She stared Linda in her eyes.

'Get over to my room, NOW, and wait for me!' she ordered.

Linda picked up her briefcase and embarrassedly walked across to Miss Blake's room. She sat on one of the benches in the changing room outside the gym.

After ten minutes, Miss Blake came across and shouted, 'What's your name, girl?'

'Linda MacGregor, Miss', Linda replied.

'I'll ask again, why are you wearing these ridiculous colours?'

'This is the uniform my mammy bought me', Linda said, terrified.

'Why did she buy these colours? Did she not find out the proper uniform before she spent her money?'

'These were the colours my cousin wore when she came to The Adademy', Linda replied in a low voice.

'Who is your cousin?', Miss Blake asked Linda.

'Jessie Murdoch. She left the school two years ago Miss', said Linda.

Miss Blake knew Jessie well. She was a star pupil, but that didn't stop her from whacking Linda with her mean leather belt. She told Linda that the school colours had changed since then, so she had better tell her mother to get her the proper ones as soon as possible.

She finished up by saying, 'Every day you wear a grey skirt to school, my girl, you will get the belt'.

Linda walked out with a very sore wrist and hand on her very first day at Secondary School. She wasn't sure that she was going to like it at The Adademy, and wished that she had gone with all her friends to Possil Secondary instead.

That evening, she told her mammy that she had the wrong school colours, but didn't have the heart to tell her that she had to get her a new one as soon as possible. She also didn't mention that Miss Blake belted her and was going to belt her for every day she wore a grey skirt. She knew that her mammy had struggled to get the price of the uniform in the first place. Linda wore one of Douglas junior's old school blazers and suffered a very painful hand and wrist at the mercy of Miss Blake every day for two further weeks until her mammy finally had the money to buy her a new navy blue skirt.

Norah and her brother had decided after the first week to take a different route to school, as they lived at the opposite end of the housing scheme. They could catch a bus from near their house that took a much longer route, but involved less walking. Douglas junior had gone into school early, as he had prefect duties. Linda set off for school that Monday morning, relieved that this would be her first day at school that she wouldn't be getting the belt. She left at her normal time and crossed the fields. She ran past Colston School to taunts of 'academy snob'. She stood waiting for her bus and she waited and waited as the queue grew longer. Finally, a bus came and she just got on it by the skin of her teeth.

'Whit's happened tae the buses this morning, we're a' late fur work', one woman angrily asked the conductor.

'Oh, the driver of the bus before wis sick and there wisnae a replacement tae drive his bus', replied the conductor.

Linda's tummy was turning over with anxiety, panic stricken in case she would be late. She jumped off the bus at Springburn Woolworth's and ran up the avenue, which was really steep and no easy going. She approached the gates and Norah's brother was there on prefect duty. She breathed a sigh of relief, thinking that he would let her slip through and not take her name. She was to think again and was devastated when he asked her name.

'You know my name', she retorted in disbelief.

'I am on prefect duty and I have to do my job', he said with a sick, sly smile. He took her name and sent her to Miss Blake.

'Well, well, well!' said Miss Blake, 'seems that you can't get enough punishment, Linda MacGregor. At last you have a navy blue skirt! But now, you've come in late. At least you are wearing the right colour of skirt and that has saved you from getting two of the best'.

Linda started her third week at The Academy with the usual painful swollen wrist and hand. She told Norah what she thought of her two faced nasty brother.

Norah said, 'Don't worry, I don't like him either. He's such a big head!'

Linda and Norah made friends with girls in their year who were from Springburn. On Saturday afternoons, Linda and Norah went to their houses to meet them and then they all went to the Princes Picture House in Gourlay Street. Linda was fascinated when she saw how some of them lived in wee one or two room and kitchen apartments. Some still had outside toilets on the staircase to share with other families on the same landing, others were lucky enough to have an inside toilet. None of them had the luxury of a bathroom. It made Linda realize how lucky she was to have a proper house with living room, kitchenette, bedrooms, bathroom and large back and front gardens, even though it was a council house!

Linda and Norah found out from their Springburn friends that the school in Gourlay Street did elocution lessons one evening per week. Linda told her mum, and Margie said it would stand her in good stead for her future. Norah's mum agreed as well, so the two girls trotted off every Tuesdsay night for their lessons. Amongst other things, they were taught how to pronounce letters and vowels properly, mouth exercises, how to use their diaphragms, to breathe properly and also, how to speak each word clearly before starting the next one. The girls thoroughly enjoyed their evening class, especially the poems and expressions. Linda especially loved, 'The Owl and the Pussycat', it became her party piece.

Christmas 1960 and they went to Granny Nixon, Mary and David's house. Betty and Duncan were there too. The sisters got a bit tipsy and Mary whispered something to Betty and Margie. The next thing they had disappeared out of the living room door. Ten minutes later they appeared dressed in Mary's sons scouts' outfits.

Douglas looked at them in bewilderment and said, 'In the name…whit is this?'

They all looked a picture in khaki shirts, shorts, neck scarves and toggles.

Margie stood in front with a big wide brimmed scout hat and a pole and started to march up and down singing, 'For I'm a Scout, Scout, Scout and you'll always hear me shout'.

Everyone was in fits of laughter as she jokingly put on her serious face with her two sisters saluting in the background. That got the singing and merriment underway.

Margie said to Linda, 'Say your poem for everyone'. Margie stood back proudly as Linda recited 'The Owl and the Pussycat', pronouncing her vowels in a perfect elocution trained voice.

Mary, who was a bit of a snob and always regarded herself as a cut above the rest, said in her put-on Kelvinside accent, 'That was beautiful Linda, who teaches you?'

Everyone roared with laughter when Linda answered, 'Och! It's a wee fat wuman!'

So much for elocution!

What's For Ye, Won't Go By Ye

Late Spring 1961 and Douglas junior had his 'Highers' exams. These were very important to him and would help him on his way to University. If he failed, he would have to stay at school to re-sit them. His dad was already nagging him about getting out to earn a living and bring money into the household. His year was allowed two weeks off before the exams to swot up. Douglas junior sat in his bedroom and studied hard. The day before his first big exam, his dad came into his bedroom and dragged him out, telling him that it wasn't good for him to be cooped up there all day. He ordered him to get out and dig the garden, making out that this would help him to clear his head and think better. When Linda came home, she saw her brother out digging the garden, throwing the spade into the ground in temper and frustration. His eyes welled up as if he couldn't take any more.

'What are you doing, why are you not studying?' she asked him.

'He's made me stop my studies to do this', he said, his lips quivering with upset and anger.

Linda was speechless and wished that she could do something to help her brother, but she knew that she was powerless against her bully of a dad. It was as if he was willing his son to be a failure. Just before Margie was due in from work, Douglas called his son in and told him to get upstairs and carry on studying, making out that he really cared and telling him that his head would be nice and clear now. He knew fine well that his son wouldn't mention anything to his mother, but he didn't reckon on Linda. She was becoming more independent as she was growing up. She longed to be grown up just so that she wouldn't have to put up with her dad's beatings and bullying. Margie came in the back door looking tired after her hard day in the factory. Her husband took her in his arms and gave her a warm welcoming kiss. It wasn't very often that he made a fuss of her, so when he was in a good mood, she enjoyed every minute of seeing the nice side of him.

'Is Douglas junior ready for his exams tomorrow? Has he been working hard on his studies?', she enquired.

Before Douglas could answer, Linda piped in, 'No, he's been digging the garden all day'.

'What!' Margie exclaimed, 'what do you mean? He has a very important day tomorrow, is he off his head? Why hasn't he been studying?'

Linda looked at her dad innocently, then turned to her mum and said, 'Daddy said that it would do him good, to get away from studying and clear his head'.

Margie couldn't believe what she was hearing. One word led to another and there was an almighty row that finished up with the dinner being thrown in the bin. Linda worried if she had done the right thing telling her mammy, because all the shouting and fighting wasn't helping her brother studies at all. At the same time, she felt her mammy had to know what was going on when she wasn't there.

It wasn't very often that Margie stood up to her husband, for he had a way of winding her round his little finger and pinning all the blame on someone else. In this case, Linda got it. It wasn't long before her mammy was telling her that she shouldn't tell tales and that she had caused all this trouble. Her dad had convinced his wife that he was only concerned and it was in Douglas' best interests because he looked ill. Of course, Margie was so soft that she believed him.

Linda couldn't believe that she was being made out to be the bad one and being blamed for everything. Linda was young, but she could see that her dad was a control freak and that he loved the family to live along with his moods. When he was nice, life was wonderful and he could be a loving father when he tried, making them laugh with his funny stories. When he was in a bad mood, and especially when he had been drinking, life was just sheer hell for all concerned! Sometimes she wished that her mother would wake up and realize just how two-faced and nasty her daddy could be. If only her mammy was stronger and could face up to him, then they could all have a better life!

June 1961 and the school year had come to an end. Linda went to a dance in the Orange Halls in Springburn with her pals from the Academy. A boy called Tim, who was a 'Mod' and a friend of her brother's, came over to talk to her. Her friends looked on in envy as this 17 year-old boy chatted to Linda. She felt really flattered and became all coy and shy. Tim called round to her house often to see Douglas junior. He had a brand new Lambretta scooter and always wore a green 'Mod' parka. She had secretly fancied and hero-worshiped him, but never thought that she would ever have a chance to date him because he was four years older. He asked if he could see her home to make sure that she got back safely, adding that it was only right that he should look after his mate's sister, even although it was well out of his way. Linda felt like she was walking on air as they strolled home together. She was thirteen and very naive.

As they walked down the lane near to her house he suddenly stopped and said, 'I'll leave you here Linda. Your parents might disapprove of me seeing you home because I am so much older than you'.

Linda was puzzled and really didn't understand what he meant.

Then he said, 'Don't I get a kiss then?'

Linda felt very nervous as he bent down to kiss her. Then he frightened the life out of her by almost chewing her face off. This was nothing like the feeling of sheer heaven she had experienced when Patrick kissed her. In fact, it was quite the opposite, this was pure hell! Linda knew that her mum and dad would be home soon from Auntie Mary's and Uncle David's and she risked getting a belting from her dad for being home late. She broke away from him and made her excuses to leave.

'Can you meet me at seven o'clock next Friday night at the bus terminus in town?' he said as she left.

'Yes, OK', she shouted back, just to get away quickly.

She ran along the road home as fast as she could, feeling quite sick at the thought of his horrible kiss. He had shattered all her dreams of him being a wonderful romantic.

The next day she had a heart to heart talk with her mum and confided to her about Tim, mentioning how rough he had been. Margie told her that at thirteen she was too young for him anyway, and told her to send him a note telling him this and that she didn't want to keep the date. Margie's advice to Linda was always to make the men do the running.

She added, 'Never make yourself easy, as they will lose all respect for you. Boys talk amongst themselves and they can damage a girl's reputation very quickly'.

Linda valued her mum's advice and wrote a short letter to Tim, as she suggested. After the evening meal as she walked up that same lane to post the letter, she spotted a familiar figure walking down towards her. It was Patrick. He looked very happy to see her. They stopped and started to chat about what had been happening in their lives over the past year.

Patrick said, 'C'mon! I'll walk to the post box with you. I wasn't really going any where special'.

They posted the letter then went for a walk together. Linda felt elated and could sense that Patrick was enjoying her company too. Time just seemed to fly by and before they knew it, it was going on for 9pm. Linda knew that she had to get back home, as 9pm was her deadline on weekdays. It started to drizzle, so Patrick took his jacket off and put it over the top of their heads as they ran towards her house. On the corner as they turned and laughed at themselves, dripping wet, their eyes caught each other's gaze. The laughter stopped as Linda felt his warm lips on hers. The rain was running down their faces but they were oblivious in their passion.

Linda said, 'I really have to go now or else my dad will be out looking for me Reluctantly, she pulled away.

Patrick said, 'I'll see you tomorrow. I'll wait at the bars in the lane for you about 1 o'clock.

The lane was on a steep slope. The handrail up the middle was known to the local children as 'the bars'. It was a common meeting place and, from a young age, they practiced their gymnastics on them, twisting, turning and tumbling over. Linda couldn't wait to see Patrick again. She got up early. It was a wonderful summer's morning and she got round her chores in no time at all. She left her house at five minutes to one and hurried along to the lane. Just before she got there, she slowed down so as not to look over anxious. She remembered her mother's advice about always letting the boy do the running, and that he would never respect her if she chased after him.

She got to the top of the stairs and in the distance she could see about five of the summer gang waiting at the bars in the next lane over the road. As she approached them, she nodded shyly to Patrick. She felt her heart turn over as he smiled back, his white teeth gleaming and his blue eyes twinkling. There were two other boys, Jack and Andy, and a girl called Joanne, who lived in the next street to Linda.

Joanne said, 'Let's go for a walk over the fields to Bishobbriggs. I'll bring my transistor radio and we can listen to pop songs'.

As they walked along, Patrick waited for Linda. She felt relaxed in his company and felt shivers down her spine as he nervously put his arm around her. She complimented him by putting her arm around him. She felt him breathe a huge sigh, as if he was relieved that she didn't object. She had a wonderful day out with the gang. They walked for miles, laughed and told stories. They got back just before 6pm. Patrick took Linda in his arms and kissed her tenderly as the rest of the gang walked on in front. Linda had been dreaming about his kiss all day and went home dancing on air.

He shouted after her, 'I'll see you at seven tonight at the bars'.

She replied, 'OK then', before she ran indoors.

'Where've you been all day?' said her daddy.

'I've been out with all my friends. We went for a long walk in the country-side. You've always told me that it was good exercise to get out into the fresh air', replied Linda.

She daren't mention that she was out with Catholics, never mind having a Catholic boyfriend, it would have started World War III.

'Well, you'd better get the table set for dinner, your mammy will be home any minute. I have made mince and potatoes for dinner. I have to leave at nine o'clock to get away back to work for an overtime shift', her daddy said.

Linda ate her dinner at double speed.

'Linda, don't gobble your food like that, you'll get indigestion!' exclaimed Margie.

She waited anxiously for everyone to finish so that she could clear the table and get the dishes done.

She kept trying to remove items from the table, until finally her dad said, 'Hang on Linda. What's the big rush, we're still using that!'

At last, she was able to start clearing up. 'I'll wash and you dry', she said to her brother, knowing that she could get away quicker doing that.

'I'm away out now', Linda shouted as she made her way to the back door.

'Hold on, where are you going?' said her dad.

'I'm just meeting my pals along the road',

'Well, see and be back for nine o'clock, no later, I mean it!' he bellowed.

It was five past seven. Linda ran along the road, hoping that Patrick hadn't gone without her. She was relieved to see him standing there with the others, waiting for her.

'Sorry I'm late', she said, ' I had to wait until everyone had finished before I could do the clearing up and dishes'.

'Do you have to do the dishes?' asked Joanne.

'Yes', said Linda, looking puzzled at Joanne's question 'I have chores to do every day, don't you?'

'No', said Joanne. 'My mammy just tells me to get out of her way'.

Linda thought that was strange, she never minded doing her bit for her mammy and especially enjoyed doing the family shopping on a Saturday morning .Joanne's mother didn't go out to work, so she didn't really need a hand.

They all went for a walk. No one had any money to do anything else. They got back to the bars for nine o'clock. Linda knew that she should be going home, but remembered that her daddy was working and her mammy was always a bit more lenient. She was hoping that he had left to go to work and wouldn't know that she wasn't home by her deadline. She was enjoying Patrick's company so much that she didn't want to leave.

Just then, Joanne said, 'Isn't that you dad, coming up the lane Linda?' Linda's stomach turned somersaults as she saw him in the distance coming towards them. He would be furious if he knew that she had been out with a Catholic boy. She made out that she was on her way home and had stopped to talk to friends.

Her dad was having none of it and shouted, 'I told you to be home by nine'.

Next thing she knew, his heavy hand came slamming down across her jaw. She stumbled back with the force of it, feeling really hurt and humiliated in front of everyone.

'Get home now!' he demanded as he walked away to catch the bus to work.

Linda pulled herself together and ran down the road home. Patrick and the others were shocked by what they had just witnessed. Linda told her mammy. She could confide in her, although she knew that her mammy too was terrified of her daddy, so most times she just sided with him for the sake of peace.

Margie cuddled her and said, 'My father was exactly the same. I was sixteen when he died and up until then I wasn't even allowed to talk to a boy. If he had lived, he would never have allowed me to go out with your daddy when I was eighteen'.

Linda was embarrassed about meeting Patrick the next day, but he put here at ease.

He said, 'You didn't deserve that, you know. You don't have to put up with it. The next time he goes to hit you, you tell him that you will report him to the police for assault'.

Linda thought about it, but worried about what the consequences would be if she did, or what effect it would have on her mother. Would her mammy side with her dad in fear and make matters a lot worse for everyone? Linda was to find out sooner than she thought. She got home just before six o'clock and her daddy was waiting for her.

'Who was that scruffy lot that you were hanging about with last night?' he said.

'They're not a scruffy lot, they're my friends. They are all nice boys and girls', she plucked up her courage to reply.

'Well, you're not seeing them again, for you are not going out tonight, or any other night!' he shouted.

Linda felt the tears running down her face as she cried, 'I haven't done anything wrong, I don't have any other friends in this area because you sent me to a school that's miles away'.

'That's enough of your cheek', he said. 'The matter's closed'.

'Why don't you admit it', Linda shouted, 'it's just because they are boys and they are Catholics. You don't trust me'. Douglas went to bring his hand down heavy on her when Linda found herself blurting out, 'If you lay one finger on me, I will go to the police and have you arrested for assault'.

She couldn't believe that she had actually said those words to her father. He stared in disbelief, then pulled his hand back and walked away as if he knew she meant it. Her father was learning that Linda was no soft touch like her mother and would never put up with his verbal abuse and beatings. He confined her to her room that evening. The next day she went out to meet Patrick and told him what she had said.

'I wish I had threatened him with the police years ago, we might all have had a better life!' Linda said bitterly.

Gradually she was allowed out again in the evening. She just made sure that she was home by nine o'clock and never near, or in, the same vicinity as her daddy when she was with Patrick and the rest of the gang.

August 1961 and Linda was starting her second year at The Academy. She never really liked the school. She tended to enjoy the social after-school life better, although she did shine at French, arithmetic, geography and loved netball.

125

What's For Ye, Won't Go By Ye

The headmaster and teachers were very strict about areas of the school that pupils weren't allowed in, especially the separate staircases for boys and girls. The children used to wonder how, when they had seen the headmaster walk across the playground, he could suddenly appear on the third floor of the school. Then they found out that he had a small, secret staircase behind a door in the main lobby of the school, near to his office. Of course, the temptation was too much to resist for Linda. When they were walking in line to their next lesson, instead of going to the girls' stairs all the way at the end of the corridor, Linda shot in through the secret door and ran up the headmaster's stairs. Then she discovered there was another staircase that went right down into the girls' changing room at the gym. This came in handy when they were in lessons on the top floor and had to get to the girls' gym for the next period. She would be in serious trouble if the headmaster or Miss Blake ever caught her using the forbidden staircases.

One day in the playground, Linda said to her friends, 'I wonder what is behind that door in the corner by the girls' toilets?'

They went over and Linda, being the daredevil that she was, slowly and gingerly opened the door. There was a staircase going down. Linda, Norah and three other girls followed. They went down twelve stairs into pitch darkness. As their eyes became accustomed, they could make out a wall and an opening with no door.

One of the girls said, 'Come on Linda, let's go back, it's really scary and the bell will be going soon'.

They all made their way upstairs and crept out of the door into the playground.

Linda said, 'Right girls. Tomorrow, we'll bring torches and we'll find out just what is down there!' The others nodded in agreement.

The next day at playtime, the five girls all made their way with their torches to the door in the corner. Linda opened the door, then ushered them all in before closing the door behind them. They switched their torches on and crept down the stairs. They were in a large room, about the size of the classroom upstairs. They stepped through a doorway into another room, then the same again until they worked out that they had walked halfway round under the school in the foundations. They shone their torches and all they could see were brick walls. Linda felt a movement down at her foot. She shone her torch down and there, at her feet, sat a rat. The girls all screamed and ran. It seemed to take ages to get back. They had walked further than they thought. Every time they thought that the next doorway would lead to the staircase out, they were met by another brick wall. Eventually they got to the playground. The word had got round what Linda and her friends had been up to, and everyone gathered round to ask questions about what was down there. Of course, the story got exaggerated. One small rat became hundreds of massive rodents the size of cats! After that, no one would dare to go down there. They preferred to remember it the way it was, but at least they could boast that they had seen the school foundations.

Linda started to go to homework scheme classes. Norah and she stayed at school for an extra hour until 5pm. Linda found it particularly helpful. This was one way of making sure that her homework got done. There was also the benefit of a teacher there to ask, should she need any help. The biggest asset was that on Fridays, she didn't have to go home to face her drunken dad, and usually got back home at the same time as her mammy.

Christmas 1961 was approaching and the schools broke up for the holidays.

Margie said, 'There's a big grocery shop called Grandfare opened in Argyle Street in the town. It is a self service American idea, and it's massive. Can you meet me there on Friday night after I finish work and help me carry the messages home? I'll wait at the bus terminus in town for you'.

Linda was more than happy to get out of the house on a Friday afternoon.

Friday came, and, as usual, her daddy was the worse for drink. She asked him for her bus fare to go in and meet her mammy.

He slurred and said, 'What do you want money for? You've to meet your mammy at the shops up the road!'

Linda said, 'No, daddy. We're going to that new American shop in town'.

'Don't be stupid. Your mammy would never carry all her messages from there', he insisted in his drunken stupor.

'Get up to the bus stop and wait for her coming off the bus'.

It was a freezing cold winter's night and the snow was thick on the ground. Linda felt awful because she was certain that her daddy was wrong, but what could she do? He wouldn't give her the money for her bus fare and she had no way of contacting her mammy. She stood waiting in the snow. An hour had passed and she knew by this time that her daddy had got it completely wrong. She ran home to tell him that she was worried because her mammy hadn't appeared and she knew that she would be standing waiting for her, freezing, at the bus terminus in town. She was going to be firm with him and ask him for the bus fare. When she got home, he wasn't anywhere to be seen. She went upstairs and she could hear him snoring. As she slowly opened the bedroom door, the reek of booze hit her. She screwed up her face in disgust at the smell and left the room, knowing that there would be no chance of getting any money from him now. She went back up to the bus stop to wait, and hoped that her mammy would realise that there had been a mix up and get the bus home before the local shops closed. Another hour and a half later, the shops were closed and Linda stood there, blue with the cold. A steady stream of buses came and went and, at last, one pulled in and she could see her mammy waiting to get off.

'Where have you been?, Margie demanded, not knowing whether to be angry or worried.

After Linda told her what had happened and that her dad wouldn't give her the fare, Margie calmed down and said, 'Well, he shouldn't have interfered. Don't listen to him. I'll make sure that you have the fare in future!'

They both went home and had a big cup of cocoa to warm themselves up before making tea. They left him slumbering. The next day Margie told him that he had got it all wrong and because he stuck his nose into something he knew nothing about, Linda and she were both standing freezing for over two hours in different places. He was sober, so he was in a different frame of mind, and actually looked apologetic, although he never said sorry, that was not Douglas' style!

In between Christmas and New Year's, Linda was feeling very down. Margie asked her what was wrong.

'I don't know mammy. I can't help it. I have a feeling something sad is going to happen!' Linda cried.

Margie laughed and said, 'Oh don't be daft! What can happen?'

On 4th January1962, David, Mary, Betty and Duncan pulled up at the door in David's posh company car.

'Oh, we've got visitors', said Margie, 'Go and open the door Linda'.

Mary and David entered with very serious expressions.

'What's up with you two?' Margie joked, 'you both look miserable!'

'You had better sit down Margie', said David.

'Why, what's up?' said a puzzled Margie.

'It's your mother', David replied.

Margie started to panic. 'What's happened to her?'

Mary's eyes filled up as she told Margie that their mother had died in her sleep. Mary had taken a cup of tea into her in the morning and found her lying there.

'She was very peaceful and at least she didn't suffer any pain', said Mary.

Margie was devastated. She couldn't take it in that she was never going to see or speak to her mother again.

Two days later on Saturday, Linda was told to take her cousin out for the day to the afternoon matinee at the local picture house while the adults attended Peggy's funeral. She was buried in the same plot as her husband. Afterwards, the mourners went to the local tearoom for lunch and refreshments. They cried and laughed with fondness as they remembered the wonderful lady. Margie recalled the time when Peggy had to have her eye taken out because of glaucoma and was getting used to wearing a glass eye. She went into Woolworth's and was standing looking over the jewellery counter. Suddenly, there was an awful crash. The assistant ran up to see what was wrong and Peggy said very casually, 'Oh, it's just my eye. It's fallen out and hit off the glass counter. Can you pass it back to me please?' The young assistant ran away screaming. Peggy always had a good chuckle when she told that story. She was such a kind, forgiving and peace-loving woman who would help anyone. The family could not begin to conceive how life could go on without her.

CHAPTER SIX

Douglas junior was eighteen. He had passed his 'Highers' with distinction and was working as a junior chemist in the laboratory of the local brewery. He was still studying hard at evening classes to get the qualifications to go to University to study chemistry. His father made sure that he handed every penny of his wages over to his mother, leaving Douglas junior with nothing in his pocket. This, his father told him, would help pay back a portion of what he had spent on him over the years. His mum bought him what he needed in the way of clothes and bus fares, and gave him pocket money every week. It was never in Douglas junior's nature to argue. In order to get a bit more pocket money, he kept on doing his milk run, which meant that he was up at 4.30am every morning. Then he went to work all day and evening classes at night. His dad never at any time seemed to think that he was pushing the lad too far, nor did he ever encourage him. Instead, he felt hard done by in life, with being taken out of school at fourteen to help support his brothers and sisters and then being forced to join the Army and fight for his country. He just couldn't help himself being jealous of his son's academic achievements.

One spring day in 1962, Douglas junior came home and told his parents that the lady who bred dogs in the big house in Bishopbriggs had offered him a puppy.

Immediately his dad said, 'No dogs in this house!'

Douglas junior and Linda were disappointed. They pleaded with him.

Margie saw how her children would love a pet and said, 'Let me have a word with your dad'.

She picked the right moment and told him, 'Well, it's company for Linda, we're all out working now and she is on her own'.

After a bit more persuasion, he finally gave in and was adamant that it had to be a dog not a bitch, that Douglas junior and Linda had to walk it, feed it and generally look after it, not Margie or himself. Linda was ecstatic. She couldn't wait to see their new puppy.

Douglas junior brought the timid six-month-old puppy home the next morning. It was a cross between a bull terrier and a fox terrier. It had a white coat with faded black spots like a bull terrier and the cute little face of a fox terrier. The only problem was, it was a bitch. Douglas junior knew his dad had said it had to be a dog, but the lady had already promised all her dogs to buyers and as this one was free, he thought he would bring it home for approval. The poor puppy was terrified because it was used to being with other dogs. The lady breeder was trying to create a new breed of dog by crossing bull and fox terriers. Linda spent the day cuddling and reassuring the puppy until her dad came home from work. She didn't tell her dad that earlier it had peed over the linoleum in the corner. She made sure it was all cleaned up by that time. Douglas was a bit apprehensive about the whole thing.

He took one look and said, 'It will have to go back, it's a bitch. We don't want a bitch'.

Margie came home that evening and said, 'Oh, it's so cute. The poor wee thing is terrified!'

The dog had got used to Linda by this time and was following her around everywhere. All the family was hoping that Douglas would take to it and let them keep it. Later on in the evening, the dog came up to Douglas' feet and sat by his leg as if looking for reassurance. At this point, Douglas proved that he did have a heart after all.

When he looked at everyone, smiled and said, 'What are we going to call her then?', everyone breathed a sigh of relief.

'I know', said Linda, 'let's call her Chienne. It's French for dog!'

'That sounds different', said Margie.

They all agreed that was a good name and so it was unanimously decided that Chienne it was. They pronounced it 'Shen'

Linda went out the next day to buy Chienne a collar and leash. The dog hated them, as she had never worn them before and tumbled over, struggling to get free. Linda persevered and finally Chienne was walking smartly on her leash. Only problem was, she wouldn't go with anyone else other than the family. If any of Linda's pals took hold of the leash, Chienne stood still and refused to budge. Linda thought that the reason for this might that Chienne remembered being taken away from her breeder's home and was frightened that the same thing might happen again. Linda taught her to beg, give a paw, sit, lie down and count by barking. After a few months, they couldn't imagine life without her.

Her cousin Anne had been bought an expensive cairn terrier pedigree by the uncles. Linda had got used to them spoiling Anne and ignoring her, but she never complained about it. They looked down their nose at Linda's mongrel, but Linda wouldn't change her for the world. She was a loving happy puppy, whereas Anne's dog was a grumpy thing that would take your hand off if you went near it to pat it.

What's For Ye, Won't Go By Ye

Linda took Chienne up to Auntie Dot's one day. The grumpy cairn showed its teeth, growling and snarling as Chienne tried to play. The cairn was really fat and fussy. Auntie Dot only ever fed it roast lamb, so this was all it would eat. Chienne, on the other hand, ate anything. Then, the inevitable happened. Suddenly there was fierce fighting and barking coming from Auntie Dot's kitchen. Chienne had wandered in, liked the look of the roast lamb, and had tucked in and scoffed the lot. The cairn came in just in time to see the last morsel of her dinner disappear down Chienne's throat, so she went for her. Chienne wasn't having any of it as she wasn't a fighting dog. She ran away and jumped up onto Linda's lap, with ears back and tail wagging in fear.

'I think you had better take her home Linda', said Auntie Dot.

'Yes, OK, Auntie Dot. I think you're right'.

Auntie Dot hung onto the cairn's collar, holding her back as she growled and attempted to attack Chienne, who was secure in Linda's arms and wagging her tail, happily unaware that she had done anything wrong.

Every morning, Douglas junior took Chienne on his milk round with him. She soon got into the habit and was at the door at 4.45am, wagging her tail and waiting for Douglas junior. It was great exercise for both of them. She ran alongside him, off the leash, through the fields to the diary in Lambhill, and she loved it. One morning, when Douglas junior delivered the milk to the breeder he had got Chienne from, Chienne wandered into the garden. She darted off to see her brothers and sisters. There was about fourteen other Chienne look-a-likes. They all made a fuss of her and they played and ran around the garden together. Douglas junior wondered if it would be a problem to get her to come back with him now that she was back with the family that she had fretted so much for when he first got her. He shouted on her and started to walk away, but she carried on playing. He made his way to the gate and out into the street. Suddenly she dashed out after him, looking up and down the street as if in a panic that he had left without her. When she spotted him, she ran over, licking and making a fuss of him. Douglas junior knew then that she had finally accepted life with the MacGregors.

Douglas junior loved to run. He had joined the local harrier's club and, at weekends, he ran for miles cross-country. He became very fit. He was one of their top runners and entered competitions. Every weekend he was at different Highland games gatherings, running for his club. He also took part in the Ben Nevis race, which involved running up a mountain. He ran for the Scottish Cross Country team as well. Every week, his picture and a report about him taking part in that week's event appeared in the sports section of the Scottish newspapers. He was proving himself to be a fine sportsman and a top academic too. Although his dad boasted to all his family and friends about his son's achievements, he didn't show Douglas junior much encouragement. For everything

Douglas junior did, his dad had stories of himself being able to do it better. In a strange way, Douglas junior used his dad's criticisms of him to his advantage, pushing himself to do better to impress his dad, looking to his dad as his mentor.

It was Linda's fourteenth birthday and she had £1/5/- in birthday money from relatives. She was going to use some of it to buy Cliff Richard's new hit record 'The Young Ones'. One of her cousins already had the 45 and wasn't too keen on it. She asked Linda to swap it for 'It Doesn't Matter Anymore' by Buddy Holly. Linda agreed, even though it was her brother's record. He wasn't very happy with her when he found out, and Linda felt quite guilty. She knew how much he idolised Buddy Holly, for he was always singing his songs. A new young fourteen-year-old singer called Helen Shapiro arrived on the pop scene. She was appearing at The Glasgow Empire. Linda spent 7/6d of her money on a ticket for the show. Anne went along too. A very shy Helen Shapiro came on the stage to meet her audience. She was wearing a sleeveless lemon dress, fitted down to the hips, then gathered and full, with bouncy petticoats under. She had the short haircut that she had made famous and that all the young girls, including Linda, had copied. The boys in the audience were all wolf-whistling and Helen appeared to be embarrassed. She laughed and continued to sing, turning her back to everyone. Linda found her songs very easy to sing because she had a deep singing voice very similar to Linda's. Many a time Linda stood in her bedroom holding her hair brush for a mike and belted out Helen Shapiro's hits, 'Don't Treat Me Like A Child', and 'You Don't Know'.

Spring 1962 was coming to an end and everyone was looking forward to summer. Linda had just finished clearing up the dinner dishes and was in the street outside her house talking to her pals. In the distance, she could see two women walking along the street. She recognised one of them as her cousin Jessie. She felt a panic inside and her stomach churned.

She ran into the house and blurted out to her mammy and daddy, 'Jessie's coming along the street with another lady. Something has happened to Uncle Jack, he's dead!'

Her mother and father looked at her in shock. 'What do you mean? Just because Jessie is walking along our street, it doesn't mean that anything has happened to anyone', exclaimed Margie.

Douglas piped in, 'Uncle Jack is very healthy. If anything happens to anyone, it will be Auntie Joyce. She has a weak heart! Anyway, stop this silly talk now!'

At that, there was a knock on the door. Margie and Linda stood back as Douglas opened the front door. Jessie stood there with her godmother. Her face was ashen and her eyes red as she stepped in the door. She blurted out, 'My dad has died!' She then burst into tears.

Margie and Douglas stared in disbelief at her and then Linda. How could Linda have known this? Linda loved her Uncle Jack. She was distraught and sobbed uncontrollably.

'I knew it was Uncle Jack', she said, over and over again.

'What happened?' said Douglas in complete shock. 'He was only forty two, for God's sake'.

'He died in his sleep of natural causes. His heart gave in', replied Jessie's godmother quietly.

'Joyce will need help', said Douglas, 'She's on her own now!'

He instructed Linda to go to Auntie Dot's house and tell her to come round immediately, but not to mention what has happened, as they would break the sad news to her. Linda ran up the road as fast as she could, running past all her friends and crying her heart out. They all looked at each other puzzled, wondering what was the matter with her. She banged on Auntie Dot's door over and over again, shouting her name, but there was no reply. In a way, Linda was glad that there was no one in, as she didn't know how she was going to say to Auntie Dot without letting her know that something awful had happened, because she couldn't stop sobbing. She ran all the way home again and told them that Auntie Dot wasn't at home.

'She'll probably be at the bowling green', said Douglas. 'Jessie, you get back to look after your mother. We'll walk round and get Auntie Dot and Uncle Tom and we'll be there as soon as we can'.

The day of the funeral approached. Linda wanted to go and say goodbye to her beloved Uncle Jack, but she wasn't allowed to because it just wasn't the place for a young girl to be. In any case, she had school to go to. Linda cried herself to sleep for weeks thinking of her Uncle Jack and remembering with fondness how he used to call her his brown-eyed beauty. Margie came into Linda's bedroom one evening and, on seeing her upset, cuddled her to reassure her.

'Unfortunately', she said to Linda, 'it was time for Uncle Jack to go. He won't be far away. How did you know, Linda?' said Margie inquisitively.

'Know what?', replied Linda.

'When you told us Uncle Jack had died before Jessie had even got to the door', Margie replied.

'I don't know', said Linda, 'I just had a feeling'.

'The same feeling you had when you told me that something sad was going to happen, days before your Granny Nixon died?' Margie queried.

'Aye, something, like that', said Linda.

Margie shook her head in amazement and said, 'Well, we'll have to start calling you psychic Linda!' she exclaimed.

Douglas and Jack had been very close and he took the death of his brother very badly. He seemed to go into a depression and turned even more to drink for comfort. One evening, in one of his drunken temper fits, he was threatening to beat Linda. She hadn't done anything wrong but, as usual, in his boozed-up frame of mind, he had fabricated something from nothing. She was at the end of her tether, exhausted and exasperated with her dad's tantrums. When was he ever going to learn that alcohol wasn't going to help or solve anything? All it did was numb the pain for him, but made everyone else's life hell. Anne never even got as much as a smack from her parents, never mind a beating. Dear Uncle Jack would never have hurt a fly.

As her daddy's heavy hand came thundering towards her face, she stared into his eyes and shouted, 'I wish that it was you who had died, not Uncle Jack. He was a much nicer person than you will ever be!'

She couldn't believe what she had said, but at that point, his hand stopped in mid air. He gazed at her with a hurt and questioning expression, unable to believe what he had just heard. Then he turned and walked away. Douglas was very quiet for days after that, as if trying to work things out in his head. As a result, the house became very relaxed and peaceful for a change.

Douglas junior changed his job and went to work in a laboratory for a company down in the west coast of Scotland. The train fares were taking their toll on the family purse strings, so when he got the chance of a flat share with two of his workmates, he came home and discussed it with his parents. His father agreed, but insisted that he still contribute to the household finances, as his income was needed. Margie didn't think that this was right, but she would never disagree with her husband. Poor Douglas junior would never argue with his dad either, so he struggled for survival on next to nothing, trying to pay his rent while sending a good percentage of his wages home to his mum and dad. His flat mates had only their rent to worry about and had the rest of their wages to themselves. They couldn't understand why Douglas junior never had any money. They began to think that he was mean because he never went to the pub on a Friday nor brought anything extra into the house, other than what was needed.

He carried on studying very hard at evening college to achieve his qualification for entry into University. This was his ultimate goal. His father had it drummed into him so much that he was wasting his time and would never be as clever as his dad. Douglas reminded his son constantly that he had been Dux of his school, but was never allowed the privilege of going to University because he had been taken out of school to work and bring money in to feed and clothe his brothers and sisters. Douglas had a bad chip on his shoulder and felt life had done him an injustice by not allowing him to take the path he wanted. He felt very hard done by in not getting the opportunity to go to University, even though he had the intelligence to get a place. His years in the Army, fighting for his country, left him a very bitter and changed man. He wanted to be proud of his son, he loved him so much, but he couldn't show his feelings or help himself being jealous. He made everything that Douglas junior attempted very difficult. Douglas junior battled on. He wanted to prove to the world that, in spite of all the drawbacks, he could and was going to do it!

Summer 1962 was here and Linda took her friend Norah to meet her Catholic friends. Patrick was there. He had brought along a tall, gorgeously handsome friend called Mick, who had dark hair combed into a bop style. Mick took a shine to Linda. They flirted, and he teased her. It became very obvious that they fancied each other. Patrick didn't look too happy about it. Linda didn't want to hurt him, so she encouraged him to take an interest in Norah. Norah liked Patrick a lot and was delighted that Linda wasn't interested in him anymore. The four of them spent the summer together but, when it came time to go back to their respective schools and other friends, Linda lost touch with Mick. Norah and Patrick carried on seeing each other. Linda had grown out of her childhood crush on Patrick and was happy for them both. They seemed besotted with each other. Patrick left school and started a job on shift work. Every day, he stood at the school gate waiting for Norah and they walked home with their arms wrapped around each other, stopping to kiss, over and over again, on the way.

Late Spring 1963 and Douglas junior got the news that he had been waiting for. He had been accepted for Strathclyde University to study chemistry. He applied for all the necessary grants to cover all his costs and expenses. Margie and Douglas agreed to keep their son while he studied for the next three years at University. He was to start the new term in September and worried about moving back home, but he knew that there was no other way that he was going to do it. Margie was especially very proud of her son. Amazingly, Douglas was too, and the both of them could be heard boasting about Douglas junior to all their family and friends. Douglas junior had lived away from home for a year. His relationship with his dad wasn't good before, but now it had became rather distant. Douglas junior didn't have a bad bone in his body. He always showed respect for his dad and seemed to blank all the nightmare years of the past out of his memory. They never went anywhere together or had a father-son relationship. He was almost twenty now and his dad seemed to have backed off, realising that his son had great ambitions, was highly intelligent, and that there was no holding him back.

June 1963 was fast approaching. Linda had decided that she had had enough of school and wanted to get out and work in an office. If she stayed on another year to do 'O' levels, she could miss her best opportunity of getting into an office, as most companies preferred to take on fifteen years olds as juniors to train up into their office routines.

There were always plenty of offices and trades taking on young, fifteen year olds every summer when the schools broke up. The schools arranged interviews with local businesses that required office juniors. Linda trotted off, dressed in her best outfit to impress, only to find forty or more girls from her school sitting in the waiting room, waiting to be interviewed for one vacancy. She attended six more of these particular interviews and was not successful in any of them. She began to feel that there was something wrong with her as, one by one, her friends got work in offices in the town, boasting about their earning of £2 10/- per week.

Douglas' knowledge of the big companies in the city from his years as a postman came in very handy. He wrote them all down for Linda, helped her draft out a letter introducing herself to them, telling them why she would like the opportunity of working for them. Night after night, she sat and wrote off letter after letter until she had writer's cramp. She waited in anticipation for the replies to arrive. Some companies never bothered to answer, others replied with an apology that they had no vacancies but would keep her details on file. The summer holidays were almost over. Linda was getting very despondent and considering going back to school. She couldn't see what chance there was of her getting a job, as the majority of all the school leavers were now employed and all the vacancies were filled. Margie kept an optimistic outlook and told her not to worry. It was only because there was something better waiting for her.

On Monday morning of the third week in August 1963, a letter dropped through the letterbox addressed to Linda. She tore it open and jumped up and down with excitement as she read she was invited to come on Friday for an interview with an international company in the city centre. On the Thursday night, she soaked in the bath and then set her hair in rollers. In the morning she got up, carefully removed her rollers and back-combed her hair into a neat bouffant with kiss curls at the side before spraying it stiff with hair lacquer. She put on a little black mascara to curl her eyelashes, and pink lipstick. Her interview was at 10.30am. After breakfast, she donned her new boucle beige/brown mixture straight skirt, white blouse, best blue/grey coat, black patent shoes with matching handbag, black gloves and, carried a long, gold walking umbrella. She cut through the lane past the bars where she used to hang around with her gang. They were building houses in the field there now. She blushed and hurried on towards the bus stop as the builders hung over the scaffolding and whistled at her. This made her feel very grown up.

What's For Ye, Won't Go By Ye

Linda got off the bus at the terminus in town and walked towards West Nile Street. She checked the numbers on the way down the hill until finally she came to the big red building with the words 'Royal Edinburgh House'. Her stomach churned as she walked through the doorway and studied the sign with the names of all the companies and which floors they were on. She waited for the elevator. Finally it arrived and three businessmen in bowler hats got out. Linda got in. It seemed to take an eternity to get to the sixth floor. There were two glazed double doors leading to the reception. Linda went in. The receptionist slid back a glass window and asked whom she had come to see. She took her details and told Linda to take a seat. The office manager, Mr. Vernon, a tall and very distinguished, but eccentric looking, grey-haired English gentleman opened the door. He invited Linda to come up to the seventh floor for her interview. He seemed very friendly, although she had trouble understanding him because he stammered and laughed his way through his accent. He led her into a very plush office belonging to Mr. Robb, the area divisional manager. Mr. Robb was in his mid thirties, balding, with thick, black-rimmed glasses. He was a public schoolboy type with an attitude like a strict headmaster.

The two bosses interviewed the very nervous Linda, Mr. Robb taking the roll of Mr. Nasty and Mr. Vernon that of Mr. Nice. Her elocution lessons stood her in good stead, just like her mammy told her they would one day. She put on her best posh voice so that the Englishmen understood her. They fired different questions at Linda, asking her how she would deal with certain situations and awkward customers, why she wanted to work from them, and where she had found out about the vacancy. Then, they gave her a verbal arithmetic test. Linda managed this no bother, as arithmetic was her best subject, and she actually enjoyed mental arithmetic. At the end of the interview, they both shook her hand and told her that they had more people to interview, but would let her know by the end of next week. Linda walked out of the room, breathed a huge sigh of relief that her ordeal was over, and hoped that she would hear good news from them. She was a bit pessimistic because of the past disappointments she had in finding work, and had heard that line before 'We have other people to see, but we'll let you know'.

The weekend passed and, on Tuesday, Linda got a letter requesting her to go back on Friday for a second interview. Her mammy and daddy told her that could be good news, because it usually meant that she had been short-listed for the job. She donned her best clothes again on Friday morning and set off for her second interview.

The receptionist greeted her with a big smile saying, 'Oh hello again. Just take a seat and I will call Mr. Vernon for you'.

Mr. Vernon escorted her again up to Mr. Robb's posh office. There, waiting for her, was a short haired, very slim, smart, typical spinster type lady dressed in a grey/blue tweed suit and in her mid fifties. Mr. Vernon introduced her to Linda as Miss Drummond, the head clerkess, and told Linda that it was in Miss Drummond's office the vacancy for the junior clerkess was. If she were successful, then Miss Drummond would be her direct boss. The interview was more relaxed this time, with just Mr. Vernon and Miss Drummond. Linda got the impression that Miss Drummond was present at this interview to give her approval or disapproval of the final candidates.

After ten minutes, Miss Drummond asked Linda if she would like a cup of tea. Linda, thinking it would be rude to refuse, shyly agreed. Miss Drummond left the office to get the tea and returned about five minutes later, holding a tray with a steel teapot, cups and saucers, and a plate of custard cream biscuits. Linda noticed that there were four cups and saucers on the tray. She was wondering whom the other cup of tea was for when Mr. Robb appeared. He sat in his big black leather swivel chair behind his big plush desk.

His eyes twinkled and, with a wry smile, he said to the two other bosses, 'Well, what do you both think? Shall we offer the job to Miss MacGregor?'

Linda's heart thumped in her chest. She couldn't believe her luck and could hardly control her excitement as Miss Drummond nodded in agreement.

Mr. Vernon replied, 'Yes, I think we'll give her a go!'

'Can you start on Monday?' asked Mr. Robb.

A big, gratified smile spread across Linda's face and she blurted out, 'Yes, oh yes! I would love to start on Monday. Thank you so much!'

One by one, they shook her hand and warmly welcomed her into the company. Linda put two and two together and realised that Miss Drummond had used the excuse of going for the tea to give her approval to Mr. Robb.

Mr. Robb seemed a lot more relaxed now that the interview was over. He told Linda that they were all impressed by her initiative in writing to the company to enquire about vacancies instead of waiting to see if any were advertised. The best news was yet to come, though, because her office was a division of the London office, she would receive the London rate of pay of £4 16/-. She couldn't believe it. This was almost double what her pals were earning and her job was a junior clerkess, which meant she would be trained in all aspects of clerical and statistical work, and not just be a dog's body office junior like the majority of her friends. There were also company perks, including a subsidised canteen, free samples of company products, members' club and a pension fund. She ran faster than she ever thought possible all the way to the bus terminus and willed the bus to get her home faster so that she could break the wonderful news to her daddy.

He was delighted. 'Another wage coming in will help a lot', said Douglas.

Linda was waiting at the door for her mammy and brother to come home that night. Linda felt that she had achieved something worthwhile and wonderful as they hugged and congratulated her.

What's For Ye, Won't Go By Ye

'See, I told you', said Margie proudly. 'Something better was waiting round the corner for you. You were lucky enough to enjoy all of your school holidays, and now you're earning double what your friends are. You've lost nothing. Your pals went straight from school to work and had no holidays!'

Monday morning came and a very nervous Linda arrived fifteen minutes early at her new place of work. Miss Drummond introduced her to Katherine, an attractive dark-haired girl, who wore dark rimmed secretary-type glasses. She was very trim and neat in a plain straight skirt and white blouse. Katherine was the clerkess that would train Linda. She was from the Hebrides and had a beautiful Highland lilt to her voice. Katherine also spoke Gaelic. There was just the three of them in the office, and the atmosphere was a bit like a classroom with Miss Drummond's big desk at the other side of the room, opposite theirs. Miss Drummond was a chain smoker. She lit up one cigarette after another, looking up as she did so, her eyes glancing from side to side between Katherine and Linda to make sure that they were both getting on with their work.

In the afternoon, Miss Drummond told Katherine to take Linda and introduce her to the other staff. First of all, they went along the corridor to meet the two secretaries. Vera, Mr. Vernon's secretary, was a small, pleasant churchy-type with tight, curly dark hair. Connie, Mr. Robb's secretary, was about 5ft 6in with cold staring eyes, a pointed nose and mousy brown hair cut in a straight bob. Connie had the biggest bosoms ever and skinny legs that seemed to knock her out of proportion. Linda wasn't too sure about her. She could feel an invisible barrier and, if she did indeed have psychic powers, they were certainly working and giving her some sort of warning.

Then they went downstairs to meet the staff in the big open plan office. There were about sixty people working there, and Linda was trying hard to memorise all of their names. She met Geraldine, the office junior. She was sixteen and Linda thought her job was boring. Geraldine's job seemed to consist of wrapping up parcels, running errands, filing the outgoing post into the pigeonholes and delivering the incoming post to all the different departments. At the end of the day, she took all the envelopes from the pigeonholes, sealed them up, weighed and franked them. She then put the London post into a big green material bag and took the lot to the post office. Linda couldn't understand why Geraldine had not applied for the vacancy of junior clerkess in Miss Drummond's office where she would have had the opportunity to learn more. Katherine told her discreetly that Geraldine was interested in the job, but an excuse had been made to her, because Miss Drummond didn't think she was suitable. Linda was pleased about this, because if Geraldine had got the job of junior clerkess, then Linda would probably have been left with Geraldine's boring job.

The old-fashioned plug-in switchboard in the reception area fascinated Linda. She was introduced to Heather, the receptionist, a tall, very attractive, pleasant model like girl with gleaming white teeth, a wide smile and black hair up in an immaculate French roll.

'Oh, you will soon get to know all about the reception and switchboard', Heather told Linda. 'This will be part of your training. The company likes to teach juniors the reception and switchboard so that they can cover lunch breaks, emergencies, holiday and sickness when necessary'.

Linda was excited about this, although she did feel a bit apprehensive when she looked at all the crossed wires plugged into different holes on the board.

It was afternoon teatime and Katherine said, 'Come on into the kitchen Linda, and meet Agnes, our tea lady'.

Agnes was a cheery wee woman, very thin and ordinary. Linda felt sorry for her when she learned from the others that Agnes had a hard life, with five children and a lazy drunken husband who never worked and beat her up. Agnes came in to work regularly with her eyes blackened. The staff rallied round her at times like these and offered her help, but Agnes was a very hard-working, proud woman and never ever admitted to anyone that it was her husband who hit her. She always laughed and made an excuse about bumping into a lamp post or walking into a door.

Within a week, Linda was organising orders, uplifts of goods from shops, percentage comparison figures to compare sales from last year's to this, and representatives' expenses. She took to it like a duck to water and looked forward to going in to work each day. Miss Drummond was very strict and didn't allow her girls to chat, but if she felt like talking, they had to stop and listen. Linda and Katherine didn't mind this, because she always reminisced and had interesting tales to tell about her past and the olden days. When Miss Drummond left the room for any reason, Katherine and Linda downed their pens and had a blether. Unbeknownst to Miss Drummond, they nicknamed her Fanny. Miss Drummond had worked with the company since she left school at the age of fourteen, and she was now fifty-six. Mr. Thompson, the office manager downstairs, was the same age as her, and he too had started work with the firm at the age of fourteen. So, the two of them had worked together and known each other for over forty years, but unfortunately, they never saw eye to eye. They argued about everything and anything. Often, there were scenes in the office as the two of them shouted at each other while Katherine and Linda kept their heads down and sniggered under their breath.

At the end of her first week, Linda took her wages home. She didn't pay any tax and got the whole amount of £4 16/- in a brown envelope. She was on a probationary period for the first three months. After that, if all went well, she would go on to a monthly salary. She thought she was well off until her dad took charge, instructing Margie to take £4 10/- and give Linda back 6/- pocket money.

'We will buy all your clothes and necessities, pay your bus fares and feed you', said Douglas. 'You'll have 6/- to do what you want with. I think you have a good deal, don't you?', he continued.

Linda wasn't so sure, but she knew that there was no point in discussing it any further, as that was how all families worked. Her friends were the same, they got approximately 5/- pocket money per week back out of their wages. Margie talked Douglas into allowing Linda to keep her first week's wages to herself so that she could by outfits for work.

'It's tradition', Margie told Douglas. 'It's all one anyway, because I would have to buy her nice clothes for the office. She can't go in her school uniform!'

Margie went out with Linda and bought her two smart skirts and two smart blouses for work. It all came to just under £5. Linda told Margie about a top that was all the fashion at the time and that she was going to save up to buy for going out with.

'How much is it?' asked Margie.

'19/11d', replied Linda.

Margie slipped Linda £1 and said, 'Don't tell your dad!'

Margie went home while Linda went to buy herself the top. She was hoping that the shop she saw it in hadn't run out, because they were very popular. She asked the lady in the shop if she had any left and was delighted when she brought one out to her.

'You're very lucky, it's the last one', said the kindly shop assistant.

Linda was meeting her friends at the Dennistoun Palais that night and couldn't wait to wear it.

That evening, she got herself ready. She pinned her hair up, put her make-up on and wore her new top, along with a grey skirt. She was in the height of fashion. She felt a million dollars and couldn't wait to show herself off to her friends. Linda came downstairs, expecting compliments from her parents on how good she looked.

Instead, her dad stared in disbelief. 'What on earth are you wearing?' he angrily demanded.

'What do you mean, what's wrong with it?' Linda replied, confused.

'You're not going any where wearing that, you look like a prostitute!' her dad replied.

The top was printed with labels saying 'New York', 'Paris' and 'London'. They were all the style and all the young girls were wearing them. Linda's dad, however, was having none of it.

'Only good time girls wear clothes like that, with labels attached to them!' he insisted.

Linda was stunned, how could he think like that? She wasn't a bad girl, she just wanted to follow the fashion. Douglas made her change and put a blouse on. Linda was very upset. She went to meet her friends that evening and they were all wearing the new fashionable tops. Linda was devastated when Douglas made Margie take her back to the shop the following week and change the top for a frilly blue blouse.

There was great excitement. The Beatles were coming to town, and they were to perform live on stage at the Odeon in Renfield Street. The tickets were 10/6d each and Linda didn't have that sort of cash to spend. So, she resigned herself to the fact that she couldn't afford to go and see them. It was a complete sell out. Two days before the gig, one of Linda's friends told her that a pal of her sister's had a ticket but couldn't go. She was happy to let Linda have the ticket and pay her later over a couple of months. Linda couldn't believe it. She remembered one of her Granny's Nixon's favourite sayings, 'What's for ye, won't go by ye'. She was so grateful to this girl who could have sold her ticket for more. She sat up in the balcony and watched in wonderment as her idols sang the songs that she had played over and over again on her record player, 'Please, Please Me', 'From Me To You' and, her favourite, 'She Loves You'. She came out of the theatre dancing on air, nipping herself to believe that she had actually seen The Beatles.

In November 1963, a letter came through the letterbox offering them a brand new, three bed roomed house in a very posh area to the west of the city. Margie and Douglas had been trying for over two years to get a council house out in that area of the city to be near Margie's sisters, but, up until now, they hadn't had any offers. They only had two bedrooms and Linda had been sleeping on the bed settee in the living room for two years. It would be nice to have three bedrooms, allowing Douglas junior and Linda to have their own bedroom each.

They all went out to view the house and fell in love with it. There were eight semi-detached houses standing off the beaten track up a lane. The houses were surrounded by open space and fields. Their house was the very first one. It had the very latest under-floor heating, a modern kitchenette with an electric cooker, a drying cupboard to hang washing, a utility room, a 24-foot long lounge with large windows looking out to the back and front. There were gardens at the back and front, albeit that the back garden was on a steep slope. The best thing of all was that the house had three bedrooms. Straight away, Linda claimed the small cosy room to the front of the house. Margie was amazed that she didn't want the big bedroom at the back but didn't question her decision.

What's For Ye, Won't Go By Ye

The family moved to their new home a week before Christmas. Margie, Douglas and Douglas junior worked with the removal men. Linda couldn't get time off. She went to work from the old house and returned very excited to her new house in the evening. That evening they sat down to tea and Margie reflected on the original reasons why she wanted to live in this part of the city.

'If only this had happened two or more years ago, then I could have spent some more time with my mother', she said thoughtfully. 'Oh well, for what's for ye, won't go by ye! She's probably looking down and very happy for us now!'

Linda became very good friends with Katherine from work. They often went out together or to each other's houses. Linda liked going to Katherine's. Her parents were lovely and she got on so well with them. They taught her Gaelic, as that was the only language spoken in their household, so you had to understand it if you wanted to join in the conversation. Likewise, Katherine was a regular visitor at Linda's house. Margie and Douglas loved her and she thought the world of them too.

New Year 1964, and Douglas and Margie threw a big house-warming party in their new house. All the family, from both sides, came along, and so did Katherine. Douglas junior brought a few of his fellow students along, and everyone was impressed when his professor and wife called in too. Douglas junior amazed everyone by drinking a pint of beer while standing on his head against the wall. All his student pals gathered round clapping and cheering him on. Later, Linda noticed that Katherine and her brother Douglas seemed to be very chatty towards each other. Linda took Douglas junior aside and asked him if he was interested in Katherine.

He said, 'Yes, she's a really nice girl. I wouldn't mind getting to know her better'.

Then Linda went over to Katherine and asked her what she thought of Douglas junior.

Katherine answered, 'I think your brother is gorgeous. I wouldn't say no if he asked me out'.

So, Linda set the wheels in motion and before long, Douglas junior and Katherine were courting. Linda was delighted because they all got on so well together . She visualised them getting married one day, Katherine becoming the sister she always wanted.

There was one drawback, nice as Katherine was, she came from the Outer Hebrides and had a strict Catholic upbringing. Douglas wasn't at all happy about the prospects of Margie and him having a Catholic daughter-in-law, nor was Katherine's family pleased at the prospect of having a Protestant son-in-law.

Katherine's mum often said to Douglas junior, 'Don't worry son, we'll soon make a good Catholic out of you!'

This made Douglas junior feel very uneasy. The religion thing didn't worry Katherine or himself, so why should everyone else make such a big deal out of it? Even Miss Drummond took Linda aside and told her to warn her brother about getting caught up in the Catholic religion. Linda and Margie seemed to be the only two that never mentioned or worried about the two of them being of different religions. Douglas junior and Katherine were like soul mates. They were made for each other, and struggled on happily together, trying to ignore the interference of their families.

February 1964, Douglas' sister Emily was very ill and in the hospital. She had been given weeks to live. It was terrible for the family, as her daughter Maureen was an only child and only twelve years old. During all this, Pop MacGregor died very suddenly from natural causes. The family all gathered round for his funeral. It was a very sad time. They decided not to cause Emily any more distress and never told her about Pop. Emily passed away not long after. Amazingly, her very spoiled daughter became a woman overnight, taking care of everything, refusing help from aunts and uncles, doing the cooking, cleaning and washing for herself and her dad.

Linda had been working for seven months. She carried out every task with efficiency and Fanny Drummond was always congratulating her on her excellence. She got on very well with everyone at the company office, apart from two people whom she was very wary of. One was the office junior Geraldine, who was very jealous of Linda, who had a more important job than her. Geraldine complained to her manager, Mr. Thompson. She felt Linda should be helping her with the company mail and taking turns at going to the post office. Mr. Thomson spoke to Fanny Drummond about it and, as usual, they had an unholy row. Fanny Drummond told him that Linda's job was more important than wrapping up parcels and sorting out company post. In the end, for peace's sake, Linda agreed to go downstairs half an hour before finishing time every night to help Geraldine with the evening mail, taking turns at dropping it off at the post office.

Geraldine had got her own way. Linda was annoyed, but she never complained, even when she saw Geraldine wasting time talking. Geraldine's job had no pressure or deadlines. Linda often had to leave important sales figures unfinished, just to help this whimpering, lazy girl stick down the envelopes and post the mail. Mr. Robb, unaware of the situation and the pressure that Linda was under, would get annoyed and harass Linda to get the figures finished. Of course, Connie, his mouthy secretary, didn't help things. She was a friend of Geraldine's, and was also annoyed that she didn't get Linda's job. Connie persisted in making life hard for Linda by reporting her at every turn for anything that she could think of.

On one occasion, Linda asked Miss Drummond if she could extend her lunch break by half an hour and come in half an hour earlier at 8am the next day to make up for it because she was meeting her mother. Miss Drummond knew that Linda was a worker, and had no hesitation in agreeing to it. After lunch, when Linda returned to her office, she was just getting her coat off when Mr. Vernon, looking very angry, called her into his office.

'Where do you think you have been until this time?' he questioned.

Linda told him exactly where she had been and that she had asked Miss Drummond's approval. He blurted out in his stammering voice that Connie had needed to get the sales figures for typing and, because Linda was late, it would mean that the figures wouldn't be ready for the meeting in time. It became obvious to Linda that Connie had been into the boss, stirring it up. This was Tuesday, and Linda always gave Connie the figures on a Wednesday to be ready for the meeting on Friday.

'What would happen if we were all late? Nothing would get done', he continued.

'Excuse me', Linda found herself blurting out loudly. She felt the tears welling up in anger and frustration and couldn't contain herself anymore. "I am never late and I wasn't late today! I asked permission to extend my lunch hour, and I am coming in half an hour early tomorrow morning to make up for it. On the other hand, if you want to talk about timekeeping, then I suggest we discuss Connie. The starting time is 8.30am and she never gets in until 8.50am at the earliest, always making some silly excuse about her train being delayed or late. Why doesn't she get out of bed earlier in the morning? She's working at least an hour and a quarter less than the rest of us every week, and approximately five hours less than us every month, never mind the hours she's saving in a year. Why don't you bring her in and have a word with her?'

Linda suddenly stopped and realised who she was speaking to, but it was all so unfair and she couldn't help herself.

'Don't be so insubordinate!' bellowed Mr. Vernon. 'Send Miss Drummond in, I want a word with her!'

Linda went back along the corridor. She was upset and quickly blurted out to Miss Drummond what had happened, and that Mr. Vernon wanted to see her. Miss Drummond took an angry breath, bit her lip, and marched through to his office. Linda could hear shouts, but couldn't make out what was being said. Ten minutes later, Miss Drummond banged in through the door, red with anger. Linda wondered what was going to be said to her. She was waiting for a dressing down for answering Mr. Vernon back.

Instead, Miss Drummond said to Linda. 'Ignore everything Linda, and don't you worry. You never did anything wrong. Mr. Vernon had no right to question you without seeing me first. I am your boss and I make the decisions, not Connie! That woman is nothing but a troublemaker. She sticks her nose into everyone's business, instead of getting on with her own work. I've just told Mr. Vernon that you had every right to complain about her time keeping. Why should she get away with it when she's the first to complain about anyone else? Mr. Vernon will be calling you in and apologizing to you for not checking things out with me first. He is also going to have a word with Connie about her time keeping'.

True to word, Mr. Vernon called Linda back in to tell her that he had it explained to him and will know in the future not to listen to Connie, but to check it out with Miss Drummond first.

Connie was annoyed that Linda had found out that it was she who had reported her, and even more annoyed that it had backfired on her. Often Linda would take work along for Connie to type, only to find her and Geraldine gossiping. The room would go silent when Linda entered. It was obvious that they were talking about her. One day Linda left the room, making sure the door wasn't closed. She pretended to walk along the corridor by standing on the spot and making the noise of footsteps. The conversation quickly started up.

'That Linda gets away with blue murder', said Connie quite clearly. 'She gets her own way and has Miss Drummond right round her wee finger'.

'I know', replied Geraldine 'I had to fight to get her to help with the evening post. She thinks she's too good for that!'

Linda had heard enough. She stormed into the room and the two women's mouths fell open as they stared in disbelief.

'Have you quite finished now?' enquired Linda defiantly.

The both of them stood looking very sheepish as Linda asked them if they had nothing better to do with themselves.

Linda said, 'I suggest that both of you get your facts right before you bad-mouth people. That's how you end up losing your job, or even in court! Now, if you don't mind, unlike you two, who have all the time in the world to gossip, I have a job to do!'

At that, Linda turned smartly on her heels and marched out of the room. She felt satisfied that she had caught them both red-handed and got the opportunity to put both of the bitches in their places. After that, she was treated with a bit more respect, but it didn't mean that she liked Connie or Geraldine any better. She knew that neither of them was to be trusted. Not long after that Geraldine left, leaving Connie with no allies.

What's For Ye, Won't Go By Ye

In May 1964, .a new girl called Alice started work as the office junior in place of Geraldine. She had thick, bright red hair and a lovely cheery personality. Linda and Alice hit it off right away and worked well together. She was always willing to help out and lend a hand. If Linda was busy, Alice told her not to worry, that she would manage the post herself and say honestly that her job wasn't a busy one anyway. After she took over the job, it became obvious to everyone just how lazy and how much of a skiver Geraldine had been.

The atmosphere in the big office was much better without the bitchy Geraldine. The girls got a chance to know Linda better. Often there could be heard a choir of voices coming from the ladies' toilet at lunchtime as Linda led the girls in singing the popular songs from the hit parade.

June 1964 and it was Linda's week for covering the switchboard at lunchtime for the receptionist Heather. This meant that she had a late lunch from 2pm until 3pm. She was quite expert at it by now, and loved criss-crossing all the plugs and wires. There weren't many calls coming in, as most businesses closed between the hours of 1pm and 2pm. Norah and a few other of Linda's old school friends also did lunchtime cover on their company's switchboards. Linda called Norah, who was talking to another friend, so she connected Linda up to their line. After that, another friend, Lena, called Linda. Eventually there were eight of them all linked up through their company switchboards, talking about everything from clothes, make up, boys to pop stars. Every now and then, one of them would break away to answer a company call.

Lena said, 'Hang on girls, be back in a minute, I have a call coming in'. Two minutes later, she was back, saying, 'Now listen girls. I have two blokes on my line called Clive and Benny from a chartered accountants office in West Regent Street. They came through to me a couple of days ago on a wrong number and now they keep calling me. They're all a good laugh. Do you want to talk to them?'

'Yes', the girls all echoed, 'put them through'.

The party lines became a regular occurrence at lunchtimes and sometimes there were up to twenty people on the line as the circle of friends grew.

One day Clive called Linda and said, 'Where exactly is your office? We're coming round that way at lunchtime and thought that we would pop in to see you'.

'Oh', said Linda very hesitantly. She thought, *what the devil, at least I'll get to see what they look like!*

So she gave Clive instructions on how to get to her office, but warned them not to come before 1pm or after 2pm, because Miss Drummond would go mad if she knew Linda had boys visiting her. Linda wasn't on lunchtime switchboard duty, but she sat at the reception area and ate her sandwiches with Heather.

Linda knew that both the lads were 19, three years older than her. She wondered if they would keep to their word. The girls were blethering when they heard the 'ding' of the lift arriving at their floor. They waited, quietly giggling, to see if it was Clive and Benny. The door slowly opened and two lads entered.

One, a small, thin, dark haired, pale-skinned ordinary looking boy said, 'We're looking for Linda'.

Linda said, 'Linda who? This is a big office, do you know her surname?'

'Well, er, no', he replied.

'Who shall I say wants her?' asked Linda.

'It's Clive. Tell her Clive and Benny', he answered.

'You are Clive then?' enquired Linda.

'Yes', he replied.

'Well, it's nice to meet you at last, I'm Linda!'

'You're Linda? Oh! You really had me going there!' Clive exclaimed.

'And this must be Benny', she said to the other lad.

Linda felt an instant attraction to Benny. He had a good build, blond hair, blue eyes and a wide smile. Clive was the talkative one, and Benny was very shy. He seemed to have more confidence when he was talking on the phone, but both lads had a very good sense of humour. After half an hour, the boys went back to their office.

Heather said to Linda, 'You like Benny, don't you?"

'He's OK', said Linda, pretending it didn't matter.

'Yes, you do like him, I can tell!' said Heather.

That same afternoon, Clive called Linda in her office. Fanny Drummond frowned on personal calls, but fortunately, she had gone to the kitchen for a second cup of tea.

Clive said, 'Have you seen that new James Bond film, Linda? I'm going to see it tonight and I don't like going on my own. Would you like to come with me?'

Linda thought for a moment. She was secretly disappointed that Benny hadn't asked her.

She said, 'Oh go on then. I'm not doing anything else tonight'.

'Great', said Clive. 'I'll meet you at the Odeon in Anniesland Cross at quarter past seven'.

Linda got home just after six o'clock, had her tea, and then quickly washed and changed. She always made a point of being five minutes late, because she didn't like standing on her own waiting for boys. She got off the bus outside of the picture house and there was no Clive She felt silly standing there and was getting really annoyed. She wasn't particularly bothered about seeing the film, she only agreed to keep Clive company because she felt sorry for him. She knew people would be thinking that she had been stood up but, it wasn't a real date.

She waited another ten minutes and was just about to cross the road and get a bus home when she saw Benny strolling towards her.

'What are you doing here, and where's Clive?' she asked firmly.

'Clive phoned me at the last minute to say that he couldn't make it. He asked me to meet you, because he didn't want to let you down'.

Linda was secretly delighted. She much preferred the idea of going out with Benny, but she wasn't sure how he felt. He was a perfect gentlemen. He insisted on paying her in and bought her a box of Maltesers at the kiosk. Once inside, it was dark, as the film was about to start. They fumbled around to find their way and sat three rows from the back, in the middle. After half and hour, Linda opened the Maltesers but, as she pulled the cellophane off, the box slipped from her grip. She managed to catch it, but not before half of the boxful went rumbling loudly under the seats, down the whole length of the cinema. *Oh no,* thought Linda embarrassedly. *That had to happen, and at a quite tense moment in the film.* She turned to Benny to see him doubled up, trying desperately to stifle his laugh. This started her off, and others around saw the funny side and laughed too. That box of Maltesers certainly broke the ice!

After the film finished, Linda thanked Benny for a lovely evening and went to cross the road to her bus stop.

'Where are you going?' he asked her.

'To catch the bus home', she replied.

'I'll drop you home', Benny said.

Linda was astonished. She didn't know that he had a car. They walked round the corner and sitting there was a lovely grey Morris Minor. Linda got in, feeling quite a toff. Not many young lads had cars. They pulled up at the lane in front of her house. Linda was hoping that he would suggest going out again, but he never mentioned anything. She was disappointed and resigned herself to the fact that he was just doing Clive a favour and didn't fancy her.

The next day Clive called her at lunchtime.

He said, 'How did you enjoy the film?'

She told him it was very good and asked him why he couldn't make it.

'Well!, said Clive, 'do you really want the truth?'

'You don't have to tell me if you don't want to', said Linda.

'No, I think you should know, but don't tell Benny that I told you', replied Clive. He went on. 'Actually, I never was going to the cinema last night. Benny was too shy to ask you, so he got me to pretend to be meeting you. We then arranged for him to come along and tell you the cock and bull story about me not being able to make it!'

Linda pulled a puzzled face, then said, 'Wouldn't it just have been easier for him to have asked me himself?'

'Oh no', said Clive, 'he just couldn't pluck up the courage'.

'Where is he now?' Linda asked.

'Oh, he had to go out today. I wouldn't be telling you this if he was here'.

Linda was confused now. Benny seemed to like her, but didn't have the guts to ask her out. Instead, he had to get his pal to do it for him. And he just said goodbye at the end of the night, with no mention of seeing her again or phoning her at lunchtime!

The following Monday, Linda went to the Dennistoun Palais with Alice and her friends. They danced the night away to the Beatles, the Searchers, Herman's Hermits (Linda loved Herman, she even named her teddy bear after him). and all the other sounds of the Sixties. At the end of the evening they all walked to the train station together. The girls saw Linda on her train first. She went in the opposite direction to the rest of them and had to travel all the way back from the east of the city to the west. She got home just before midnight and her mum was waiting for her.

Her mum said, 'You had a visitor tonight, Linda'.

'A visitor?' enquired Linda. 'Who?'

'Benny came to the door about nine o'clock. He's an awful nice lad. He came in and stayed and blethered for about half an hour', Margie replied.

'What did he want?' said Linda, becoming more confused by the minute.

'Oh! He said if it's all right, he will come and pick you up on Wednesday night about half past seven and take you out somewhere'.

Linda was delighted, but found it hard to understand why Benny had the courage to come to her door and spend half an hour with her mum and dad, yet didn't have the guts to phone and ask her out himself.

Wednesday came and, sure enough, Benny was at the door at half past seven. He came in and made himself comfortable. He seemed to be at ease with Linda's parents.

Margie said, 'I'm just popping up to Betty's. I'll see you later'.

Benny chimed in, 'Where does she live?'

'Oh! It's only half an hour's walk away', replied Margie.

'Well, I'll drop you off'. said Benny.

'I'll come for the run too, then', said Douglas, 'it's not very often I get a chance of a hurl in a car!'

They all climbed in to the Morris Minor, Douglas in front and Margie and Linda in the back. They were at Betty's house in just over five minutes.

'When do you plan to leave again?' asked Benny.

'Oh, no later than ten o'clock', said Margie, 'we've all got work in the morning'.

'Then we'll go for a run and come back and collect you', Benny offered.

Margie never liked to put anyone out. 'Och no!' she said, 'it's OK, we'll walk'.

'No, I insist', said Benny, 'we'll see you later!'

Linda sat in amazement at this confident lad chatting away to her mum and dad like he knew them all his life, yet not once had he mentioned to her about going out, or hinted that he liked her. He took her down to Helensburgh. It was a nice evening. They got out of the car and had a walk along the prom and stopped off to buy some chips before returning back to Auntie Betty's and Uncle Duncan's flat.

They got there just before ten o'clock, parked the car and got the lift up to the eleventh floor of the tower block. Linda couldn't make heads or tails of Benny. He seemed to enjoy her company, but all the time they were alone, he never made any attempt to put his arm around her or even kiss her. Auntie Betty made them welcome and Benny charmed her and Margie with his sense of humour and good manners. As promised, he dropped everyone off. It was eleven o'clock by then.

'Are you coming in for a cup of tea before you drive home Benny?' asked Margie.

'Oh, no, it's a bit late. I'll get on my way', he answered.

Off he went, without mentioning to Linda how he enjoyed her company or asking to see her again.

This happened three more times. Benny would just turn up out of the blue and spend the evening with Linda and her family. By this time, all Linda's aunties thought he was wonderful. He was always good mannered and it was never an effort to run them home. Benny obviously was attracted to Linda and enjoyed coming to her house, but somehow he couldn't pluck up the courage to ask her out personally or even to give her a goodnight kiss. Linda noticed that he never ever came to see her on the weekends, only midweek. He never made any plans in advance and she never knew when he would turn up next, nor did he give her his home telephone number or address.

Alice's aunt asked her if she would mind babysitting for her and staying over with the kids until she and her husband returned on Saturday morning. Alice asked Linda if she would like to come and keep her company. Alice's aunt lived just outside Glasgow, so straight after work on Friday, the two girls got the train to the aunt's house in Coatbridge. About ten o'clock, there was a knock on the door. The girls got scared because they didn't know the area. They grabbed Alice's uncle's Alsatian dog by the collar and gingerly opened the front door. There on the doorstep stood Benny and Clive.

'What on earth are you two doing here? Who told you where I was, and how did you find your way?' Alice gasped.

'Oh! We went to your house and your mum gave us this address', Clive answered.

They stayed for an hour then left again.

Benny carried on like this for another six weeks, just popping up at Linda's house unexpectedly and taking her out. He never made any arrangements in advance.

One lunchtime, Linda called him at his office and said to him, 'There's a good group playing at the club on the corner of Botanic Gardens next Sunday night, do you fancy going?'

She waited for his answer. This would be the first time that an actual date had been made, and she was the one who was doing the asking.

He said, 'Can I let you know about that?'

Linda waited, but he didn't get back to her.

Then, on Sunday morning at eleven o'clock there was a knock on her door. Benny stood there and said, 'What time was it for tonight?'

'Half past seven', replied Linda.

She was beginning to get really concerned about his deepness.

They went along to the club, but she noticed that Benny was a bit uneasy. He took her home that night and actually gave her a goodnight kiss. Linda was disappointed after all this waiting. It wasn't that great. She never heard from Benny again. He never called or came to her door. She still spoke to Clive at lunchtimes, but he was very evasive and wouldn't commit himself to say what he thought the problem might be. He just brushed over the subject, telling her he did not want to get involved, and she should speak to Benny.

Linda twisted her ankle and was ordered to rest at home. She was listening to the local radio station when she heard the DJ say, 'This a request for Benny Martin from Patsy. She says the message is in the song. Oh dear Benny, it looks like you are in the doghouse! The radio then belted out Nancy Sinatra's song, 'These Boots Are Made For Walking'. Linda couldn't make heads or tails of it. Who was Patsy and what had Benny done?

One Saturday afternoon in August, Linda was in Partick. She was walking through the crowds in the main shopping area when suddenly she spotted Benny, arm in arm with a very pregnant young girl. Suddenly it all made sense. That's why he never phoned her in the evening, why he couldn't commit himself to a certain time, and only came to her house during the week. He was married! This must be Patsy, and she had obviously found out about them the night they went to the club in Botanic Gardens. He had been seen there by someone he knew and they told his wife that Benny was with another girl. He had been very uncomfortable that night and never contacted Linda again. Linda was horrified. He caught her staring at him. She gave him a filthy look and he looked away. He seemed to become uneasy and led his completely unaware wife in a different direction. Linda thought, *What a despicable rat! Thank God I didn't become involved with him. Poor Patsy!*

What's For Ye, Won't Go By Ye

It was a Monday morning in September 1964. Linda got into work and Fanny Drummond had a serious look on her face.

'We have to report downstairs at 9am for a staff meeting. I know what it's all about, as I was instructed to attend a meeting with all the bosses after every one left on Friday night. I can't say anything, Mr. Vernon will tell you himself!'

Everyone gathered in the big open plan office with looks of worry and bewilderment on their faces. Mr. Vernon and Mr. Thompson stood in front of them with very serious expressions. There was no sign of Mr. Robb, as he was in London. The staff gasped and sighed when they heard the news that their office was to move to Leeds and they were to be made redundant. Only a hand-ful of people would be kept on to run the small sales office. They were to be told throughout the day who was going and who was staying. Linda waited with baited breath. She loved her job. Surely she wasn't going to lose it? It was announced that Mr. Vernon was to be pensioned off and that Mr. Thompson was moving upstairs to the sales office. All the staff in the big office was made redundant. Miss Douglas, the two secretaries and Katherine were staying, but there was still no word for Linda about her job.

Eventually, she was called into Mr. Vernon's room and he told her that she would be staying. The reason the decision took so long was that Mr. Thompson wanted to keep on his own office junior Alice, but Miss Drummond and Mr. Vernon fought tooth and nail against him. Linda found out later from Miss Drummond the extent of the heated debate. They had reminded Mr. Thompson that the job title was 'junior clerkess', which was a lot more involved than an office junior's duties. They argued that he couldn't make Linda redun-dant, because her job in the sales office was still required. Miss Drummond told Mr. Thompson that he was treading on dangerous water and could end up in court if he made Linda redundant from a job that was still ongoing. She also informed him that she wasn't prepared to start training another junior, because she was more than satisfied by the efficient way that Linda carried out her duties, and would stand up in any court and say so! Mr. Thompson had no choice but to reluctantly give in and agree to make his junior redundant.

By November 1964, the big open plan office had closed, leaving just five staff and two bosses in the small sales office. The office furniture was being sold to dealers and Linda asked if she could buy one of the old desks for her broth-er for his bedroom. She knew that he would love it for his studies. Mr. Thompson agreed on a knock down price of £5. Her parents raised £3.50 and Linda scraped up the other £1.50. Delivery vans were coming and going all the time, in and out of the big office, and Mr. Thompson very kindly arranged for one of them to drop the desk off at Linda's house.

Linda's duties increased and she now had the responsibility of a small modern switchboard on her desk. Katherine always took a turn when Linda was busy, and they would both muck in with the evening mail. Katherine and Linda could never go out for lunch together now because they had to stagger their lunch breaks to cover the switchboard. Agnes the tea lady had been made redundant too, because there wasn't enough staff to justify keeping her on. So it became Linda's responsibility to make the tea for everyone. The little cleaner's cupboard out in the landing was transformed into a small kitchen. Every morning at 10am and afternoon at 3pm, Linda went to the kitchen and put the kettle on. She prepared a tray for each of the bosses consisting of a plate with two biscuits, a cup, a saucer, teaspoon, sugar and milk. She took the trays into the boss's offices and then came back to the kitchen to make a big pot that held at least ten cups of tea.

She started off by serving Fanny Drummond and Katherine first, because Fanny had a stomach ulcer and liked her tea very weak. Then Linda served the two bosses, followed by Vera and Connie. She always left the pot in the secretary's office because they preferred strong tea and liked to drain it for a second cup. Linda got sick and tired of Connie's constant moans about everyone having to suffer weak tea because Miss Drummond liked it weak. One afternoon, as Linda served the tea, when Vera was in Mr. Thompson's office taking dictation and had her tea in there with him, Linda nipped back into the kitchen and placed two tablespoonfuls of coffee into the big teapot. She stirred it in, knowing that what she was doing was wrong and that she would probably get into terrible trouble for it, but she felt Connie was a nutter who just talked and complained needlessly and endlessly.

Linda decided on the spur of the moment that Connie needed to be taught a lesson. She walked into Connie's room, smiling cheerfully and announced it was teatime. She stifled a giggle as Connie poured out the dark brown liquid. Then she left immediately, running back to the kitchen before bursting into hysterics. She composed herself and went into her office and sat back at her desk, waiting for the fireworks to start. The switchboard buzzer went. *Oh no, though Linda, It's Connie's phone!*

Linda picked up her telephone and answered innocently, 'Switchboard. Can I help?'

She was dumbfounded when Connie congratulated her and said , 'At last, you have learned to make a decent cuppie, Linda. Well done, keep it up!'

Linda couldn't believe what she was hearing and had to leave the office and run to the toilet to have a good laugh. When she got back to the office, Fanny Drummond went to the toilet. Linda then told Katherine what she had done.

'Good on you Linda. Somebody had to teach that bitch a lesson!' Katherine said, as the two of them doubled up in uncontrollable laughter.

What's For Ye, Won't Go By Ye

Linda followed a local band called the 'Beatstalkers'. They played in the Barrowland and other different dance halls in the city. They were to play a special open-air gig at lunchtime in George Square. Linda secretly arranged with Katherine so that she could have a double lunch hour to go and see them. She would work through another day, so that Katherine could have a two-hour break. Fanny Drummond knew nothing about this little scheme. She let the girls sort out their own lunchtime cover rosters, and always stayed out for the full hour between 1pm and 2pm.

Linda met her friends in George Square. It was packed solid with teenage girls. The stage was set up in front of the City Chambers. The compare announced that the band was almost ready. Then the whole area erupted as the band walked from the City Chambers on to the stage. Their songs could hardly be heard above the noise of the young fans screaming. Suddenly, a few girls broke through the barrier to get onto the stage. Everyone else followed and, after only four songs, the band had to run for their lives and take refuge in the City Chambers. The fans waited outside, chanting over and over again, 'We love you Beatstalkers', but they never came back out.

Linda got back to her office and Fanny Drummond said 'What have you been up to Linda?'

Linda got worried, thinking that her and Katherine's double lunch hour perk had been rumbled.

Fanny just laughed and told her, 'Mr. Thompson had been on a business lunch and came back quite confused. He said he saw you running wildly across George Square screaming your head off!'

Luckily, Fanny was no wiser to the fact that Linda had taken a two-hour lunch break.

It was the first Saturday in January 1965 and the family all gathered round at Auntie Dot's for her annual New Year's celebrations. The family next door to Auntie Dot came in to join the party. They had two sons who played in a folk/country band and they popped in with their guitars, squeezebox and tambourine. Linda loved the squeezebox. Katherine 's family had one and she had learnt to master it over at their house. She picked it up and amazed everyone with the tunes she belted out. Her mum and dad weren't even aware of her musical talents or that she could play it. She backed the boys in a few numbers.

Then the eldest brother, Harry, said to her, 'Can you sing too?'

Linda blushed and said, 'Well I can try'.

The boys played the intro to 'Made Of Sand', and Linda sang with all her heart. The room fell to a hush as everyone listened intently. The lads in the band nodded to each other with a knowing, satisfied smirk on their faces. When the song was finished, everyone erupted into a rapturous applause with cries for more.

Harry said to Linda, 'How would you like to join the band? We've been looking for a girl singer'.

Linda was floating on cloud nine and quietly replied 'yes'. Harry told Linda to meet them at a hall in Anniesland Cross the next Thursday evening. Anne said that she would come along with her. Thursday came and Linda had butterflies in her stomach as she waited at the bus stop for Anne to arrive. The girls walked up the road and found the venue, which was actually the staff club of a large company. It was an informal folk gathering with lots of friendly people getting up to entertain the audience.

'We meet here every Thursday', said Harry. 'It's excellent, because it's great for rehearsals. We try out new numbers and get a true reaction from the crowd'.

'Ladies and gentlemen, put your hands together for The Honkydos', announced the compare.

Linda looked around wondering who 'The Honkydos were. Then she saw Harry and the lads take the stage. She had forgotten to ask them the name of their band. They played a few numbers.

Harry then announced, 'We have a surprise for you all tonight. We were at a party last week and were knocked out by this girl's singing and musical talents. We asked her to join the band and she agreed. So, ladies and gentlemen, we would like to introduce you to our new girl singer, LINDA!'

Linda nervously took the stage. The band struck up and she sang 'Made Of Sand'. The audience loved her and she went on to sing another four songs. Harry smiled proudly as his new discovery sang her heart out. They went to the canteen afterwards for soft drinks.

'Well, you went down very well Linda. Can we show you our gig list and you can let us know which ones you can make?'

In the following months, Linda became more relaxed and played at different venues and folk clubs with the band. Her brother Douglas bought her a guitar for her seventeenth birthday. She bought herself a book to learn how to play the guitar, and sat in her bedroom every spare chance she had, strumming and singing. Harry and the boys helped her with guitar tuition and it wasn't long until she was strumming and backing the boys. Linda was in seventh heaven. She loved singing and playing in the band. It was hard work though, because they only ever got enough for expenses, and never made any money from it. They played two, and occasionally three, mid-week nights in folk and country music clubs. Linda didn't have a vast wardrobe and wanted to have the right folksy-type clothes to wear when she was with the band, so she got herself a Saturday job in a large store to help pay for new outfits. Fortunately, her dad agreed that she could keep her Saturday money for her own pocket.

Herman's Hermits were making a special appearance at the Barrowland. Linda and Lena managed to get tickets for it. Linda could hardly contain herself, she was so excited. She had only seen them before on television and couldn't wait to see them for real. The girls got there early and managed to secure a place standing right in front of the stage. They watched the support acts. Then, Herman's Hermits appeared, but where was Herman? Everyone was calling for him and after five minutes he appeared and the fans went wild. He was within touching distance of Linda and Lena. The crowd surged forward. Linda got crushed against the stage. She couldn't move her arms, for they were stuck by her sides, and she felt the breath go from her body. The next thing she knew, she was in a corridor with people around her and a lady holding smelling salts under her nose. Poor Lena was standing over her with a worried look on her face. They had missed most of their favourite songs. Linda got to her feet and the girls stood safely at the back and listened. The girls were disappointed that they couldn't see much, but they realised that it was too dangerous to get any closer.

Towards the end of January 1965, Fanny Drummond couldn't stand working with Mr. Thompson any longer. She was 58 and two years off of retirement. She had worked for the company for forty -four years since 1921. She requested early retirement, which meant that she didn't get her full pension, but she had already been for an interview to work part-time in the office of a small jeweller's shop and they had offered her the job. This meant that her income would still be the same. Everyone was shocked by her decision, but she was adamant that she had had enough. Mr. Thompson and the new office divisional manager, Mr. Wright, offered Miss Drummond's job to Katherine. Katherine knew the job well because she covered the position for Fanny Drummond when she was on holiday. Linda was offered Katherine's job, which she accepted gladly because she always enjoyed covering for Katherine when she was away. Miss Drummond worked her month's notice and left on the last Friday at the end of February.

On the following Monday, a new office junior started. She was a smart, pleasant fifteen-year-old girl called Sally. It was Linda's job to show her the ropes. She was a quick learner and soon everything was running as smoothly as if Fanny Drummond had never been there.

It was April 1965, the new divisional office manager, Mr. Wright, called Linda into his office. He told her that she was to get a very good birthday pay rise at the end of the month, taking her annual income up £100 to a staggering £400 per year. This was because of her promotion, all the extra duties she had, and the excellent way she carried them out. She was absolutely delighted. It meant that she could now be possibly clearing around £25 per month after tax. She decided that it was time to ask her parents if she could go on her own can, which meant that she would give her parents housekeeping and keep herself. This would enable her to give up her Saturday job and concentrate more on her guitar practice and singing with the band.

Linda found it a hard struggle. Although her parents kept her, fed her, paid her travel expenses to and from the office and bought her the necessary seasonal clothes, coats, shoes and such., she had to buy her own stage clothes, make-up, nylons and girlie essentials off of her Saturday job earnings and the pocket money her parents gave her. All her pals were on their own can and they were earning much less than her. Her dad created a fuss, saying that she was too young to deal with her own expenses. Margie, on the other hand, thought that it would do her good and plucked up the courage to get Douglas to agree to a month's trial run.

Linda said, 'So if I give you £10 per month house keeping and I have £15 left to keep myself, I'll even buy my own food too!'.

Douglas said, 'You'll give your mother £12 per month, and no arguments!'

Linda replied, 'I will never be able to pay for everything off of £13 every month!'

Her dad said, 'It's that or nothing. You must learn to pay your way'.

Linda retorted, 'Well, I think you should set an example and put more into the house. If you had paid your way years ago, mum would never have had to slog over sewing machines for hours on end for all these years!'

Linda couldn't help herself from being honest. Of course, this made her dad see red. A big row erupted.

Margie said, 'Why did you say that Linda? You know what he's like'.

Linda said, 'But mum, you should have stuck up for yourself years ago. I would never let a man get away with treating me like that!'

'Yes, but I know how to handle him, just leave me to it'.

Linda could never understand how her mother always knuckled down. Before long, she was again getting the blame for being an upstart and trouble-maker, when all she was doing was sticking up for her poor, over-worked mother.

Linda took her mum aside and reminded her of the time not so long ago when Margie was pressing Douglas' postman uniform and his wage slip fell out of his pocket. Margie would never ever have gone through his pockets, but this was lying for all to see. He never told Margie what he was earning. He gave her £9 per week to buy the food and pay all the household bills. Margie always assumed that he was honest with her, giving her the bulk of his wage and taking the minimum for pocket money. She was astounded and very hurt when she read on this slip that he cleared £18 per week. She called Linda over as if she needed someone to confide in.

What's For Ye, Won't Go By Ye

Margie said, 'I would never have believed that he could do this. He's got the same in his pocket as I have to keep the house, and I have to work all hours myself to just to make ends meet!'

This made Linda feel very angry towards her dad. He wasn't playing fair. Her mum was tired working long hours and trying to make the housekeeping stretch. He didn't seem to notice and it didn't bother him, as long as he had money in his pocket for his booze and cigarettes.

For her mother's sake she handed in £12 per month, but it was a hard struggle. She gave up her Saturday job and instead took on an evening job as a waitress three nights a week in a restaurant to make ends meet. She went there straight from her office on Tuesdays and Wednesdays and worked until 10.30pm and didn't get home until 11.15pm. On Fridays, she worked until 11pm. She had to run to catch the last bus and didn't get home much before midnight. When she wasn't working, she was singing in the band or going to dance halls and gigs with her pals. Linda wasn't at home much in the evenings.

It was a sunny afternoon in the city. There was great hysteria in the streets below Linda's office. The Beatles were arriving in town again. The crowds lined up on West Nile Street because the word had got out that their car would be driving up there to the stage door of the Odeon. Linda stood outside her office door for her hour lunch break, but was very disappointed when they hadn't appeared and she had to go back to work. She couldn't see the street below from her office window because there was a balcony round the top floor and there were no doors out to it. The screams were getting louder.

Suddenly Katherine, Linda and Sally got the fright of their lives when a face peered at them through their office window. It was their trendy young manager Mr. Wright! He had climbed out of his office window to watch the scene below and he gestured for them to do the same. The girls threw down their pens and clambered out of the window just in time to see an open-topped limousine below with the Fab Four onboard.

The girls waved and shouted, 'John, Paul, George, Ringo'.

Paul looked up to the balcony where the girls were standing, nudged John, and they both laughed and gave the girls and Mr. Wright a wave. The girls found it very hard to concentrate that afternoon after their experience. They decided that they would go up to the Odeon's stage door at five o'clock. The Searchers were due to arrive around that time. They made their way to the building two blocks away where they were met with about fifty other office girls that had the same idea. The crowds began to grow when a van appeared and some young men got out carrying guitars. Girls started screaming. The young men couldn't get to the stage door, so they started running in the opposite direction up West Regent Street, carrying their guitars. Linda and the girls joined the rest and made chase up the hill.

160

As they were running up the hill Linda said to another fan, 'Are they the Searchers?'

'I don't know', said this girl, 'but they've got guitars!'

At that point, Linda stopped in her tracks. She realised that they had been hood-winked. While everyone was chasing these unknown decoys, the real band was quietly going in the stage door without disturbance.

A new company moved into the offices across the hallway. It was a subsidiary company of the one Linda worked for. The manager, Mr.Thorn, was a cheery man in his fifties. He had a secretary about the same age, called Mrs. Black. She was a lovely smiling, obliging lady. She mentioned to Linda they had a big promotion coming up and would need a helper over the next six weeks to work with them in their office. Linda immediately told Mrs. Black about her brother Douglas, who was just finishing his second year at university, would be looking for summer work before starting his final year in September. Douglas junior never had problems getting temporary work at Christmas time because his dad always got him into the post office, sorting and delivering letters. Summer was a different matter. Usually, students had to go down to the coast and get live-in jobs in hotels.

Douglas junior came in for an interview and hit it off immediately with Mr. Thorn and Mrs. Black. He started after his exams in June 1965 and got on like a house on fire with everyone, including the people in Linda's company. It was a bonus too, because he could see Katherine and they spent their lunch hours together every day. He got a good wage, as this company was also paying London rates. He was able to take home £7 clear every week, of which he dutifully gave £4 to his mother to help make up for the rest of the year when he wasn't earning. By means of a thank you to Linda for getting him the job, he bought her a big teddy bear that he knew she had been admiring in a local shop's sale for £1.

Douglas junior and Katherine were made for each other. Their romance would have blossomed had people left them alone, but they faced constant criticism about their different religions. In the end, they couldn't take it anymore and they went their separate ways just before Christmas 1965. Katherine was very upset, as was Douglas junior. Linda was there for both of them. She said over and over again, 'Don't listen to others. It's what you want out of life!' The pressure was just too much for them both. Linda and Margie were both very sad. They saw Katherine as one of the family. She was a lovely girl and fitted in so well, she was like another daughter to Margie.

January 1966 and Katherine decided to leave her job and go to London to work. She had gone as far as she could in the company. Her cousins had a flat in Archway and they told her that she would have no problem getting an office job in London. Linda couldn't bear to think about it. She was really going to miss Katherine. Meanwhile, Linda had been doing her new job for almost one year. She loved it and was getting on very well. Mr. Thompson had changed his views and was happy that he had kept Linda on, and not Alice. He realised what a smart girl she was, nothing was too much effort for her. One morning he called her into his office, Mr. Wright was there.

Mr. Wright said to Linda, 'We are just discussing replacing Katherine'.

Linda was dreading this. She had got on so well with Miss Drummond and Katherine and didn't know how she would take to a new boss in her office.

Mr. Thompson had a wry smile on his face and he said to Mr. Wright, 'You know, I think I know the very person. She already knows the job very well'.

Linda was puzzled as he carried on.

'She carries out the duties with no effort whatsoever when Katherine's on holiday'.

Everything began to fall into place. Linda's heart started beating faster with excitement as she thought to herself, *could the really mean me? I'm only seventeen. Surely they can't be offering me the position of being in charge of the sales office?*

Mr. Thompson said to Linda, 'Well, what do you think Linda? You already know the job, you would have to train the new person, and it would be silly for you to teach your new boss her job, wouldn't it?'

'Well, yes, yes it would and yes, I definitely would love to accept the job. But I'm only seventeen, Miss Drummond was in her fifties'.

'You will soon be eighteen and anyway, Linda, age doesn't come into it. We know that you are the right person, and that's why we have made this offer to you', said Mr. Wright.

Linda shook hands with both her bosses. She waltzed back to her office on cloud nine. She was still upset at Katherine leaving, but this took the edge off it. Katherine was happy for her too and congratulated her.

At the beginning of February, Linda went down to the Central Station on a cold Saturday morning. Katherine was about to board the London train. Both girls were very tearful.

Suddenly Katherine said, 'Why don't you come to London too, it'll be great!'

Linda loved the idea but knew that her mum would go to pieces if she even suggested it to her, so Linda said, 'I'm only seventeen. I'll wait until I am eighteen in April then I'll think about it'.

She sobbed as she watched the train disappear into the tunnel.

The two friends wrote regularly and kept in touch with each other. Katherine landed a good job in the accounts department of a manufacturer's office in the centre of London. She told Linda that there were tons of office jobs on offer with great pay. Linda was getting tempted, but she enjoyed her new job. She had a wonderful appraisal on her eighteenth birthday and an equally wonderful pay rise, taking her annual salary up to £550. By the time she paid tax and insurance, she was clearing just under £35 per month. Her junior clerkess, Sally, was promoted up to the clerkess job and she had a new junior called Beverley. She ran the sales office well and the girls enjoyed having a young trendy boss. Linda decided that she was happy where she was, but would see the summer out and then consider thinking about joining Katherine in London.

Linda was able to give up her evening job as a waitress. She loved to treat her mum and buy her little gifts. With the extra cash in her bank account, she bought her a quilted floral dressing gown, which was all the rage. Linda wrapped it up with love and proudly presented it to her mum.

Margie looked surprised. 'What's this?' she said, for she wasn't expecting anything.

She removed the wrapping paper and stared at the dressing gown in disbelief. She was so overcome and tearfully said to Linda, 'Did you buy this for me pet? Oh you are a good girl'.

Linda was overcome by her mum's emotions and the two of them were crying and laughing together.

Herman's Hermits were appearing in town again, this time at the Odeon Theatre. Linda had never really got to see them properly the last time at The Barrowland, so she decided this time she would treat her little cousin for her twelfth birthday. She paid 8/6d each for the two tickets. She rushed home from work and her Aunt Mary brought Katy down to Linda's house. The two girls then got the bus into town to see the show. Young Katy was mesmerised as the fans screamed in frenzy when the band came on stage and they continued screaming throughout the show. Katy was just a year off of her teenage years and had all this in front of her

Linda wanted to buy herself a suede coat. They cost in the region of £20 and she knew that she could never afford to pay for it in one go, so she asked her mum if she would come shopping with her one Saturday to one of the big suede and fur shops and go guarantor for her. The posh lady assistant wore a fitted black dress and had short black hair, neatly curled back. Linda described to her what she was looking for and the lady brought different styles out to her. While the lady was out in the back shop, Linda spotted a beautiful three-quarter length pale blue suede coat. She tried it on. It was unique and she fell in love with it. The coat cost £19/19/11d. She asked the assistant what the easy payment terms would be. The lady took a pen and paper and worked out a few figures. She came up with £3 down and over a year, would work out at £1/19/6d per month, with interest.

Linda got very excited. She knew that she would have to be sensible and pay the H.P. installment at the shop as soon as she got paid every month. As she sat down with the assistant to complete the H.P. paperwork, she noticed her mum was trying on a beautiful imitation beige fur coat. She looked so elegant in it. Linda excused herself from the lady assistant and went over to her mum.

'Do you like that coat mum?' she asked.

'Oh it's gorgeous! I am just passing the time while you are sorting out your business. I could never afford this coat!' Margie answered.

Linda felt a real sense of guilt. Here was this woman who had worked her fingers to the bone and done everything for her and she could only dream about owning a coat like this, while Linda was selfishly treating herself.

'How much is it?' said Linda as she searched for the price tag.

'There's no point in even looking at that', laughed Margie.

The price tag read £21. Linda went over to the assistant and asked her to work out what the two coats would be over a year. The assistant got to work with her pen and paper again. The two coats would be £5 down and £3/17/6d per month. Linda gave her agreement. She knew that it would be a struggle, but her mum more than deserved it and it was worth every penny to do this for her.

She went over to her mum and said, 'OK then, is this definitely the one that you want mum?'

Margie laughed, thinking Linda was joking. 'Yes, sure thing', she said.

'Don't you want to try anything else on?' Linda asked her mum.

Margie looked puzzled, her smile turning to serious confusion. 'What are you on about Linda?'

'I'm buying the coat for you mum, so you had better make sure that you picked the right one!' said Linda.

Margie stepped back in disbelief. 'You, you can't afford that Linda. How will I ever repay you?' stammered Margie.

'Mum, I could never ever in my lifetime afford to repay you for what you have done for me, but I can afford to buy you that coat. Now, do you want it or not?' Linda said with a smile.

Margie said, 'Are you sure, are you really sure?'

Linda nodded and gave her mum a big hug. Margie's eyes filled up as she admired herself in the shop mirror.

'I never ever thought I would own a coat like this. Thank you, thank you so much Linda!'

The two of them proudly walked out of the shop with their posh bags, carrying their new coats.

'Well I never for a minute thought that I would be going home with a new fur coat today. I can't wait to show it off to Betty and Mary, and wait until your dad sees it', Margie said, full of excitement.

It was April 1966 and Linda had just turned eighteen. Her brother Douglas got her and her old school friend Lena in to the student's union at the local University every Saturday night. They had a great time there because there were always some very good bands performing. This particular Saturday night, Linda tied back the top of her long dark, shiny hair and let the rest hang loose. She put on her pan stick makeup, thick black eye liner, mascara, false eyelashes and pale pink lipstick. She then got dolled up in her black and white Mary Quant 'Op-Art' mini-dress, along with white calf-length boots that had bits cut out and bows on the front. She completed her outfit with big, round black and white plastic earrings and equally big black and white plastic beads hanging loosely round her neck.

Well into the evening, a tall, dark handsome boy came over and asked her to dance. He introduced himself as Steve. They ended up dancing the night away and she lost Lena. At the end of the evening, she excused herself, telling Steve that she would have to find her friend. Linda searched in vain. She waited at the cloakroom, hoping that Lena would turn up for her coat. She stood there for half and hour until all the coats had been handed out. Then she got worried that she might miss her bus home. She had just decided that she had better make her way to the bus stop on her own when Steve appeared again.

'Are you still here?' he enquired.

'Yes, I've lost my friend. She must have left earlier', Linda replied.

'Hang on a sec', said Steve. 'We can't have you walking through the town on your own at this time of night, I'll walk you to your bus stop'.

They got to Linda's bus stop in Bath Street.

'My bus is not due for another ten minutes yet', said Linda. 'You had better go in case you miss your last bus home'.

'Oh, it's OK', said Steve. 'I have to go back to the student union to pack up. Then I'll take the van home!'

'Pack up what?' asked Linda.

'Oh, we didn't get round to talking about that, did we?' said Steve. 'I'm the roadie with the band. I take care of all their gear and pack it up and get it to their next gig for them'.

Linda said to Steve, 'Oh, here's my bus coming in the distance'.

Steve blurted out, 'Can I see you again? Have you got a phone number?'

Linda quickly took his pen and wrote her telephone number on the back of his hand.

What's For Ye, Won't Go By Ye

Two days later, the phone rang. It was Steve. He said that the band had Wednesday night off and asked if she would like to go to the pictures with him. She wasn't doing anything else, so she agreed. On Wednesday night, she got the bus into town to meet him, but she couldn't for the love of herself remember what Steve looked like! As usual, she arrived five minutes late so that he would be there first. This would give her a chance to refresh her memory and know whom she was going out with. Steve was standing at her bus stop in Charing Cross, waiting for her.

Over the next month, they went out at least twice a week. He was a nice lad. He was one year older than her at nineteen, and they got on very well together. Linda didn't feel that magic in the air. She liked him as a friend and she was getting worried because she could feel that he was becoming very attached to her. She dreaded when he kissed her, because it did nothing for her, she didn't feel herself responding and didn't want to insult him or hurt his feelings by making this known.

She decided that Steve was becoming too serious, so it was time to call everything off. She felt really sad about it, because she did enjoy his company and he was a nice respectable bloke, but she knew that he was looking for more than a friendship and she couldn't offer him that. It was the first Wednesday in May. They met up as usual and went to the pictures. Linda was dreading telling him that it was over and thought if only there was a way that she could put him off of her, so that he would hate her, that would make things a lot easier! Her stomach churned all evening. She just couldn't find the words to say.

Finally, as he waited with her at her bus stop, he said, 'Oh, I have Sunday night off. Where would you like to go?'

Linda looked up at him and blurted out, 'Steve, I think we should call it a day'.

He looked at her in hurt and disbelief and questioned, 'Why…why Linda, what do you mean? Are you telling me that you don't want to see me again?'

Linda felt awful and tried to soften the blow by saying, 'It's not you Steve. It's just that. I am really not looking for a serious relationship. I am only eighteen. I have a lot of living to do and I plan to go to London to work in a few months. There really is no future in it for us. I'm sorry, I thought that it was better to stop where we are now before one of us gets really hurt'.

She looked up at Steve and there was this tall handsome, well built boy standing with tears running down his face.

'But Linda, I really do love you. You're the girl of my dreams and I thought we were made for each other', he said, trying to fight back his tears and not appear to be a sissy.

Linda felt very cruel and struggled to fight back her tears but what could she do, it would be wrong of her to live a lie and let him think that she loved him.

166

She said to him, 'We can still be friends and go out occasionally. I'm just not ready for settling down'.

'What about next week? Can we meet up next week?' said Steve enthusiastically.

Linda told him that it would be best to have at least a month's break to sort themselves out. 'Who knows?' she said, 'you might meet the real girl of your dreams'.

Steve didn't seem impressed by this comment and Linda jumped on her bus, leaving him standing very sad and solemn at the bus stop. She looked down at him from the upstairs of the bus as it pulled away from the stop. Her heart was breaking with guilt as he blew her a tearful kiss.

It was Saturday 14th May and just one week after Linda had finished with Steve. Margie had got some beautiful, dark blue Chinese silk material and she was making Linda a dress to go out with in the evening. That morning, Linda drew the design that she wanted and, by late afternoon, the dress was complete. Linda knew that her mum was a genius when it came to making clothes. She sometimes wished that she had inherited her skills, but Linda just didn't have the patience to sit down and make something from scratch. She remembered how it had taken her a year to make a pair of knickers at her sewing class in school. Margie did teach her to take up a hem, sew on buttons, fancy stitching and embroidery, and she mastered those quite well.

Margie and Douglas were going to visit Margie's old school friend in East Kilbride. They packed an overnight bag to stay over and waited to see Linda in her new dress before they left. Linda felt great as she and Lena made their way to the Students Union, but they were very disappointed when they got there to find that there was a 'FULL' sign at the door. A very popular band was playing and it had brought out all the students in droves.

'What do we do now?' Linda said to Lena.

'What about the 'Locarno?' replied Lena.

'Oh! I don't know. I've never been there. It's full of American sailors and you know if you're even seen talking to one of them, you're reputation is gone!'

'Oh, we can look after ourselves, we're not silly little girls', said Lena. 'Let's give it a go!'

The two girls made their way to the top of Sauchiehall Street. They got to the big magnificent neon lit entrance to the Locarno.

'Are you sure we should do this?' Linda said nervously to Lena.

"Oh c'mon, stop it! We're going in now!" retorted Lena.

They paid their 10/6d at the door. Linda was amazed, she had never been in such a grand ballroom before. There was a balcony all the way round where you could sit at little tables with softly-lit table lamps and have a tea, coffee or a nonalcoholic drink. A live band was playing and, every now and then, the whole stage revolved round to reveal another band. Linda and Lena were mesmerized by this new grown up world they were experiencing. They danced the night away, but made sure that they kept away from the corner where all the Americans sailors were hanging out.

Near to the end of the evening, Lena went to the ladies. Linda was standing by a pillar at the edge of the dance floor watching everyone dancing and listening to the band.

Suddenly she felt a tap on her shoulder and a man with a Glasgow accent asked politely, 'Excuse me, would you like to dance?'

Linda turned round and found herself looking at the most handsome man in the hall. He was tall, with the most gorgeous dark curls and stylish brown suede jacket. She couldn't believe that he had picked her to dance with him. She shyly accepted and they had a couple of dances together. She was just about to leave the floor as the band struck up the last waltz.

'Aren't you going to give me the honour of the last waltz then?' he asked Linda.

'Oh, all right then', she replied, not believing her luck.

She found out that his name was James. He and his pal, Alan, were actually going to a dance hall in the south side of the city, but as their car had broken down near the Locarno, they decided to try it out.

As James and Linda finished the last dance, he said, 'Can I walk you to your bus stop?'

They waited at the stop and Linda asked James how he was going to get home.

'Oh, I'll get the blue country bus. It runs a bit later than the corporation bus. My mate's a mechanic. We'll come back tomorrow for the car'.

Linda discovered that he lived about half an hour's walk from her house, but they were on different bus routes and there was no direct bus route between their areas.

Her bus pulled up at the stop. She was quite disappointed when James never asked her if he could see her again, or for her phone number. She thanked him for waiting with her and jumped on the bus. She climbed up the stairs, got a seat by the window and looked down to wave to him, but he was gone. She was just thinking what a quick get-away he had made and accepting that it wasn't to be when she suddenly she felt someone sit beside her.

She couldn't understand this, because there were plenty of empty double seats. She turned round to find James sitting beside her.

'You didn't think that I was going to let you get away that easy', he said.

Linda felt her heart flutter with excitement.

She said, 'But how are you going to get home?'

'Let me worry about that', he smiled.

They got off the bus at the stop nearby to Linda's house. He walked her right to her door and said, 'Well, can I see you again?'

Linda was just about to give him her telephone number when her brother Douglas walked up the lane. Douglas junior was always very friendly and welcoming. Linda introduced him to James.

'I'm just going in to make myself a coffee. James, would you like to join me?'

Linda blushed with embarrassment. She had only just met James and here was her brother inviting him into the house. Their parents weren't at home, and Linda didn't want James to get the wrong idea about her. Her mother always told her to play hard to get and let the boy do the running, and she respected her mum's good advice.

As the three of them sat chatting, Linda thought to herself, can this night get any better? I was going somewhere else tonight and so was James, but we both end up in the Locarno. Now, here we are sitting in my living room and drinking coffee just after midnight. Could this be fate?

CHAPTER SEVEN

June 1966 and the romance between Linda and James was beginning to blossom. On the first date, James took Linda into the lounge of a little pub in the Charing Cross area of Glasgow. This was a new experience for her. Linda had never really gone into a pub before with a boyfriend, only on a couple of very rare occasions on holidays in Rothesay, when she was sixteen and her dad asked the landlord if she could come into the snug lounge and sit with him and Margie. Linda learned that James was an apprentice joiner and worked for his cousin, who had a joiner's shop in Maryhill.

Linda still went to her folk club every Thursday night and sang with the band, although they didn't do many gigs anymore because two of the lads were very busy studying at University and couldn't spare the time. The other one was seriously 'winching' and preferred to spend his spare time with his girlfriend. James came with her on a couple of occasions and although he was proud of her talents, it wasn't really his scene.

Sometimes James and Linda went to the cinema in Anniesland. They came out of the Odeon one evening and went up to the chip shop in the Temple area for a bag of chips to eat while walking home. As they strolled along arm in arm munching the chips, James told Linda that he had just bought a little puppy for his mother.

'Would you like to come up to my house on Sunday and see him? His name is Shandy', enthused James.

This was James' roundabout way of asking Linda to meet his mother. Sunday came and James came down to collect Linda. She had only been going out with James for five weeks and was very nervous at the prospect of meeting his mother. She dressed smartly in a floral shift style dress, with cream sling-back shoes and a handbag to match. Linda stopped at the café and bought James' mother, Mrs. Alexander, a box of Maltesers. As they approached James' home in a corner tenement block in Drumchapel's Number One Scheme,

170

which was apparently the up-market part of Drumchapel, being right next to Blairdardie and Old Drumchapel village, she felt her stomach churning with butterflies.

James laughed and said, 'Don't worry, she won't bite you!'

They climbed up to the third floor flat. James put his key into the lock and opened the door. They walked along the long hall to where James' mother was sitting by the fireside.

'Ma, I'd like you to meet Linda'.

Linda politely shook Mrs. Alexander's hand and gave her the Maltesers,

'Oh! Ah cannae stand Maltesers', said Mrs. Alexander.

Linda was embarrassed, she had never met anyone before who didn't like Maltesers, and James never said anything about his mother not liking them.

'That's all right', said James, 'if you don't want them, then we'll eat them'.

The atmosphere was strained to begin with. James's mother was a thin, bespectacled serious, church-going woman with a strict Victorian attitude. She was very outspoken, but James was her pride and joy. He was her only son, very spoiled and a late surprise, for she discovered that she was pregnant at the age of forty-two. It was two years after the Second World War had finished. She already had two daughters when she was in her thirties and found it very embarrassing to be expecting a baby at her age, especially as all her sister's children were in their twenties by this time, and she hadn't been planning any more additions to her family. James was the only young child in the family and the apple of all his aunts, uncles and cousin's eyes.

From the age of seven onwards, he often stayed weekends with his mother's sister, Annie. Annie's husband had died a few years earlier. James loved his Auntie Annie. She was a big plump, happy, cuddly lady. She and Molly didn't even look like they were related, never mind sisters. Annie never went in for style and was more comfortable in her flowery cross-over apron which she wore permanently. Her house was warm, friendly, tidy-ish and welcoming.

Molly often critisised Annie on having no dress sense and for her ideas of cleanliness. One particular year, Annie's family bought her a beautiful new black cocktail style dress for Hogmanay. Everyone complimented her on how lovely she looked. The following week, Molly went to visit Annie. As she climbed the stairs to Annie's flat, she turned round the corner on the third floor landing and was met by the sight of Annie's backside wiggling backwards and forwards as she vigorously scrubbed the stairs on her hands and knees. Molly was horrified, not only was Annie wearing her beautiful cocktail dress, with NO apron, but she was also using her big soup pot as a basin. Molly didn't mince her words, telling Annie what a clatty bitch she was. Annie just laughed and ignored Molly.

What's For Ye, Won't Go By Ye

Auntie Annie fascinated James. She could knit a jumper (with no pattern), play cards, read a book, listen to a play on the radio and have a conversation, all at the same time. The fact that Annie used her soup pot to wash the stairs never put anyone off from eating from it. It was a known fact that Annie's soup was the best in the neighbourhood. She made a big pot every Saturday and it fed the family until Monday. James' cousin, twenty-two-year-old Ernest, loved his mother's soup so much that, on Monday mornings, when Annie made his work pieces for lunchtime, she spread the cold jellified soup on the buttered plain bread. Ernest looked forward to this treat every Monday.

James tucked into his Auntie Annie's homemade soup every Saturday at teatime. This was followed by her equally delicious mince and tatties. After all the dishes were cleared away, Annie's youngest daughter, nineteen-year-old Cassie, popped down to their favourite café on Maryhill Road for the regular Saturday night treat of ice cream. During the evening, James munched his way through a mound of sweets bought for him by his cousins. Around seven o'clock every Saturday night, Auntie Annie sent James to the pub on the corner to tell his cousin Wullie, that his dinner was getting dried up and ruined in the oven.

Wullie was a confirmed batchelor in his early thirties. He worked on the railway. To say that he liked a drink or two was an understatement. James ran out in the cold with his short grey trousers, tackety boots, Fair Isle tank top, school blazer and balaclava that Auntie Annie had knitted for him. He stood outside the pub and every time the door opened he tried to attract Wullie's attention. He always ended up asking some man if he could give Wullie the message and then went back to Auntie Annie's on his own.

After the pubs had closed at ten o'clock, Wullie always staggered in, eating a fish supper out of a newspaper. He had fish suppers for his mother and James to share in one coat pocket, and a bottle of Irn Bru in the other pocket. James wired into the fish supper and washed it down with Irn Bru. Needless to say, in the middle of the night, he was up sick. It happened every weekend, but no one ever learned a lesson from it. Auntie Annie cuddled James into her big bosom, sympathising with him and telling him that he was her wee pal. She always gave Wullie and the other cousins a ticking off for feeding James all the rubbish and making him sick, but she never blamed James for eating it!

Every Christmas morning, Cassie always turned up on Molly's doorstep laden with presents from her and all the family for James. His mum and dad were very grateful for this because they weren't that well off and this eased the financial strain for them. One year, when James was ten years old, he got up on Christmas morning and went through to the living room to see a shiny blue bike propped up by the handlebars against the wall. The bike looked familiar to him. He was so excited and went to climb on it.

Hs dad jumped up and said, 'Careful James, don't touch it yet. Leave it a couple of hours until the paint dries!'

No wonder the bike was recognizable, it was his cousin's old one that James used to play on every time he visited him. His dad had painted it late at night from black to the same blue that they used for the ships in the shipyard. This was a very popular colour in the area. Lots of men worked in the shipyard and used this blue paint 'on loan' from the company for many things!

From 1960 on, James' dad Joe had lived in London. James' two sisters were now married and he and his mother lived on their own. Joe moved out when James was only thirteen. James told Linda that he found it very hard at first because he missed and needed his dad, but that his dad was a heavy gambler. His mother couldn't tolerate it anymore and life became unbearable. She never knew who would be knocking at the door next demanding money, so she told him to leave. Mrs. Alexander and James had been living on their own for a few years now. She depended on him being the man of the house.

Linda sensed that James mother was very wary of her. She gave the impression that no one was good enough for her son. When the conversation dried up, Linda diverted her attentions to Shandy, the collie dog. Gradually, as the evening went on, the atmosphere became a little more relaxed. At half past nine, Linda made her excuses to leave, because she had to get up early for work in the morning. James walked her home. It was a twenty-five minute walk to Linda's house. They stood at the side of her front door for a few minutes to make arrangements for the next night. They had a long, lingering good night kiss. Linda's stomach turned over with butterflies whenever James' lips touched hers. She had never felt like this about any boy before, and was very much in love with him.

The journey home again only took James fifteen minutes because he ran all the way. Linda worried about him walking back on his own because he had to walk along a quiet dark lane that went under an unlit railway bridge. Linda had paid for the installation of a telephone for her mum and dad and contributed for her share of the quarterly bill, but James' mother didn't have a telephone, so she couldn't check that he had arrived back home safely.

Douglas and Margie were shocked when they got a tearful phone call from Dot to tell them that Douglas' second eldest brother, George, had signed papers and put their younger brother, Andrew, who suffered from Downs Syndrome, in a mental home. Douglas and Margie got their coats on immediately, caught a No.2 bus to George's Cross, then a No. 18 tram to Ruchill. Dot and Tom were already there and Dot was sobbing uncontrollably. Douglas was furious that he hadn't been consulted with this major decision on his brother.

'We can't cope with him anymore now that Pop is not here to look after him', Angus told the rest of the family. 'We have a life to live too, and besides, Ina is tired out!'

Douglas' eldest brother Angus was very caring and easy going, but he was bullied by George and Ina and did as they told. The rest of the family was stunned by George's hard heartedness.

'I thought the whole reason for Ina giving up work was to care for Andrew. Besides, he doesn't take much looking after. He can wash, bath and dress himself, help with housework and washing up. He can make a pot of tea and cook simple things', said Douglas.

'He's no bother, we could all have taken it in turns of having him', said Dot, sobbing.

'Yes we could have worked something out', said Douglas angrily. 'Why didn't you discuss it with us first?' he demanded.

'We didn't think that you would be interested, being that you are all married with your own families', answered George in a temper.

'Well, you should have confided in us. This should have been a family decision, not just yours!' shouted Douglas.

'Well, it's done now, and there's no going back', snapped George.

'He'll never settle in there. He's 31 and been at home all his life', Douglas said as he felt tears welling up with anger at his brothers selfishness.

That Saturday morning, Linda set off with her mum and dad for the trip to see Andrew in the home out by Kirkintilloch. It was on massive, landscaped grounds. They found the ward he was in and their heart bled for him. He looked at them with big sad eyes and refused to speak at first.

'What's up Andrew, don't you like it here?' said Douglas, fighting back his emotion and tears.

Andrew looked down and never answered him.

'C'mon, we'll take you to the tearoom for something nice to eat', said Margie.

Andrew took Linda's hand and they strolled through the grounds. Linda started singing some of his favourite songs to him to try to cheer him up and Andrew giggled as she got to the chorus. This broke the ice and Andrew joined in. They spent the whole afternoon with him and as it drew to a close, Andrew could sense that they were going to leave him. He went quiet and moody again. He kept his head down and refused to speak to any of them. They cuddled him and gave him a kiss, telling him that they would be back again soon, but he just ignored them as tears welled up and fell from his eyes.

The following Thursday afternoon, Linda got a phone call from James. He sounded very shaken, but was trying to be brave.

'My mother's been run over, she's in Killearn Hospital', he told Linda.

'Oh God!' she answered. 'What are you going to do?'

'I'll be OK', he said bravely. 'I'm just worried that my ma's not going to be OK'.

'Is it very bad?' asked Linda.

'All they have told me is that she has leg injuries. They won't let me in to see her tonight. They say that I will have to wait until tomorrow', answered James.

'Oh, that's awful James. You can't stay on your own. Why don't you come and stay at our place, my mum won't mind!' said Linda.

'I can't do that. I have lots to see to, now that my ma won't be at home for a while', replied James.

'Don't worry James. I'll come up and help you with anything that you want', she said.

'Thanks Linda, you don't know how much I appreciate that', said James.

James went up to see his mother on Friday. She was in a bad way. Her pelvis had been crushed and she needed to have a hip replacement. His two sisters were there. The elder sister, Iris, insisted that James come back to stay with her and Kevin in their flat in Drumchapel. Mrs. Alexander was happy about that because she worried about James coping on his own. After they left the hospital on Friday evening, Iris went with James to his mother's flat and picked up some of his clothes and belongings. James wasn't looking forward to this. He didn't really like or get on with his brother-in-law Kevin.

Kevin and Iris got married when he was nineteen and Iris was eighteen. James was only eleven at that time. Kevin was from a rough and ready family from Partick. He had thick red hair and was known as a hard man. Many times Iris appeared at her mother's house with a black eye.

Mrs. Alexander would say, 'For goodness sake Iris, what's happened now?'

Iris replied, 'Don't worry mother, this is nothing, you want to see Kevin!'

Sure as fate, Kevin would appear, limping, with two black eyes, cut lip, and a bashed nose. James never understood why they stayed together. They battered hell out of each other. Kevin had pushed James around and bullied him from the first day he met him when James was just nine. James was now taller than Kevin and he stood up to him, but he didn't like Kevin's constant sarcastic remarks.

James tried to settle in at Kevin and Iris', but as usual, the couple rowed constantly and, at times, James had to pull them apart. He felt really uneasy under their roof. He kept out of their way as much as possible. After three days, all hell let loose when Kevin accused James of being stupid and leaving his razor on the bathroom shelf where their three year old son, Jamie, could have picked it up. James apologized. He wasn't used to living in the same house as a child, and he did admit that it was a silly thing to do. That wasn't enough for Kevin, he ranted and raved and threw a punch at James. James retaliated. Iris got in the middle of them. Then, Iris and Kevin started screaming at each other. James left the two of them going at each other's throats and went into his bedroom, threw his things into his bag and left.

He called Linda to tell her that he was moving back home.

He said, 'OK, it might have been stupid to have left a razor on the bathroom shelf and I certainly know now that it wasn't a clever thing to do with a toddler around. I will learn by my mistakes and never do anything silly like that again, but Iris and Kevin will never learn. They constantly scream and tear each other's hair out in front of their wee son. They never think just what damage it might be doing to the boy!'

James told Linda that Iris always had a very quick temper. She wasn't one for showing love and affection and it didn't take much for her to fly into a rage. When James was young, she was very protective of him and scared of no one. She used to beat up boys in the street if they dared to upset her brother. On the other hand, she gave her sister Maria, who was two years younger, a terrible time of it. She was very envious of Maria from the day she was born, always pulling her hair, kicking and punching her. Maria didn't let Iris' constant threat of attacks and verbal abuse affect her. She had a lovely personality and remained calm and happy.

When Iris was a teenager, she was always very well dressed and stylish. She cost her parents a fortune, insisting on the best, and never having the slightest concern that her parents couldn't really afford it. She never showed any appreciation and it totally escaped her notice that everyone else went without. Iris worked as a clippie on the country buses. She handed in her wages of £3 per week to her mother, but expected a lot more in return. Her attitude was that it was her parents' place to provide for her.

On one occasion, when Iris was seventeen and Maria was fifteen, Iris conned her mother when they went out shopping for new clothes.

She said to her mother, 'Oh, there's no point in Maria coming too. I know what she likes!'

After making sure that she got exactly what she wanted, she then convinced her mother that Maria would love a long, navy blue, pleated, granny-style skirt. When they got home, Iris threw Maria's package at her, then went in to her room to change into her new togs. Maria excitedly opened the parcel and her face fell when she looked at the old-fashioned skirt. Meanwhile, Iris walked out of her bedroom parading up and down in her very modern rock 'n' roll style dress with umpteen petticoats underneath, making it bounce up and down as she moved. Iris had done this so many times before, but Mrs. Alexander never learned.

It was the same conversation every time, 'What's up Maria, don't you like it? Iris chose that for you. She assured me that's what you wanted'.

Maria felt her eyes welling up, she looked and said nothing as she compared Iris' new outfit to hers.

Mrs. Alexander felt guilty and said, 'Right. I'll see if we can take it back. You can come with me and pick something for yourself'.

The following week, Mrs. Alexander and Maria took the horrible skirt back to the granny shop that she had bought it in. Luckily, they accepted her story that it didn't fit and then they went into C & A in Sauchiehall Street. Maria picked out a black pencil skirt and pink blouse with an open neck and stand up collar. She was always a grateful girl, unlike Iris. She never asked for much and kept thanking her mother on the way home on the bus, for she couldn't wait to get home and try it on. When Iris saw Maria's new outfit, she was tight-lipped with envy. It didn't matter that Maria didn't own a fraction of the clothes that Iris had. Iris even tried to spitefully damage Maria's outfit by trying it on and attempting to rip the seams by stretching her arms and legs awkwardly. Iris hated the fact that Maria was such a likable girl and was everyone's friend. Maria always managed to joke and make light of everything, which is probably why Iris managed to get away with her anti-social behaviour towards her.

Maria had a vivid imagination and loved Scottish poetry, her favourite being, 'The Sair Finger' by Walter Wingate. She recited it with all the feeling that it entailed.

> *"You've hurt yer finger, puir wee man,*
> *Yer pinkie? Dearie me!*
> *Noo, Juist you haud it that wey 'til*
> *I get ma specs and see!*
>
> *My, so it – an there's the skelf,*
> *Noo, dinna greet nae mair,*
> *See there- my needle's got oot!*
> *I'm sure that wisnae sair?"*

She also had the gift of exaggerating uninteresting, every-day stories and turning them into exciting, powerful dramas. For instance, if she had seen a man at the shops being annoyed by a poodle, Maria would come home and tell everyone convincingly that a vicious dog had severely attacked a man outside the newsagents, having pushed the man into the shop window, smashing it, and seriously cutting him to bits. No one could get near to help him because it was too dangerous, so the police had to be called and the man was taken away in an ambulance, fighting for his life. Everyone was used to Maria's exaggeration of events and took it all with a pinch of salt. Her mother said, 'Maria, one day something really will happen and just like the boy who cried wolf, no one will believe you because of your story telling!'

Iris' attitude to Maria didn't change, even after the sisters both got married. Iris was still nasty to her younger sister. It didn't help that Iris' husband Kevin was a Grand Master in the Orange Lodge. He was a staunch Protestant and Orange man, and had instilled his beliefs into Iris and his toddler son, teaching him to sing all the Orange and Glasgow Rangers songs as soon as he could talk and to hate the Catholics.

Maria, on the other hand, married Pete, who was a bitter Catholic and hated Protestants, especially Orange men. The atmosphere in the room when the two men were present was nerve-wrackingly electric, to say the least. Pete was a small, stocky, crude and selfish man with greasy combed-back hair. He had it in his head that he looked like Billy Fury. His language was dotted with expletives. He had no manners and didn't know the meaning of the word, share. He would rather sell you something as loan it to you. As Mrs. Alexander always said, 'He wouldn't give you daylight in a dark corner'. He controlled the purse strings, purchasing all the household necessities and furniture. He even bought Maria's clothes for her, which is the reason why, after Maria got married, she never looked stylish or smart. She never got the pleasure of going out to buy herself a new outfit. Pete decided what she needed and then brought it into her. He shopped at the Barra's Market in the east end of Glasgow, always looking for a bargain or something off the back of a lorry. Maria had no choice, but being Maria, she just went along with everything

Linda learned that James' father's (Joe Alexander) family was staunchly Catholic and Joe's sister, Bridget, was a nun. James's mother (Molly Alexander) had changed her religion from Protestant to Catholic when she married Joe. Both Iris and Maria had been baptised Catholics. This caused animosity with Molly's family. They didn't like the idea of them being Catholics, and were always trying to make them see the light against Catholicism. When Iris was five and starting school, Joe was still in the Marines and Molly wasn't sure which way to turn. She wrote to him, telling him her concerns. She wanted Iris to have a good education, but the Catholic schools weren't subsidised like the Protestant ones were, relying heavily on the Church to support them. She was worried that Iris would learn more about religion than the three 'Rs'.

Joe wrote back telling Molly to do whatever she thought was best for Iris, so Iris went to Protestant school. When Joe's parents and his family found out, all hell broke loose. They refused to have anything more to do with Molly or the children. On Joe's next leave from the Marines, the priest was at the door, demanding to know why Iris wasn't at Catholic school. Joe told him that it was his wife's and his decision, and nothing to do with the priest or the Church.

At that, the priest shouted very angrily to Joe, 'If your children go to Protestant school, and I see any of you ill on the pavement, then I will step over you, like a dead dog!'

Joe saw red and threw the priest out of the house. 'Right, the decision is made', said Joe. 'I'm not having any man, priest or not, telling me what me or my family should do or believe in. From now on, we are Protestants!'

Molly heaved a sigh of relief. She never really enjoyed all the rig ma roll of being a Catholic.

'Anyway', continued Joe with a smile, 'It now means I can have a lie-in at the barracks and no longer have to get up for early morning mass'.

Of course, his parents and family were livid and disowned him. By the time James came along, he was baptised a Protestant. Joe had left the Marines and was working in the shipyards. He was also an elder in the Church of Scotland. He worked very hard raising money for the Church and helping the old and needy. When Iris got married to Kevin in 1959 in The Church of Scotland, Joe's parents and the rest of his family refused to attend the wedding. When Maria got married to Pete in the Catholic Church in 1964 Molly's family stayed away from the ceremony in protest. They only attended the reception afterwards.

On Tuesday evening, Linda went up to see James at his mother's flat. She pulled out the twin tub washing machine and bunged in his clothes. Then she tidied round and vacuumed the carpets. She knew that Mrs. Alexander liked to keep her flat neat and tidy and James wasn't exactly house-proud.

On Thursday afternoon, exactly one week from when Mrs. Alexander had her accident, James called Linda after five o'clock at work. He told her that his dad had died very suddenly from a heart attack while working as a security/first aid attendant at a building site next to St. Paul's Cathedral in London. Linda couldn't believe it. She felt so sorry for him. She sensed that he was trying to be brave but she could hear the quivering in his voice.

He blurted out, 'I have a lot to attend to tomorrow, but I will call you during the day'.

Just after mid-day on Friday, James called Linda to tell her that he had to go to London the next day to identify his dad and make arrangements for his body to be brought back for the funeral.

'My uncle is going to come with me', he said.

Linda's heart bled for James. She couldn't think of anything worse than having the worry of his mum in the hospital and having to go down to a big city where he'd never been before, and at the age of eighteen, and taking on all that responsibility. She told James to be careful, and that she would be thinking about him and would see him when he got back.

'I should be back within a week. Can you come up to my ma's house and see me when I get home again, please Linda?' he asked her.

'I'll be there', said Linda.

James called her from London to tell her that he would be flying home early Thursday morning. Linda went to James' house that night. He was bearing up. He had been brought up to believe that boys don't cry and Linda could see that he was fighting the tears. He told her all what had happened, but she couldn't believe it when he told her how he had found out that his dad had passed away. He was coming home from work and was climbing up the stairs in his close. He used to always work late on Thursdays. That particular night, he decided to finish early and get home quickly to go to the hospital to see his mother.

As he came up to the top floor, Mr.Burrows, his next door neighbour, came out and said, 'The polis huv been here looking fur ye. You're dad's deed!'

James looked at him as if he was talking nonsense. In a daze, he opened his door, went in and flopped down on the chair. His brain was in turmoil, not knowing where to turn next. After five minutes, he pulled himself together and went straight up to his sister Iris' house. Maria was with her, they had just got the news from the police and were about to come and find him. They were all stunned.

'What do we do?' said Maria.

'Let's go down to the police station and ask them', said James.

Iris waited in for Kevin to get home from work while James and Maria set off for the local police station. The sergeant on duty was most understanding and helpful. He told them that the first person they must go to was an undertaker to give him all the details, and that he would take care of everything. The sergeant recommended the Clydebank Co-operative Undertakers.

The next morning, the three of them went down to Clydebank and explained their dilemma to the undertaker. He told them not to worry, and that he would take care of all the procedures. He explained that someone would have to go to London as soon as possible, tomorrow preferably, to see to the necessary paperwork and identify the body. After lots of discussions between James, his sisters, Kevin and Pete, it was decided that James would be the best person to carry out this difficult job. His sisters just weren't up to it. Although James didn't know his dad's side of the family, his Uncle Michael (Joe's only brother), was concerned about his eighteen-year-old nephew going to London on his own. It was a terribly daunting task for a young lad to carry out, so Uncle Michael decided to escort and support him and went to the station to purchase their tickets for the train journey to London the next day.

Later that same afternoon, James and his sisters caught the bus for the long run out to the country hospital to see their mother. They hadn't had a chance to see her since they got the bad news of their father's sudden death. There were too many things to be seen to.

As the bus trundled through the countryside, they sat there wondering what on earth they were going to say to their mother. They worried how she was going to cope, for she had just had a hip replacement operation and was in a lot of pain. They didn't even know if she was aware that her husband had passed away. When they got there, they looked into the ward to see their mum sobbing. The doctor had taken her into a side room to break the sad news to her. Although she and Mr. Alexander no longer lived together because of his gambling, they still cared a lot for each other. Due to her accident, he was actually planning to come home to spend his two weeks annual holiday with the family in two week's time.

'What have we done to deserve all this?' Mrs. Alexander sadly asked her children.

They couldn't answer. They all huddled round their mother, sobbing, and trying to comfort her the best they could.

Early Saturday morning, James and his Uncle Michael boarded the train for London at Glasgow Central Station. Eventually they arrived at Euston where they got on a tube and made their way to Joe's digs in Elephant and Castle. It was late Saturday afternoon. They went along to the police station and set things in motion. James didn't like what he had to do, but he bravely and dutifully carried on. His uncle wasn't very bright and not much help. He was giving the police and the undertakers all the wrong information and details. James was glad of his Uncle Michael's company, but had to tell him to stand aside and leave it to him.

The police put him on the right track and James and his uncle travelled all over London to different buildings to collect all the necessary paperwork. James was advised that the easiest and cheapest way to return his dad's body to Scotland was to fly him home. So, once everything was sorted out in London, he arranged for his dad's body to be flown home on Thursday afternoon for the funeral on Friday. An ambulance brought his mum home from the hospital on Thursday. It was too soon after her accident and hip replacement operation, and the doctors wouldn't normally have allowed a patient out so early. They understood that she wanted to be there, and allowed her out for her husband's funeral on the condition that she didn't over do things.

What's For Ye, Won't Go By Ye

James was home by lunchtime. He and his sisters sat in their mother's flat, watching the planes flying past the living room window on their way to land at Glasgow Airport. They were wondering which plane was the one carrying their father's body. Linda didn't stay long on the Thursday evening, she felt that the family needed to be alone. She didn't go to the funeral the next day, as she didn't think it was her place to intrude on the family's privacy, having never met James' dad. Mrs. Alexander was hobbling about on crutches and unable to make the journey to the crematorium. Her sister stayed with her and kept her company. Linda went up to the flat afterwards and helped make tea and sandwiches for everyone. She was introduced to James' uncles, aunts, cousins, family friends and neighbours. It was very sad, and not the way she had imagined that she would be meeting them.

Mrs. Alexander was supposed to go back into hospital the day after the funeral, but she refused, telling the doctors that she could manage. The truth was, she just didn't want to go back to the hospital, and preferred to convalesce at home. She also liked to keep her eye on things and didn't like the idea of James and Linda being alone in her house. She had got friendly with a young nurse who lived in scheme No.2 in Drumchapel.

Molly wasn't happy about James' attention being diverted from her to Linda and, in an attempt to break them up, she invited the young nurse up to visit her one Monday evening. Molly then insisted on the nurse staying until late, assuring her not to worry, for James would walk her home when he returned. James ran all the way home from Linda's and was looking forward to getting home and into bed because he had to be up at 6.30am for work the next morning. He was annoyed with his mum when he got back after midnight, only to be told that she had promised this young girl that he would walk her home. He never showed his anger, but he could tell that the young nurse was very embarrassed.

When he returned, Molly told James that the young nurse was very keen on him. The nurse had hinted on coming to the house to try to see James, so that's why Molly had invited her.

'After all', Molly said to her son, 'you're too young to be going steady. You should be enjoying life and going out with different young women!'

James replied, 'Well, you needn't have bothered trying to match-make, mother! She hasn't got a patch on Linda!'

James asked Linda to come up to his house on Sunday evening. Linda assumed that it was because his mum was not very mobile and he didn't like to leave her on her own for too long. About ten minutes after she arrived at his house, James told Linda that he had to go for a message with one of his pals. Linda assumed that he wouldn't be too long. She felt uncomfortable alone in the house with Mrs. Alexander. She tried to make polite conversation with her, but Mrs. Alexander wasn't the easiest woman to talk to. She snapped at Linda, disagreeing with every subject she spoke about. She made it quite clear that she was unhappy about the situation. James still hadn't returned after two hours, and both women were feeling very awkward. Mrs. Alexander said James had told her he had to see his old friend, Ronnie, because he had just lost his dad and wanted to spend some time with him. It was embarrassingly quiet. Linda and Mrs. Alexander had nothing in common to talk about.

Linda plucked up the courage and asked her hesitantly, 'Have you got any old photos we could have a look at?'

Mrs. Alexander seemed to like that idea, and told Linda where she kept a box of photos on a top shelf in the hall cupboard. It helped to ease the tension, as Linda showed an interest in looking at photos of James when he was young. By this time, she had realised that she dare not pass comment or make any jokes about the old photos, like most people would normally do. Mrs. Alexander wouldn't have appreciated the humour. Just after ten o'clock, Linda told Mrs. Alexander that she would have to leave and walk home, as it was getting late and she had to get up early for work the next morning. She was very annoyed with James and wasn't looking forward to walking home alone through the dark lane and under the railway bridge.

Just then she heard a key in the door. It was James and he was grinning like a Cheshire cat. Linda could feel the anger building up in her as she realised that he had been out all night drinking. She politely thanked Mrs. Alexander for her hospitality, and then turned and walked out the door. James ran after her.

'What's the problem?' he asked her.

Linda told him that she had no objections to him seeing his friends, and that if he had wanted her to sit with his mother, then he should have just asked her outright. Instead, he had pulled the wool over her eyes and made her believe that they were both going to have a night in. She told him how embarrassing it had been because she and his mother hardly knew each other. She told him how selfish and thoughtless he had been. The only reason she came up to his mother's house was to spend time with him, not his mother.

Linda felt used and was angry with James. She told him that she didn't want to see him during the week. James reluctantly agreed, and asked her if they could meet up the following Saturday. She told him that she wasn't going to put herself out for him. If he wanted to see her, then he would have to come to her house. He told her he would come and pick her up at her parent's house on Saturday evening at half past seven. He got worried that he had gone too far, and was going to lose her and telephoned her at work every day. She told him that she was too busy to talk to him. He tried calling her in the evenings, but she went up to her room after tea every night, telling her mum that she was having an early night, and that if James called, to tell him that she was asleep in bed.

What's For Ye, Won't Go By Ye

Linda got home from work on Friday night. She was feeling depressed because, the month previously, she had booked the two weeks off from work to coincide with James' holidays. All trades, including his cousin's joinery business, closed down for the last two weeks in July, which was also the Glasgow Fair Fortnight. Auntie Dot, Uncle Tom and Anne were in Rothesay for their annual month's holiday. Linda was beginning to doubt her feelings for James. She wasn't sure that his feelings for her were genuine. She decided that she would pack a case that night and get up first thing and travel to Rothesay to spend a week with Auntie Dot, in order to clear her head. She didn't bother to tell James her plans, because she was still annoyed with him for using her the way he did on the previous Sunday. She felt that to lie to her and do what he did meant that he had no respect for her. She wasn't sure that there was any trust between them.

She went down to the Central Station the following morning and caught the train to Wemyss Bay, then, the ferry across to Rothesay. Auntie Dot was delighted to see her and Anne was glad of Linda's company. They had a good time, but Linda couldn't get James out of her head. This was what she needed the break for. She wanted to find out if she could forget him. She soon discovered that she missed him terribly. She had never had these feelings for anyone before, and actually got quite annoyed at herself. Everything was swimming around in her head.

She said to Anne, 'Why did I have to go and meet this boy that I can't get out of my mind? He has come along and messed up all my plans. I could be in London with Katherine now, working and having a great time!'

Deep down, Linda knew that London didn't matter any more. All she wanted was to be with James. She had to know that he would never disrespect her again by lying . She wanted them to have an honest relationship. In any case, he might never get in touch with her again, for by this time, he would have been at her house and discovered that she had gone off on holiday without telling him. In a way, Linda felt that she had given him a taste of his own medicine. She wondered how he liked having the wool pulled over his eyes. She sent him a postcard telling him how much she was enjoying her holiday, casually making out between the lines that she wasn't missing him. She also mentioned that she was returning the following Saturday.

Linda had been going out with James for just over two months. After a week of deep thought, she decided that she wasn't going to chase after him. She liked him a lot and had special feelings for him, but concluded that if he couldn't return these feelings, then it wouldn't be fair for her to try to force him to respect and love her. There would be no point in pursuing the relationship any further. Linda had made her mind up that if James didn't get back in touch within one week, then she would try to forget him and go to London to meet up with Katherine.

Saturday morning came and Auntie Dot, Uncle Tom and Anne saw Linda off on the boat for her return to Glasgow. She felt butterflies in her stomach. She was hoping that James missed her as much as she missed him, and that he would call her. She arrived back home about half past two in the afternoon. Just after four o'clock, the phone rang. Linda nervously answered it. It was James, and he sounded very nervous. He asked Linda if they could meet up to have a talk that night. She agreed and met him in Anniesland at half past seven. He seemed quite sheepish as she approached him.

He said to her, 'Why did you go away without even telling me?'

Linda replied, 'Why did you ask me to come up to your house, only leave me with your mother while you went out with your pal for the evening?'

James didn't have an answer for that one, he seemed to realise that what he did wasn't the right way to treat a girl. Linda wasn't going to be messed around with, and if he wanted a relationship with her, then he would have to show her a lot more respect.

One Friday morning in August 1966, Douglas and Margie got a frantic telephone call from Dot, telling them Andrew had escaped from the home. They all got out there as quickly as they could. The police had been informed and had spread the word to look out for him. Douglas questioned the male nurse who had discovered that Andrew was missing.

'When did you last see him? How could you let this happen?' These were just two of the questions he fired at him.

The nurse couldn't answer. He didn't know where Andrew was or how he had got away. Eventually, everyone was relieved when the Glasgow Police phoned to say that they had Andrew in Glasgow. He had got on the country bus and the conductor had surmised that he was from the home, because he had slippers on and didn't have any money. The conductor wisely kept him on the bus, chatting to him to make sure that he didn't get off at any stops. When they got to the terminus in Glasgow, he took him into the office and called the police. Andrew was really upset when he was brought back. He shrugged past everyone, he really didn't want to be there.

Douglas said to Dot, 'We have to do something. He can't stay here, he's too unhappy!'

Douglas made enquiries and found out that George had wrangled it that he was Andrew's legal guardian, so no one else had a say. Only George could release Andrew from the home, which had now become his prison.

'How can George live with himself?' Dot said to Douglas. 'I can't believe how heartless and selfish he has become. Can't he see what this place is doing to our wee brother?'

'Legally, our hands are tied', replied Douglas. 'We will just have to keep visiting Andrew when we can and cheer him up!'

What's For Ye, Won't Go By Ye

Happily, the romance between James and Linda became more serious. They saw each other every night, except for Tuesdays and Thursdays, when James worked late. Linda gradually fell away from the folk club on Thursdays. She needed the two nights indoors every week to catch up on her ironing and mending, altering the hemlines of her few dresses and skirts up or down, to suit the style. Most importantly, it was the only chance she had to catch up on her sleep and have an early night. Linda and James didn't have much money, so James spent a lot of time at Linda's house. If it was a nice evening, they went for a walk.

Every Sunday evening was a ritual when Linda visited James' house. She always took with her a box of Cadbury's half-covered chocolate biscuits (James' favourites), and a box of chocolates for his mother (not Maltesers of course). Iris, Kevin, their son Jamie, and Maria started visiting Molly on Sunday nights too. Maria's husband, Pete, wasn't a sociable person and never visited his mother-in-law. He never invited her or made her welcome in his house. Although Kevin was a tough-nut, he did have a heart in there somewhere. He was the one who did most of the cooking at home and always made Molly welcome, insisting that she stay for dinner. He also had a devilish sense of humour. He and Maria had everyone in fits of laughter. Their personalities bounced off of each other and they had a joke for everything. Maria deliberately embarrassed James and had everyone laughing at her exaggerated stories about him when he was wee. Red-faced, James told Linda to ignore Maria, that the stories weren't true. The more he said this, however, the more Maria exaggerated and the louder the laughter got. Iris didn't like Maria being the centre of attention. She was like a red rag to a bull and everyone had to be wary of her. When she had enough and thought the jokes had gone far enough, she would suddenly raise her voice and shout hysterically at either Kevin or Maria and the atmosphere quickly changed.

One Sunday evening in particular, Maria was proudly wearing a string of beads that her mother had bought her for her birthday. Iris didn't like the fuss that everyone was making over Maria and her birthday present. During the fun and laughter, suddenly, without warning, Iris lurched at Maria. In front of everyone, Iris yanked the beads from around Maria's neck and clenched her hands tightly around Maria's throat. The beads scattered in all directions. Maria was gasping for breath and Molly screamed.

Kevin yelled, 'You psycho bitch!' as he jumped up and pulled Iris off.

Maria was stunned and very upset with Iris for breaking her birthday gift from her mother. Maria didn't have much and treasured little things like this. Linda was utterly shocked by Iris' behaviour. James was totally the opposite from Iris. He was respectable, caring, loving and ambitious. He never looked for trouble.

Molly or, Mrs. Alexander, as Linda respectfully called her, always bought a wee tin of tuna for Sunday evenings and baked a sponge cake. Linda and James went into the kitchen just after eight o'clock every week. James made the tea and put out the cups and saucers, while Linda made up a plate of sandwiches, struggling to make the meager supply of tuna go as far as possible. Everything was laid out on the coffee table in front of the fire. Kevin and Maria opened their sandwiches, making out that they were having a job finding the tuna, even Molly joined in with the laughter.

Linda weighed up the situation and came to the conclusion that Kevin wasn't all that bad. It was Iris who brought out the worst in him. Linda and Maria became great friends. They got on very well together. Iris, on the other hand, kept her distance from Linda and made it quite clear that she didn't like intruders in the family. Iris was the black sheep of the family. She always had been a problem, causing numerous arguments between her parents since she was small, and especially throughout her teen-age years.

Molly knew deep down that she was bad news. She had broken her mother's heart over and over again. Iris constantly borrowed money from her mother. She made arrangements to meet her mother to go shopping, but never turned up, leaving Molly standing outside in the freezing cold and rain for hours. Molly never gave up, and kept forgiving Iris, hoping for a miracle. This annoyed James and Maria. Their mother spent much time with Iris, convinced that this time she would change. Mrs. Alexander neglected to recognize she had a good son and daughter in James and Maria. James often tried to make his mother see sense, telling her to be much more firm and say no to Iris.

'Let her get on with her own life and don't freely hand out money to her', he advised his mother.

Maria and James could both see that their mother was being used by Iris, and that Iris was never going to change. Molly carried on being at Iris' beckon call, allowing her to control her. She listened to Iris' made-up stories, taking in the lies she jealously spun about Maria, James and Linda. Molly would then challenge the others on Iris' hearsay, which would result in disruption, rows and distress within the family. This happened over and over again, causing Molly more upset. Instead of nurturing and enjoying the good relationship that she already had with James and Maria, she carried on believing in Iris.

At the end of September 1966, Douglas and Margie got the call they had been dreading. George told them that Andrew had had a series of fits and had passed away during one of them. He was very unfeeling and cold about it. Margie broke down and cried.

Douglas' lip quivered as he said to George, 'It was that place that did it to him. How can you ever live with yourself for what you have done?'

George calmly said, 'Well he couldn't live forever'.

'Our mother would turn in her grave if she knew what you had done. Her one wish was that if anything happened to her, we would care for Andrew. You betrayed her George!' Douglas told him as he hung the phone up.

The following week, at the beginning of October, the family attended Andrew's funeral. It was very sad and everyone was in tears, except George, who didn't show any emotion or remorse. It didn't seem to bother him that Andrew had spent the last few months of his life desperately unhappy.

James decided that he needed to supplement his income. He was only on apprentice joiner's wages and that didn't go very far, especially when his widowed mother only had a basic pension. Although Linda went Dutch with him whenever they went anywhere, he was still scrimping and scraping towards the end of every week. He found out that an Italian ice cream company in Whiteinch was selling franchises in their company. There was no money to pay up front and they supplied the van, equipment and all the stock. At the end of every shift, they did a stock take and you paid them for the stock that you sold, plus a percentage for their commission. It sounded like easy money to James. He would be able to take the van out a couple of evenings per week, besides Friday, Saturday and Sunday nights.

He talked to Linda about it. She always fancied working in an ice cream van, and she agreed to give it a go. James went to the ice cream company to enquire, and they told him that before they could set him up with a van, he needed to go to the Glasgow Corporation and get his street trader's license. This would allow him to trade anywhere in the streets of Glasgow. Within a couple of weeks, this was organized and James was all ready for his new venture. He told Linda that he would take the van out on his own the first night to get used to it, as one of his bosses was going to show him the ropes and go through all his stock and prices with him.

Linda couldn't stop thinking about James on his first night and waited anxiously to hear how he got on. He called her just before midnight and told her his takings were OK for his first night, although it was quite hard going. He hadn't actually established a route for himself yet. He was driving round and stopping where he thought there was a good spot but, most times, another ice cream van stopped behind him and all the customers went to the second van. This was because they were the regular ice cream van, which left him with the odd person.

'Oh never mind, we'll soon work out a good route!' Linda told him.

She arranged to meet him at the van in one of the streets in Drumchapel at eight o'clock on Wednesday evening.

'Just come round to the driver's door and hop in', James told her.

Linda got off the bus just before eight o'clock and nervously walked up the hill, where she could see the van halfway up. There were many people round the window and she thought, *Oh great! Business looks like it is good.* She opened the driver's door, only to be faced with a hard looking Italian man in his twenties.

He stared at her and, in a broad Glasgow accent questioned, 'Whit dae YOU want?'

'Ooo-h, I-I'm awful sorry. I-I've got the wrong van. I-I thought you were someone else', Linda stammered.

Then she spotted an identical van further up the street with one wee boy getting served. As she walked up to it, James leaned over the counter smiling and waving. He indicated for her to come in the driver's door. She told him how she had gone in the wrong van and they had a good laugh about it.

'There seem to be too many vans in this area. The one behind us is from the same company and sells the same things, but he's getting the custom. I don't know where else to go. All the routes are already taken', said James.

At that, four teenage boys appeared and ordered four double nougats, four ice lollies, boxes of chocolates, toffees, two bottles of lemonade and umpteen other things. James was a bit suspicious, and wondered where they would get the money for all these goodies. Wanting to make sure that they were going to pay him and not do 'a runner' on him, he told them to show him their money before he served them. They piled about £5 worth of shillings onto the counter.

'A've bin savin' up 'n' um treatin' ma pals. Is that a problum fur ye?' said the tough looking, ginger curly haired, lad.

James answered, 'No, no problem at all!' and took their money in return for the ice cream and goods.

They walked away laughing loudly and then the smallest one shouted back, 'Hey mister, it wisnae his money, he's jist done somebody's meter!'

Linda looked at James in shock. 'You don't think he's serious, do you?' she said.

'I don't know, and I'm not hanging around to find out! Let's try the new houses in Bearsden and see if we have any luck there!' replied James.

Linda couldn't believe everything that was crammed into the van. They sold all sorts of groceries and sundry items as well as ice cream. They entered the road where the new 'bought' houses were and, as soon as they played their chimes, people came running out in droves.

'This is great!' said a very happy woman. 'We wondered when we were going to have the luxury of an ice cream man. Can I have two double sponges and two 3d pokey hats please? Oh, how much are these wee macaroon bars?'

'They are 2d each, but if you get one with pink inside instead of white, then you get a free one', answered Linda.

'Is that right?' the customer responded. 'Well, I'll take four of them as well, please'.

The other customers heard this and were clambering to buy the macaroon bars as well as ice cream, ginger, sweets, chocolate, tea, cigarettes, biscuits and even babies' dummies. James and Linda had a great night and sold out completely in macaroon bars, giving away four free ones. Their shelves were almost cleared and the lemonade crates were full of empty bottles. They drove back towards the depot, very pleased with themselves. James stopped to drop Linda off home on the way. He went through to the ice cream fridge and made up four big double nougats for her to take indoors for her family.

'Oh, are you sure James? It doesn't seem right to eat the profits', Linda said.

'We've had a really good night. We've found the right area and got it all to ourselves. I just hope the other vans don't discover our goldmine! If we continue like this, we'll be millionaires in no time', he laughed.

The next day, James phoned Linda at her office and told her that the boss was delighted with his takings. When James told him where he had been trading, his boss shook his head and told him that he wasn't allowed to take his van into that area. It was outside the Glasgow boundary and James didn't have a license to sell goods there. James' boss told him he was lucky the police didn't see him. James was devastated. So that was why the other vans were nowhere near him! No wonder he had done so well. It was all too good to be true.

The following Friday evening, Linda met James in the van in the same street as she had met him on Wednesday night.

'I'm afraid we'll just have to stick to this area and share the trade with the other vans', James told Linda with a glum look.

'It seems so stupid that the people who live ten minutes away are crying out for an ice cream van, and we can't sell to them because it is one street away from Glasgow. If we took in all that money on Wednesday evening, just imagine, we could do a roaring trade tonight, being it's Friday!' said Linda.

They drove round the streets for two hours, but everywhere they stopped, another van stopped behind them, stealing all their trade.

James said, 'I'm beginning to think that this wasn't such a good idea. There are too many ice cream vans and not enough customers to go round for us all. I'm the new boy, so I don't stand a chance. I'll have to think of another way to increase my income. We'll just do one more stop and then we'll call it a night'.

They stopped in a road that had houses on one side and, on the other side, a field stretching for about 400 yards across to another street with houses. As they pulled up, another ice cream van pulled up behind them.

'Oh no, here we go again! They're just not going to give us a break, are they?' James said to Linda.

A few seconds later, a bigger van pulled in front and backed up towards James' van. James noticed that the van in back was edging up close to him.

He realised something wasn't right and shouted, 'Quick Linda, close the window, NOW!'

He jumped into the driver's seat. Linda was confused, but did as he told her. While she was trying to get her balance and make her way to the front passenger seat, James skillfully drove the van out of the tight spot and raced across the field to the other street. Linda looked back to see four Italian-looking men running after them with broken bottles.

She shouted to James, 'What's going on? What's happening?'

'I don't think they like us, James exclaimed. Sod this! All I wanted was to earn a few extra honest bob. I didn't want to get involved in the Italian mafia!'

James took the van back that night and told the boss that he was finished. He and Linda were both very innocent and hadn't realised that it was such a cut-throat business. They weren't aware that this sort of thing went on. They certainly had their eyes opened

One Sunday night in October 1966, Maria arrived at her mother's flat, very excited.

'I've got some news for you all. I'm expecting, and they think it's twins again!'

Maria longed for children and had miscarried three times over the past two and a half years. She lost the first two babies within ten weeks of pregnancy. The last pregnancy was twin girls, who were delivered dead when Maria was six months' pregnant. Molly, James, Linda and Kevin stood up and took it in turns to hug and congratulate Maria.

Iris remained seated, lifted her teacup to her mouth and said sarcastically, 'Oh, that's nice for you', and then sipped her tea.

Molly desperately wanted a granddaughter and beamed, 'When are you due?'

'Not until the early May', replied Maria. 'Who knows? If it is twins again, it could be earlier. Because they know my history now, the doctor said they are going to keep an eye on me this time. He said they might even consider taking me into the hospital to rest for the last couple of months and stitch my womb so that I won't go into early labour. There is also a professor at The Queen Mother's Hospital who uses this new machine called a scanner. Apparently, you can see the baby in the womb and he uses this technology for problem cases like mine. My doctor says that there is a very good chance that he might want to see me!'

What's For Ye, Won't Go By Ye

Maria bubbled with excitement for the rest of the evening, talking about her baby. She wondered if she would have a boy or girl, or twins. She considered whom he or she would look like. hoping that the baby would be healthy.

'You will all have to get your knitting needles out and get busy, because I am useless and I might need two of everything', she laughed.

'God, listen to you Maria', said Iris as she stood up. Iris stared menacingly at Maria. 'You'd think that you are the only woman ever to have a baby. There's nothing great in it. Millions of woman in the world before you have done it. Stop going on about it. All this baby talk is making me sick!'

'Leave her alone. She's been through a lot with her miscarriages. Why can't you be happy for her?' retorted Molly.

Iris raised her voice and stared into her mother's eyes, shouting, 'I had a hell of a time giving birth to him', she said, pointing at Jamie, 'but nobody was concerned or pampered me!'

'You went through a normal childbirth, like every woman does. At least, you were in hospital and got gas and air and pethadine to ease the pain', Molly answered back. 'Would you like me to tell you the torture that you put me through? I had you at home, in a single end, with only a woman neighbour present, and nothing to ease the pain!' Molly replied.

'Stop it! I really don't need all this arguing. I want you all to be happy for me!' shouted Maria.

Iris scowled as she lit up a cigarette and threw herself down into the armchair by the fireside.

'Ignore your sister. We're all very happy for you Maria', Molly said, reassuringly

Linda loved kids, and James' three-year-old nephew, Jamie, loved the attention that he got from her. His parents weren't the type to make a fuss of him and, often as not, left him with either his Nana Alexander or friends. The poor little soul had so many aunts and uncles that weren't really his aunts or uncles, only people who looked after him when his mum and dad went out, that he got confused. He always a made a bee-line for Linda as soon as she came in the door, patiently waiting for her to sit down so that he could climb on to her lap. She spent valuable time with him, teaching him nursery rhymes, the alphabet and street songs. He loved the cuddles that she gave him and snuggled into her.

'You'll make that we'an soft!' said Molly sharply. 'Boys are not meant to be kissed and cuddled. They have to learn to be tough!'

Linda couldn't understand Molly's Victorian attitude. She knew through her own experience of life that a reassuring and loving cuddle was the right way to treat children and certainly didn't do them any harm. She ignored Molly's strange advice. Linda was quite firm on the idea that when she had children of her own, they would never go short of love and affection.

Avril Dalziel Saunders

It was nearing Christmas. Jamie had not long turned four years old and Linda asked Kevin and Iris if she could take him out Saturday to visit Santa Claus at Lewis' Department Store in Argyll Street. Kevin and Iris were always glad of anybody that took James off of their hands, so they readily agreed. Linda and Jamie waited at the stop on the Boulevard in Drumchapel for the No. 20 Cream, Green and Orange Corporation bus to take them into town. Jamie was so excited. He couldn't wait and talked about it non-stop.

The bus arrived and they clambered on board and went upstairs to the front seat. Jamie started singing all the songs that Linda had taught him at the top of his voice. He had been passed around from pillar to post and had so many different baby-sitters in the past that he wasn't shy and spoke to anyone. The bus was packed and Linda worried that passengers who were trying to read their newspapers would be annoyed at all the disturbance. She told Jamie to sing quietly. He looked at her, confused. He wasn't used to being asked nicely to stop doing something. Usually, he got a smack on the legs with no explanation of what he had done wrong.

As no smack was coming his way, Jamie didn't understand, so he started singing louder. Then, the most unbelievably embarrassing thing happened. He started to sing the songs that his dad had taught him, and at the top of his voice. In a bus packed full of people, Jamie belted out 'The Sash', 'Follow Follow' and more. The more Linda pleaded with him to stop, the more he laughed and the louder he sang. Linda sank down into her seat, wishing that the floor would open up and swallow her. She was never so glad to get off that bus. She tried to explain to Jamie that he shouldn't sing those sort of songs in public, but he did-n't understand. He didn't even know what he was singing about. He was only repeating, parrot-fashion, what his father had taught him.

They got to Lewis' and queued up the big staircase for almost two hours to see Santa. Every time they turned a bend on the stairs, Jamie hoped that Santa would be there. Eventually, there was Santa, beckoning Jamie to sit on his lap. Linda laughed as Jamie went completely quiet and shy. If only Santa had heard him earlier, belting out these songs, he might have had second thoughts about this little angelic blonde boy with freckles.

Santa asked him what he wanted and Jamie told him, 'A garage for my toy cars'.

'Well, we'll have to see about that, won't we?' Santa answered. 'You'll have to promise to be a good boy and do everything that you are told'.

Jamie nodded in agreement and Santa gave him a toy gun.

Linda thought to herself, *Oh No! He's going to be singing those songs AND shooting people with his gun on the bus on the way home again.* Linda reminded Jamie what Santa had said about his being a good boy and doing what he was told. She reiterated to him that he mustn't sing his dad's songs on the bus, that if he wants to sing, then to sing the ones that she taught him, and quietly, so as not to disturb other folk. Fortunately, he seemed to understand. He appeared worried that Santa wouldn't bring him his toy garage on Christmas morning, so he was on his best behaviour on the return journey. Linda heaved a sigh of relief.

When they got back to Iris' and Kevin's flat, Linda told them about Jamie singing Orange and Rangers' songs at the top of his voice on the bus. They doubled up in fits of laughter and thought that it was hysterical.

Kevin said, 'That's my boy!'

Linda was dismayed. All the good work that she had done to instill, and get through to, little Jamie's head that it was wrong to sing these songs in public, was undone in two minutes flat!

CHAPTER EIGHT

Two weeks before Christmas 1966 and Maria had to attend the prenatal clinic for her routine check. Linda took a day's holiday from work to go with her. She got to Maria's wee room and kitchen in Partick in plenty time.

'I won't be long', said Maria as she went into a cupboard under the sink and took out an empty lemonade bottle. 'Just got to do my sample urine for the clinic!'

Linda was puzzled. She thought to herself, *what on earth is doing with that lemonade bottle?* Maria came out of the toilet, clutching the now full bottle.

'That's that done, now we can go', she said to Linda.

'What in heaven's name have you got in that bottle, Maria?' Linda asked her.

'It's my sample for the clinic', she answered.

'Maria! They only need a wee drop. Haven't you got one of these wee empty shampoo bottles or something similar that you can rinse out and use?' Linda said, stifling her laughter

'Oh, are you sure?' Maria said with an embarrassed and inquisitive look on her face. 'I thought that every drop counted'.

The two young women fell about in fits of uncontrollable laughter.

Maria said, 'I've always taken a lemonade bottle full, nobody ever told me otherwise. God, what must they have thought. I feel so stupid!'

Then, realising the time, Maria found a wee shampoo bottle, transferred some of her sample into it, and poured the remainder down the pan. They quickly sorted out their running mascara.

Maria said, 'I don't suppose it would be right to take this bottle back to the shop for the threepence deposit after what's been in it, would it?' she joked with Linda as she threw it into the bin.

This started the two women off laughing again.

'Stop it!' said Linda. 'We'll never get to the hospital at this rate!'

Maria and Linda got on very well. Linda was more like a sister to her than Iris was. The women walked up to the hospital arm in arm, giggling and laughing all the way. Linda sat in the waiting room while Maria went in for her checkup. Maria was five months pregnant now and was beginning to fill out all around.

Molly was a firm believer in old wives' tales and had convinced her daughter that she was having a girl.

'Girls always are carried all the way round, while boys tend to be all to the front!' she told Maria seriously.

After thirty minutes, Maria came out beaming. 'Guess what? It is twins! They can hear two heartbeats!' She gushed excitedly to Linda just like a wee girl, 'Oh, I can't wait to tell my mammy'.

The doctor had advised Maria to be prepared to go into hospital from the end of February onwards. Now that they were certain that she was carrying twins again, they wanted to make sure she wouldn't miscarry and lose the babies. They decided it would be best to stitch the bottom of her womb closed to hold everything in place. The only problem was that it would be dangerous if she went into early labour while the stitches were in place. If this happened it would have to be undone very quickly This was the reason that she would have to be under medical supervision in hospital for the last couple of months before the babies were born.

A week before Christmas, Kevin and Iris decided to foster an eighteen-month-old boy called Jason. He was adorable, with platinum blonde hair and beautiful big blue eyes. He was very quiet and clingy. His dad had left his mother with three kids, and Jason's mother had taken ill and was admitted into hospital. The poor wee boy looked very confused. Iris sat cuddling him to reassure him, which seemed unusual for her, because she was never very maternal towards her own son. Linda had an idea that this was Iris' way of getting the attention away from the excitement of Maria's two anticipated arrivals, and worried about the effect this would have on the little boy.

Molly was having none of it and said sharply to Iris, 'If you wanted another baby, why don't you have one of your own? I can't understand why you want to look after someone else's!'

'I'm not going through that again for anyone', Iris retorted. 'In any case, we're better off doing it this way. We don't have to buy anything for Jason. The Social supplies his push chair, cot, bedding, nappies, clothes, and anything else he might need. We even get paid for keeping him!'

Linda was quite shocked at her cold attitude of being intrigued into looking after a foster child because of the money.

Little Jamie wanted a toy garage, but was also desperate for a seesaw. He had asked his parents if Santa would bring him one, now that he had a wee brother to play on it with. This was a luxury toy, and there was no way that Iris and Kevin could afford it, or the toy garage. Linda and James decided that they would skin themselves to get a see-saw for Jamie. Two days before Christmas, they went down to a big toyshop in town and picked out the one Jamie had seen. They sneaked it into Iris' and Kevin's flat on Christmas Eve when Jamie and Jason were fast asleep in bed.

On Christmas morning Jamie got up at 6am. Excitedly, the four-year-old tore the wrapping paper off, half believing that it could be a seesaw. His eyes lit up as the blue and yellow metal stuck out through the paper. He couldn't talk and was gasping with delight. He ran backwards and forwards, asking his mum to wake Jason up so that he could play on it with him. Molly went up to Iris' and Kevin's for Christmas dinner and James and Linda arrived later on.

'Uncle James, Auntie Linda, guess what Santa brought me?' wee Jamie screamed with delight.

'I don't know, what?' said James.

'A seesaw', Jamie told them, with his eyes popping.

'What! How did he get that down the lum?' said James.

'I don't know, he's magic', replied wee Jamie.

James pretended to sit on the see saw at the opposite end from Jamie and pushed it up and down, as his nephew giggled with enthusiasm.

Towards the end of January 1967, Molly went with Maria for her regular check-up at the hospital. They told Maria that it would be best if she came into hospital immediately to rest, because the twins were lying quite low down. She went home and made sure she had everything that she needed in her already packed case. Molly waited with her until Pete came home from work at three o'clock. He quickly got washed and changed, ready to take her straight back up to the hospital. Molly left to go home and told Maria that she would call in to tell Iris on the way. James got home from work at quarter to five. He met his mother making her way up the stairs of their close. She told him about Maria. James was very concerned. He cared a lot for his wee sister. He called her this because she was only 5ft 2 inches and he was a good bit taller than her, at 5ft 11inches.

'I'll go over to the phone box and call Linda and we'll all go up to see her tonight', he said.

Maria had settled in by the time that Linda and James got there. They had stopped off at the corner shop and bought her some Orange Squash, tissues, magazines and a bar of chocolate. Maria was delighted to see them and started telling them all about the troubles of the five other women in her six-bed ward. This was typical of Maria. She hadn't even been in there three hours and she knew everybody's names, where they came from, what their husbands did for a living, who their grannies were, and what they had for breakfast!

Pete rolled his eyes back and moaned. 'I'm f*****g starving! I haven't eaten anything since this morning. My belly thinks my throa's been cut! Noo that James and Linda are here to keep you company, I'm off! I'll buy fish and chips and eat them on the way to the pub. I desperately need a f*****g pint, too'.

Maria waved good-bye to him.

As he walked down the corridor, she said to her mother, James and Linda, 'Promise that you will never breathe a word of this to Pete'.

They wondered what she was about to tell them as she went on.

'Linda, do you remember telling me that the shampoo bottles were the best thing to take my urine samples to the hospital in?'

Linda nodded her head.

'Well', continued Maria. 'I used a nice wee bottle today and I did my sample, but I forgot to take it with me, and left it by the sink. I had to do another one when I got to the clinic'.

'So what's wrong with that? And why can't we tell Pete?' asked Linda.

Maria began to shake with laughter. 'Aye, but because I came home in a rush to get my things, I forgot all about it. Pete was quickly washing himself to bring me back to the hospital and he shouted through to the room, *Maria, where did you get this f*****g shampoo, it's f*****g useless, there's nae lather in it!* I had to stifle my laughter. I didn't dare tell him that he had washed his hair with my pish! This is the first that I have been able to let go and have a good laugh. Now, you really won't tell him will you?'

'We promise,! said Linda, trying to calm Maria down. 'Stop it Maria! Control yourself!' Linda said as they all fell about laughing. 'You don't want to be going into labour yet, it's too early!'

James introduced Linda to one of his old school pals, Eric, and his girlfriend, Morag. They had been going out together since they were fourteen, but it was an on/off relationship. Every now and then they would get fed up with each other, have a fling for a couple of months, only to get back together again.

Eric had been raised by his gran and granddad after his parents split up when he was a baby. Eric was spoiled rotten as a child and had wanted for nothing. His grandparents gave him everything that he wanted. His mother and father visited him on separate occasions and gave him toys and amounts of money that other children in the 1950's could only dream about. This affected him in such a way that whenever he decided to take up any new sport or hobby, he had to have the full uniform, gear or kit concerned before he would first attend. When he was ten, James talked him into coming to the Cubs with him.

He turned up the first week in a brand-spanking new Cub's uniform. That was the only time he ever attended and he never went back again. At the age of eighteen, he decided that he would take up diving and again, his grandparents bought him the best of gear. That cost a bob or two. Again, Eric went once and never went back again. He wasn't a sticker. The same thing happened with fishing, martial arts classes, and umpteen other things.

Morag was small made and very thin, with a pointed chin and black hair. She was a 'nebby', common sort of character from a rough and ready family. She had expensive tastes and was money mad. Everything she did in life seemed to have financial gain attached to it. She worked for a football pools company. She had started there at the age of fifteen and, because of her efficiency in dealing with the financial side of the business, she got on very well with the top management. When she was eighteen, she was promoted, put in charge of a staff of ten and given her own office. Weekends were the busiest time in Morag's office. All the agents had to pay in their takings by midday Saturday, then the cash had to be counted and distributed. Morag asked Linda if she was interested in either Saturday or Sunday work from 8am until 3pm. Linda jumped at the chance to work both days and earn a bob or two more. James worked overtime on Saturdays and she never saw him until late Saturday afternoon, so it wouldn't interfere with their lives.

Linda looked forward to the weekends. The job she did in the pools office was similar to working in a bank, only it was a much more sociable environment. She was on the counter, checking the agents' pay-in books, counting their takings and stamping their books paid. She couldn't believe the wages she was paid for the two days, £4 per day! She earned the same in two days that she earned in a week, for all the slog and responsibility that she had with her main job.

The joinery business started by James' cousin was doing well. They had plenty of work, so he continued to work overtime on Tuesday and Thursday evenings and Saturday mornings. With her extra income, Linda was able to save too, so she and James decided that they would use their extra money and have a holiday in the Isle of Man in the summer of 1967.

Back at Linda's house, nothing much had changed regarding Douglas' binge drinking on Saturdays and Sundays. The only difference was that there was no one at home on Friday afternoons for him to pick on. By the time everyone got home after 6pm, he had slept and sobered up. Saturdays were a different matter. Linda's brother, Douglas junior, usually went cross-country running with the Harriers and was out all day every Saturday. Linda worked at the pools office and went shopping when she finished at 3pm. She didn't get home until nearer 6pm. She could sense an atmosphere most Saturdays at teatime, and more than once asked her mother if her dad had been drinking and picking on her. Margie always denied everything, protecting her husband, which only made life worse for herself in the long run. Linda was worried. At times, she could see that her mother had been upset and crying.

'Why don't you come into town on Saturdays and meet me when I finish work? We can go shopping together'. Linda encouraged her mother.

'I would love to Linda, but now that you're not at home to do the shopping on Saturday mornings, after I have finished that, I come home to do the washing and ironing. It takes me all day. It is teatime before I know it!'

'What we need is a washing machine. It will make life a lot easier. Then, we can bung clothes into it in the evenings and hang them in the drying cupboard. That will save washing a whole week's washing on Saturday by hand and praying for a dry day to hang it on the outside line. Leave it to me! I will pick the right moment and speak to dad', said Linda confidently. 'That way, you could come in and meet me after work on Saturdays. We can go to the supermarket in town and bring the shopping home together'.

Margie liked the sound of it all, but didn't hold much hope in Douglas agreeing to purchasing a washing machine.

That Monday lunchtime, Linda went to the Electricity Board to price up washing machines. She saw a Twin Tub for £28, and the assistant told her she could have it for a small deposit and easy terms over one year. Linda went home that night and spoke to her father. She knew Monday was a good night because he had spent all his money at the weekend and would be sober.

'I think that it is only fair to mum', she told him. 'She works all week and spends all Saturday washing, ironing and shopping. I will chip in a bit extra per month to help pay for it'.

Douglas agreed with her that it would be a great asset, so Margie and Linda met up on Tuesday lunchtime and ordered it.

'We can deliver it next week, madam', said the assistant to Margie.

'Oh, can you make it an afternoon, please?' answered Margie.

'Oh, not Friday', said Linda, remembering the state her dad would be in.

'Would Wednesday after 3pm next week do, madam?' asked the assistant.

'That would be ideal', said Margie.

On Wednesday evening the following week, Margie and Linda met at the bus stop in Bath Street after work. The bus was packed, so they went upstairs. They sat in the three-seater in the back, by the stairs. At the next stop, a gentleman with a bowler hat, black umbrella and brown leather briefcase appeared at the top of the stairs. He spotted a seat in the middle of the bus but, as he made his way to it, the bus suddenly jogged to a halt. He was sent running up the passage, banging off the front window. That was enough to set Margie off. She had a devilish sense of humour. At first, she tried to conceal her laughter, muffling it with pretend coughs. Then, she couldn't contain herself anymore and burst out into a loud, hearty laugh. Linda was giggling too, but embarrassedly told her mum to stop it.

'I can't help it', replied Margie with tears running down her face. 'It was the way he ran up the passage'. She laughed and couldn't help herself from blurting out aloud, 'His wee hat was bobbing up and down!'

Margie's laugh was infectious and it started the rest of the passengers off. Just as Margie was beginning to calm down, the gentleman in question turned round and gave her a disconcerting smile as if to say, 'Are you quite finished now?' Well, this was enough to start Margie off again. She nearly choked and couldn't help herself. Linda couldn't wait to get off the bus and wished that it would go faster, not only for her mum's embarrassing sense of humour, but also to see the new washing machine.

At last they arrived at their stop and got off the bus. As they hurried up the lane, Linda had her keys in her hand at the ready. They fell in the door, laughing, to find Douglas in the kitchen with the washing machine all set up.

'This is great', he said. 'I don't know why we didn't get one before. Look! The bit in the middle is called an 'agitator', and it will swirl the clothes back and forth'.

Setting it up was as far as he could go. He wouldn't have attempted to put any clothes in, in case he ruined them.

'Right. Linda, go up and get some washing. Bring down all the whites and I will get it going while I make dinner', said Margie, gushing with enthusiasm.

Linda did as she was told. Margie read the instructions and filled the machine up with hot water.

'Look, even if you don't have hot water in the tap, the washing machine has a heater and will heat it up by itself! This is unbelievable, what a great invention!' said Margie.

Linda set the table for dinner, stopping every now and then to watch the agitator work the clothes back and forth while Margie got on with making dinner.

After dinner, Margie picked up the wooden tongs and transferred the clothes into the spin dryer. 'While this lot is spinning, we can put the dark clothes in for washing in the tub'. She was delighted with her new washing machine. 'Life is going to be a lot easier in future', Margie beamed.

The following Saturday, Margie came into town and met Linda. They went to C & A to look for a new coat for Linda. She bought a lovely dark green boucle one with a buckle belt. Then, they went to Boots to buy makeup before heading for the big supermarket in town to get the weekly groceries. They got on well as mother and daughter, and Linda was pleased that she had got her mother out of the house on a Saturday. She knew her mother never really had much of a life. She worked all week, spent Saturdays doing shopping and housework, Sundays cooking lunch and catching up on more ironing before returning back to work on Monday mornings.

Margie enjoyed listening as Linda told her all about the latest styles, music and films. They stood at the bus stop in Bath Street loaded down with bags of messages and waiting for the number eleven bus home. It was the busy time, as all the shops were closing for the evening and the buses were packed. They struggled on to the downstairs of the bus with their bags. Margie gave a big sigh as she flopped down onto the seat, while Linda stood beside her When they got home, Douglas was asleep upstairs in bed. Margie and Linda unpacked the groceries and then Linda went upstairs to get ready to go out with James while Margie dutifully cooked the dinner.

'Don't bother cooking for me mum', said Linda. 'James and I are going to that new Chinese restaurant in town'.

'Which one is that?' asked Margie.

'It's called 'Hong Town' and it is above the Classic Cinema in Renfield Street. We're going with Eric and Morag'.

'Oh giggles', said Margie. 'I don't know how you can eat that foreign stuff! It can't be as good for you as a good plate of mince and tatties!'

Douglas junior came home from his cross-country running and quickly got washed and changed. He was heading out to the Student's Union at Glasgow University.

'Are you not waiting to have dinner?' Margie said to him. 'It'll be ready in about half an hour'.

'No, I will just make myself a quick omelette', said Douglas junior. 'I am meeting someone, and I don't want to be late. I won't be home tonight. I am staying with a friend'.

'Ooooh', teased Linda. 'And what's her name?'

'It's none of your business! Anyway, who said that it was a girl?' replied Douglas junior. 'I think you have just let the cat out of the bag', laughed Linda.

At that, their dad came downstairs. They all knew that he had been sleeping off his afternoon drinking binge but not a word was mentioned about it.

Maria was doing well with her pregnancy. The professor at the hospital regularly scanned her to check her progress. Maria was fascinated by this and kept the photos of her unborn twins on her bedside cabinet. The professor told her many times how lucky and honoured she should be, because she was one of the first women to experience this new technology. It would take at least twenty years before pregnant women all over the world would receive this as routine. She had rested in hospital for ten weeks and had carried her twins for eight months. This was a great achievement for her, after her past record.

When she went into labour at the beginning of April 1967, her surgeon and his team rushed her into the operating theatre and very quickly removed the stitches from her womb. Maria gave birth almost immediately to a baby boy, followed ten minutes later by another baby boy. They were hereditary twins and not identical. The first baby was almost bald but had a very light wisp of fair hair and weighed in at 3lb 1oz. The second boy weighed in at a tiny 2lb 10oz and had a clump of dark hair. They were immediately cleaned and put into incubators. It had been a tough night for Maria. She was shattered and doped up on pethidine. She was so proud of herself and couldn't wait to speak to her husband, who had been waiting outside in the corridor. Pete was beaming. It never occurred to him to tell Maria what a good job she had done. He actually took all the credit for the twins, telling everyone that he had fired two f*****g darts with the one f*****g arrow.

Molly came up to the hospital with James and Linda the following day.

'Oh well', said Molly with a sigh. 'Another two grandsons. Maybe one day I'll get my granddaughter!'

'Well, don't look at me mammy', said Maria. 'I never want to go through that again! I'll leave that to James and Linda. I'm just happy that my babies are well'.

'Och, every woman says that!' replied Molly. 'You'll soon forget!'

Maria came out of the hospital ten days later but had to leave her babies behind until they got stronger and put on some more weight. Pete built a box, which resembled a large drawer. He lined the bottom of it with a spongy foam and screwed on four black legs from an old coffee table to each corner. This was to be the babies' first bed when they got home. They called the eldest and biggest twin Adam, and the smaller one, Greg. Within three weeks, Adam had reached 4lb 12oz and was allowed home. He rolled about in the big box all by himself for another three weeks until Greg came home, weighing a healthy 4lb 10oz. Now Maria had her work cut out! Pete acquired a big, old-fashioned green and cream, hard bodied, bouncy, twin pram and Maria was as pleased as punch with it. She couldn't wait to take her babies out in Partick and show them off.

Eric's girlfriend Morag passed her driving test. It was just before her eighteenth birthday and her parents bought her a Singer Chamois car. James had passed his driving test not long after his seventeenth birthday. His dad had bought him a car, but it was an old Vauxhall Velox. It cost £25 and lasted about three months before being scrapped, so Linda never had the privilege of even seeing it, never mind being taken out in it.

What's For Ye, Won't Go By Ye

One Saturday at work, Morag said to Linda, 'Do you fancy the four of us go for a run out to the Duck Bay Marina Hotel at Balloch tonight? I'll drive us there. I've heard that they have a discotheque and we can get something to eat too!'

Linda told Morag that she would love to go but, that James and she had already agreed to go out for a drink with his best friend Alan and his new girlfriend Helen.

'Oh! Ask them if they would like to come. I'd like to meet her too! The six of us can easily squeeze into my car!' replied Morag.

Linda thought that it would be nice to do something different for a change. She got home from work, soaked in a nice warm bath and then took out her little blue mini skirt outfit with matching jacket. James arrived at her house at 7pm.

'Wow, you look gorgeous!' he told Linda. 'Are you expecting to go somewhere nice?' he chuckled.

'Well, actually, Morag's offered to drive us down to Balloch for a meal and a discotheque. She said that Alan and Helen can come too!'

'Oh? That's very nice of her. I wish I'd known. I thought we were just going to the pub. I would have put my suit on!' said James.

'You're fine as you are', said Linda. 'There's nothing wrong with grey trousers and a blue jacket. Besides, you always look smart! You really need to talk to your mother about getting a telephone installed. Nearly everyone has got one now, and it would be so much easier for us all to keep in touch. Maria could call her when she needs motherly advice, Iris could call and let your mother know when she's not going to turn up to meet her, instead of leaving her standing frozen on a street corner in town, and, most importantly, I could have let you know about tonight!' Linda said with a cheeky grin as she locked her arms round James and kissed him tenderly.

'Aye, yer right', said James. 'My mother's getting on and I'm never in. She should have a phone for her own safety, if nothing else. Can you arrange it Linda? I will pay for the installation'.

'Consider it done', replied Linda. She was quite relieved because being able to communicate by telephone would make life easier for everyone concerned.

It was a beautiful Spring evening when Morag and Eric pulled up in the car outside Linda's house at 7.30pm. James and Linda clambered into the back seat.

'Hey, it's great having a bird that drives', said Eric. 'Not only does it mean that I get to go to lots of places impossible to get to by bus, but I can have a drink and not worry about what time I get home!'

'Don't be too sure, pal!' replied Morag. 'I might just dump you out at Loch Lomond. Then how would you get home?'

'You wouldn't do that…would you?' questioned Eric.

'Just try me! You better not step out of line Eric!' answered Morag.

He tried to make light of Morag's remarks by laughing them off. He would have liked his friends to believe that he was the boss in the relationship, but everyone knew that Morag wore the trousers and he was right under her thumb.

'We have to go and meet Alan and Helen at the bar in the Boulevard', said James. 'I told them we'd be there at 7.30pm. They should be waiting for us, but mind you he's never on time!'

Morag parked outside in the pub car park, while James ran in to get Alan and Helen.

When they came out, Alan took one look and said in disbelief, 'The six of us will never fit into a Singer Chamois!'

'Want to bet?' said Eric, as he greedily climbed into the front passenger seat

'Oh, aye! Pull up the ladder, I'm in. Some people never change. He always makes sure he's got the best!' muttered Alan sarcastically under his breath.

James and Alan sat on the outsides of the back seat while Helen and Linda sat in between them with their legs over their boyfriends' laps.

'Oh, you should see what your missing Eric!' teased James and Alan. 'This is really cosy, much better than sitting in the front on your own!'

Eric gave them a look and said, 'Who are you kidding?'

Linda told them that she and James were going to Isle of Man for the Glasgow Fair Fortnight.

'Ye'r daft!' exclaimed Morag. 'Ye can go to Spain for half the price and yer guaranteed sunshine. That's where we're gauing. The Bacardi's cheaper than the coke tae! Why don't ye cancel it and come wae us?'

Linda and James told Morag that they would think about it, but they knew that they had no intention of canceling. They were excited about having a holiday on their own. They hadn't ever been to Isle of Man before and were looking forward to the experience.

They arrived at their destination. It was a beautiful mild night. Later in the evening, they walked down through the hotel grounds to the Loch. Ben Lomond stood tall in the background as if he was the chief mountain, while the other hills proudly bordered the Loch. The light of the moon in the glorious red sky shone down on the calm waters and lit up the mountains, showing off their different shades of green. In the distance, they could see a mild ripple as a man in a wee canoe rowed across to the pub at the other side of the Loch.

'This is wonderful. It's a different life!' said Linda.

'Aye, we must do things like this more often, now that I have a car. It's not far!' said Morag.

'Oh! We'd love to!' said Linda enthusiastically as they all climbed back into the car for the journey home. 'It's great to go somewhere else other than into town on a Saturday night. I love the country side. Thanks very much for bringing us out here tonight Morag!'

'Yes, it's been brilliant Morag, thanks for asking us!' echoed Helen.

'No bother, next time us girls will leave the boys at home, then we'll really enjoy ourselves!' Morag laughed.

They were nearing Dumbarton when Morag said, 'You know what? I desperately need a pee. I should have went before we left!'

Linda said, 'Me too, but there is no way that we'll find a toilet open at this time of night!'

Just at that, Morag pulled into the side of the road on the outskirts of the town and stopped the car.

'This'll do nicely', she said, pointing to an advertising billboard. "Let's go behind there!'

'Oh, now that you two are talking about it, I need to go too', said Helen.

The girls climbed out of the car and ran around to the back of the billboard, breathing a sigh of relief. When they got back to the car James, Alan and Eric were in stitches.

'What's so funny?' demanded Morag.

'You three thought that you were being so discreet', replied Eric.

'You would have been just as well to have gone in the gutter!'

'What are you on about?' asked Morag.

'Well, look at that billboard. The bottom of it is trellis. We could see everything and, what's more, it has spotlights at the top of the board shining down. You gave everyone that was passing a lovely show of bums!'

Morag, Linda and Helen looked in disbelief. He was right! How could they not have noticed that?

'Och well, who cares?' shrugged Morag. 'They might have enjoyed the bum show, but nobody saw our faces, so they'll never know who the bums belonged to!'

James saw a wee white Ford Anglia van for sale and decided to buy it. It cost him £120, he paid £20 down and the balance in monthly payments over two years. It made a big difference to his and Linda's life. At work, he was able to get round his jobs much quicker than he ever did when he had to travel by bus, so his cousin gave him a small rise. Linda and he went for runs all over the place and discovered beauty spots in Scotland that they never knew existed. Loch Lomond and the Trossachs were their favourite places to go. Most of all, they loved to drive to Balmaha with a picnic and sit at the wee pier, taking in the breathtaking beauty of the hills and mountains surrounding them. As the warm summer evenings approached, it became a regular thing to take James' mother out with them. She would only have been sitting on her own at home otherwise, and Linda never minded her tagging along. Linda always climbed into the seat that James had fitted in the back, to allow Molly to sit comfortably in the front, although Molly never showed any gratitude for Linda's understanding. She carried on childishly, making it clear that it was her son's car and she had more rights than Linda. She still couldn't help herself from being envious of the attention that James gave to his girlfriend.

Maria told Linda not to worry about Molly.

'It's not you Linda!' said Maria. 'It would be any girl. My mother likes to possess her children. She would be quite happy for us all to stay single and keep her company for the rest of her life. She is selfish and never considers anyone else's feelings. She was the same with Iris and me when we were going out with Kevin and Pete. You have got it worse though, because she has been on her own with James for such a long while. Not only is he her only son, but he is also the last one at home. You are another female, stealing her limelight. Just ignore her and don't let her get to you Linda!'

Linda was very good to Molly. She tried to win her round, but Molly never recognised this. She seemed to bear a grudge against life and her attitude was 'Blood's Thicker Than Water' She continued to keep Linda at a distance and took her generous nature for granted. Eventually, Linda reluctantly gave up trying and treated her with the contempt she deserved. Linda would have liked nothing better than to have had a good relationship with James' mother, but came to the conclusion that there was no point. There was nothing else she could try. She could not force Molly to like her, but, at the same time, Linda couldn't help thinking that Molly was a fool to be missing out on a good friendship. James was always telling Linda that his dad would have loved her and would have put Molly in her place. Somehow, James never had the courage to face up to his mother himself and continued to ignore the hurtful remarks and insults that she threw Linda's way.

June 1967 and the twins were three months old. Poor Maria was absolutely shattered. No sooner had she fed and changed one twin when the other one wakened up, needing the same. By the time the second one was seen to, the first one needed attention again. This went on twenty-four hours a day. Pete wasn't any help whatsoever. He wouldn't feed either of the babies with a bottle and most definitely would never change a nappy, saying it was women's work. Meanwhile, Pete came home every day at 3pm after the pub closed. A local firm employed him to do 'job and knock' and although he got a full day's rate of pay, he never worked more than five hours. He sprawled out on the settee with his working clothes on, cigarette in his hand and a beer on the floor beside him, getting in Maria's way. Although they owned their wee flat, it was very small. They couldn't afford to upgrade and buy a larger one.

Maria couldn't take anymore. She was getting claustrophobic. She went to the council housing office and, almost in tears, explained her predicament. She explained to them about how overcrowded they were in a one bedroom flat, that they desperately needed a bigger place with at least one more bedroom. She said how difficult it was for her to get out with twin babies because they lived three stairs up. After much form filling over the next few weeks and many interviews, Maria was delighted when a letter arrived from the housing department, offering them a ground floor, three apartment flat near her mother in Drumchapel. Maria was over the moon. Pete sold their flat for £120 and they moved into their council flat within weeks.

On Sundays, after Linda finished working at the pools office at three o'clock, she made her way to Maria and Pete's house. She helped Maria get the twins dressed. Then the two of them set off to catch the bus to Molly's house, with one baby each wrapped in the shawls that Molly had crocheted for them. Maria looked forward to this every week. It was the only break that she got from the twins. Every one wanted to fuss over the babies, so it gave her a chance to have some quality time to herself. Iris had given up on the idea of fostering children, it interfered too much with her social life. At the end of the night, James dropped Maria and her babies back at their house in his van before taking Linda home.

The Fair Fortnight arrived and James and Linda were full of excitement at the thought of their first holiday together. They took their cases down in the van the night before to the Central Station and put them in left luggage. Saturday morning came and James said goodbye to Molly. She was very quiet. She didn't relish the thought of being on her own for two weeks. She couldn't stay with any of her daughters. There was no peace and quiet in Iris and Kevin's house, and Pete never made her welcome for a visit, never mind living there. James parked his van in the street at the back of Linda's house. Margie had made Linda and James some sandwiches and a flask and gave them a box of chocolates to eat on the way. Douglas and Margie wished them a safe journey and told them to enjoy their holiday. They reminded them to send a postcard.

As they stood at the door and waved them off, Margie pointed to her hip and discreetly mimed to Linda, 'Have you got your money OK?' Margie had sewn a secret pocket inside a corset for Linda to keep her money in.

Linda laughed and shouted 'YEESSS mum!' as she and James walked hand in hand up to Knightswood Cross to catch a bus into town.

They got to the Central Station in plenty time. There were one and a half hours to spare before the train left for Stranraer to meet up with the ferry for Isle of Man. As they approached the left luggage lockers, James went into his wallet to get his key for the locker.

'Oh no, where is it?' he panicked. 'Oh God, I remember now. I was sorting out this wallet with my holiday money and I took the key out and left it on my dressing table'.

'What are we going to do now?' said a very worried Linda.

'I'll phone my mother and ask her to pick up the key and get a taxi into town. She should be here in half an hour!' James answered.

They hurried to the phone box and quickly dialed Molly's number, but their hearts fell when there was no reply.

'Oh, I don't believe it! She never said that she was going out this morning! There's only one thing we can do now. We'll have to jump in a taxi and ask him to wait while I pick the key up. He can bring us back to the station again!' James said.

By this time, he was feeling angry with himself for being so silly. It had been his idea to take the luggage down the night before in his van so that they could relax and travel into town by bus with no cases and save the taxi fare. Now, they were going to have to rush like mad, pay a taxi fare to Drumchapel and back again. There was the horrible thought that they might not make it. There wasn't another train until Monday and the fare wasn't refundable. So, stomachs churning, they hailed a taxi and told the driver of their dilemma. They got to James' house within twenty-five minutes. He ran up the stairs and appeared five minutes later with the key. Linda breathed a sigh of relief, but it wasn't over yet. They had to get back to the station and the Saturday morning traffic was beginning to build up. Then, they had to get to the left luggage lockers before getting to the platform to board the train. The taxi driver took back streets to avoid the jams and whizzed as fast as he could back to the Central Station. James pressed a £10 note into Linda's hand instructing her to pay the driver while he ran on to collect the luggage. Linda did this and then ran towards the left luggage lockers.

James was just getting the second case out of the locker when he shouted to Linda, 'Start running towards the platform. I'll see to the cases'.

The train was full as she ran up the outside to look for seats. James wasn't far behind her. Linda looked down and saw the guard preparing to blow his whistle. Luckily, it was a corridor train.

'Let's just get on board and we can walk through and find a seat', she shouted to James.

Eventually, they found a compartment with only two people in it. They flopped down on the seats, exhausted after their experience. They started to laugh about it all and congratulated themselves on their wonderful timing, although they were already down on their holiday money because of the taxi fare. They were famished and ready for Margie's sandwiches now and tucked in before settling down for the long journey to the Isle of Man.

Luckily, it was a beautiful sunny day. The Irish Sea was calm and they sunbathed on the deck as they sailed across the waves to the Isle of Man. The big ship docked at Douglas Pier at 3pm and James and Linda looked all around them, trying to take in all the sights as they disembarked. They had a little map from the landlady of the bed and breakfast boarding house. This wasn't far from the pier, only up a hill and three streets away. They had both saved hard for this holiday. Linda had £30 in cash and James had £60 in his post office savings account. They stopped off at the post office on their way to the boarding house to collect the remaining £10 balance owed for their stay from James savings account.

'What say we don't go mad and just try to manage on your cash for the first week. Then, we can really go to town and have a ball the second week with the £50 left in my savings account', James offered. Linda thought this was a good idea and went along with it.

They knocked on the door of the big Victorian house and a little thin old lady with a big smile answered.

'Oh, you must be Mr. Alexander and Miss MacGregor', she said with an eccentric giggle as she beckoned them into her home.

Before leading them up the big staircase, she introduced herself and her spinster sister as the two Miss Jeffreys.

'I am the elder and she is the younger, but only by eleven months', she teetered.

She showed Linda into a wonderful big front upstairs room, then she said to James, 'Right young man, come with me and I'll take you to your room'.

She led him up a narrow, steep staircase to the attic and into a small front room with a sloping ceiling which anyone over 5ft 4ins would have a problem with. James, being 5ft 11ins, could only stand straight up on one side of the room.

James and Linda decided to leave their unpacking until later and go out to discover the resort of Douglas. They walked back down to the front and hopped onto a horse-drawn tram, which took them all the way along to the other side of the promenade. They got off and walked back, stopping off for an ice cream on the way. Then they had a stroll around the town. They got back to their boarding house and washed and changed, ready to go out for dinner. They found a nice little restaurant in the town and enjoyed a meal of steak pie, potatoes and peas before heading for a pub for a singsong. They got back home again late. James gave Linda a goodnight kiss outside her bedroom door then climbed upstairs to his room. It didn't take long for them to fall fast asleep after such a long day.

They got up bright and early the first morning and were first down for breakfast. The younger of the old sisters did the cooking, while the elder served breakfast. She was bent over with age, hard of hearing and had an infectious, cheeky giggle. She welcomed the young couple into the dining room and showed them to their table. This was a new experience for Linda. She had never stayed at a hotel or boarding house before. James had though, because, years ago, his dad used to organise trips for the neighbours to Blackpool for the illuminations, and James always went along with his parents.

The elder Miss Jeffreys told Linda and James to help themselves to cereal and orange juice, and that she would bring their fried breakfast through when they were ready for it. Just as they finished eating their corn flakes, a grumpy Glaswegian man in his sixties sat at the next table. He ordered the two old ladies about and they jumped to attention for him. Linda and James gathered that he was a regular at their boarding house.

The elder Miss Jeffreys brought him a cup of tea, he took a mouthful, spat it out and bellowed, 'I don't take sugar! How many times do I have to tell you that!'

The poor old lady apologised and got all panicky. She quickly picked the cup up and it rattled around the saucer as she nervously hurried back to the kitchen with it.

Linda and James soon learned that this was the first of many times that this grumpy man was to shout at the old, eccentric sisters. Every morning, when his cup of tea came through, James and Linda looked at each other, smiled and waited for it.

'I don't like sugar! How many times do I have to tell you?' he rudely complained at the top of his voice, without any concern for the other guests.

The weather was wonderfully hot and sunny and the first day they went onto the beach, they hired deck chairs and Linda got her orange bikini on.

Just as they were about to settle down, this voice suddenly belted out across the beach, 'James Alexander! What are you doing here?'

Linda couldn't believe it. The beach was mobbed and there were hundreds of folk on it. Who was standing about five feet away from them but James' friend Ronnie, with a couple of his mates. Ronnie was the one that had almost split James and Linda up when they went out that Sunday night and left her sitting with Molly. He was the last person she had hoped she'd ever bump into. The boys pulled up deck chairs alongside and talked to James, while Linda lay quietly sunbathing.

After about half an hour, Ronnie held his hands out, looked up to the sky and said, 'Well boys, it looks like rain. I think we better make for the pub!'

It was a blissfully hot day with not a single cloud in the sky. The lads laughed and folded up their deck chairs.

'Are you coming James?' his mates sang out. Linda couldn't believe what she was hearing and stared at James.

'No, I'm quite happy here', he said. 'I'll catch up with you another time'.

That was the last they saw of the lads and Linda didn't complain about that.

The first week seemed to go in very quickly, they packed so much into it. They went up Snaefell on the Manx Railway, went to lots of shows, hired bikes and cycled to Ramsey, went on a coach tour to the other side of the Island and said good morning to the fairies. James took Linda to her first wrestling match. She wasn't really looking forward to it and only went to please James. She couldn't believe how much she got into it, and couldn't control herself. She was standing up shouting at the baddie and telling the referee how useless he was. The final straw came when she really embarrassed James by running down the aisle and belted the referee with her handbag. James swore blind that he would never take her to another wrestling match as long as they lived.

Linda laughed and said, 'Well, how was I to know that I would get so carried away? Anyway, I really enjoyed myself, if you must know!'

Linda's cash lasted up until Thursday night. On Friday, they went to draw the cash from James account for the remaining nine days. They were shocked to learn from the post office assistant that James was only allowed to make one withdrawal of £10 per week, then, £3 per day afterwards. As James had already withdrawn £10 the previous Saturday, he wouldn't be allowed another £10 until the next day. They only had £3 on Friday for entertainment and food.

'It's just as well that breakfast is included at our boarding house, otherwise we would starve', said Linda.

They wondered how on earth they were going to manage for the next nine days. They had spent £30 in the first six days alone. The £3 for Friday, then the £10 that they were allowed on Saturday, plus, the next seven days until they left, at £3 per day, only amounted to £34. This was never going to be enough to pay for everything for the rest of their holiday! They hadn't bought presents, sent post cards or bought stamps yet! They tried to explain their predicament to the post office assistant, but he didn't want to know. James was angry and felt annoyed with himself for not checking this out beforehand. If he had known this, they could have drawn £3 per day from the day they arrived. That, along with the £30 cash Linda had would have been more than enough. There was only one thing for it, the second week they had to calm down and spend most of the time walking and sitting on the promenade eating one portion of fish and chips from the paper between them for their main meal.

'It's so annoying', said James. 'I have all that money in my account. It's mine and they won't let me have it! When I get back, I am going to withdraw the lot and put it into a bank'.

They sailed out of Douglas Harbour for Stranraer early on Saturday morning before the post office opened, so they had no money for the journey. They were famished and thirsty when they finally reached Glasgow Central Station and were very glad to be home. Linda sat with the cases while James ran round to the post office to withdraw £10 before they closed for the day. Wearily, they got into a taxi to Linda's house. James said that he would be back down for her at 8pm, then he got into his van and drove home.

Margie and Douglas were waiting to hear all about her holiday and were very concerned when Linda told them how they couldn't get their money out of the post office and had to cut down on everything for the second week.

'Never mind, you're home now!' said Margie, hugging her daughter. 'You must be starving. What would you like me to make for you?'

Molly was pleased and relieved that James was home again, and made a fuss of him. She didn't enjoy being on her own one little bit. James unpacked and then had a shower. Molly asked him why he was ironing his shirt.

'Surely that can wait until tomorrow', she said.

'No, I'm wearing it to go to Linda's tonight', he replied.

'What! Haven't you two seen enough of each other over the past two weeks?' retorted Molly 'I thought that you would be spending a nice evening in with me, being that we haven't seen each other for two weeks!'

James felt badly, but he wanted to see Linda. He pacified his mother by telling her that Linda and he would both be spending the next night at home with her as they usually did on Sundays, so she could look forward to that. Molly wasn't happy, but she didn't argue.

New Year 1967 and James was down at Margie and Douglas' house to bring in 1968 with Linda and her relatives. Not long after midnight, there was knock on the door.

'Quick Douglas. You get the door, that'll be our first foot!' said Margie.

Douglas opened the door to see his son's university friend Charlie standing there with an open bottle of whisky in one hand, a lump of coal in the other and a silly grin on his face.

What's For Ye, Won't Go By Ye

'Happy New Year, Mr. MacGregor', slurred Charlie as he shoved the bottle and coal into Douglas' hands and walked in the door.

He was followed by his girlfriend and a string of sixteen students. Ten minutes later, Douglas junior's University professor, along with his wife, arrived. Douglas junior had invited them for New Year's also. This wasn't unusual for Douglas junior to invite everyone round to his parents' house. Often, on a Saturday night, he called his parents to ask if they would mind if he brought a few pals round. Mary and Betty, and their husbands, were usually there too, and it always ended up a rousing party, which was enjoyed by all. As often as not, the pals would stay the night and Margie got up on Sunday morning and made breakfast for everyone. It was a godsend for Margie, because her husband always behaved himself on these occasions. He liked to be the centre of attraction and the life and soul of any party. Fortunately, when others were around, his Jekyl and Hyde nature would never show.

After almost an hour of wishing everyone 'A Happy New Year', Linda and James left to first foot Iris and Kevin, who were throwing a party. Molly, Maria and Pete were already there. James and Linda plowed through the deep snow on the Great Western Road. It was a long, long walk to Iris and Kevin's house and would probably take them the best part of an hour. They were hoping to catch a taxi, but they were all driving past with their 'For Hire' signs down. Linda saw a taxi in the distance and stepped out to the edge of the pavement. Suddenly she heard a 'crack' and fell over in the snow. She had actually stepped off the pavement and on to the road without realizing it because the snow had leveled off the road and pavement. It was a deep step down and her ankle ached. Fortunately, she was wearing long boots, which helped to support her leg. They got into the taxi and headed for the party.

James was concerned about Linda's foot. 'Don't worry, the pain will soon go. I've only sprained my ankle', she said.

She hobbled up the stairs to the party and was relieved to find an empty armchair to flop down onto. James helped her remove her boot, which was a painful process. Linda sat resting her sore foot on a stool, still convinced that she had only sprained her ankle. The party started off with everyone being friendly and polite. Then, as they got more to drink, they had the usual Glasgow sing-a-long. Everyone had their own songs. Iris and Kevin's neighbours were a rough and ready Irish couple called Theresa and Danny. They had seven children ranging from eleven years down to eighteen months, who were all tucked up in bed next door. They sang all the Irish rebel songs, which delighted Pete, who joined in loudly with 'The Wild Colonial Boy' while Kevin sat seething.

Kevin lost his temper and ordered them to stop singing these songs in his house, or get out. An argument erupted and James got between Kevin and Danny while Theresa and Iris screamed at each other. Linda sat there absolutely dumbfounded, while everyone was throwing punches. She had never seen anything like it and couldn't even move to help James. Molly was crying and upset, telling Linda that this was how all of Iris and Kevin's parties turned out. Meanwhile, tight-fisted Pete was using the distraction of the occasion to fill his glass with more whisky.

Theresa was over by the window and screamed out, 'Quick Danny, some bastard's siphoning petrol from our van!'

Everyone rushed to the window to see a lone figure standing there, tube in hand, filling a can from the few cars that were in the street. This distracted everyone from the original fight. They all united and rushed off down the stairs to catch the fuel thief. Pete had downed almost a bottle of whisky by himself during all the commotion and was more than ready to go home. The twins were fast asleep in their big twin pram. Fortunately, they were only a five minutes' walk away from their house. Danny and Theresa went home.

As soon as they left, Kevin said, 'Right! Now we've got rid of the Tim's, let's have some proper music!' He played, 'The Sash' at top volume and kicked his legs high.

The next thing, the front door was getting banged as if someone was about to break it down. It was Danny. The Orange music was thumping through the wall to his house and he was furious. Another punch up started. By this time, it was 6am and Linda had had enough. Her ankle was so swollen that she couldn't get her boot back on.

James said, 'I'm taking you to the hospital to have that x-rayed'.

Linda protested.

'Don't argue', said James. 'That ankle needs looking at!'

He went down to the street and hailed a taxi and helped Linda down the stairs and into it. They got to the Western Infirmary and waited in the casualty department. It was very busy, there were a lot of unfortunate people with different injuries ranging from cutting themselves on broken glass at parties or, like Linda, fallen over in the snow.

While they were sitting there, James apologised to Linda for his family's bad behaviour saying, 'You can choose your friends but you're stuck with your family!'

He seemed embarrassed for them and told her that whenever there was a family party and Pete left first, the Orange songs got big licks as soon as he was out of the door and, vice versa, if Kevin's the first to leave, then the Irish rebel songs get played.

James told her that he didn't see the point in it all and couldn't understand why people were so bigoted. 'If that's what religion does for you, then I don't want any of it!' he said.

Linda told him that it wasn't his fault and she knew that he wasn't like that.

Eventually Linda's name was called and the nurse got her a wheelchair and took her through to see the doctor. She was sent for an x-ray and the doctor broke the bad news that she had broken her ankle. She would have to have her leg plastered up to the knee for six weeks. Linda was warned not to put her foot down on the ground and they finally left the hospital at 10am, with Linda on crutches. They managed to flag down a taxi outside of the hospital and went back to Linda's house.

Margie was shocked when she saw Linda hobbling up the lane. 'What on earth has happened?' she asked, very worried about her daughter.

James and Linda told her how Linda had stepped off the pavement in the snow without realising it, and that she thought she had just sprained her ankle. It got worse as the night went on. Margie fussed over Linda in her usual caring way and got a stool to rest her leg on. Linda laughed as her mum asked her if she wanted a blanket. Then Margie told James to sit down and relax while she made them something to eat. Margie set up one place at the dining room table.

Linda said to her, 'What are you doing mum?'

'Well, you can have you're food on a tray over on the settee', she answered.

'Oh, I'm all right to sit at the table with James', said Linda.

'Are you really sure?' replied Margie with a worried expression.

'Of course', said Linda. 'They've given me crutches to get around with!'

James and Linda tucked into Margie's homemade Scotch broth, followed by the traditional New Year's meal of steak pie, peas and potatoes. Linda didn't tell her mum about the punch-up at the party. She didn't see any point in worrying her mother or in embarrassing James.

February 1968 and Maria discovered that she was two months pregnant. She hadn't reckoned on having another baby quite so soon. She worried how on earth she was going to cope. Just over a week later, Maria was rushed to the hospital with a miscarriage. She was devastated but convinced it was for the best as she didn't have the time for another baby right now. Six weeks later she told Linda that she hadn't had a period. She thought that it was because doctors at the hospital had scraped and cleaned her womb out after the miscarriage. She thought that this had probably upset her monthly cycle. Over the next couple of weeks, Maria wasn't at all well and kept throwing up. Linda convinced Maria that she should see her doctor because she might be expecting again. One week later, Maria got it confirmed that she was indeed having another baby, but she got the shock of her life when her doctor told her that she was at least eighteen weeks pregnant.

'But how can that possibly be?' asked Maria. 'I had a miscarriage two months ago!'

The doctor told her that the only explanation was that she was carrying twins and one had come away at eight weeks.

'But they scraped and cleaned my womb out at the hospital!' she said, unconvinced.

'Then he or she is a tough little character, because you are definitely around four months pregnant!' replied the doctor.

Maria walked home in a daze, consoling herself with the fact that at least there would only be one more baby. How on earth would she have managed with two sets of twins under eighteen months old!

One fine spring evening as Linda and James were walking home from the pictures at Anniesland, She noticed that James seemed a bit uneasy. He hadn't been himself all night. Linda surmised that he might be trying to tell her something and got worried that he had fallen out of love with her and wanted to call everything off. Linda had asked him two or three times during the evening if anything was the matter, but he had just mumbled, 'nothing'.

Finally, as they were approaching Linda's house, she said to James, 'Look, I know something's not right. You can cut the atmosphere with a knife. Are you going to tell me what's wrong or not?'

James kept his head down and said, 'There's nothing wrong... I... I... Well, I just want to ask you if you will marry me', he blurted out shyly.

Linda hugged him tightly. 'Is that what this is all about?' she said. 'Of course I'll marry. you, you daft galloot!' I wondered when you were ever going to ask me', she laughed excitedly. 'You know that I want to spend the rest of my life with you, James Alexander!'

James sighed with relief that he had managed to pluck up the courage to propose to Linda.

He told her, 'I wanted to buy you a ring, but I wasn't sure what kind you would want and, as you will be wearing it for the rest of your life, I thought it would be best if we go to the jewellers and choose one together. You've made me the happiest man on earth, Linda MacGregor. I can't wait to grow old with you!'

'When were you thinking about us getting married then?' Linda asked him.

'As soon as we can afford it! Just think, we'll have our own wee house and, in the near future, a couple of kids running around. You do want children, don't you?' said James, worried that he might be jumping the gun.

'The more the merrier', said Linda in elation Then she continued, 'How many would you like James? I think four would be nice'.

'That sounds great by me. Two strapping lads', James laughed 'and two beautiful daughters, just like their mammy'.

'Let's go home now and tell my parents!' said Linda.

What's For Ye, Won't Go By Ye

James suggested they wait until they had bought the ring, so they could announce their engagement properly. Linda could hardly contain herself, she was dying to tell her mum and her friends but she did what James wanted and kept quiet about their news.

'What about announcing our engagement on my twentieth birthday in two weeks' time?' said Linda to James.

'We'll see', replied James.

Linda could sense that something was wrong. 'What's up James. Have you changed your mind about us getting married?' she asked him.

'No, it's not that. I would get married tomorrow, but I don't know how to break the news to my mother. She is going to be devastated that I am leaving home and I do worry about how she will manage on her own!'

Linda realised that this was going to be a problem. James knew that Molly was going to be difficult about him and Linda getting engaged. She was always telling him that he was too young to be going out seriously with a girl and she would have been happy to see him and Linda split up. He was a very caring person, and his mother knew this and played on his emotions. He loved his mother and didn't want to hurt her, so knuckled down to her. As much as he wanted to get engaged to Linda as soon as possible, he just couldn't pluck up the courage to tell his mother of their plans.

CHAPTER NINE

It was a beautiful evening in May. James and Linda had taken Molly down to Helensburgh for the evening. They had a slow stroll along the prom then went into a restaurant on the front for fish and chips. They got back to Linda's about 11pm after dropping Molly home. Aunt Mary and Uncle David were there. Linda noticed that her mother's tartan shopping trolley was in the corner of the living room with her big teddy bear sticking out of it.

'What's Herman doing in your trolley?' (Linda had renamed her teddy after her idol, Herman, of Herman's Hermits). And what's your shopping trolley doing in the living room?' she asked Margie.

Margie looked at Mary from the corner of her eye and, smiling, bit her lip and said, 'Well! Aunt Mary has something to tell you both!'

Linda and James looked at Aunt Mary while Uncle David puffed on his big cigar and chuckled.

'Go on Mary, tell them!' encouraged Margie.

'Well', started Mary, looking a bit embarrassed. 'Your going to have a new wee cousin!'

Linda looked puzzled, then, her face broke into a big smile when she realised what Aunt Mary was trying to tell them.

'What, you mean you are having another baby?' she quizzed.

'Yes, and what a shock at my age. I thought that after having four, I was fin-ished having kids. I'm 42 for goodness sake!' said Mary.

'Oh, that's wonderful news!' answered Linda 'It'll be great to have a baby in the family!'

'That's what I told her', agreed Margie excitedly.

Mary wasn't so convinced, she never really was the maternal type like her sister Margie. None of her children were planned, they just happened

'When is the baby due?' asked Linda.

'November, just in time for Christmas!' answered Mary.

'You haven't answered my question though', said Linda to her mother. 'Why is Herman stuck in your shopping trolley?'

'I'm practicing!' answered Margie, giggling. 'When the baby comes along, Mary can push the pram and I will take Herman out in my shopping trolley to keep her company!'

Everyone roared with laughter at the thought of it.

By this time, Douglas had charged the glasses. 'Congratulations Mary and David, here's to your new baby!'

Everyone echoed Douglas' congratulations as they drank the toast.

Time went on. It was July and still no sign of an engagement ring. Meanwhile, Linda's brother Douglas junior had graduated, been offered and accepted to study for a PhD in chemistry at the University, and got engaged to his girlfriend Norma in June. They had set their wedding date for the end of August, 1969. Linda had confided to Morag that James and she were going to get engaged. Morag and Eric didn't like to be outdone, so she and Eric got engaged in July. Of course, Eric bought Morag a huge rock of a diamond set in platinum. Eric's granddad was a retired jeweller, so he was able to get them a huge discount through his trade contacts. Even then, it cost £90. Linda couldn't believe that they had paid that much for a ring.

'Are you going to get it engraved?' Linda asked Morag.

'Oh naw', replied Morag with a look of amazed bewilderment. 'That wid devalue it if ah wanted to sell it!'

'Why would you want to sell your engagement ring?' Linda asked her inquisitively.

'Well, if Eric and I ever split up, it will be a good investment fur me', answered Morag quite categorically.

Linda was stunned by her answer. 'If you think that there is a chance you might break up, then why get engaged in the first place?' she asked Morag.

'Well, it's aboot time he goet me a ring. We've been guan oot since I wis fourteen. That's nearly six years!' answered Morag, quite emotionless.

Linda concluded to herself that there were no deep feelings there and they had just got engaged to keep up with her and James. Meanwhile James just seemed to keep talking about becoming engaged and getting married, but wasn't making any headway. Linda was beginning to lose interest and was wondering if she was doing the right thing. Much as she loved James, she could see that there could be trouble with an interfering mother-in-law.

She put it to James, 'You are just going to have to face up to your mother. I'm not going to wait forever! It's four months since you asked me to marry you, and you promised me a ring. There is only one thing stopping that from happening, and that's your mother. If that's the way things are going to go on, then what chance do I have? I don't know if I want to marry a man who's so scared of his mother!'

James was pretty shaken by Linda's words and said that he would sort it out.

'Right!' said Linda. 'We get engaged on your twenty first birthday in August, and that is final! It's what we want that matters, and no one else!'

James agreed to August, but said that he didn't want a fuss on his birthday, so they decided to make it the following week. James knew that he would have to ask Linda's dad and, as it was only a few weeks away, he would have to do it soon. Strangely enough, that didn't bother him. It was the thought of breaking the news to his mother that worried him most. He knew that once he had asked Linda's dad, he would have to tell his mother. She would be annoyed if everyone else knew except her.

The following Friday evening, James arrived to take Linda out. He came in and sat in the living room.

Suddenly, he came out with, 'Mr. MacGregor, I would like to marry Linda. Can we have your ,and Mrs. MacGregors', permission to get engaged?'

Linda was taken aback. She wasn't expecting him to come out with it like that. It turned out that he had been thinking about it all the way down the road and decided to jump in at the deep end and get it over and done with. Douglas gave them both his blessing.

He called Margie through to the living room and said, 'Margie, we have good news, Linda and James are getting engaged'.

'Oh! When?' said Margie excitedly.

'In three weeks' time', replied James.

'Gosh, two engagements in two months, it's all happening at once!' said Margie.

Douglas poured the two women out a glass of sherry each and James and himself each a whisky to celebrate.

'Have you got the ring yet?' Douglas asked James.

'No, we're going to buy one tomorrow', answered James.

Linda looked at James in amazement. This was news to her. Linda fetched her coat and they left to go into town.

As they walked up the lane, Linda said to James, 'I take it that you've told your mother then?'

'Not yet!' replied James.

'Then when do you intend to break the news to her? Shouldn't we go and see her tonight?' Linda asked him. 'It seems only fair, she won't like it if she finds out that my mum and dad know, and you haven't said anything to her', Linda continued.

I will talk to her when I get home tonight. I prefer to break the news to her myself!' said James.

What's For Ye, Won't Go By Ye

Linda knew this was because his mother would not be over the moon about their announcement, and would be more concerned about herself than her son's future happiness.

James and Linda agreed to meet at three o'clock the next day, after they were both finished work.

'How did your mother take it then?' Linda enquired.

'She's OK'. answered James, intimating that he didn't want to talk about it.

They walked up and down Sauchiehall Street pushing their way through the usual Saturday afternoon hustle and bustle, looking in jewellers' windows. Linda couldn't see any ring that she liked for the money that they had. All the ones that she really loved were too expensive. They decided to go down to Argyll Street. They went through the arcades and under the Heilan' Man's Umbrella, but to no avail. Linda was on the point of giving up.

'Maybe we'll leave it until next week', she said disappointedly to James.

They walked up Hope Street and noticed a little jeweller's shop amongst the offices.

'I never knew that shop existed', said Linda.

'Let's have a look', answered James.

'Oh, it's probably too expensive', said Linda as she perused the window of diamond engagement rings.

Her eyes lit up as she spotted a beautiful solitaire diamond ring with high platinum shoulders in a tray in the window. It was just the ring that she had been dreaming about.

'Oh, that one is so beautiful; but we probably couldn't afford it', Linda told James.

'Well, we can go up to £30. If it's more than that, then maybe they will hold it for us and we can come back when we have the balance', said James encouragingly.

They held hands tightly, went into the shop and asked to see the tray from the window. Linda tried the ring on, but it was too big for her.

'Never mind madam, we can get it adjusted for you, and it can be ready in two weeks', said the jeweller.

'How much is it?' enquired James, holding his breath and waiting for an answer.

'That ring is one of our old lines of stock and it has been reduced, down from £27 to £21', the man answered.

They looked at each other in glee.

James smiled and asked Linda, 'Do you want that ring?'

'Oh James, it's gorgeous! I would love to have it!' Linda beamed back at him.

'Then, that's it then, it's yours!' James laughed.

The jeweller measured Linda's finger. James paid the £5 deposit and agreed to come back in two weeks' time to collect the ring. They walked on air up the road. They were so much in love and Linda couldn't wait to tell her mum all about the sparkling ring that James had bought for her.

The next evening, James and Linda went down in the van to pick up Maria and the twins and take them to Molly's house for the usual Sunday evening get-together. Maria was very pregnant and Linda climbed into the seats in the back of the van with the twins to let Maria sit in the front. Maria was very excited about James and Linda's engagement.

'My mother phoned yesterday morning to tell me. You know, she is not very happy about it', she said.

'She's all right', lied James, not wanting to upset Linda.

'She's not, you know', replied Maria honestly. 'I told her to watch what she is doing. If you and James love each other, nothing's going to stop you from getting married. If she interferes, then she could end up losing her son. As much as a man loves his mother, it's his wife he's chosen to spend the rest of his life with, so it's just too bad if his mother doesn't approve! I don't know what gets into her. She is abusing the privilege of having a lovely daughter-in-law like Linda'.

All this talk made Linda uptight, it was taking the good out of the happiness of their engagement. It only made Linda more determined. She loved James, and his mother was not going to come between them. They got to the house and Linda was dreading facing Molly. James and Maria's Aunt Bessie, and Molly's friend Mrs. Tweedie, were visiting. Aunt Bessie was a small round jolly lady who always wore dark tweed suits with a matching hat. She was more masculine than feminine and loved to crack cheeky jokes. The twins were teething and were a bit irritable.

'Here! Never mind waiting for your own teeth to come through, have these instead!' said Auntie Bessie, and she cackled as she took out her false teeth and gave them to the toddlers to play with.

She chuckled loudly, showing a big gummy smile. Her shoulders bobbed up and down as they examined them and grabbed them out of each other's hands clapping them together.

'Aye, don't talk to me about teeth! They're bloody painful to get and cause you nothing but trouble all your life. Yer better off without them!' exclaimed Aunt Bessie.

Linda was bemused by Aunt Bessie's antics. Then, she looked across at Molly's friend, Mrs. Tweedie. She was a tall, lanky, country type, with no curves and a straight up and down figure. She was sitting on the chair by the fireside opposite the couch. She was wearing a red and white checked gingham skirt, which she had obviously made herself, there were big white tacking stitches along the hem. Her legs were wide apart and she was showing off her big white bloomers underneath. She talked about all the property that she was buying and selling, while telling Molly that she wouldn't phone because it was 'cheaper tae write'.

Instead of excitedly talking about their forthcoming engagement, Linda said nothing about it until Molly frostily said, 'So, you and James are getting married? You know married life isn't a bed of roses and it's not glamorous! Men can be very difficult to live with. You just become a drudge to them'.

Maria looked at Linda and then looked up into the air. Linda felt quite upset. She knew that Molly was trying to change their minds. She went through to the kitchen, making the excuse that she was needing a glass of water.

Maria followed her and said, 'Ignore her remarks, don't let her get to you Linda'.

Linda answered, 'Would it have been too much for her to say congratulations and welcome me into the family?'

It was one week to go until James' twenty-first birthday. Linda wanted to get James something that he would really appreciate, and asked him if there was anything that he would like.

'I could do with a new tyre for my van', answered James seriously.

Linda couldn't believe what she was hearing. 'A tyre, for your twenty first birthday? Are you having me on?'

Linda realised by the expression on James' face that he was perfectly serious.

'Well', James answered, 'they are expensive, and the treads are getting really low. I can't really afford to buy one at the moment'.

Linda knew that was because all his savings were going on her engagement ring. 'If that's what you really want', she replied, screwing her face up in disbelief.

'It's not just a case of wanting, it's a case of needing. Otherwise, I will have to take the van off the road until I can save up for one'.

Linda didn't want James to take a risk driving about with a worn out tyre and decided that it would make sense to think practically and buy him the tyre for his birthday. James was delighted when, a few days later, he and Linda took his van into the tyre place in Maryhill and drove out with a brand spanking new tyre to replace the dodgy one.

I can't thank you enough Linda. That's the best present I have had in a long time and I really do appreciate it. It was a worry for me. Cars are OK until they go wrong or need new parts. That's when they can run away with the pennies', said James. He stretched across and squeezed Linda's hand lovingly, then he continued. 'Maybe it's a good idea to think about trading this van in before it gets any older and anything else goes wrong. Maybe next spring we'll get a wee car. It will make life a lot easier for taking our parents and family out and about, instead of you having to climb in the back every time. It'll be a lot more comfortable for everyone'.

'Oh. that would be great', said Linda. 'Do you think that we will be able to afford it?'

'Well, I am due to get a rise, now that I am twenty-one. My wages should go up and we should be able to pick up something decent for around £200. We can use the van for the deposit and pay it up over a couple of years, shouldn't be anymore than about £1 per week', replied James enthusiastically.

'Oh. that should be OK', answered Linda, excited at the thought of them having a nice car instead of a van.

Linda and James wanted to get engaged in private, so they planned to go out for a nice meal on the last Friday night in August before going to the Gaumont in Sauchiehall Street to see Julie Andrews in her new film 'Star'. James picked the ring up three days before the official engagement day and, as much as Linda pleaded with him, he would not let her see it, telling her that she would get it on Friday and have the rest of her life to admire it. The big night came and Linda waited in anticipation. They went for the meal to Hong Town Chinese Restaurant in Renfield Street. James never even let on whether he had the ring on him or not. After that, they made their way up to the Gaumont Cinema. Linda was beginning to wonder what on earth was going on when, just before the interval, James took her hand and slipped the ring on to her finger. He kissed her tenderly and told her, you'll soon be Mrs. Alexander. Linda was breathless with happiness. James went to get them an ice cream. Linda held her hand at different angles, looking at the ring and how it sparkled. She looked across and caught James laughing. She smiled back at him admiringly, thinking how lucky she was to be marrying such a handsome caring man. She was walking on air when they left the cinema at the end of the evening. They strolled round the corner to Renfrew Street to where James' van was parked. Linda felt very conscious of the diamond ring on her finger and was sure that everyone else noticed it too. When they got home, Margie and Douglas were waiting to see the ring.

'Oh, it's so beautiful!' said Margie. 'I wish I had got a solitaire instead of three in a twist'. Douglas poured them a drink and welcomed James into the family.

Douglas and Margie threw a party for James and Linda on Saturday night, and invited all James' family along. Linda was hoping that Iris and Kevin would behave themselves. Margie loved the twins and sat talking and playing with them. When they were tired, Margie and Linda took them upstairs and put them in the big double bed. The weather was hot and Margie made a lovely chicken salad meal with new potatoes. Douglas gave a nice speech to welcome James and the joining of the two families. Margie had baked a delicious cake for Linda and James. The happy couple giggled as they cut the cake together. Then, James gave Linda a present. She opened it and it was a 45 record of Solomon King singing, 'She Wears My Ring'. Linda was overcome by James thoughtfulness and she put the record on the record player to play. They lovingly danced in the middle of the room, while everyone looked on, clapping and cheering.

Kevin shouted over to James, 'Hi James, has Linda no' bought you a ring tae?'

'Aye', replied James, 'it's oan my van'.

Of course, he meant the tyre that Linda had bought for him. They doubled up laughing at Kevin's bemused expression.

Linda played some party music, while everyone blethered and got to know each other better. Of course, a party wasn't a party without the usual sing-a-long. So, they all sang their party pieces. Even Molly, after a couple of sherries, seemed to be enjoying herself. She sang 'Bonny Scotland'. Linda noticed her laughing and thought how different and attractive she looked when she smiled, instead of wearing a perpetual frown. She normally had a very matter of fact attitude. However, during the celebrations of the evening, accompanied by alcohol, which she normally never touched, she spoke to Linda.

'You widnae huv hud a man if ah hudnae washed ma feet!'

Linda, not sure how to take her, asked her what she meant.

'Well!' Molly continued. 'After ah hud the lassies, they telt me that ma womb had gone tae the back, and a widnae be able to huv any mer we'ans. Ah wiz quite happy aboot that, but wan day ah goet a bowl of water tae steep ma feet, as ah cerried it away ah slipped oan some water spilt oan the linoleum and came thuddin' doon oan ma back. Next thing ah knew, ah wiz expectin' an' the docter said it must huv been the thump oan ma back that knocked ma womb back intae place!'

Linda laughed, but didn't prolong it because she still wasn't sure whether Molly was telling her this in seriousness or as a joke. Linda was hoping that now that the engagement was official, Molly would be happy for them both and accept her. Little Jamie enjoyed the fuss everyone made of him, he wasn't used to it. Maria hit it off straight away with Margie. She complimented Margie on the excellent meal and they both went into fits of laughter as Margie unwittingly demonstrated, by holding her hands to her breasts, about the lovely chicken breasts that she had bought from the local butcher. Maria only had two weeks to go, and was feeling uncomfortable. So, just after 10pm, Pete and she decided it was time to go. Linda's Uncle David took them home in his car.

As soon as they had left the party, Kevin started singing his usual Orange songs. He was drunk and got up in the middle of the room, kicking his legs high. His six-year-old son Jamie joined in and everyone laughed at them. They thought that he was a bit of a nutter and didn't encourage him, so Linda was relieved when, after five minutes of high kicks, he flopped down on an arm-chair, tired out. The evening was a great success and enjoyed by all. The last of the partygoers tripped out of the door in the wee small hours, thanking Douglas and Margie for a wonderful evening. Douglas had drunk a skinful but, thankfully, with all the events of the evening, he was very tired and went straight to bed. Margie was relieved and sat talking to Linda until she was sure that he was fast asleep. She didn't want to tempt Providence by going into the bedroom and waking him up, in case he started going into one of his foul drunken tempers.

The following Saturday afternoon, the phone rang. It was Margie's sister Betty.

'I'm having a couple of friends round this evening. Would you and Douglas like to come along? Mary and David will be here'.

'Hang on, I'll see what Douglas says', answered Margie.

Douglas agreed to go. He enjoyed a good sing-a-long at parties and knew that there would be no shortage of whisky and beer.

That evening, when Linda and James got home, the house was empty. Linda made some coffee before James set off home. She was only in bed for about half an hour when she heard the key in the lock. Thinking it was her parents return-ing she rolled over to go back to sleep, but heard footsteps coming up the stairs in what seemed like a panic. She got out of bed to see her mother very upset and tearful.

'What's wrong mum, and where is dad?' Linda asked.

Margie was upset and hyperventilating. 'Oh, he's started again Linda. He gave me a right showing up as we were walking home. He was shouting at me, accusing me of flirting with Duncan. He knows that I can't stand Duncan near me. Why is he doing this? I crossed the road to the other pavement down at the park to get away from him and he carried on shouting. There were people there and I was so embarrassed. I can't take anymore. What am I going to do?'

'Right', said Linda. 'I will have a word with him when he gets home. Where is he now?'

'I don't know', said Margie. 'I took a short cut through the park to get away from him'.

'You shouldn't have walked through the park on your own mum, that's very dangerous!' said Linda.

'Yes, I know. I would never normally have done that. I had no option. Please Linda, don't say anything to him, you'll only make it worse for me!'

At that, they heard his footsteps approaching.

Margie dived into Linda's cupboard behind her hanging clothes to hide and said, 'Just pretend that you are sleeping. If he asks, you haven't seen me, OK?'

Linda did as her mother requested, but she wasn't happy about it and couldn't understand her reasoning. Surely she could see, that by not standing up to her husband, she was allowing him to bully her all the more. Margie, being a quiet, kind-natured person, didn't see it that way. She was happy to wait for her husband to sober up again and pretend it didn't happen.

Douglas stormed into the house shouting, 'Where are you, you bitch, how dare you try to get off with your sister's husband under my nose?'

Linda could hear him opening and slamming doors, looking for Margie.

The next thing, he threw Linda's bedroom door open and shouted, 'Where's your mother?'

Linda did as Margie had asked and pretended to be asleep. He shook Linda, demanding to know if she had seen Margie.

'What are you on about, you have just woken me up', said Linda. She panicked as he opened the cupboard door and pulled some of the clothes apart. Poor Margie was crouched down at the very back of the cupboard trying to be as quiet as possible. Luckily, he didn't see her. He stamped back out of the room, went to the bathroom and then in to his bedroom. It wasn't long until Linda could hear him snoring.

She went to the cupboard and said to her mum, 'It's OK, he's sleeping now. You can come out!'

Margie was sore and stiff. She had been uncomfortably doubled up while hiding in the cupboard for just under an hour. Linda was disgusted with the way her dad was treating her poor harmless wee mum, who would never have hurt anyone. She felt so sorry for her.

'He's not getting away with this mum', she said. 'I can't stand by and watch your life being ruined by his drinking. He needs to be told what a horrible person he is when he is under the influence of alcohol. We should stand up to him and tell him what he's like and that we're not going to tolerate it anymore. The shock might make him do something about it! It is not in his nature to be so bad, you know how nice he can be when he's not been drinking. He needs help. As long as you are covering up for him, he will never see that he is doing any wrong!'

Margie just nodded with a pained, tearful expression.

The next morning when Douglas was sober, Margie was spoiling him again and quietly pleading with Linda not to bring anything up about the night before, in case it started another row. Linda was unhappy about the whole situation. Deep down, she knew that her mum was protecting her dad because she didn't want friends and family to find out just how bad her husband's addiction to alcohol was. She actually believed that they hadn't noticed. This secrecy wasn't helping anyone, if anything, it was encouraging him to drink more, because no one ever told him how evil he was and what a fool he made of himself when he was inebriated. Linda felt her hands were tied. She wanted to help, but her mother wouldn't allow her to.

Not long after that, Margie developed a bad chest infection and had trouble breathing. The doctor diagnosed asthma and prescribed an inhaler for her. Linda was worried about her mum. She knew that her mum's dad had died in his fifties with breathing and bronchial complications and was very concerned when her mum suddenly developed asthma in her mid forties. Margie needed time off work to recover. She didn't get paid while on the sick from her factory job. As she only contributed to the small national insurance stamp for women, she didn't get any sick pay from the government. She couldn't help but worry about household finances and paying bills. Linda tried to ease the situation by putting more money into the house and helping with the housework and shopping. Douglas toed the line and hurried home from his postman's job every afternoon to nurse his wife, collecting necessary groceries on the way. He vacuumed and tidied the house before preparing the evening meal. All this sudden responsibility kept him out of the pub, meaning there was money for essentials, which was a blessing for all.

On Saturdays, Linda went for all the grocery shopping after she finished work at the pools office, and rushed home to see her mum. One particular Saturday she thought it was strange that the house was empty. She saw a note on the mantelpiece from her brother saying that he had gone to run in a cross-country race. *That's funny'*, she thought, *mum must be feeling a lot better and has gone out with dad!* She felt quite happy about this because it upset her to see her beloved mother so ill. She washed her hair and set it in rollers. She was just making herself some beans on toast when the phone rang. Linda answered, and it was Molly.

'Oh Linda', she said with a caring and sympathetic voice, 'I was just calling to see how your mother was'.

'What do you mean?' replied Linda.

'Oh no', said Molly, 'don't tell me that you don't know!'

'Know what?' said Linda, who was, by this time starting to panic.

'Oh, I wouldn't have called if I knew that you hadn't been told', said Molly, prolonging the agony for Linda.

'Told what?' demanded Linda, practically shouting down the phone at her in worried exasperation.

'Your mum was taken into Ruchill hospital this afternoon. I only know because James came down with some butcher meat for her, and he got there as your mum was being taken into the ambulance. Your dad is with her. They had no way of letting you know, because you had left your work. I just thought that maybe someone would have called you by now'.

Linda burst into tears and told Molly that she knew nothing of all this. Molly felt dreadful for being the one to break the news.

Linda said to Molly, 'I've got to go and find out what is happening. Is James there?'

'He's just this minute walked in the door. Here, I'll let you speak to him'.

Linda was distraught and James tried to calm her down.

'I'm on my way down now Linda, try not to get too upset', he said. 'I'll take you to see your mum'.

Linda called the hospital and was told that her mum was comfortable, but she wouldn't be allowed visitors until seven o'clock that evening. It was quarter to five now and Linda felt she couldn't wait that long. She was desperately upset and wanted to know what was wrong with her mum. At that, she heard a key in the door. It was her dad! Linda ran straight to him in tears.

'What's wrong with mum? I have just found out from Molly that they took her to hospital. Why, dad?'

Douglas was very emotional as he told her, 'I had to call in the doctor because she couldn't breathe. The doctor called an ambulance and had her admitted to hospital. Did you not read the note I left on the mantelpiece?'

'What note?' replied Linda.

'This one', answered her dad, as he lifted the note off the mantelpiece.

'But that's from Douglas junior saying that he is running a race today', said Linda.

Douglas looked puzzled, then turned the note round. He held his head in disbelief and reeled as he flopped down onto the armchair.

'He's turned it round. I don't believe he did this! He turned my note round and then went running, how could he do that?'

Linda took the note from her dad's hand and read it. Sure enough, her dad had scribbled details of her mum being taken into Ruchill Hospital with breathing problems.

'I had no way of letting you know, so I left a note for you both'.

He then went through to the kitchen and sat at the corner by the back door, where he broke down in floods of tears. Linda cuddled her dad and tried to console him.

'Yer poor wee mammy, she was so ill Linda. She couldn't breathe at all', he sobbed.

Linda's stomach was churning. She had never, ever seen her dad cry before and she fought back the tears. She badly wanted to be with her mum, but she controlled her emotions to help her dad. He had been very brave for Margie and, now that he was home, he couldn't hold back anymore.

'C'mon dad', said Linda, 'James will be here soon. I'll make you something to eat and then we will all go up to the hospital to see mum'.

James arrived, followed five minutes later by Douglas junior.

'Why did you turn the note round?' Douglas asked his son in anger. 'Because of that, Linda wasn't aware that anything was wrong!'

'Oh, I'm sorry dad', answered Douglas junior. 'When I read the note, I assumed that Linda knew. I had to go running. They're the trials for Scotland and I would have let the team down if I hadn't turned up. I know mum wouldn't have liked it if I did that'.

His dad couldn't argue with that, as Margie was proud of her son's running achievements and the many medals and trophies that he had already won. She would certainly have been annoyed if he hadn't turned up for this important race.

'How did you get on then?' asked his dad.

'Our team got through and we will be running for Scotland in the national cross country race next month'.

'Ah, yer mammy will be proud o' ye son!' said his dad, forgivingly.

Linda lost her appetite, she just wanted to see her mum.

At half past six, they climbed into James' van and set off for the hospital. It was an old red sandstone building with big old-fashioned wards and annexes. Margie was in an annex right at the back of the grounds.

'Now try not to get upset when you see your mum, because she will just worry about you', said Douglas as they went through the entrance into the hallway leading into the ward Margie was in.

Linda peeped in. Margie was in the bed directly opposite the door. Linda got the shock of her life when she saw her mum. Margie was wired up with different drips and an oxygen mask, gasping for breath. Linda, her brother and her dad made their way towards her, only three visitors were allowed to a bed, so James waited out in the corridor. It was a big long ward with a cold atmosphere and eight beds lined up either side. Linda controlled herself and gave her mum a big hug and kiss. She tried to cheer her up and jokingly gave her mum a telling off for being admitted to hospital instead of meeting her in town. She told her mum not to worry about anything and that her dad, brother and herself were more than capable of looking after everything while she relaxed and concentrated on getting herself well again. Margie looked delighted when her son told her that he had been selected to run for Scotland.

'Oh, I'll have to get out of here by then son, won't I?' she said.

After fifteen minutes, all the concerned family members were starting to arrive, so Linda cuddled her mum and said she and her brother would pop out for ten minutes to let Margie's sisters, Betty and Mary, into the ward. Once she got out to the corridor, Linda couldn't control her emotions any longer and fell into James' arms, bursting into tears. James had been through his own share of grief, and Linda felt safe in his strong arms as he consoled her.

The next few days were very worrying as Margie's health yo-yo'd, improving one day and deteriorating the next. After eight days in hospital, the doctor told her that they were going to put her on steroids because her respiratory system needed help. This seemed to do the trick. Margie called the steroids her 'magic pills'. They gave her relief and allowed her to inhale and exhale with ease
. She was discharged from hospital into the care of her local doctor after two weeks. The family doctor explained that steroids were the new wonder drug on the market. She was still pretty weak and had to rest. Linda's boss was very understanding and told her not to worry about coming into work on time every morning, but to see that her mother was all right first. Margie was confined to bed and Aunt Betty or Aunt Mary, who was almost seven months pregnant by now, took it in turns to take over from Linda in the mornings. They kept Margie company and looked after her for a few hours until Douglas got home from work at half past one.

One week after she came out of hospital, Douglas called in the doctor because Margie was getting breathless and a bit panicky again. It was after hours, the surgery was closed, and the area radio doctor came out. He was a nice young lad and asked Margie lots of questions before giving her an injection to relax her. She seemed a lot more settled and sleepy. Douglas had made dinner, but he decided to let her rest and have it later. He went downstairs to have dinner with his son and daughter. Douglas junior wolfed his dinner down. He was going over to a family party at Norma's and had to make sure he left in time to catch the bus. He took his empty plate and cutlery through to the kitchen, washed them and put them on the draining board before grabbing his jacket from the newel post at the bottom of the stairs.

'I'm off now! Bye mum', he shouted up the stairs. 'I'll see you tomorrow night. I'm staying at Norma's tonight!'

There was no reply, so Douglas junior assumed she had falling asleep and dashed out of the door. A strange feeling came over Douglas, and he went upstairs to check on his wife.

He shouted down the stairs, 'Linda! Linda, call that radio doctor back, QUICK! NOW!'!

Just at that, the phone rang. Linda answered and it was Margie's brother, John, calling to see how she was.

'Get whoever it is off the phone, now! Linda, get that doctor back pronto!' her dad demanded.

Linda panicked as she shouted to her uncle John, 'Get off the line! I have to call the doctor for my mum!'

She cleared the line and nervously dialed the surgery number with a shaking hand. It seemed to take forever as the dial turned round. She quickly explained to the operator that it was an emergency and she needed the doctor back as quickly as possible. After giving the details, Linda ran up the stairs three at a time to help her dad. She went into her parents' bedroom to see her mum was blue and not moving. Douglas was trying to get her to sit up.

'Don't let her fall asleep', he instructed. 'Speak to her, sing to her, get her to respond!'

They propped her up, holding on to an arm each and supporting her back. Linda sang her mum's favourite party piece, encouraging her to join in.

'C'mon mum, you know the words, sing to me!' she shouted anxiously. 'I know a millionaire…'.

Margie muttered and hummed the song along with Linda for what seemed to be an eternity but was, in fact, only minutes, before the doorbell rang. Linda ran down the stairs and threw open the door. The doctor ran past her straight up to the bedroom. He lay Margie flat and raised her feet, then gave her another injection. Linda and Douglas both had very worried expressions on their faces and they gave a huge sigh of relief as Margie gradually opened her eyes and came round, the colour returning to her face.

'Will she be OK, doctor?' asked Douglas.

'Aye. Her blood pressure dropped dangerously low. That first injection I gave her must have reacted with her medication. It can happen, but there is no way of knowing. Just keep an eye on her now, and make sure she drinks plenty of water. She should be fine. If there is any cause for worry, call me straight back. I'm on call until the early hours of the morning'.

Douglas wasn't taking any more chances, and he sat up in the bedroom looking after Margie for the rest of the night. The events of the evening suddenly hit him. He was so worried about her. She was the love of his life and he couldn't imagine being without her. Linda and James stayed downstairs and popped up frequently to make sure that all was well.

The next morning, Linda went in to see how her mum was, and she was surprised to see her sitting up in bed eating toast and drinking tea. Douglas was by her bedside.

Margie laughed as she said to Linda, 'What a song to get me to sing!'

Linda replied, 'What do you mean?'

'I'm at death's door and you have me singing, 'When I Leave The World Behind?'

Linda suddenly realised that was the title of Margie's favourite song.

'Oh mum, I never thought! I just wanted to keep you from slipping into a deep sleep and I knew that you knew all the words of that song', said Linda apologetically.

'Don't worry Linda, you and your dad were marvelous! You saved my life. I can remember everything, but it was like I was in a dream. I just felt my feet were turning into blocks of ice and I couldn't keep my eyes open. I never want to experience anything like that ever again!' said Margie.

'Don't you worry about that, we're going to look after you and get you back to the best of health again, mum! We need you and love you too much. What would we do without you?' said Linda as she sat on the bed beside her beloved mum and cuddled into her.

Meanwhile, in mid September 1968 and after a trouble free pregnancy, Maria gave birth to a healthy, whopping bouncing baby boy weighing in at 10lb 4oz. Everyone was amazed because Maria was so tiny and no one could understand how on earth she managed to give birth to such a big baby. He was beautiful with a fair complexion. She decided to call him Darren. Luckily, he was a very good natured, happy baby. He never demanded much attention, eating and sleeping at the right times. It was as if he knew that his mother was already overworked and exhausted.

Also at this time, Linda unfortunately had to leave her well paid weekend job at the pools office because, as the business expanded, they took on more full time staff and so didn't need week-end workers anymore. She missed the extra income, but enjoyed spending time at home with her mum on Saturday mornings. She attended to the family chores and went up to the local co-op with the shopping trolley to get the week's messages in.

On Saturday afternoons Linda went to Maria's. She loved to make a fuss of the boys and spend some time with them before taking Darren out to allow Maria to get a break. Linda carried Darren in her arms and caught a bus home. He was a happy, smiling baby and a pleasure to look after. Margie loved children and looked forward to seeing him on Saturdays. Maria didn't have much, and couldn't really afford nice baby clothes. Darren grew rapidly and so was mostly dressed in hand-me downs. Once a month, when Linda got paid, she took him into town and bought him a new outfit. On one particular occasion, when he was about six months old, she went into the baby store and saw this beautiful white fur coat. Although it was expensive, she couldn't resist it. She skinned herself to buy it, along with a white knit pom-pom hat that tied under his chin. She bought the twins, Adam and Greg, a wee toy car each because she didn't like to leave them out. When she got home to her house, Linda tried the coat and hat on Darren and he looked so gorgeous and cuddly. He seemed to know this, and chuckled as she tied the bow under his chin. Linda decided to keep the outfit on him and surprise Maria. Maria was overcome when she saw Darren. She thanked Linda over and over again.

As she held him tightly into her in his new furry coat she said, 'Just wait until your Nana sees you tomorrow. She'll think you're a right wee toff!'

Pete never put himself out to visit his mother-in-law so, unless James was able to pick her up in the van, Maria only took one of her children, in turn, with her on Sunday to visit her mum, leaving the other two at home with their dad.

In the early hours of a mid November Sunday morning in 1968, David called Margie and Douglas on the telephone from The Queen Mother's Hospital. He telephoned tell them that Mary was in labour.

'Everything is moving pretty fast, and they reckon the baby will be born within the next few hours', he told them excitedly.

Margie could hardly contain herself. She was so excited at the prospect of a new baby in the family.

'Keep us in the picture, David, and let us know as soon as you can when the baby is born!' she instructed him.

Every time the phone rang in the MacGregor household that morning, everyone raced to pick it up, while the others stood round on tenterhooks to find out if it was news from David. Eventually, just after eleven o'clock in the morning, a jubilant David called to say that he and Mary were the proud parents of a gorgeous, healthy baby girl. She was 7lb 8oz with beautiful fair skin and blond features. Mother and baby were well.

Margie and Linda couldn't wait to get to the hospital the next evening to get a glimpse of the new addition. Linda met her mum and dad outside of the hospital after she had finished work and together they made their way to the ward that Mary and her baby were in. As they passed the waiting room, they saw Mary and David's two eldest sons sitting in there.

'We're taking it in turns', Neil told them. 'The matron only allows three visitors to a bed. Our dad is in there with Jon and Katy. I'll show you what ward mum is in'.

They followed Neil along the corridor until they came to the second to the last door on the right. They looked into the modern six-bed ward. Mary was sitting up, drinking a cup of tea, and David was on the armchair at the side of her with a big proud beaming smile on his face. Katy was tucking her new little sister into the 'pyrex dish' cot and telling her all about their bedroom at home. Katy was delighted. She was fourteen, the only girl, and the youngest in the family. She had prayed for a wee sister. Jon was at the other side of his mum, eating her grapes and asking her when they would be getting their new wee sister home.

'C'mon Jon and Katy', said David. 'We'll go out to the waiting room with Neil and Billy and let your Auntie Margie, Uncle Douglas and Linda spend some time with mum and your wee sister'.

Katie reluctantly left her wee sister, kissing her own hand and placing it gently on the baby's forehead.

'Oh Mary, I can't believe it! Isn't life wonderful? She's a wee beauty! How do you feel?' Margie gushed all at once, without taking a breath.

Mary laughed. 'I feel great!' she replied. 'It was over and done with so quick! My waters burst at home. I didn't have any warning signs. It was just as well it was a Sunday and David was at home. He rushed me straight up to the hospital in the car. The labour pains weren't really very fierce and, within four and a half hours, she was born. I suppose after four kids on the production line, it just gets easier', Mary laughed.

'Have you got a name for her yet, Auntie Mary?' asked Linda.

'Yes, Katy would like her to be called Lisa, and we all approve. So that will be your new wee cousin's name', answered Mary.

'Awe, that is a lovely name', said Linda, adoringly.

Early December 1968 and Margie's health had gradually improved, although she was now a chronic asthmatic and had to rely on steroids and an inhaler to help her have a quality of life. Douglas junior came home from University and told Margie that they were looking for a lab assistant in the university.

'Why don't you go for the job mum? You're clever, you could do it easy!' Douglas told his mum.

'Me! I wouldn't have a clue. How could I work in a scientific lab? I left school at fourteen and never even studied science!' Margie told her son.

'It's only common sense. Everyone is really nice, and I'll be there to help you too. So, come on mum! It'll do you good', Douglas junior encouraged her.

Eventually, Margie gave in and agreed for her son to put her name forward for an interview. She never thought for a minute that it would go any further and got the shock of her life when her son's professor invited her to come in for an interview. Margie went along. She was very negative and wasn't sure what a lab assistant did. Douglas junior had invited the professor and his wife to Margie's house many times, so she knew him quite well. He was a very laid back pleasant man, and a bit eccentric. He told Margie all about the job and then showed her round the lab that she would be working in if she got the job.

She was in the interview for over an hour, when he said, 'Well, the job's yours if you want it!'

Margie was astounded and answered, 'Are you sure? I mean, I've never done this sort of work before', but quickly added, 'I am a quick learner!'

The professor laughed and said, 'Was that a Yes?'

'I guess so', answered Margie, in a daze.

'Right, then you can start Monday at 8.30am!' the professor said in finality.

Margie came out of the University nipping herself to make sure that she hadn't been dreaming. She had worked in factories all her life and now, here she was about to embark in a new career in the University at the age of forty-seven!

'See, I knew that you would sail through the interview! My mammy's no' daft', said Douglas junior with a satisfied grin when she told him the good news.

Christmas that year was very exciting. Margie had taken to her new job like a duck to water and settled in to it really well. She was very popular with her workmates, the students loved her and she made a lot of new friends. Then, there was the excitement in the family of the new baby, Lisa. She was inundated with all sorts of baby toys and lovely new clothes from all the family. Linda and James bought her a pink furry baby siren suit. Meanwhile, Linda couldn't help comparing the difference with Maria's kids. The twins were twenty-one months old, and delighted with their second-hand kiddie car and toddler tricycle that their dad bought at the Barras for them for Christmas. He also got them wee red coats from the kids' clothes stall. Nana Molly knitted them identical blue jumpers each. Darren was only three and a half months old, and he got a wee cuddly toy that Pete had purchased from the Barras. Nana Molly knitted Darren a blue matinee coat and pantaloon set. James and Linda bought the twins Fisher-Price learning toys and Darren a lovely furry blue warm and cosy baby siren suit. Iris and Kevin's son, Jamie, was six years old by now and Linda and James got him the toy garage, complete with a ramp and car lift, that he had always been asking for.

It was coming up to Linda's twenty-first birthday in April 1969. She knew that her mum and dad couldn't afford to throw the big party that some of her friends and cousins had enjoyed in a local hall, so she opted for a party at home for all her friends. Margie and Douglas were going over to visit Margie's lifelong friend and her husband in East Kilbride, she had invited them to stay overnight with them. Linda was so excited! She had invited approximately forty guests, including old school friends, work colleagues, new friends, James' friends and their girlfriends, and her cousins. The only ones that she wasn't sure about were Iris, Kevin and Pete. She knew she had to invite them, because they were James' family, but, with Iris and Kevin's drinking, arguing and fighting, and, with Pete's foul language, Linda was embarrassed. Linda and James paid for all the party food and drink out of their own pockets. Linda made her own sausage rolls from scratch. Amongst other things, she had cheese, onion and pineapple chunks on cocktail sticks stuck into grapefruit halves, and a selection of filled bridge rolls, meats and cheeses, crisps and savouries. Her work colleague, Sally, had a cousin who was married to an officer in the American Army. He was able to get them cheap booze from the base.

What's For Ye, Won't Go By Ye

The special evening arrived and the party was all organized. James told Linda how beautiful she looked in her new black halter necked mini-dress. The food looked very inviting laid out on the table. In the middle was big a pink and white iced birthday cake that Linda's parents had bought for her, with 'Happy 21st Birthday Linda' piped onto it in pink, with twenty-one candles arranged around the outside. There was every drink that you could think of in the walk-in cupboard off the kitchen, which James and Douglas junior had set up as a bar.

All they needed was for the guests to start arriving, and one by one they did. There was a lovely and happy atmosphere as everyone mingled well. Linda was worried because Iris, Kevin and Pete seemed to be spending the whole party in the wee room off the kitchen where all the booze was. She asked James to keep his eye on them, because, apart from the fact that they were guzzling all the booze, she didn't want them showing her up. Somehow, Iris realised that she was being watched and she didn't like it.

She approached Linda and slurred , 'Whit's your problem then?'

Linda realized that this wasn't good,. It was usually Iris' opening line before a fight broke out. She tried to calm Iris down, telling her she didn't have a problem, and tried to interest her in the food. Linda thought if she could get Iris to eat something, it might help to sober her up, but Iris was having none of it. She was showing the same jealous streak towards Linda that had made her sister Maria's life hell for years. Maria got James and, together, they tried to calm Iris down. James went to take her by the hand, intending to take her over to the other a side of the room to speak to his friends.

Suddenly, Iris broke loose and, without warning, screamed, 'Don't patronise me!'

She then threw a punch at Linda, thumping her in the eye. Linda reeled back in shock and surprise, wondering what on earth she had done to deserve that. She never wanted Iris at the party in the first place. She didn't like her, and only invited her out of good manners. Douglas junior ran over when he saw what had happened and pulled Iris away from Linda, demanding that she leave the party now, before he called the police and had her arrested for assaulting his sister. This was very embarrassing for Linda in front of all her work colleagues, friends and cousins, but she needn't have worried, because they all saw that it was a completely unprovoked attack, and rushed to Linda's aid. Kevin was furious with Iris. He liked Linda and knew that she didn't deserve this. He grabbed Iris' coat threw it on her, ordering her out of the house. He apologed profusely to everyone for his 'nutter of a wife's behavior'. Douglas and his fiancée, Norma, bathed Linda's eye, which, by this time, was beginning to close and swell up black and blue. What a terrible present for her special birthday.! The guests made excuses and left.

Maria was looking for Pete. 'Did he leave with Iris and Kevin?' she asked James.

'I don't think so. Come to think of it, I never saw him during all the commotion!' answered James.

'Hold on. Wait a minute, there's one place we haven't looked'.

James opened the door of the wee room off the kitchen and, sure enough, there was Pete, sitting on a chair with a smiling, sozzled face and empty spirit bottles all around him.

'You greedy bastard, Pete!' said James in disgust. 'While we have been trying to calm Iris down and stop her from causing an almighty row, you have been in here guzzling all the booze. Get your jacket on and leave, now!'

What a terrible way for Linda to celebrate her twenty-first birthday! She had been looking forward to it so much, and this mad woman that was to be her future sister-in-law had spoiled it for her. Instead of having lovely memories of her special birthday, Linda would remember for years to come what that evil, vindictive woman did to her.

After this incident, Linda had second thoughts about marrying James. What with his mum so obviously opposed to their relationship and making Linda feel so unwelcome at times, and his disturbed sister creating trouble at every turn, Linda wondered what sort of family she would be marrying into.

I'm not marrying any of them, she thought. *I'm marrying James, and he is not like them. Besides, Maria and I get on very well, better than she and Iris do. If James and I were to part company, that would be right up his mum's street, because I would be off the scene and she would have her son back.*

Maria had told Linda in confidence that her mum had once said to her, 'I wish that you girls had never got married. I never wanted any of my kids to marry after what I suffered. You'd all be better off and have much more of a life if you were single and stayed at home with me'.

Even Maria admitted that her mum had a very selfish attitude.

The next time Linda went to James' house, Molly was very cold with her. She never mentioned Linda's black eye or showed any commiseration towards her for her Iris' disgraceful and embarrassing behaviour. Obviously, Iris had got to her mum first with a cock and bull story about Linda. As usual, Molly believed her because, as far she was concerned, the sun rose and shone out of Iris' backside. Molly brought up the subject of the party with an accusing attitude towards Linda. Linda, however, didn't take her on. Instead, she told Molly firmly what had happened, and that she had not said or done any of the things Iris was making up. Besides, Linda pointed out, Iris was too drunk to even be aware of, or remember, the fight SHE caused, and how SHE had ruined the party.

James said nothing, and never got involved as Linda battled it out on her own with Molly. On the way home afterwards, Linda had serious words with James and told him that she expected him to speak up for her and not allow his mum to get away with her rude, hurtful, outspoken and uncalled for remarks. She told him that he was capable of putting a stop to everything before it spiraled out of control by just facing up to his mother and putting her in her place once and for all.

James agreed that he would do this in the future, but Linda had serious doubts about his courage to challenge his mum. She had the feeling that he was listening to her, but not paying attention to the seriousness of the whole matter. His mother had some sort of a hold over him, and he seemed scared to cross her. Linda knew that indirectly, James was to blame for allowing matters to continue.. Instead of nipping things in the bud and being firm with his mother by giving her an ultimatum to stop listening to Iris and stirring up trouble, he would walk away. By not passing any comment, it only prolonged the agony, as it allowed his mother to become more confident in getting away with her insulting behaviour, causing greater rows to develop.

Meanwhile, Margie and Douglas were furious when they heard about Iris' fighting and picking on Linda in their house. They knew that this had no reflection on James, because he was a different person entirely from his psycho sister. Linda's parents told James in no uncertain terms that his sister was not welcome in their house ever again.

Margie warned Linda to stay away from Iris and have nothing to do with her. 'She's a very dangerous woman and you don't want to be mixing with that type of hard person'.

She was concerned for her daughter. She needn't have worried because, by this time, Linda had already made her mind up that she would be avoiding Iris' company as much as possible. Nothing, not even James' family, was coming between her and the man she loved and planned to marry.

As an outsider looking in Linda, could see that Iris and her mother were trying to poison James against Linda. The more they tried to interfere, the more determined Linda became. James was wearing blinkers and seemed to be oblivious to everything. Linda got very hurt by all this. She couldn't understand what Molly's problem was. Surely she should be glad that her son had found such happiness and was going to marry a girl that loved and respected him, and would be a very good wife and daughter-in-law. Linda didn't blame James, because he loved his mother no matter what, and Linda understood this. She didn't want him to fall out with his mother, just to gently make her see that she would be far better off to ignore Iris and accept Linda. If only Molly did this, everyone's life would be far happier.

Avril Dalziel Saunders

Douglas gradually slipped back to bad old ways, coming home drunk and being abusive to Margie at weekends. Linda worried herself sick about this. In spite of the fact that Margie battled on with life, carrying on working and never looking for any sort of sympathy and refusing to give in to her illness, Linda knew her mother was not really a healthy woman. Linda came home one Saturday afternoon and found her drunken father casting up to her mum how he had saved her life. Margie's face was swollen with crying and she was gasping for breath. Linda pushed past her dad and cuddled her mother. She went into her mother's handbag and got her inhaler for her.

'Leave mum alone! How could you do this, after all mum's been through? You are an evil alcoholic. You seem to forget the buckets that you cried when mum was in hospital. Just go to bed and sober up. You are no good to anyone like that!, she angrily told her dad.

He gave Linda a horrible staring look and then turned on his heels, disappearing upstairs. Linda found it hard to tolerate her father who, in sobriety, was a very decent, loving and caring family man. She knew that if he could see the way he behaved under the influence of alcohol, even he would be shocked and despise himself. Linda sat her mum down on the settee and made her a cup of tea.

'Did he really cry, Linda, when I was in hospital. Did he really cry for me?'

'Yes mum, he cried like a baby'. Linda answered.

Margie seemed to find a new confidence. It was as if she was never sure of his love for her but, knowing he cried for her, comforted her and confirmed that he still had feelings. Linda wasn't so sure though. At the time, she felt really sorry for her dad and was convinced that was crying for his very sick wife. She thought all that had happened would be enough to make him change his ways and turn against drink. But now, here he was, back and as bad as ever. Now, even worse, he was making her mum feel guilty about his having saved her life. Linda couldn't understand why he was doing this. She worried about how her mum would cope when both she and her brother married and their mum would be left alone with their dad. She couldn't help herself from thinking that his tears had been because he was feeling sorry for himself, not for Margie.

CHAPTER TEN

After Linda gave her mum housekeeping and paid out for her travel expenses, meals and clothes each week, there wasn't anything left in the kitty. There was nothing for it but for her to find another part-time job to boost her income, otherwise, she would never be able to save up to get married. A new law had been passed, allowing public houses to be opened in housing schemes that were originally dry areas. 'The New Inn' opened just ten minutes' walk away from Linda's house on the main road.

One Saturday lunchtime, Linda plucked up all her courage and went into the lounge. She introduced herself to the manageress and asked her if there were any jobs going. She was a smart, attractive woman in her late thirties with a well-proportioned, shapely figure. Her face makeup seemed very professional. She had a sharp nose. She wore blue eye shadow, thick black eyeliner and long false eyelashes. This made her eyes big and emphasized them as her best feature. Tangerine lipstick outlined her wide mouth, showing off her perfect, pearly white teeth. She seemed very confident and gave the impression that it wouldn't be wise to be her enemy.

She swung her shoulder length, thick wavy black hair to one side and then the other before asking Linda, 'Have you done this sort of work before?'

'Well, I have never worked in a pub, but I've waited on tables in a restaurant. Is it similar?' asked Linda.

'Hmmm', said the manageress. 'Let me see now. I need someone to assist in the off sales department. Would you be interested in working there one night mid-week as well as Friday nights, Saturday afternoons and Saturday nights, but also be willing to help out in any of the bars when we are busy?'

'That sounds good to me', answered Linda. 'When can I start?'

The manageress replied, 'This evening, if you like. We open at six o'clock. Can you come in at five for some training?'

'OK, see you at five o'clock', answered Linda.

'That's great! By the way, my name is Donna', said the manageress.

Linda practically ran down the road, as pleased as Punch with herself. She couldn't wait to tell her mother, James and everyone else the good news.

'You're starting tonight? Do you think that's wise, Linda? What's James going to think of you working every weekend?' asked Margie.

'Oh, he'll be fine, mum. It means that I'll be earning instead of spending at the weekends, so I should be able to save now', Linda answered.

Linda rang James, but he wasn't too happy when he heard that she got herself a job in a pub, that she was working that night, and would be every weekend from now on.

'What am I supposed to do while you are working, then?' James asked Linda.

'You can come down just before I finish at ten o'clock. It'll still be early. We can spend a few hours together after', Linda replied.

She felt quite upset that he wasn't pleased at her using her initiative to work hard and earn more money to help build their future together.

'I'm doing it for us, James', she said more seriously. 'It's not as if I'm going to go out gallivanting with my pals. C'mon, I was understanding when you wanted to give the ice cream business a try!'

James reluctantly gave in and said that he would come down to the off sales before ten o'clock to pick her up when she finished.

Linda pulled the top of her long, dark hair back and secured it with a blue elastic hair band, leaving the rest flowing down over her shoulders. She applied her makeup, carefully painting an even, black line along her top eyelids with liner and blackening the inside of her bottom lid with eye pencil. After lengthening her eyelashes with black mascara, she finished off by livening up her lips with bright orange lipstick. She donned her blue mini-dress and black patent, block-heeled shoes and then set off, with butterflies in her tummy, for her new part time job.

'This is Isa', Donna said to Linda. 'Isa, this is your new part-time assistant, her name is Linda. Isa's the off sales department supervisor and she'll show you the ropes, Linda.

Isa was a large, plump and happy lady. It was obvious that this was her space and it was to be run her way. She told Linda that she had been doing this sort of work all her life and she certainly seemed to know her stuff. She went through all the stock with Linda, telling all the different sizes of spirits to her. There were miniatures, double-doubles and upwards. Then, there were all the different beers, and those which were most popular. Isa showed Linda the stock room and told her how important it was to stock the shelves in the shop from the back, in order to rotate the stock so that it didn't go out of date.

'But then, I don't know why I'm telling you that', she laughed. 'It never sits on the shelves long enough to age'.

Linda learned all about the different types of cigars, tobacco and cigarettes that they sold. Linda was a non-smoker and never realised that there were so many brands. She had a sweet tooth, so she didn't have any trouble absorbing the information about the different types of chocolates and sweets that they sold, she knew it all already. Isa furnished Linda with three sheets of foolscap paper stapled together. On them were typed everything that they sold and all the prices.

'You can take this home and study it', Isa told Linda.

By this time, Linda was beginning to wonder if she had done the right thing. She never thought that there would be so much to take in.

'Don't look so worried, you'll soon grasp it all and, before long, you'll be so confident you won't even need to look at the list', Isa consoled Linda.

'Oh, I don't know about that! My head's birling already, and I haven't even started my shift', answered Linda.

'Well, you better unbirl it', Isa admonished her, 'because we're opening in five minutes, and you'll be straight in at the deep end. Look at the queues starting outside already!'

Linda looked out through the pane of glass on the door to see at least eight people standing outside. Her stomach started churning.

'Och! Don't panic, Saturday night is constantly busy. It's the best night to learn. By ten o'clock you'll be an expert!' Isa encouraged.

Linda wasn't so sure. She wished to herself that the door would stay locked and never open. Isa picked up the big bunch of keys and walking towards the door.

She said, 'Well my dear, are you ready? Cos this is it'.

As she unlocked the door, at least a dozen people pushed past Isa towards the counter where Linda was standing.

A wee bachely man got to the counter first and blurted out to Linda, 'A double! Double o' Bells, please'.

Linda reached to the shelf behind her and quickly wrapped the wee bottle up in brown paper as she said to him, 'Will there be anything else, sir?'

'Aye hen', he smiled, 'Four cans o' Carlsberg Special'.

Linda reached below the counter for the beer and put them into a brown paper 'carry-out' carrier bag, then placed the wrapped up whisky bottle on top. She wrote the prices down, ready to tally up on the next sheet of brown paper.

'Is that it, then?' she asked the customer.

'Whit dae ye mean, is that it! Is that no enough?' he answered.

Linda looked concerned, in case the man thought that she was being cheeky.

Then, he laughed. 'Don't worry, hen, and don't look so worried. A'm only kidding ye. If the wife gied me mer money, then I wid buy the shoap. Bit this is a' A cin afford the night!'

Before the evening was out, Linda was right into the swing of it. She enjoyed arithmetic and was very quick and efficient when adding up the orders. This impressed Isa. Linda got to know the regular patter and confidently joked with the customers, giving as good as she got. As the last customer left the shop at 10 o'clock, James came in the door just as Isa went to lock it.

'Sorry, we're closed', she said to James.

'Oh Isa, this is my boyfriend, James. James, this is Isa'.

'Nice to meet you! I've heard lots about you already, and it's all good', Isa said to James. 'Your girlfriend worked very hard tonight. She's a smart girl'. Isa turned to Linda. 'How did you enjoy your first experience of working in an off sales?'

'I loved it', said Linda. 'I'm looking forward to my next shift'.

'Well, you certainly took to it, like a duck to water. I hope you'll not get fed up working Friday and Saturday nights. I could really do with someone like you on a permanent basis!' replied Isa.

'I don't see any problem, every little helps towards James' and my future', answered Linda. She looked towards James as she said this, and couldn't help noticing that he appeared uneasy.

'I could really do with you working Thursday nights, because some people get paid that night, and we can get very busy. I'll understand if you don't want to, because it would mean three nights in a row', said Isa.

'Well, if you don't mind, I'd rather not. If I am working Fridays and Saturdays, then I would prefer not to work Thursdays', Linda answered.

'Well, how do Wednesdays suit you then? Can you do Wednesdays for your mid week nights?' asked Isa.

Linda nodded. 'Yes, that should be no problem, but remember, I don't get home from my office job until just after six o'clock, and I have to wash, eat and get changed'.

'Half past seven will be fine Linda. See you Wednesday then!" replied Isa.

Linda couldn't wait to tell James all about her evening, but he wasn't interested. In fact, he wasn't happy about it at all.

'C'mon Linda', James said. 'It's not right, you working all weekend. When are we meant to see each other?'

'10 o'clock is not too late, is it?' answered Linda.

'It is if we want to go to the pictures or into town for a meal or a show. I won't pretend or beat about the bush. I'm not happy about you working in a pub!' replied James defiantly.

Linda was dismayed. She couldn't think what all the fuss was about. All she wanted was to save money for their future together.

What's For Ye, Won't Go By Ye

Linda turned up for her job in the off sales the following Wednesday night.

'Well! Are you ready for another night slaving behind the counter, Linda?' Isa joked. 'Mind you, it won't be as busy as it was on Saturday night', she continued.

'Well, I'm ready. I enjoy it, but James isn't happy about me working here at all, so I don't know how long I will be able to stick it out for', Linda informed Isa.

Isa looked very disappointed. Linda was pleasant and efficient, and had a way with the customers. 'Well, I hope you won't leave. You fit in so well', she responded.

'We'll wait and see', replied Linda.

It wasn't too busy in the off sales Wednesday night. Linda was bottling and stocking up when Donna came in behind the counter from the side door in the bar.

'I need you in the lounge bar, Linda. We are quite busy through there, and as it's not too bad in here. It would be a good time for you to learn what goes on through there', Donna said.

Isa didn't look very happy about being left on her own, but Donna was the boss, and no one argued with her. Donna took Linda through the bar area, which was filled with only men. She got dozens of wolf whistles as she ploughed her way through the crowd and smoke to get behind the bar.

Linda felt herself blush as Donna told the punters, 'Oh behave! Have you never seen a young girl in a mini skirt before? Anyway, you're all old men! She wouldn't look twice at any of you!'

Donna turned to Linda and said, 'Just ignore them! They imagine that they are Romeos, but they're all past it!'

Linda followed Donna through the door to the stock room and then out through another door that led behind the bar of the lounge.

'Right', said Donna, 'We'll put you on waiting at the tables'.

At that, she shoved a tray into Linda's hand. Then she went below the counter and fished out an old tobacco tin, took out £3 worth of change from the till.

Then Donna said, 'Right Linda, that's your float. The six tables over in the far left corner are yours for the night. You take their orders, come back to the bar where one of the barmaids, June or Barbara, will serve you. You pay them out of your float, go back, and collect the money from your customer when you serve them their drinks. At the end of the night, you pay in your £3 float and any tips go into the kitty to be divided up between everyone. It is waitress service only in here, and punters are not allowed at the bar. June and Barbara are slaving away all night, and it is only right that they get a share of the tips!'

Linda grasped her tray apprehensively. 'Can I not learn the work behind the bar instead?' she asked Donna nervously. 'I would much rather do that as serve the tables'.

'Oh, don't be daft!' Donna said. "You have to start at the bottom and bar work is for the much more experienced!' 'You will get a chance to be trained in that eventually', she promised Linda.

Linda soon got the hang of it, and was doing quite well, until six young men came in and started chatting her up. Linda got their six pints of heavy from the bar. She carefully carried the loaded tray over to far corner where they were sitting. She rested the corner of the tray on the table. She was about to start unloading the tray with the drinks nearest to her, when two of the young men grabbed their pints from the corner of the tray that was resting on the table. Disaster ensued. The top-heavy tray tipped over and drinks went everywhere.

Linda's skirt was wringing wet with beer, and she was really embarrassed. The place was packed and everyone was looking at her. She felt herself shaking as she apologised to the young man nearest to her, whose trousers were soaked. He seemed to sympathise with her predicament and told her not to worry, assuring her that it was the fault of his idiotic mates for grabbing their drinks and not having the good manners to wait to be served. He assured Linda they would pay the cleaning bill for her skirt, and that he would see to it. Linda then went back to the bar, to get more drinks. By this time, everyone knew about it.

June, the barmaid, said, 'That's nearly eight shillings' worth of drink that you have wasted! You should really pay for that yourself'.

Linda was very uncomfortable, right through to her underwear. On hearing June say that, Linda felt like putting her tray down and walking out. Eight shillings would be whack out of her wages.

Donna overheard June, and instructed her to serve the drinks to Linda, saying, 'The only way to learn is by your mistakes. You'll know next time to be wary of greedy, grabbing punters. C'mon, June! You're not telling me that in all your years working in bars, you've never done anything wrong! I did the very self same thing as Linda in my young days. I soaked a man, and, what was worse, it wasn't even his order! We've all done it at sometime. You're not a bar waitress until you baptise a punter with alcohol!'

June muttered under her breath, annoyed that Donna had overruled her. One-by-one, the five other waitresses all told Linda not to worry, and just to ignore June. They had all spilt drinks in their first week or so. They also told Linda that June was a moaner—everybody ignored her. They advised Linda not take any notice of her.

What's For Ye, Won't Go By Ye

James came round to the off sales to meet Linda at quarter to ten. He wasn't very happy to find her working in the lounge bar. He sat at a table in the corner, waiting for her to finish her shift and cash in her float. She had made nearly eight shillings in tips. She put it into the kitty and got six shillings back after it had been divided between the eight staff. She was quite delighted with this, because nobody gave tips in the off sales department.

'You did very well Linda. Now I know I can call on you in an emergency', Donna told her. Then she added, 'In a couple of weeks I'll train you behind the bar, pulling pints and such, because I need someone else to fall back on in emergencies'.

Linda was delighted, this was something she was really looking forward to. She tried to talk to James about her evening and her dilemma but he wasn't interested.

'How much longer are you going to stick to this stupid job?' he asked her.

Linda was upset with his remark. Why couldn't he see that she was working really hard, doing something that she really enjoyed, and that anything she saved was going towards their future together?

That Friday, Linda reported to the off sales for her evening shift.

Isa said to her, 'I hope Donna doesn't come and whip you away again. Friday nights are busy and I need the extra pair of hands'.

'James is still not happy about me working here every weekend, Isa. If it causes a problem with us, I might have to think about packing it in!' Linda told her.

Isa was dismayed. 'Does he fancy working in the bar? They need another barman in there', she said to Linda.

Linda replied by shaking her head, 'Oh no, Isa. He works very hard manually during the day. He already does two nights and a Saturday morning for overtime. He wouldn't be interested in working anymore hours in the week, especially in a pub!'

'That's a shame', said Isa thoughtfully. 'Donna won't be too happy about losing you, especially when she's training you up to cover all the different jobs'. She stopped for a minute and then continued, 'Leave it to me Linda!'

Linda asked her what she was up to.

'Never you mind!' Isa smiled

James turned up, not too happy, as usual, just before ten o'clock.

Isa was busy praising Linda to him when she quickly threw in, 'Why don't you go for a job in the bar, James?' Before he could answer, she carried on quickly, 'It makes sense! It's dead easy. Linda picked everything up very fast. You'll enjoy working here and it can be quite sociable. You finish at ten o'clock, there's still plenty time to spend with each other and, the best thing is, you'll both be saving and earning together!'

Before James had time to absorb what Isa was on about, she continued, 'Will I ask Tommy, the manager in the public bar, what shifts he has going?'

James was stunned, and looked like he didn't believe what he was saying when he found himself agreeing. Isa wasted no time and decided to strike while the iron was hot.

'Come through here with me', she said to James as she stood by the side door into the bar. Isa ushered him with her outstretched arm. Isa appeared back in the off sales a few minutes later with a cheeky grin on her face.

'I've left them to it', she said to Linda.

'That was very sneaky of you, Isa!' said Linda. 'I knew that you had something up your sleeve. You didn't even give him a chance to think anything out properly!'

Isa laughed and said, 'I know, but I don't want to lose you, and it is the only solution. Besides, he will enjoy it and thank me eventually, trust me!'

Linda gave Isa a look as if to tell her that she wasn't so sure about that! James came back through to the off sales after about fifteen minutes.

'Well, how did you get on, then?' Isa asked him.

'I start tomorrow night', James answered, turning his head towards Linda with a confused smirk, as if to say, I know that I have been set up here!

Just like Linda, James got on well and was very conscientious about his work. He carried out every task with efficiency. He worked in the men-only public bar, and it wasn't long before he was the star barman. Meanwhile, Linda carried on working in the off sales. By this time, Donna had trained her to work behind the lounge bar, serving and pulling pints and doing the cashier's job. No one was allowed to touch the till other than the cashier, in either the lounge or public bar. The barmen and barmaids told the cashier how much their order added up to. The cashier rang their money into the till and gave them their change back.

Linda was amazed when she saw what went on behind bars. Donna told her that on no account was the waste, or 'Ullage', beer, to be thrown away. There were a couple of big metal buckets of it, out of sight behind the bar. A large jug was dipped into one of these metal buckets, and then a lot pint glasses were lined up behind the Guinness pump. About an eighth of a pint of Ullage was poured into each pint glass for unsuspecting customers.

'Guinness is the best way to lose Ullage. I keep my stocks in profit that way', Donna told Linda.

Linda thought it was disgusting, and warned all her friends and family not to drink Guinness because of this unethical practice.

She thoroughly enjoyed pulling pints though, and preferred doing that to waiting tables. In the lounge, the waitresses took the last orders at half past nine because the police came, dead on ten o'clock, to make sure that all customers had left the premises and that the law wasn't being broken. It was different in the public bar. The last orders were taken by ten minutes to ten and no drinks were served after that. Glasses had to be empty, and all punters out, by ten o'clock. When the staff had finished their shifts and cashed up, they shared out the tips and sat down together. They were allowed to buy two drinks each before they left, which were served to them by the managers. The police came in and sat down with them to enjoy a couple of free pints each. This was considered their privilege, and no one argued.

Linda and James got friendly with all the other young folk working in the pub, especially another young engaged couple, Mickey and Natalie. Mickey was tall and gangly with thick, mousy brown hair. He was a born comedian. He got up to all sorts of tricks to make people laugh, it was difficult to get angry with him and he was always good fun to be with. One particular Saturday afternoon, Donna sent Linda through to the storeroom to get a tray full of pies to warm up in the oven by the bar. As she walked back with the full tray, she met Mickey in the corridor. He grabbed the pies, two or three at a time, and held them to his backside, farting on them before placing them back on the tray. Linda couldn't do anything! There was no place to put the tray down. She was helpless with laughter, telling Mickey to put them back and not to be so disgusting. Eventually, when Mickey was satisfied that he had farted on every one, he let her past him. Linda couldn't help giggling to herself as she and Donna put the pies into the oven. She warned her family and friends not to eat them, and swore blind that she would never eat another pie in a pub ever again. Natalie complimented Mickey's humour. She was small and petite, with short brown hair styled in a very modern 60's style which swept over one eye. She always dressed in fashion. She was characterised as the dumb blonde. It always took a little longer for jokes to sink in, and she had to have everything explained and spelt out to her.

There was usually a party to go to afterwards at weekends when they finished work. One particularly warm and balmy Friday night, about eight of them were all heading off to a house party in Drumchapel. James had his van parked in the car park. The noisy partygoers, with a couple of drinks each inside them, piled into the back of the van. James and Linda got in the front. It was pitch black in the car park. James slowly reversed out when suddenly, there was a loud 'BANG'. The van shuddered to a halt and the passengers in the back fell towards the back door of the van. There was silence as they all sat up in shock, not knowing what to think. James gingerly got out and went to the back of the van, followed by Linda and the others.

'Oh, God! I've gone into someone's car! They must have had too much too drink and decided to leave it. I wasn't expecting another car to be here at this time of night!' said a worried James.

There wasn't much damage to the van, but the car headlights were smashed. Just at that, a police car drew up in the car park. Two policemen got out and were walking towards the back door of the pub.

'Oh no!' whispered James to Linda. 'I'm for it now! They'll accuse me of being drunk and in charge of a vehicle'.

At that, the police clocked what had happened, about-turned double quick, jumped into their panda car and sped off.

'Wow, that was lucky! Don't hang around folks. Everyone get back in the van. Let's get out of here, fast!' said Mickey.

James couldn't believe his luck and nobody could understand why the police did a runner, it was the topic of the conversation all the way to the party.

They arrived at the party. Someone who had been drinking in the pub that evening had invited them all along, but they didn't know whose house it was. The girls left their coats in the van. It was the 'zip age': coats, dress, jumpers, cardigans and jackets all fastened up with zips with a metal ring to pull them up and down. Mickey and Natalie walked into the party in front of James and Linda. Suddenly, a roar went up. All the guys' eyes lit up and they were wolf-whistling and cheering. Linda wondered what was going on. Then, she realised that Natalie, in her usual dizziness, had forgotten she had left her coat with the front zipper in the van. She walked into the party and, in front of everyone, had absentmindedly pulled the zip right down in her dress. It wasn't until everyone cheered that she realised she was giving the lads a free show of her bra and pants.

Natalie stayed cool, smiled sweetly and said, 'Oh dear silly me!' and pulled the zip back up. She then made her way to the kitchen for a drink. The house was packed with folk and the drink was flowing. There were parties in every room, and everyone was tipsy. In one room, someone was strumming a guitar and singing a slow, labourious song about the deep blue sea. He had already sung some of the revelers to sleep and they were snoring in unison on the floor.

Suddenly, a head slowly and sleepily rose up from one of the bodies and shouted in a drunken slur, 'Will someone shut that Fucker up? He's making me sea sick!' Nobody came to his aid, and the folk singer carried on singing his lullabys.

Linda reported for work the next afternoon. She was working in the off sales. Isa loved to gossip and knew all what was going on. Linda was amazed how she found everything out.

'Did your James hit a car in the car park when he was leaving last night?' Isa asked Linda.

'How do you mean?' Linda answered.

'Well, Jessie, who works in the public bar, has been having it off with one of the punters. He arrived just before closing time and parked his car in the car park. When they left, the front of his car was all bashed in and his headlights smashed. He told Jessie that the only vehicle in the car park when he parked up was a white van. He can't make an official complaint to claim his insurance, because his wife thinks he was working night shift, and she will want to know what he was doing parked here, when he works in town', laughed Isa.

'Oh, well, I'll tell James. Now that we know who the car belongs to, we will pay for the damage', Linda responded. 'There was another strange thing that happened last night. Two policemen were heading for the pub and when they saw the crash, they jumped into their police car and drove off very fast'.

'Oh, that'll be Noreen's and May's fancymen. They have been seeing these two coppers for months and they always come in at closing time. They are out of their area when they come here, and would get seriously disciplined if they were caught, so don't worry about that,. If they were to open their mouths about James, you could shop them, and they know that!' confided Isa.

Everything was making sense now to Linda. James had a word with Jessie, and she told him that the repairs to her boyfriend's car would cost £25.

The following weekend, Mickey came over to James, handed him a brown envelope and said, 'There you go pal. We can't have you and Linda paying out all that money. It was more our fault for being so loud and making you lose your concentration. We've had a whip round and we have raised £21 towards the cost of the repairs for Jessie's fella's car'.

James and Linda were grateful for their workmates' generosity. It certainly was a big help. They would have had to work weeks to replace that money in their savings.

There was a cashier's job going in the public bar and Tommy asked Linda if she was interested. She told him that she wasn't, because she enjoyed her work in the off sales and helping out in different areas at busy periods. However, when she mentioned this to Maria, she said that she wouldn't mind a few nights a week.

'It'll do Kevin good to look after the kids. I could do with the break away from the house and, we could certainly do with the extra money'.

Linda had a word with Tommy and Maria started that weekend.

All the family were up in Molly's for the usual Sunday evening when Iris piped up, 'Are there any more jobs going in that pub you work in, Linda?'

Now, the last person that Linda wanted to be working alongside of was Iris. It would be a constant worry that she might give James, Maria and herself a showing up with her drinking and explosive temper.

'No, I don't think so', Linda lied, having no intention of asking Donna or Tommy.

'What about that new pub our boss is opening next month in Drumchapel? I'll ask about that one for you', Maria came out with, in all innocence.

'Oh, is that the same chain as yours? That'll be even better, because it's just walking distance for me. I'll save on bus fares', Iris enthused.

After Iris left, Linda said to Maria, 'Are you sure that it's a good idea to speak for a job for Iris? You know what she's like on alcohol. You don't want it all to come back on you, do you?'

Maria looked worried. 'Oh, I didn't think about that, you're right Linda! Me and my big mouth! What am I going to do now? I can't not very well say anything now, she'll kill me!'

Maria asked the area manager, Iris went for an interview, and got a job as a barmaid. The pub didn't open for another couple of weeks, but they asked her to come in the week before to help set it up. Linda and Maria prayed that she wouldn't let them down, but they needn't have worried. The pub needed someone like Iris to control a certain element that drank in there. Nobody in their right mind messed with Iris, and she was soon kingpin. She got Molly a job as the pub cleaner.

Linda chuckled to herself as she thought, *James wasn't too happy about me taking on this job but, within months, he and his whole family are working for the same pub chain! All because of me wanting a part time job to help save up for our future!*

Meanwhile, James and Linda were making plans for their wedding the following year in 1970. They decided on a low-key affair, mainly because that's all they could afford. They knew that their families didn't have the finances to help. They agreed on 28th March. This was a popular time of the year for weddings because the tax year ended on 5th April and, if you married just before that, you got your tax allowances back for the whole year. They thought about a church wedding and attended every Sunday for a month before changing their minds. Besides the fact that James was completely tone deaf and seemed to knock the whole congregation out of key, they were both uncomfortable with it. They only went to church for weddings, christenings and funerals, and felt a bit like hypocrites. They plumped for a civil registry office wedding instead.

Molly, being a devout church-goer, wasn't at all happy about this. 'They are not proper ceremonies! They don't mean anything. You are in and out so quickly because the next couple is waiting. It's not right! You won't feel married', she told James and Linda in frustration.

What's For Ye, Won't Go By Ye

To Molly's dismay and anger, Linda stood firm on her decision. The hall above the City Bakeries in Byres Road was a popular party venue. They went along to see if it was free for that day and were in luck, because another wedding had just been cancelled.

'I hope that's not a bad omen', said Linda as they paid the £12 deposit.

They intended to invite just the immediate relatives and a few very best friends. The problem was that Linda's mum and dad both came from large, close families. The best she could break the invitations down to, for her side without offending anyone, was forty seven, and that wasn't counting friends.

'Perhaps we should just have parents and witnesses, and forget all this expense', said Linda disappointedly.

'No', insisted James. 'We'll have the best we can afford. I won't have any more than sixteen people on my side. My two sisters, their husbands and kids, my mother, her two widowed sisters and four cousins. I won't be asking the Alexander side of the family, because they don't talk to my mother. Our friends should bring it up to approximately seventy guests. With my apprenticeship finished and the increase in my wages, along with our part time jobs in the New Inn, I think we will be just about able to cover it'.

'Oh! It's going to cost an awful lot James! Just think what we could buy for our first house with all that money. It seems such a waste!' said Linda.

'Don't worry, we'll get by', James told Linda positively.

'That's another thing, though James. We're going to have to start looking for a place, and for £50, we could put down a deposit to buy a wee room and kitchen to start us off, instead of blowing everything on one day for a wedding', Linda said.

James looked at her in deep thought, as if to tell her he knew that what she was saying made sense.

Linda and James sorted out the wedding list with Margie and Douglas for Linda's side of the family. Then they went to see Molly.

'So, what you are saying is that you are having forty seven family guests and we are only to have sixteen? That doesn't sound very fair to me!' said Molly in her usual argumentative way.

'Yes, but that's all the family we have, mother. You wouldn't want the Alexanders' there. Besides, Linda and I are really stretching our budget to cover seventy guests. It's going to be a real struggle for us!' James said.

He and Linda tried hard to reason with Molly.

'Well, if Linda is having forty seven family guests on her side, then it is only right that we have the same amount on our side! We can invite my friends to make up the numbers, that'll balance things out', Molly said defiantly.

'But we can't afford to pay for that amount of people! In any case, my parents don't have any friends coming. My forty seven guests are all close family. We can't put ourselves to the expense of inviting friends of yours that we hardly know, just to make numbers up on your side. I've never heard anything so stupid!' Linda told Molly with determination.

Molly was being very stubborn and wasn't giving in easily.

Later, Linda said to James, 'I don't know what we are going to do! You're mother is adamant that she should make up the numbers with friends. That is very selfish. She knows we are struggling! You will have to tell her that she is welcome to bring as many friends as she wants but that she will have to pay the difference! I am not going to waste time arguing with her anymore, because she doesn't listen!'

James just pursed his lips, thinking how on earth he was going to get round this one and still keep his controlling mother happy.

Iris had only been in her new job a few months when, true to form, she was causing disruption in the family. Molly discovered that she was carrying on with one of the punters who drank in her pub. Every night, he walked her home and they sneaked into a back close for a bit of hankie-pankie on the way. Molly was disgusted by her daughter's behaviour and tried to talk to Iris about it, but, as usual, she ignored her mother. Iris was selfish and was only concerned about her own happiness. Molly never gave up hope that one day Iris would see the light and reform.

Iris shocked and embarrassed Molly by turning up for work one morning with a black eye. 'Did Kevin do that to you?' she asked Iris.

'Aye! He accused me of carrying on with another man', answered her daughter.

Molly pleaded with Iris, saying, 'Iris, you're a married woman! You shouldn't be doing this. You have a wee son to consider too'.

Iris gave her mother a filthy look and turned away, as if to tell her to mind her own business.

Molly continued with, 'But, even so, it's still no reason for Kevin to lift his hands to you. You're going to have to stop all this nonsense though. I think you should give this job up. What with the drink and the men, it is too tempting for you'

Iris answered with, 'I can't give my job up! I need the money more than ever now, because Julie has rented an apartment in Kelvinside and she has asked me to share with her'.

'What! How are you going to manage? And what about Jamie?' Molly worriedly asked her.

'Jamie can come with me, there is plenty of room', Iris announced.

What's For Ye, Won't Go By Ye

Iris always twisted her mum round her wee finger and it wasn't long before she had convinced Molly that it was the right thing for her to do.

Iris' next step was to ask James to come up to her house with his van when Kevin was working late, to remove her belongings and some of the furniture. James wasn't happy, and didn't want to get involved. but his mum talked him into it. She explained that he would be helping Iris get out of a violent relationship with her husband. Iris arranged for James to be at her house at 4.30pm one afternoon. He was very nervous. He only had three hours to get everything that Iris needed out, because Kevin would be home by half past seven. It would take at least two runs back and forward. James worked very fast. He had a horrible, sick feeling inside that Kevin might come home early, and he didn't relish that thought. He got all Iris' belongings to her new address, then he drove home feeling uptight about the whole thing. Although he didn't really have much time for Kevin, he couldn't help thinking how lousy it was going to be for him to come home to find out that his wife had cleared off with his son and half of the household belongings.

James felt quite guilty about the whole thing. Over his dinner, he was thinking of all the problems that Iris had created over the years, the worry and disruption she had caused his whole family, and yet, his mother kept forgiving her, only for to Iris do it all over again. He wondered if one day his mother would ever come to her senses and realise that there was very little chance of Iris ever changing or being normal.

James and Linda took Molly down to see Iris in her pokey wee flat. Molly was horrified to see that little Jamie slept in a 'hole-in-the-wall' bed in the kitchen, while Iris slept on a bed settee and Julie had the bedroom.

Iris ignored Molly when she said, 'This is no place to bring a we'an up! You're going back the way, instead of forward! Anyway, where is Jamie?'

'He's playing with his new pals on a swing. He's settled in really well and loves it here', Iris said, trying to convince everyone.

After an hour had passed and Jamie still hadn't come home, James went out to look for him. He returned after just over half an hour and was infuriated.

'Do you have any idea where this swing was that he and his pals were playing on, Iris?' James demanded.

'No, I knew it couldn't be far away, though', she answered, unconcerned.

'It was over the River Kelvin! Do you know how dangerous that river can be?' James shouted to her in disgust.

Iris just laughed. Then she said, 'I don't know why you're getting so worked up—he's OK, isn't he? Nothing has happened to him!'

'But what if I didn't get there when I did...', then James threw his hands in the air and said, 'A-h-h, what's the use! You're a useless mother and you won't listen to anyone!'

James then said to his mother and Linda, 'C'mon, we're going. I've seen enough to last me a lifetime!'

Two weeks later, Iris arrived at her mother's house with a small suitcase. 'What's in the case?' Molly asked her.

'It's Jamie's clothes', said Iris. 'I've got a hotel job down in England for a few months and I'm leaving Jamie with you'.

'But Iris! I'm sixty-four and, much as I love Jamie, I don't have the stamina to look after a six-year-old on my own, and on a permanent basis. Besides, I have my nights out at the Women's Guild and day trips with the church to consider! I can't take a we'an with me to them!' Molly answered.

'Well, I've had him all winter!' Iris told her mother indignantly.

Molly couldn't believe her ears! She raised her voice and shouted 'You're his mother Iris! You're supposed to look after him!' She then caught sight of Jamie, who was standing in the corner, anxiously glancing back and forwards at the two women. 'C'm'ere son. I will always be here for you', Molly said gently.

Iris cold heartedly said, 'Well, that's that, then. I best be off! I have to catch an early train in the morning. You be a good boy for your Nana. I'll be back for Christmas!' She gave Jamie a quick kiss on the cheek and ran out of the door before Molly had a chance to change her mind.

It was June 1969. Linda was sitting at her office desk reading the newspaper during the afternoon tea break.

'Here, Beverley!' she said to her office junior. 'The Citizen is looking for young local girls to appear on their 'Daily Dolly' page. It says here, if you know of any young attractive girls, send in their details to them, and they will be invited along to have their photos taken for the national newspaper. Are you up for it?'

Beverley blushed. 'Oh, God no! I'd be dead embarrassed!' she answered.

'You've got nothing to be embarrassed about! You're a very attractive eighteen year old and you have a gorgeous figure! If you've got it, flaunt it, that's what I say!' Linda commented.

Sally joined in, 'Yes, go for it Bev. Linda's right, they'll love you!'

Beverley reluctantly agreed, and Linda filled out the form and sent it into in the newspaper's Glasgow headquarters. Three days later, a letter arrived for Beverley. It was from The Citizen, inviting her to come along to their studio and have her photo taken. She was to phone in and make an appointment.

'Oh God, no! I can't go through with this', she told Linda.

'Well, you don't have to if you don't want to! Nobody's forcing you. Calm down, let it sink in, think about it, and then decide', Linda replied.

An hour later, Beverley came over to Linda's desk and asked, 'Can I have a word with you, please?'

Linda put her pen down and said, 'Certainly Beverley, don't worry. Do you want me to call them up and cancel the photo session? I understand completely. I shouldn't have talked you into it, it was wrong of me. It's just that you see some of these girls and you would beat them all hands down'.

'No, No, it's not that', Beverley interrupted, stopping Linda in her tracks. 'Oh God, I've decided you're right. Deep down I really want to do this. I need to have more confidence in myself. I won't get anywhere running away from things, so I'm going to call them and make an appointment. There's just ONE thing. I would feel really stupid going on my own. Will you come along and keep me company, please Linda?'

'Of course I will', said Linda, and she continued, 'Oh, I can't wait to see your photo in the paper! You'll be really popular after that, you'll be fighting all the lads off!'

'Oh God! I should be so lucky', Beverley laughed, as she answered Linda.

The appointment was made for Friday lunchtime. Linda did Beverley's make up for her. She put thick, black eyeliner round her eyes with lashing of mascara and juicy, pink lipstick on her lips. Sally helped style her hair, it was short and hanging long on one side, in a Mary Quant fashion.

'Oh God', Beverley said with a proud, satisfied smile as she looked in the mirror. 'I feel like a different person. I,... I feel quite beautiful! Oh God, you'll think I'm so vain!'

'You are beautiful, Beverley. You must stop putting yourself down', said Linda.

Beverley disappeared upstairs to the ladies to get dressed in her black mini skirt, white baggy-sleeved blouse, short black waistcoat and black mod shoes. Linda loaned her a pair of dangling Mary Quant black and white plastic earrings. Fifteen minutes later, the office door opened and in glided Beverley.

'Oh God.....you are gorgeous', echoed Linda and Sally together.

Then they all collapsed laughing.

'Oh God! Do I really keep saying that? It's just a nervous habit', giggled Beverley.

At quarter to one, Linda set off with a very nervous Beverley for the newspaper offices at the other side of George Square. They went into the big building and told the girl at reception that Beverley had an appointment with the photographer for quarter past one. A young 'camp' lad came down to reception and met them. He took them up in a lift. Then they followed him for what seemed like miles along corridors and through an open plan office where the young men stopped what they were doing. The girls could feel their eyes penetrating them as wolf whistles filled the air.

'Hey look lads, we've got a couple of 'Daily Dollies' here!' announced one young Paul McCartney look-alike, complete with long Beatles' hairstyle and collarless jacket. He was sitting casually on top of his desk with a note pad in his hand and a pencil stuck in his ear.

'Have you lot never seen girls before?' shouted their young escort with a grin to the admiring young males.

He turned to Linda and Beverley and joked, 'You've got to excuse them, the poor souls are stuck up here on the eighth floor, deprived of women'.

Eventually they arrived at a studio door. 'Just sit there', the lad told them, pointing to some chairs in the corridor. 'I'll tell him you're here'.

'Oh God, no. I want to run away, I've got awful butterflies', said Beverley.

'Just relax and take deep breaths, you'll be OK', Linda told her.

'Oh God, you don't think that he will expect me to take my clothes off! I'm not doing that!' said Beverley in a panic.

'No, don't be so daft! It's not that sort of photo they're looking for Beverley. It's respectable, attractive local girls', said Linda, trying to calm her down and wishing that she had never suggested this.

'Oh God, are you positively sure, Linda?' Beverley moaned.

'YES!' answered Linda in a loud, exasperated tone.

The next thing, a large man in his forties, with long, brown, straggly unkempt hair, half rimmed specs sitting halfway down his nose, a black polo neck underneath a well worn baggy brown suede jacket, which was hanging open and untidy, appeared at the studio door.

'Ah, what do we have here, not one, but two 'Daily Dollies?' How lucky can a man get!'

Linda felt herself getting flustered as she stuttered and told him, 'No, No, I'm not here to be a 'Daily Dolly'. It's Beverley who has the appointment with you. I'm just keeping her company!'

The photographer put his head down, looked over the top of his specs, gave a wry smile and said, 'We'll see! Right girls, come this way'.

Linda felt close to panic and began to realise what poor Beverley had been going through. She wished she had never suggested this and that the ground would open up and swallow her. In the corner of the studio, there was a dark backdrop with a brown leather chaise longue in front of it.

'OK Beverley, climb onto the sofa', the photographer said. Beverley nervously sat down on the chaise longue. Then he said, 'I need a pose, Beverley. Swing round and put your legs up on the sofa, now lean back to one side, head down, and look up at me. Tease me with your eyes!'

What's For Ye, Won't Go By Ye

Beverley looked uncomfortable as the camera flashed. After less than ten minutes, the session was over. Linda walked towards Beverley and held out her handbag for her. Linda's conscience was checking her for putting poor Beverley through all this. There was only one thing on her mind and that was for them to get out of there as quickly as possible.

'Not so fast! Where do you think you're going, young lady? You don't think that you're getting away that easy!' the photographer said to Linda.

'Oh, we have to get back, this is our lunch break, we'll be late!' Linda feebly tried to convince him.

'Oh come on Linda, we have at least half an hour, the session only takes ten minutes! We'll get back to the office in plenty time. If I can do it, then so can you!' said a now much more confident Beverley.

Linda looked at Beverley in disbelief at what she was saying. As Beverley smiled sweetly back at her, Linda couldn't help thinking that it was pay back time. She had convinced Beverley that there was nothing in it, so now she had to eat her words and prove it. She climbed onto the chaise longue and sat there with her legs straight out in front of her.

'OK Linda, pull one leg up, place one hand on your knee and the other one behind you. Now, tilt your head round slightly to me, chin down and look up at me cheekily with your eyes', the photographer said.

Linda felt herself shaking, she had a mini skirt on and was hoping against hope that nothing was showing. She just wanted to get off of that sofa and was thinking to herself, *What on earth is James going to say about this when he sees my photo plastered over the inside page of the daily newspaper?* Eventually the torture was over. Before they left, the photographer took their details and told then that their pictures would be appearing within the next month or so. Linda and Beverley felt their hearts palpitating as they found their way back through the building and out into the street.

'Phew! I'm glad that's over! The next time I see anything in the paper like this again, just ignore me, Beverley!' said Linda.

'Actually, it wasn't as bad as I thought it would be Linda. It was quite tame, but, Oh God! I would never do it again. I am quite looking forward to seeing our pictures in the paper though. Just think what all our pals will say, and wait until we tell Sally what happened!' Beverley said excitedly.

Sally laughed hysterically when they told her how the photographer had insisted on Linda having her photos taken too. She crossed her legs and tears were running down her face with laughter as they exaggerated all the different poses.

'Well, all I can say is I am glad that I wasn't there. It's a blessing that we have staggered lunch breaks and I had to stay and hold the fort. I would have been mortified if he had asked me to pose like a haddy!' Sally chuckled.

That evening, Linda told James what had happened.

'What? You mean you are going to be in the paper as a 'Daily Dolly?' I hope you kept your clothes on!' said a concerned James.

'Of course not, I was as naked as the day I was born!' answered Linda with a cheeky grin, giggling at the shocked look on James' face. Then she continued, 'Don't be so daft! You don't think that I would stoop that low....do you? It was just respectable poses'. Yet, at the same time, she worried that she wouldn't be showing too much leg or look tarty.

Linda and James' savings were coming along well. They traded in James' van for £80 and bought a maroon Ford Anglia car for £195. Linda refused to discuss wedding guest lists with Molly because she wasn't showing any signs of giving in.

Out of the blue, James said to Linda, 'I think we should get away from it all for a week. Let's book up to go to the Isle of Man for the last week of the Glasgow Fair at the end of July'.

'But James, where is the money going to come from for a holiday? We need to pay for our wedding, find a place to live, buy furniture, plus, we are paying HP on the car! We have my brother's wedding in August and we have to buy them a present! I will need a new outfit. Besides, your mother will wonder how we can go on holiday, but won't pay for her friends to attend our wedding', Linda pointed out.

James answered defiantly, 'We need a holiday! I can't listen to my mother going on about it anymore. Her friends won't be coming to the wedding!'

'Have you told her this?' Linda quietly put to him.

'How can I? She wouldn't listen to me, anyhow. I just don't want to talk about it', answered James in desperation.

Linda replied, 'Well, it's not going to go away by itself. You are going to have to tell her this. She can't read your mind. She won't take any notice of me but, if you are firm with her for once, she might stand up and take notice and finally realise that you mean business!'

'I wish we could just disappear off and get married without all this hassle! I don't know why she's being so difficult!' said James sadly. Then he continued, 'C'mon Linda, let's have a nice relaxing holiday! It might be the last one for a while. We both want children. If you're pregnant by next summer, not only will we not be able to afford it, you'll probably not feel like going anywhere'.

Linda could see that all the pressure was getting to James and had to agree with him that it would be a good thing for them to get away completely on their own. The following day, she went to the travel agents in her lunch break and booked a week for them again in the boarding house belonging to the two Misses Jeffreys at the end of July.

261

What's For Ye, Won't Go By Ye

The weeks weren't long in passing and before they knew it, James and Linda were on their way to Isle of Man. They knew that they couldn't really afford this holiday, but with Molly's lack of co-operation on the subject of the guest list, the whole thing was becoming a headache rather than a day to look forward to. It was lovely and sunny as they sailed out of Stranraer.

They were sitting on the top deck enjoying the warm breeze when James suddenly said to Linda, 'You know, there is one way round all of this'.

'Round what?' asked Linda.

'The wedding problems! All we want to do is get married. We want to start a family right away, so why don't we go in for a baby now? We can just have a registry office wedding with a wee party afterwards for the immediate family. We can afford that, and there won't be any interference from anyone!'

Linda knew what James was getting at. It would be much easier for him to tell his mum that the wedding had to be rushed now, so it would only be a small, simple ceremony and reception.. Although James knew his mother would be furious and that this would be totally against her religious beliefs, he felt more comfortable with this because she would have to go along with whatever was decided. She wouldn't be able to make demands on what type of wedding they were to have, or how many guests to invite. The pair of them decided that they wanted to be in charge of their own wedding day and that to go ahead with this plan was the best solution.

They got off the boat and climbed up the hill to the boarding house. The two Miss Jeffreys greeted them warmly at the door, and welcomed them back for another holiday. The following morning at breakfast, it was the same procedure as their stay there two years previously. The elder Miss Jeffreys told Linda and James to help themselves to cereal and orange juice, and that she would bring their fried breakfast through when they were ready for it.

Just as they finished eating their corn flakes, they heard a familiar voice bellowing in the corner, 'I don't like sugar! How many times do I have to tell you?'

They both burst out laughing! It was the same grumpy Glaswegian man that was there the last time.

After breakfast, they went for a ride along the prom on the horse-drawn tram. At the end of the line, they decided to get off the tram and walk all the way back. The sun was splitting the pavement. They popped into a little café for ice-cold soft drinks and then continued on their way, walking hand in hand and happily chatting about what the future would hold for them.

As they were nearing the town and the shops, James said, 'Look Linda, is that your Auntie Dot coming out of that telephone box?'

Linda looked in disbelief. 'No it can't be!' she replied.

'Well, if it isn't, then there's a man with her who looks just like your Uncle Tom!' answered James.

Linda stared for a second, then said, 'It is them, isn't it?' She ran after them, 'Auntie Dot, Uncle Tom!'

Dot and Tom turned round in amazement at who was shouting their names. 'It's Linda!' Auntie Dot exclaimed to Uncle Tom.

'What are you doing here?' the two women asked each other at exactly the same time. Then they started to laugh. 'When did you arrive? Did you fly or sail? How long are you here for? Where are you staying?' They fired questions, talking over each other without taking a breath.

'We sailed over yesterday', Linda told her aunt and uncle.

'Actually, we only arrived last night. We just took a last minute notion to come here and managed to get the last two seats on the aeroplane', said Auntie Dot. She continued, 'But Linda, I've got to tell you this. We were sitting on the plane and the man in the next row up, opposite us, was reading The Evening Citizen, and you know how big that newspaper is. He was holding part of it out in the aisle. I glanced over and then looked again. I couldn't believe my eyes! I nudged Uncle Tom and said to him, is that Linda as a 'Daily Dolly?' He had a look and said, Aye it looks like her. We tried to get The Citizen at the airport when we landed, but they don't sell it here'.

'Oh no, have they put my photo in? Thank goodness I'm not at home to take all the stick!' said Linda.

She called her mother and told her, but Margie and Douglas already knew and had bought a bundle of the newspapers to show off to all their friends and family.

Linda and James intended to hire a car the next day to drive round the island and invited Auntie Dot and Uncle Tom to come with them for the run. The four of them met up in front of the Villa Marina after breakfast the following morning and set off on their trip. They had a wonderful time. They said good morning to the fairies, stopped off at a small zoo, had lunch in a nice restaurant in Ramsey, and then continued all the way round the island. Auntie Dot and Uncle Tom had to be back before six o'clock for their evening meal, and James pulled the car up outside of their hotel at half past five. It had been a long day, they were all tired out, but they had thoroughly enjoyed themselves.

'We'll see you tomorrow morning at half past ten in the Villa Marina for morning coffee', said Linda.

She knew that they wouldn't want to go to the young lively bars that James and she intended to go to that evening.

They met up with Auntie Dot and Uncle Tom every day after breakfast and went somewhere different. The week just flew and, in no time, they were on the ship sailing back to Stranraer. Auntie Dot and Uncle Tom came to see them off at the pier because they were not flying out until early the next morning. The

Irish Sea was rough and the further out they sailed, the worse it got. Linda had always been a good sailor, but she was feeling rather queasy. Downstairs, people were lying in the luggage racks, moaning, groaning and running to the toilets to be sick.

'I can't understand this. I've sailed over to the Islands in rough seas before and never felt this ill...unless, of course, ...I'm expecting', she said to James hesitantly, with a worried, concerned expression.

'So, what if you are? It'll be the most loved baby ever. This is something we both want isn't it? It just means that we will get married sooner rather than later, with no interference from anyone'.

When they got back to Linda's house, Douglas showed them The Evening Citizen, with Linda's picture in it. It wasn't too bad. She was showing a bit of leg, but in a tasteful way. James seemed quite proud and took a couple of the newspapers to show to his friends and family. When Linda went into work, the girls teased her, calling out, 'how's Miss Scotland today?' She was embarrassed to find out from Sally that Beverley's picture still hadn't appeared in The Evening Citizen.

When James and Linda went back to their part time jobs in the pub, young lads were using the chat-up line to Linda, 'Didn't I see your photo in the paper a couple of weeks back?'

Donna would interrupt them with, 'I would give up now if I were you lads, you don't stand a chance. Have you seen her boyfriend? He works in the public bar next door, and he won't be very happy if he knew you were coming onto his girlfriend!'

The lads usually made a quick exit while the two young women giggled.

Almost two weeks passed and Linda's periods still hadn't started. This was most unusual, because she was always on time.

'I think you better get to the doctor for a test, Linda', James told her.

'I'll wait another few days. They might start by the end of the week', answered Linda.

Deep down, she knew that she was pregnant. Her sense of smell had changed, she felt sick when she walked by the baker's shop, and she couldn't stand the smell of food cooking. She was sitting at her office desk and felt herself about to throw up. She didn't have time to run to the ladies toilet, so she turned round and was sick in her waste paper bin.

Sally came running over. 'Are you OK?' she asked Linda, worriedly.

'Yes, I'm fine now, it must've been something I ate', answered Linda.

Douglas junior and Norma's wedding was on the last Friday of August. It was a posh affair in a country church, followed by a big reception for 200 guests in a swish hotel. Norma's parents were comfortably off and paid for everything. It was the sort of wedding that Linda dreamt about, but she knew that the finances just weren't there for her and James. Linda's boss only allowed her to take the afternoon off for the wedding, so she had to make a mad dash to the hairdresser's as soon as she finished at 1pm. She didn't get out of there until after 2pm and she still had to catch a bus home. Linda had arranged for a coach to leave from her parents' house at 3.15pm and pick other guests up on the way. It was just going on for ten minutes to three and Margie and James were panicking because the coach had arrived and Linda wasn't home yet.

Just seconds later, Linda flung open the front door and flew up the stairs. She quickly got washed and dressed and, with only minutes to spare, she came back down the stairs looking radiant in her long-sleeved turquoise mini dress with checked turquoise and white sleeveless matching coat. Deep down, Linda knew that she was pregnant and that her marriage to James would be sooner than everyone imagined. No one surmised anything when she stuck to orange juice for the toasts and refused offers of alcoholic drinks as she celebrated her brother's and Norma's big day.

The following week, Linda finally took herself down to her local doctor's surgery. She saw the new young doctor. He was most understanding and told her to take a urine sample into the health department in the city centre the following day and come back to him next week for the result. Linda didn't really need the doctor to tell her, but she went along anyway. He confirmed that she was to have a baby the following April.

Linda immediately called James and told him.

'OK, we better start by telling your parents. Then we have to find a place to live and arrange a simple, quickie wedding. I'll come down this evening'. James seemed unflustered. It was as if this was what he had wanted all along. He arrived at Linda's house and they went out for a walk to talk things over.

'Don't worry, Linda, it'll be OK. I'll look after you. We'll get married before you start to show and we'll find a place to rent first, and eventually we'll buy our own house', James assured her.

Linda felt confident that James meant what he said. They made their way back to the house and, as Linda put her key in the door, James said in a whisper, 'Well, here goes!'

Douglas was sitting in front of the television doing the crossword in The Daily paper. Margie was busying about the kitchen.

'Douglas, Linda and I have something to tell you and her mum', said James nervously.

'What's that?' replied Douglas inquisitively.

'Well, we'd rather that Linda's mum was here to hear this too', replied James.

'Margie, come through here a minute! Linda and James have something to tell us!' he shouted.

Margie came through, cheerily drying her hands on a towel. 'What is it?' she asked.

'Well, Linda is expecting a baby, so, you see, we will have to get married sooner and forget the big wedding', James blurted out.

Margie and Douglas sat in stunned silence.

Then, Douglas stood up and said, 'Right We'll have to organise a wedding and find you somewhere to live. This is no one else's business. After all, it's not as if you have just got to know each other. You are engaged to be married and have been going out together for over three years'.

Margie looked a bit disappointed that she wasn't going to see her only daughter married in the traditional way, but promised to do all she could to help.

The next hurdle to cross was to tell Molly. 'Shall we both go up to your house and tell your mother now?' said Linda to James.

'No, I don't think that would be a good idea. I'll tell her myself when I get back tonight', James answered. James knew that his mother would not take this well and he didn't want Linda to be in the direct firing line.

'How did your mother take our news?' Linda asked James the following day when he called her at work.

'How do you think?' he answered, continuing with, 'She's not very happy, but she'll get used to it, she'll have to!'

Linda told the girls at work, and they were all delighted and excited for her.

'Ah! So that's why you were sick in the waste paper bin. I should have guessed, because it wasn't like you at all! Awa, James will make a lovely husband and, with your new wee baby, your family will be complete. Just think, you'll soon be Mrs. Alexander!' said Sally.

Linda replied, 'Oh no! That makes me feel ancient. I'll still be Linda. I'll leave the 'Mrs. Alexander' for my mother-in-law!'

Linda called Morag at work and arranged to meet her for lunch to tell her the news. She thought that she would get to her first before she heard through Eric's granny, who was a good friend of Molly's. Linda walked up to meet Morag at her work and they crossed the road to the restaurant.

As they sat down at a table by the window, Linda said, 'If you don't mind Morag, I'll just have a soft drink, I'm not hungry'.

'You don't need to explain. Eric's gran has already told me that you're pregnant', said Morag.

Linda was angry because she had specifically asked James to tell his mum to keep it to herself for the minute, so that she could tell people herself.

'Aye, she told her at church on Sunday. She says that you have trapped her son into marrying you', continued Morag.

By this time Linda was furious. 'How dare she say that, and how dare she tell people! She could at least have given us the privilege of telling our friends ourselves! I suppose she's gone round and told Alan's mother, too?'

'Aye, nae doubt she hus. Awe listen, jist ignore her! Ye know whit Eric's gran's like, she loves a bit of gossip. They're baith as bad as each other', said Morag.

'Aye, you're right Morag. Nothing better to do with themselves!' answered Linda.

James and Linda gave up their jobs at the pub and booked their wedding date at the registry office for Saturday 11th October. They still had a lot to do. They only had seven weeks to organise their wedding, find a place to live and furnish it. One of the better off factors who had nice properties for rent was a client of the cousin who owned the joiner's shop that James worked in. He had a word in the right direction and they told him that they had a property coming up for rent in Dennistoun towards the end of the year, and it was James', if he wanted it. The lady who lived there was terminally ill and didn't have much longer to live. While James and Linda were very sad for her, this was wonderful news for them.

Meanwhile, they had to find a place to live until the property was vacant. Douglas got to know many people on his rounds as a postman and he got talking to a local factor that had a ground floor room and kitchen to let in Parkhead. Linda and James went to view it. There was a small hallway leading into a good-sized kitchen. The sink was under the window, which looked out to the pavement, and there was a space in the corner for a cooker. The bedroom was off of the kitchen.

'But where's the bathroom?"' asked Linda.

'There isn't one, only a toilet in the back close that we share with the family next door!' answered James.

Linda looked astonished, 'Share an outside toilet, in this day and age!' she exclaimed, screwing up her face in disgust.

'Well, it won't be for long', James told her.

In the next few weeks, it was all hands on deck. Alan, Eric and James painted and decorated the whole flat. James and Linda bought blue carpet for the kitchen and red for the bedroom from a shop at The Barras. James fitted it himself. They also bought a second hand gas cooker from a stall at The Barras.

What's For Ye, Won't Go By Ye

Linda noticed an advert in the newspaper for a second hand three-piece leather suite. She phoned the man up in Clydebank and was dismayed to find that it had been sold. The man seemed to feel sorry for her and he told Linda that he had another one for only £20 and that she could have that, if she wanted. James and Linda went down that evening and they loved the black leather suite. It was as good as new with little black-sloping legs. The man selling the furniture explained that he covered the suites himself, and this was his own, but he had another one ready to replace it. The only thing was that it wasn't finished yet.

'Oh, that's not a problem because we don't get married until next month. Will yours be ready by then?' she asked him.

'Oh aye, it'll be ready sooner than that. You can have this by the end of next week. I'll deliver it for you, too', he replied.

Linda and James couldn't believe their luck. They gave the man £5 deposit and arranged for him to deliver it to their new flat the following Friday evening.

Margie and Douglas gave them a chest of drawers, a kitchen sideboard and some pots, pans and utensils that they had finished with. Molly gave them her gate leg table and her mother's old wardrobe Their flat soon took shape and was like a wee palace. It was nothing like it looked when they first went to see it.

Margie took Linda and James out to the warehouse where she held an account in the Gallowgate and let them choose a bed for their wedding present. They also chose material to make curtains for the two windows. Deep down, Margie was worried sick about her daughter going to live in a pokey wee room and kitchen with an outside toilet in the back close. She would rather that Linda and James stayed with her and Douglas.

Douglas' answered, 'Ach don't worry Margie. It's only for a short while until James' cousin gets his factor to sort out a proper place for them. When they get a house with a bathroom, they'll appreciate it all the more. You know that it's not a good thing to move in with relatives. Remember the experience we had. It's much better if they stand on their own two feet, it'll make them more responsible!'

'I just hope that they are out of there before the baby arrives' said Margie, then she continued, 'That's no place to bring up a child. It's so noisy! When the people in the street are talking, you'd think that they were in the room with you. It's not safe going out to the toilet in the back close at night time, anyone could be lurking there. It's terrible that landlords are allowed to rent out properties with no inside toilet in this day and age!'

While all this was going on, Linda was shopping around and sorting out a wedding outfit for herself. Although she longed to wear a traditional long dress and veil, she decided that it would be too fussy for the registry office. Margie's work colleague at the University told her about a lovely white lace mini dress that was in the window of a shop in Argyle Street. Linda went along to see it, tried it on and it was perfect. She bought a big floppy white hat, white round toed shoes with three inch block heels and a white beaded bag. She looked every bit the sixties bride. Linda and Anne had always promised each other when they were young that if they got married, they would be bridesmaid to each other because the two cousins had grown up together and were as close as sisters. Linda kept her promise and Anne was delighted to accept. Linda asked Anne what she would like for her bridesmaid's present, and Anne told her about this fabulous big multi-coloured watch that she had seen in Lewis' Department Store. Linda agreed to buy it for her. Linda also bought two bouquets from Lewis', a white one for her and a red one for Anne. They were only imitation cloth flowers, but they looked grand. Linda now had her new wedding outfit, so she had the 'something new' part. Auntie Betty loaned her a pearl necklace for the 'something old and borrowed', and Margie made her a blue garter for the 'something blue'. Meanwhile, James asked Alan to be his best man, because he was his life long friend and had been with him the night he met Linda.

Linda arranged her holidays so that she had one week before her wedding and one week after. There wouldn't be any money left for a honeymoon, so James and she decided the best they could afford were days here and there in their little Anglia car. Linda had already asked him if they could go through to Edinburgh the first day after they married. It was only an hour's drive and she loved to stand in the castle courtyard overlooking the Princes Street gardens and the town.

Linda went into work for the last Friday before she got married She was the first one there in the morning. She unlocked her office door and burst out laughing when she looked in the room. The girls must have doubled back after they had locked up the night before and come back to decorate her desk and chair. They had done them up with coloured crepe paper. On her desk were paper flowers, a rolling pin, tin opener, wedding jokes cut out from the paper, confetti and many other bits and pieces.

'Where am I supposed to sit?' Linda laughingly asked Sally when she arrived for work.

'Ah, you'll have to use the spare desk today. Anyway, you'll be handing over to me for the two weeks you're off, so just see to the essentials today and don't worry about anything that's not done. I will take care of next week', Sally told her.

'Just think, in eight days' time I will no longer be Miss, but Mrs. Oh, it's quite frightening. It's a complete new era of my life beginning!' Linda said to Sally and Beverley.

At the end of the day, the girls were getting ready to leave the office. Linda went over to the coat-stand and, looking puzzled, she said, 'Where's my coat gone?'

'Oh, I think I saw it in storeroom', answered Beverley.

What's For Ye, Won't Go By Ye

'I don't remember leaving it in there! I must be cracking up!' replied Linda as she went through the door into the storeroom.

Sally and Beverley bit their lips, trying not to laugh out loud as they waited for a reaction. 'Oh My God, who did this?' shouted Linda as she appeared at the storeroom door, laughing her head off. Her coney fur coat was completely covered in home made. multi-coloured paper flowers and had a big 'L' pinned to the back of it.

'I can't go home wearing this!' she pleaded.

'Oh yes you can!' insisted the girls as they locked the office door behind them and got her into the lift.

The people from different companies were coming into the lift on different floors and all Linda could do was smile embarrassedly at them.

When they got out into the street Sally said, 'We hope everything goes well for you and James next Saturday'.

Beverley chimed in with, 'Yes, we'll be thinking about you both'.

'You're not leaving me to walk up the road on my own dressed like this…are you?' Linda asked.

'Bye Linda, we'll see you in two weeks!' answered Sally and Beverley in unison as they turned and walked away in the opposite direction, giggling and disappearing into the crowds.

Linda was horrified. She drew a lot of attention as she walked up the road, unpicking the decorations from her coat. Some people stared, while others offered typical Glaswegian good wishes like, 'Guan yersel!' and 'Hard Up Hen!'

That night, Linda went out to a restaurant with her cousin Anne and her friends Morag and Helen for her last night of freedom as a single woman. James took Douglas, Douglas junior, Eric, Alan, Kevin, Pete and a few other lads to his local for his stag night. When Linda spoke to James the next day, she was glad that she had insisted on having their nights out with their pals the week before the wedding, because James was still hung over in the afternoon and wouldn't have been in any fit state if it had been their wedding day.

The night before the wedding, the MacGregor household was buzzing. The wedding cake had arrived that afternoon. It was a large square base with a medium sized second tier on pillars. The top was decorated with a large white garland. Linda was delighted. It was exactly as she had described to the baker. Linda called the hired car company during the day to confirm that the two Humber Hawk cars, decorated with flowers and white ribbons, were definitely going to be outside her door at quarter to ten on Saturday morning. She went to the hairdresser late afternoon to have her long hair pinned up. It was exactly the same style as she had for her brother Douglas' wedding, exaggerated big, soft curls and ringlets with lots of little white flowers pinned in. The hairdresser was aware that everything had to stay intact until the next morning, so she made sure all the pins were holding Linda's hairstyle securely.

'Oh my, you look gorgeous, but how on earth are you going to keep it in place until tomorrow?' gasped Margie as Linda walked in the front door.

'The hairdresser advised me to wrap a chiffon scarf loosely round my head before going to bed, and to sleep sitting up', Linda laughed.

Margie screwed her eyes up in a concerned manner. 'How on earth can you sleep sitting up?'

'Ah, it's the price we pay to be beautiful, mum', joked Linda.

Her cousin Anne arrived just after 7pm to stay overnight. Douglas was an excellent cook and enjoyed catering. He was in the kitchen wearing an apron around his waist, peeling potatoes for the traditional steak pie wedding dinner the following evening. He stopped every now again to check and stir the three big pots, each containing stew, home made soup and steepie peas that were simmering away on the cooker.

'Do you think that's enough potatoes for fifteen people?' he asked Linda and Anne as they were passing the kitchen to go upstairs to get themselves organised for the wedding.

Margie busied about getting everything up to date and making sure that the house was spic and span for the next day. The telephone rang and Douglas came out of the kitchen into the hall, ladle in one hand, and picked up the phone with the other.

'Hello, how's things at that end? I bet it isn't a fraction as hectic as it is here', laughed Douglas.

'Who is it, dad?' Linda shouted from the top of the stairs.

'It's your beloved husband-to-be, he wants a last word with you before you become his wife!' her father replied.

Linda ran down the stairs and grabbed the phone from her dad. She giggled as James said to her, 'Just think, after tomorrow you will be all mine, Mrs. Alexander'.

Then, in a panic, she said, 'Oh James, did you remember to get pennies for the scramble?'

'All organized! The conductor on the bus today was complaining about the amount of pennies everyone was giving him, so I asked him if he could spare me five bob's worth. He was happy to get rid of the extra weight from his moneybag', answered James.

'Oh ,thank goodness for that! I forgot to remind you about getting change, everyone would think we were very mean if we didn't throw them money. Besides it is supposed to bring us good luck!' said Linda.

What's For Ye, Won't Go By Ye

It was almost midnight, and the last thing that Douglas and Margie did before they retired for the evening was to lay the table.

'Oh, it's exquisite, a table fit for a king!' enthused Linda as she walked into the living room and admired the wonderful job that her mum and dad had done

They had really excelled themselves, with the posh cutlery, glasses, candelabra and napkins.

'I think you should be getting your beauty sleep Linda, you have a big day tomorrow!' said Margie.

'Yes, I know mum. I just came down to say goodnight. I want to give you both a big hug to thank you for all you've done for me'.

'Oh, I just wish we could have done more. We would have liked to have helped you financially, but we just don't have that kind of money', answered Margie with a regretful tone that was saying she felt she had let her daughter down.

'Oh, don't be daft, mum! You and dad have both worked so hard. You've paid for, and prepared, all that food as well. You have done a wonderful job. James and I really appreciate you both for holding our wedding reception at your house!'

Linda looked at her mum and whispered in a concerned voice, 'Are you going to be all right mum? I'm worried about you coping on your own with dad when he starts on his drinking binges. I'll always be there if you need me. I'm really going to miss you mum, you've done so much for me all of my life, and the most important thing you've given me is love. You're my wee mammy and I love you so much!'

'Oh, stop it, ye'll make me greet!' answered Margie, as the two woman cuddled each other tightly, with tears welling in their eyes.

The wedding was at eleven o'clock the next morning. Linda wasn't sure how many friends and family would come along to the registry office. It had been decided just to have an evening meal and a small family party at Linda's parents' house, so she only sent out official invites to the parents, brothers, sisters, spouses , children, Alan (the best man) and his girlfriend Helen and her cousin Anne (the bridesmaid). She verbally invited her mum's two sisters, Mary and Betty, to come along after the meal with their husbands, because they lived locally. Douglas junior and Norma's flat wasn't far from the registry office and they kindly offered to lay on and pay for the food for a buffet wedding breakfast for all the guests who turned up for the ceremony. Linda and James had bought all the drink for the wedding breakfast and the evening party.

It was a beautiful autumn morning, there were no clouds in the clear blue sky and the sun shone through Linda's bedroom window. Her dad knocked on her bedroom door.

'Come in', said Linda as she sat up worrying about her hair. She had gone to sleep sitting up, but had obviously slid down during the night.

Douglas walked in with a tray laden with scrambled eggs on toast and tea. 'Right, here's your last treat as a single woman, breakfast in bed!' he said.

Linda felt a lump come to her throat, as she thought of all the ups and downs over the years with her dad. Deep down, he really was a lovely person, it was just a shame that this nice behaviour wasn't consistent. He reappeared upstairs minutes later with breakfast in bed for Margie and Anne too. Linda relaxed and enjoyed her breakfast before going into the bathroom. She ran the bath water. Margie came into the bathroom and said to her, 'Oh Linda, you better not stay in the bath too long or have the water very deep, because the steam will undo your hair! Best keep the chiffon scarf on your head until you've finished!'

Linda was amazed that she wasn't feeling nervous. She went downstairs for another cup of tea with the others. Anne and she reminisced and talked about their childhood days, the fun they used to have and their family holidays in Rothesay. They forgot all about time.

Douglas came into the living room and said, 'Right girls, you'd better get a move on. The cars will be here in an hour, and you're both still sitting here in your dressing gowns!'

'Oh my goodness!' they both exclaimed in shock and ran up the stairs.

Linda removed the chiffon scarf. Her hair wasn't too bad, considering it had been done the day before and she had slept on it. She stuck the pointed tail of her comb into the pinned down curls to lift them up again, and gave her hair another spray of lacquer. She slowly and carefully applied her makeup, sticking on her long false eyelashes before drawing an even, thin line along her top lid with black eye liner. She decided to leave her pale pink lipstick until after she had got dressed, in case it smudged and marked her wedding dress. Anne came in wearing an orangey/red dress that Aunt Dot had made for her, and a straw hat that she had decorated with a matching ribbon. She helped Linda to zip the back of her wedding dress up. Linda carefully pulled her floppy white hat on over her 'big hair'.

'The cars are here!' Douglas shouted anxiously up the stairs to the two girls.

'Well, what do you think of your gorgeous 'bride-to-be' daughter?' Anne announced as Linda appeared at the top of the stairs.

Douglas and Margie both looked up and seemed dumbstruck. The both of them held on to each other as they admired their beautiful daughter and told her how wonderful she looked. She came down the stairs and they all fell into each other's arms, crying tears of happiness.

'Here, don't leave me out of this, I want a hug too!' said Anne. 'And watch your makeup, Linda, you don't want to be smudging it at this late stage', Anne said as she gave Linda a tissue.

'Where are the bouquets?' Linda asked.

'They're on the sideboard', answered Margie.

Anne went through and got them as Linda checked her make up in the hall mirror. 'Oh, my mascara has run! I'll have to go back upstairs and touch it up', said Linda.

'You haven't got time Linda, you can't be late for the registry office', emphasized her dad.

'Well, I can't get married with my eyes like this!' Linda said adamantly. Then she continued, 'Anyway, mum and Anne have to leave first. By the time they drive off, I will be ready, it won't take long!'

She ran upstairs and had a quick peep out of her bedroom window as her mum and Anne walked down the lane to their car She felt a flutter in her stomach when she saw that all the neighbours had gathered and were throwing confetti over them. The reality of the day was beginning to sink in.

'That's funny, I can't see our car. I hope they sent two, and not just one!' Douglas shouted up the stairs.

'Don't worry dad, I confirmed it yesterday. It'll be there OK, it's probably parked further up, behind the houses in front, where we can't see it!' Linda replied confidently.

'Well, you would have thought that the driver would park where we can see him, the silly bugger that he is! We're just going to have to go for it Linda. We can't hang about here! Otherwise, you won't be getting married today!' said Douglas.

Linda was remarkably calm and was determined that nothing was going to upset her wedding day.

Douglas was getting into a fluster as he made his way to the door, 'C'mon Linda, let's go! This is it, pet'. Just before he opened the front door, he stopped and admired her and continued, 'You look stunning, Linda. That James is a lucky lad! He's getting a beautiful wife!'

Linda took her father's arm and they set off down the lane. Douglas was very proud as everyone gasped and admired his daughter. Sure as fate, there was the deep burgundy Humber Hawk with white ribbons in front and an arrangement of flowers in the back window, parked in front of the house to the left of the lane. As they climbed into the car, Douglas mentioned to the driver, tactfully, and without complaining, that he was parked in a stupid place.

'We were worried that you hadn't turned up, we couldn't see you from the house!' Douglas chided.

'Ah didnae want tae park too close tae the bus stoap', was all the driver answered..

They pulled swiftly away, to echoes from the neighbours of 'Good luck, Linda!' Douglas wound the window down and threw a handful of pennies out to the excited children on the pavement. They were making good time as they drove along Great Western Road towards the town.

As they approached Hyndland, the driver said in a worried tone, 'Oh, oh!'
'What's up?' Douglas asked him.

'I don't know, looks like there could be an accident or something, nothing's moving!' the driver replied.

'Oh no! It's never as bad as this on a Saturday morning!' Linda chipped in.

'Isn't there another route we can take?' Douglas asked the driver.

'I'll try cutting up through Hyndland to Partick and go into town along Dumbarton Road instead', the driver answered.

He waited for the oncoming traffic to pass, then he quickly zoomed into a road on their right. He drove up through the side streets, then, to everyone's horror and dismay, he came to a dead end.

'Oh no, I was sure that this road went all the way down to Partick!' said the driver sheepishly, trying not to let his passengers see that he was at a loss.

Linda was starting to get a bit panicky now. 'Oh, why did this have to happen, today of all days!' she said to her dad, who by this time, was beginning to get frantic.

'We'll just have to go back into the traffic jam', said the driver apologetically.

'We're even further back now', said Douglas, as they rejoined the queue of traffic.

They crawled all the way along to the traffic lights at Byres Road, where there was a policeman directing the traffic around two smashed cars. He was just about to stop the car in front of theirs and let the other traffic go, when he caught sight of the bride's car. He stopped all the traffic and gestured for them to hurry on through the traffic lights. As they passed him, he stuck up his thumb and winked at Linda.

'Oh, thank goodness for that nice policeman! We could have been delayed there for at least another five minutes or so. As it is, we'll be lucky to get there on time. We have six minutes to get all the way through town to the registry office!' said Douglas anxiously.

'Oh, don't worry dad! We might make it on time and, even if we don't, we'll only be a little late, and that's the bride's privilege!' replied Linda.

'This is a registry off Linda, you're meant to be on time!' her dad emphasised to her.

The car made its way along Woodside Road, through Charing Cross and down Sauchiehall Street. There, they unfortunately were forced to stop at every set of traffic lights. Linda was getting uptight. She really was seriously beginning to doubt that they would get there on time and that the wedding would not go ahead after all. She felt uneasy as she nervously bit her bottom lip, waiting for the lights to turn to green. She looked out at the thronging crowds hustling and bustling by. Suddenly, she was startled by a rap on the window. There stood four soldiers in uniform!

One of them called out to her, 'Don't look so worried hen, it's no' that bad. Whoever he is, he's a lucky man. Ah'll marry ye, if ye want to change yer mind!'

This eased the tension and Linda and Douglas laughed when the soldiers all blew kisses and cheered as the car pulled away from the traffic lights. At last they reached George Square and, as the car turned the corner into Martha Street, Linda could see Alan anxiously pacing up and down. Before the car had stopped properly, Alan yanked open the door, grabbed her hand and pulled her out.

Alan shouted in a panic, 'Where have you been? They are about to cancel your ceremony and move onto the next one!'

Linda's dreams of elegantly walking along the corridor and into the marriage room on her dad's arm were shattered. She didn't have a chance to give herself a 'tidy up' or adjust her hat. She hung on to her hat with the hand that was holding her bouquet as Alan grasped her other hand and ran her along the corridor, with her dad in hot pursuit, to the room where everyone was waiting. Alan flung open the door and virtually threw her in. She tried to stop herself and retrieve a bit of dignity, but she had been running so fast that she couldn't stop and banged off of the registrar's desk. James looked very relieved as the marriage finally went ahead.

Linda was overwhelmed by everyone that had turned up to see her and James tie the knot. Aunts, uncles, cousins, friends, work colleagues, they were all there. The vows seemed to be over and done with very quickly, and Linda was in a daze as the woman registrar said, 'I now pronounce you man and wife, you may kiss your bride!' The guests cheered as James pulled her close to him and they shared a tender, romantic kiss. When they signed the register, Linda could hear the guests exclaiming 'Ah-h-h', as she bent over and gave a flash of her blue garter underneath her white lace mini dress.

After the ceremony, everyone was invited into the studio in the room next door for photos. Then, the happy couple made their way out into the street, where they were showered with confetti as Uncle Tom recorded the event for posterity with his cine camera.

'Well, we've done it Mrs. Alexander! You look so breathtakingly beautiful, and I love you very much!' said James as he pulled Linda close to him.

'And I love you very much too, Mr. Alexander! This is the best day of my life!' Linda replied.

The women gathered round to admire Linda's wedding ring while Alan brought James' Anglia car round to the door. As Helen gestured to them that it was time to go, Douglas announced to everyone that they were all very welcome to make their way to Douglas junior and Norma's house for a bite to eat and celebratory drinks. James, Linda, Alan, Helen and Anne all had to get into the car, so James and Alan stood at the car door discussing, while pointing back and forward, as to who was to sit where. Alan was driving, and at last it was sorted. Helen was to go in the front passenger seat, Anne was to sit in the back behind Alan, with Linda in the middle, and, lastly, James.

As Linda bent down to climb into the car, she suddenly heard loud voices shouting in unison, 'Linda, what about your bouquet?' It was the girls from her work.

Then her female cousins joined in, 'Yes! C'mon Linda, what about your bouquet?'

Linda started to laugh as she climbed back out of the car, turned her back to the crowd, and threw the bouquet over the top of her head and right over the car. There was a mad scrum as the women all dived for it, but Sally was the jubilant one.

'I've got it, it's my turn next!' Sally proudly called out as she waved the white flowers in the air.

'Don't make it too soon, give us a chance to save up, Sally!' said Linda as she got back in the car.

Everyone roared with laughter as Sally replied, 'I'll do my best, but I've got to find a man first!'

Alan asked James, 'Have you got your scramble money ready? I've been saving up my loose change. I'll throw some out my window, and you can throw yours out Linda's window at the opposite side'.

James wound down the window and, as the car pulled a way from the kerb, all the wee 'Townhead' kids, with their dirty faces, torn shirts, handed down clothes and ill-fitting shoes tied with string, dived around the wheels of the car, pushing and shoving each other out of the way as they tried to grab a penny or two for themselves. This wasn't just a game, this was serious, like a job of work. These children spent every Saturday morning outside the registry office waiting for the wedding scrambles. As Linda and James looked out through the back window, waving to all their guests, she glanced over to the kids. She couldn't help feeling sorry for the poor wee mites. Their faces were lit up with glee as they stood in the middle of the road counting their 'fortune'.

'I wonder what the future holds for us, James. Will we have a son or a daughter? Will we have more children? Will we ever get our very own bought house with back and front door? Where will we be twenty years from now? Will we live to a ripe old age together?' she said thoughtfully, cuddling into him.

James replied, saying, 'I will work very hard. We will buy a big house and I will make it the best house in the street, just for you. Then, we will fill it with beautiful daughters who are just like their mother, and good looking sons, just like their dad!' They both laughed as he continued, 'You have made me the happiest man alive. This is the start of a long and happy life together for both of us. I love you, Linda Alexander'.

What's For Ye, Won't Go By Ye

Linda looked up at James as if she suddenly realised that this was now her name. She gazed at her wedding ring and then she relaxed, contentedly falling back into her new husband's arms. She couldn't be happier as she dreamed about her new life, the baby in her belly, and everything that lay ahead for them.

Printed in the United Kingdom
by Lightning Source UK Ltd.
132483UK00001B/196-198/A